Critical acclaim f...

'As ever, Baldacci kee...
moving at express-train speed'
Daily Express

'Yet another winner . . .
The excitement builds . . . The plot's many
planted bombs explode unpredictably'
New York Times

'As expertly plotted as all Baldacci's work'
Sunday Times

'It's big, bold and almost impossible to
put down . . . I called this novel a masterclass on
the bestseller because of its fast-moving narrative,
the originality of its hero and its irresistible plot'
Washington Post

'Baldacci cuts everyone's grass –
Grisham's, Ludlum's, even Patricia Cornwell's –
and more than gets away with it'
People

The Will Robie thrillers by David Baldacci

The Innocent

Master assassin Will Robie is the US government's most indispensable asset. But when he refuses to pull the trigger, he's putting more than his own life at risk . . .

The Hit

Will Robie may have met his match when he's ordered to kill rogue agent Jessica Reel. With the trap set he quickly finds that there is more to her betrayal than meets the eye.

The Target

A deadly assassin from North Korea is ordered to destroy the enemy at all costs. With the stakes so high, Will Robie and Jessica Reel face their most lethal mission yet.

The Guilty

Returning home after twenty years brings back painful memories for government assassin Will Robie. His father has been arrested for murder, but could he really be guilty?

End Game

Will Robie returns to the US following an explosive mission in London to discover his boss has vanished. Calling on an old friend, the investigation begins to track him down.

The Target

David Baldacci is one of the world's bestselling and favourite thriller writers. With over 130 million copies in print, his books are published in over 80 territories and 45 languages, and have been adapted for both feature-film and television. He has established links to government sources, giving his books added authenticity. David is also the co-founder, along with his wife, of the Wish You Well Foundation®, a non-profit organization dedicated to supporting literacy efforts across the US. Still a resident of his native Virginia, he invites you to visit him at DavidBaldacci.com and his foundation at WishYouWellFoundation.org.

Trust him to take you to the action.

By David Baldacci

The Camel Club series
*(An eccentric group of social outcasts who seek to
unearth corruption at the heart of the US government)*
The Camel Club • The Collectors
Stone Cold • Divine Justice • Hell's Corner

King and Maxwell series
*(Two disgraced Secret Service agents turn
their skills to private investigation)*
Split Second • Hour Game • Simple Genius
First Family • The Sixth Man • King and Maxwell

Shaw series
*(A mysterious operative hunting down
the world's most notorious criminals)*
The Whole Truth • Deliver Us From Evil

John Puller series
*(A gifted investigator with an
unstoppable drive to find out the truth)*
Zero Day • The Forgotten
The Escape • No Man's Land

Will Robie series featuring Jessica Reel
*(A highly trained CIA assassin
and his deadly fellow agent)*
The Innocent • The Hit • The Target
The Guilty • End Game

DAVID BALDACCI

The Target

PAN BOOKS

First published 2014 by Grand Central Publishing, USA

First published in the UK 2014 by Macmillan

This edition published 2018 by Pan Books
an imprint of Pan Macmillan
20 New Wharf Road, London N1 9RR
Associated companies throughout the world
www.panmacmillan.com

ISBN 978-1-5098-5969-6

1 3 5 7 9 8 6 4 2

A CIP catalogue record for this book is available from the British Library.

Printed and bound by CPI Group (UK) Ltd, Croydon, CR0 4YY

*To Coach Ron Axselle, for being
such a great mentor and friend*

CIA Agent Profile

Name: Will Robie

Date of Birth: Classified. Early forties but doesn't look it. On the outside. On the inside, he's about 110.

Place of Birth: Cantrell, Mississippi, USA

Marital Status: Single. Never married. Too much baggage.

Physical Characteristics: 6 foot, 1 inch. 180 pounds. Athletic build, physically ripped. Dark hair, kept short.

Distinguishing Marks: Previously broken nose. Old wounds and scars over his torso and limbs. Right arm surgically repaired; scar tissue removed, tendons and ligaments all tidied up. Tattoos on one arm and also on back. One tattoo displays a large tooth from a great white because he's a predator like the shark. The other is a red slash of lightning on fire because that's how fast he strikes and what you feel like after he does. The tattoos effectively cover up old scars that have never healed properly.

Relatives: Daniel Robie (father); Tyler Robie (half-brother). Mother (current status unknown).

CONFIDENTIAL

Service Career: Began his career in the Special Forces. Robie is a dangerous and incorruptible CIA assassin. Possibly trained as part of SEAL, Delta Force, or United States Army Rangers. Details permanently classified. Reports to 'Blue Man'.

Notable Abilities: Immense endurance levels and off-the-chart tolerance to pain. Expert military-grade weapons and vehicle training. Deadly in close-quarters combat. Relies more on quickness and endurance than sheer strength. Will kill you before you even realize it with a gun, his finger, or a household appliance.

Favorite Film: *Reservoir Dogs*. He likes it because it's not nearly as violent as his line of work, so it allows him to relax.

Favorite Song: Queen's 'Another One Bites the Dust', of course.

Dislikes: Faulty scope/ammo, soulless bad guys, clueless bureaucrats, anyone pointing a weapon at him.

Likes: Jessica Reel, Blue Man, Dan and Tyler Robie, Julie Getty, Shane Connors, Nicole Vance, and last but not least, John Carr AKA Oliver Stone. Full stop.

1

Four hundred men lived here, most for the rest of their time on earth.

And then hell would get them for the rest of eternity.

The walls were thick concrete and their interior sides were layered with repulsive graffiti that spared virtually nothing in its collective depravity. And each year more filth was grafted onto the walls like sludge building up in a sewer. The steel bars were nicked and scarred, but still impossible to break by human hands. There had been escapes from here, but none for more than thirty years—once outside the walls there was no place to go. The people living on the outside around here weren't any friendlier than the ones on the inside.

And they actually had more guns.

The old man had another severe coughing fit and spit up blood, which was as much evidence of his terminal condition as any expert medical pronouncement. He knew he was dying; the only question was when. He had to hang on, though. He had something left to do, and he would not get a second chance to do it.

Earl Fontaine was large but had once been larger still. His body had imploded as the metastatic cancer ate him from the inside out. His face was heavily wrinkled, savaged by time, four packs of menthols a day, a poor diet, and most of all a bitter sense of injustice. His skin was thin and pasty from decades inside this place where the sun did not reach.

With a struggle he sat up in his bed and looked around at the other occupants of the ward. There were only seven of them, none as bad off as he was. They might leave this place upright. He was beyond that. Yet despite his dire condition, he smiled.

Another inmate from across the floor saw Earl's happy expression and called out, "What in the hell do you have to smile about, Earl? Let us in on the joke, why don't you."

Earl let the grin ease all the way across his broad face. He managed to do so despite the pain in his bones that was akin to someone cutting through them with a brittle-bladed saw. "Gettin' outta here, Junior," Earl said.

"Bullshit," said the other inmate, who was known as Junior inside these walls for no apparent reason. He had raped and killed five women across three counties simply because they had been unfortunate enough to cross his path. The authorities were working like mad to treat his current illness so he could keep his official execution date in two months.

Earl nodded. "Out of here."

"How?"

"Coffin is how, Junior, just like your scrawny ass." Earl cackled while Junior shook his head and turned back to stare glumly at his IV lines. They were similar to the ones that would carry the lethal chemicals that would end his life in Alabama's death chamber. He finally looked away, closed his eyes, and went swiftly to sleep as though practicing for the deepest of all slumbers in exactly sixty days.

Earl lay back and rattled the chain attached to the cuff around his right wrist, which in turn was hooked to a stout though rusted iron ring set into the wall.

"I'm getting away," he bellowed. "Better send the coon dogs come get me." Then he went into another coughing spell that lasted until a nurse came over and gave him some water, a pill, and a hard slap on the back. Then he helped Earl sit up straighter.

The nurse probably didn't know why Earl had been sent to prison and probably wouldn't have cared if he did know. Every inmate in this max prison had done something so appallingly horrific that every guard and worker here was completely desensitized to it.

"Now, just settle down, Earl," said the nurse. "You'll only make things worse."

Earl calmed, sat back against his pillow, and then

eyed the nurse steadily. "Can they be? Worse is what I mean."

The nurse shrugged. "Guess anything can be worse. And maybe you should've thought of that before you got to this place."

With a burst of energy Earl said, "Hey, kid, can you get me a smoke? Just slip it twixt my fingers and light me up. Won't tell nobody you done it. Cross and swear and all that crap though I ain't no God-fearing man."

The nurse blanched at the very idea of doing such a thing. "Uh, yeah, maybe if it were *1970*. You're hooked up to oxygen, for God's sake. It's explosive, Earl, as in *boom*."

Earl grinned, revealing discolored teeth and many gaps in between. "Hell, I'll take blowing up over being eaten alive from this crap inside me."

"Yeah? But the rest of us wouldn't. See, that's most people's problem, only thinking of themselves."

"Just one cig, kid. I like the Winstons. You got Winstons? It's my dying wish. Got to abide by it. Like my last supper. It's the damn law." He rattled his chain. "Last smoke. Gotta gimme it." He rattled his chain louder. "Gimme it."

The nurse said, "You're dying of lung cancer, Earl. Now, how do you think you got that? Here's a clue. They call 'em *cancer sticks* for a damn good reason. Jesus, Mary, and Joseph! With that kinda stupidity you can thank the good Lord you lived long as you have."

"Gimme the smoke, you little prick."

The nurse was obviously done dealing with Earl. "Look, I got a lot of patients to take care of. Let's have a quiet day, what do you say, old man? I don't want to have to call a guard. Albert's on ward duty now and Albert is not known for his TLC. He'll put a baton to your skull, sick and dying or not, and then lie in his report and not one person will dispute it. Dude's scary and he don't give a shit. You know that."

Before the nurse turned away Earl said, "You know why I'm here?"

The nurse smirked. "Let's see. 'Cause you're dying and the state of Alabama won't release someone like you to secure hospice even if you are costing them a ton of money in medical bills?"

"No, not this here hospital ward. I'm talking prison," said Earl, his voice low and throaty. "Gimme some more water, will ya? I can get me water in this gol-damn place, can't I?"

The nurse poured a cup and Earl greedily drank it down, wiped his face dry, and said with pent-up energy, "Got behind bars over twenty years ago. First, just for life in a federal cage. But then they got me on the death penalty thing. Sons-a-bitches lawyers. And the state done took ahold of my ass. Feds let 'em. Just let 'em. I got rights? Hell, I got *nuthin'* if they can do that. See what I'm saying? Just 'cause I killed her. Had a nice bed in the fed place. Now look at me. Bet I got me the cancer 'cause of this here place. Know I did. In the air. Lucky for me I ain't never got that AIDS shit." He raised his eyebrows and lowered his voice. "You *know* they got that kind in here."

"Uh-huh," said the nurse, who was checking the file of another patient on his laptop. It was set on a rolling cart that had locked compartments where meds were kept.

Earl said, "That's two decades plus almost two years now. Long damn time."

"Yep, you know your math all right, Earl," the nurse said absently.

"The first Bush was still president but that boy from Arkansas done beat him in the election. Saw it on the TV when I got here. Year was 1992. What was his name again? They say he's part colored."

"Bill Clinton. And he's not part black. He just played the saxophone and went to the African-American churches sometimes."

"That's right. Him. Been here since then."

"I was seven."

"What?" barked Earl, squinting his eyes to see better. He rubbed absently at the pain in his belly.

The nurse said, "I was seven when Clinton was elected. My momma and daddy were conflicted. They were Republicans, of course, but he was a southern boy all right. I think they voted for him, but wouldn't admit to it. Didn't matter none. This *is* Alabama, after all. A liberal wins here hell freezes over. Am I right?"

"Sweet home Alabama," said Earl, nodding. "Lived here a long time. Had a family here. But I'm from Georgia, son. I'm a Georgia peach, see? Not no Alabama boy."

"Okay."

"But I got sent to this here prison 'cause of what I *done* in Alabama."

"Sure you did. Not that much difference, though. Georgia, Alabama. Kissing cousins. Not like they were taking your ass up to New York or Massachusetts. Foreign countries up there for shit sure."

"'Cause of what I done," said Earl breathlessly, still rubbing at his belly. "Can't stand Jews, coloreds, and Catholics. Don't much care for Presbyterians neither."

The nurse looked at him and said in an amused tone, "Presbyterians? What the hell they ever done to you, Earl? That's like hating the Amish."

"Squealed like hogs getting butchered, swear to God they did. Jews and coloreds mostly." He shrugged and absently wiped sweat from his brow using his sheet. "Hell, truth is, I never killed me no Presbyterian. They just don't stand out, see, but I woulda if I got the chance." His smile deepened, reaching all the way to his eyes. And in that look it was easy to see that despite age and illness Earl Fontaine was a killer. Was *still* a killer. Would always be a killer until the day he died, which couldn't come soon enough for lawful-minded citizens.

The nurse unlocked a drawer on his cart and took

7

out some meds. "Now, why'd you want to go and do something like that? Them folks done nothing to you, I bet."

Earl coughed up some phlegm and spit it into his cup. He said grimly, "They was breathing. That was good enough for me."

"Guess that's why you're in here all right. But you got to set it right with God, Earl. They're all God's children. Got to set it right. You'll be seeing him soon."

Earl laughed till he choked. Then he calmed and his features seemed to clear.

"I got people coming to see me."

"That's nice, Earl," said the nurse as he administered a painkiller to the inmate in the next bed. "Family?"

"No. I done killed my family."

"Why'd you do that? Were they Jews or Presbyterians or coloreds?"

"Folks coming to see me," said Earl. "I ain't done yet, see?"

"Uh-huh." The nurse checked the monitor of the other inmate. "Good to make use of any time you got left, old man. Clock she is a-ticking, all right, for all of us."

"Coming to see me today," said Earl. "Marked it on the wall here, look."

He pointed to the concrete wall where he had used his fingernail to chip off the paint. "They said six days and they'd be coming to see me. Got me six marks on there. Good with numbers. Mind still working and all."

"Well, you sure tell 'em hello for me," said the nurse as he moved away with his cart.

Later, Earl stared at the doorway to the ward, where two men had appeared. They were dressed in dark suits and white shirts and their black shoes were polished. One wore black-framed glasses. The other looked like he'd barely graduated from high school. They were both holding Bibles and sporting gentle, reverential expressions. They appeared respectable, peaceful, and law-abiding. They were actually none of those things.

Earl caught their eye. "Coming to see me," he mumbled, his senses suddenly as clear as they had ever been. Once more he had a purpose in life. It would be right before he died, but it was still a purpose.

"Killed my family," he said. But that wasn't entirely accurate. He had murdered his wife and buried her body in the basement of their home. They hadn't found it until years later. That was why he was here and had been sentenced to death. He could have found a better hiding place, he supposed, but it had not been a priority. He was busy killing others.

The federal government had let the state of Alabama try, convict, and sentence him to death for her murder. He had had a scheduled visit to Alabama's death chamber at the Holman Correctional Facility in Atmore. Since 2002, the state of Alabama officially killed you by lethal injection. But some death penalty proponents were advocating the return of "Old Sparky" to administer final justice by electrocution to those on death row.

None of that troubled Earl. His appeal had carried on for so long that he'd never be executed now. It was because of his cancer. Ironically enough, the law said an inmate had to be in good health in order to be put to death. Yet they'd only saved him from a quick, painless demise so that nature could substitute a longer, far more painful one in the form of lung cancer that had spread all over him. Some would call that sweet justice. He just called it shitty luck.

He waved over the two men in suits.

He had killed his wife, to be sure. And he'd killed many others, though exactly how many he didn't remember. Jews, coloreds, maybe some Catholics. Maybe he'd killed a Presbyterian too. Hell, he didn't know. Wasn't like they carried ID proclaiming their faith. Anybody who got in his way was someone who needed killing. And he had allowed as many people to get in his way as was humanly possible.

Now he was chained to a wall and was dying. But still, he had something left to do.

More precisely, he had one more person to kill.

2

The men could not have looked any more tense. It was as though the weight of the world was resting on each of their shoulders.

Actually, it was.

The president of the United States sat in the seat at the end of the small table. They were in the Situation Room complex in the basement of the West Wing of the White House. Sometimes referred to as the "Woodshed," the complex was first built during President Kennedy's term after the Bay of Pigs fiasco. Kennedy no longer thought he could trust the military and wanted his own intelligence overseers who would parse the reports coming in from the Pentagon. The Truman bowling alley had been sacrificed to build the complex, which had later undergone major renovations in 2006.

During Kennedy's era a single analyst from the CIA would man the Situation Room in an unbroken twenty-hour shift, sleeping there as well. Later, the place had been expanded to include the Department of Homeland Security and the White House Chief of

Staff's office. However, the National Security Council staff ran the complex. Five "Watch Teams" comprised of thirty or so carefully vetted personnel operated the Situation Room on a 24/7 basis. Its primary goal was to keep the president and his senior staff briefed each day on important issues and allow for instant and secure communications anywhere in the world. It even had a secure link to Air Force One in the event the president was traveling.

The Situation Room itself was large, with space for thirty or more participants and a large video screen on the wall. Mahogany had been the wood surface of choice before the renovation. Now the walls were composed mainly of "whisper" materials that protected against electronic surveillance.

But tonight the men were not in the main conference room. Nor were they in the president's briefing room. They were in a small conference room that had two video screens on the wall and a row of world time clocks above. There were chairs for six people.

Only three of them were occupied.

The president's seat allowed him to stare directly at the video screens. To his right was Josh Potter, the national security advisor. To his left was Evan Tucker, head of the CIA.

That was all. The circle of need to know was miniscule. But there would be a fourth person joining them in a moment by secure video link. The staff normally in the Situation Room had been walled off from this meeting and the coming communication. There was only one person handling the transmission. And even that person would not be privy to what was said.

The VP would normally have been part of such a meeting. However, if what they were planning went awry, he might be taking over the top spot because the president could very well be impeached. Thus they had to keep him out of the loop. It would be terrible for the country if the president had to leave office. It would be catastrophic if the VP were forced out too. The Constitution dictated that the top spot would then go to the Speaker of the House of Representatives. And no one wanted the head of what could very well be the most dysfunctional group in Washington to be suddenly running the country.

The president cleared his throat and said, "This could be momentous or it could be Armageddon."

Potter nodded, as did Tucker. The president looked at the CIA chief.

"This is rock solid, Evan?"

"Rock solid, sir. In fact, not to toot our own horn, but this is the prize for nearly three years of intelligence work performed under the most difficult conditions imaginable. It has, frankly, never been done before."

The president nodded and looked at the clocks above the screens. He checked his own watch against them and made a small adjustment to his timepiece.

It looked as though he had aged five years in the last five minutes. All American presidents had to make decisions that could shake the world. In numerous ways, the demands of the position were simply beyond the ability of a mere mortal to carry out. But the Constitution required that the position be held by only one person.

He let out a long breath and said, "This had better work."

Potter said, "Agreed, sir."

"It *will* work," insisted Tucker. "And the world will be much better off for it." He added, "I have a professional bucket list, sir, and this is number two on it, right behind Iran. And in some ways, it should be number one."

Potter said, "Because of the nukes."

"Of course," said Tucker. "Iran wants nukes. These assholes already have them. With delivery capabilities that are inching closer and closer to our mainland. Now, if we pull this off, believe me, Tehran will sit up and take notice. Maybe we kill two birds with one stone."

The president put up a hand. "I know the story, Evan. I've read all the briefings. I know what hangs in the balance."

The screen flickered and a voice came over the speaker system embedded in the wall.

"Mr. President, the transmission is ready."

The president unscrewed the top of a water bottle

sitting in front of him and took a long drink. He put the bottle back down. "Do it," he said curtly.

The screen flickered once more and then came fully to life. They were staring at a man short in stature, in his seventies, with a deeply lined and tanned face. There was a rim of white near his hairline where the cap he normally wore helped to block the sun. But he was not in uniform now. He was dressed in a gray tunic with a high, stiff collar.

He stared directly at them.

Evan Tucker said, "Thank you for agreeing to communicate with us tonight, General Pak."

Pak nodded and said, in halting but clearly enunciated English, "It is good to meet, face-to-face, as it were." He smiled, showing off highly polished veneers.

The president attempted to smile back, but his heart was not in it. He knew that Pak would lose his life if exposed. But the president had a lot to lose too.

"We appreciate the level of cooperation received," he said.

Pak nodded. "Our goals are the same, Mr. President. For too long we have been isolated. It is time for us to take our seat at the world's table. We owe it to our people."

Tucker said encouragingly, "We completely agree with that assessment, General Pak."

"Details are progressing nicely," said Pak. "Then you can commence your part in this. You must send your best operatives. Even with my help, the target is a very difficult one." Pak held up a single finger. "This will be the number of opportunities we will have. No more, no less."

The president glanced at Tucker and then back at Pak. "We would send nothing less than our very best for something of this magnitude."

Potter said, "And we are sure of both the intelligence and the support?"

Pak nodded. "Absolutely sure. We have shared that with your people and they have confirmed the same."

Potter glanced at Tucker, who nodded.

"If it is discovered," said Pak. They all became riveted to him. "If it becomes discovered, I will surely lose my life. And, America, your loss will be far greater."

He looked the president directly in the eye and took a few moments seemingly to compose his words carefully.

"It is why I asked for this video conference, Mr. President. I will be sacrificing not only my life, but the lives of my family as well. That is the way here, you see. So, I need your complete and absolute assurance that if we move forward, we do so together and united, no matter what might happen. You must look me in the eye and tell me this is so."

The blood seemed to drain from the face of the president. He had made many important decisions during his term, but none so stressful or potentially momentous as this one.

He didn't look at either Potter or Tucker before answering. He kept his gaze right on Pak. "You have my word," he said in a strong, clear voice.

Pak smiled, showing off his perfect teeth again. "That is what I needed to hear. Together, then." He saluted the president, who gave his own crisp salute in return.

Tucker hit a button on the console in front of him and the screen went black once more.

The president let out an audible breath and sat back against the leather of his chair. He was sweating though the room was cool. He wiped a drop of moisture off his forehead. What they were proposing to do was quite clearly illegal. An impeachable offense. And unlike the presidents impeached before him, he had no doubt the Senate would convict him.

"Into the breach rode the five hundred," the president said in barely a whisper, but both Potter and Tucker heard it and nodded in agreement.

The president leaned forward and looked squarely at Tucker.

"There is no margin for error. None. And if there is the least hint of this coming out—"

"Sir, that will not happen. This is the first time we've ever had an asset placed that high over there. There was an attempt on the leadership last year, as you know. While he was traveling on the street in the capital. But it was botched. That was from low-level internal sources and had nothing to do with us. Our strike will be quick and clean. And it will succeed."

"And you have your team in place?"

"Being assembled, and then they'll be vetted."

The president looked sharply at him. "Vetted? Who the hell are you planning to use?"

"Will Robie and Jessica Reel."

Potter sputtered, "Robie and Reel?"

"They are the absolute best we have," said Tucker. "Look what they did with Ahmadi in Syria."

Potter eyed Tucker closely. He knew every detail of that mission. Thus he knew that neither Reel nor Robie had been intended to survive it.

The president said slowly, "But with Reel's background. What you allege she did. The possibility of her going—"

Tucker broke in. Normally, this would be unheard of. You let the president speak. But tonight Evan Tucker seemed to see and hear only what he wanted to.

"They are the best, sir, and the best is what we need here. As I said, with your permission, they will be vetted to ensure that their performance will be at the highest level. However, if they fail the vetting, I have another team, nearly as good, and certainly up to the task of performing the mission. But the clear preference is not the B Team."

Potter said, "But why not simply deploy the

backup team? Then this vetting process becomes unnecessary."

Tucker looked at the president. "We really need to do it this way, sir, for a number of reasons. Reasons which I'm sure you can readily see."

Tucker had prepared for this exact moment for weeks. He had studied the president's history, his time as commander in chief, and even gotten his hands on an old psychological profile of the man done while he was running for Congress many years ago. The president was smart and accomplished, but not that smart, and not that accomplished. That meant he had a chip on his shoulder. Thus he was reluctant to acknowledge that he was not always the smartest, most informed person in the room. Some would see that attribute as a strength. Tucker knew it to be a serious vulnerability ripe for exploitation.

And he was exploiting it right now.

The president nodded. "Yes, yes, I can see that."

Tucker's face remained impassive, but inwardly he breathed a sigh of relief.

The president leaned forward. "I respect Robie *and* Reel. But again, there is no margin for error here, Evan. So you vet the hell out of them and make damn sure they are absolutely ready for this. Or you use the B Team. Are we clear?"

"Crystal," said Tucker.

3

Will Robie, unable to sleep, stared at the ceiling of his bedroom while the rain pounded away outside. His head was pounding even more, and it would not stop when the rain did. He finally rose, dressed, put on a long slicker with a hood, and set out from his apartment in Dupont Circle in Washington, D.C.

He walked for nearly an hour through the darkness. There were few people about at this hour of the morning. Unlike other major cities, D.C. did sleep. At least the part you could see. The government side, the one that existed underground and behind concrete bunkers and in innocuous-looking low-rise buildings, never slumbered. Those people were going as hard right now as they would during the daylight hours.

Three men in their early twenties approached from the other side of the street. Robie had already seen them, sized them up, and knew what they would demand of him. There were no cops around. No witnesses. He did not have time for this. He did not have the desire for this. He turned and walked directly at them.

"If I give you some money, will you leave?" he asked the tallest of the three. This one was his size, a six-footer packing about one hundred and eighty street-hardened pounds.

The man drew back his Windbreaker, revealing a black Sig nine-mil in the waistband that hung low over his hips.

"Depends on how much."

"A hundred?"

The man looked at his two comrades. "Make it a deuce and you're on your way, dude."

"I don't have a deuce."

"So you say. Then you gonna get jacked right here."

He went to draw the gun, but Robie had already taken it from his waistband and pulled down his pants at the same time. The man tripped over his fallen trousers.

The man on the right pulled a knife and then watched in amazement as Robie first disarmed him and then laid him out with three quick punches, two to the right kidney, one to the jaw. Robie added a kick to the head after the man smacked the pavement.

The third man did not move.

The tall man exclaimed, "Shit, you a ninja?"

Robie glanced down at the Sig he held. "It's not balanced properly and it's rusted. You need to take care of your weapons better or they won't perform when you want them to." He flicked the weapon toward them. "How many more guns?"

The third man's hand went to his pocket.

"Drop the jacket," ordered Robie.

"It's raining and cold," the man protested.

Robie put the Sig's muzzle directly against his forehead. "Not asking again."

The jacket came off and fell into a puddle. Robie picked it up, found the Glock.

"I see the throwaways at your ankles," he said. "Out."

The throwaways were handed over. Robie balled them all up in the jacket.

He eyed the tall man. "See where greed gets you? Should have taken the Benny."

"We need our guns!"

"I need them more." Robie kicked some water from the puddle into the unconscious man's face and he awoke with a start, then rose on shaky legs. He did not seem to know what was going on, and probably had a concussion.

Robie flicked the gun again. "Down that way. All of you. Turn right into the alley."

The tall man suddenly looked nervous. "Hey, dude, look, we're sorry, okay? But this is our turf here. We patrol it. It's our livelihood."

"You want a livelihood? Get a real job that doesn't involve putting a gun in people's faces and taking what doesn't belong to you. Now walk. Not asking again."

They turned and marched down the street. When

one of the men turned to look back, Robie clipped him in the head with the butt of the Sig. "Eyes straight. Turn around again you get a third one to look through in the back of your head."

Robie could hear the men's breathing accelerate. Their legs were jelly. They believed they were walking to their execution.

"Walk faster," barked Robie.

They picked up their pace.

"Faster. But don't run."

The three men looked idiotic trying to go faster while still walking.

"Now run!"

The three men broke into a sprint. They turned left at the next intersection and were gone.

Robie turned and headed in the opposite direction. He ducked down an alley, found a Dumpster, and heaved the jacket and guns into it after clearing out all of the ammo. He dropped the bullets down a sewer grate.

He did not get many opportunities for peaceful moments and he did not like it when they were interrupted.

Robie continued his walk and reached the Potomac River. This had not been an idle sojourn. He had come here with a purpose.

He drew an object from the pocket of his slicker

and looked down at it, running his finger along the polished surface.

It was a medal, the highest award that the Central Intelligence Agency gave out for heroism in the field. Robie had earned it, together with another agent, for a mission undertaken in Syria at great personal risk. They had barely made it back alive.

In fact, it was the wish of certain people at the agency that they not make it back alive. One of those persons was Evan Tucker, and it was unlikely he was going away, because he happened to head up the CIA.

The other agent who had received the award was Jessica Reel. She was the real reason Evan Tucker had not wanted them back alive. Reel had killed members of her own agency. It had been for a very good reason, but some people didn't care about that. Certainly Evan Tucker hadn't.

Robie wondered where Reel was right now. They had parted on shaky ground. Robie had given her what he had believed was his unconditional support. Yet Reel did not seem to be capable of acknowledging such a gesture. Hence the shaky parting.

He gripped the chain like a slingshot and whirled the medal around and around. He eyed the dark surface of the Potomac. It was windy; there were a few small whitecaps. He wondered how far he could hurl the highest medal of the CIA into the depths of the river that formed one boundary of the nation's capital, separating it from the commonwealth of Virginia.

The chain twirled several times in the air. But in the end Robie didn't fling it out into the river. He returned the medal to his pocket. He wasn't sure why.

He had just started back when his phone buzzed. He took it out, glanced at the screen, and grimaced.

"Robie," he said tersely.

It was a voice he didn't recognize. "Please hold for DD Amanda Marks."

Please hold? Since when does the world's most elite clandestine agency have its personnel say, "Please hold"?

"Robie?"

The voice was crisp, sharp as a new blade, and in its undertone Robie could detect both immense confidence and a desire to prove oneself. That was a potentially deadly combination for him, because Robie would be the one doing this woman's bidding in the field while she safely watched from a computer screen thousands of miles away.

"Yes?"

"We need you in here ASAP."

"You're the new DD?"

"That's what it says on my door."

"A mission?"

"We'll talk when you get in here. Langley," she added, quite necessarily because the CIA had numerous local facilities.

"You know what happened to the last two DDs?" Robie asked.

"Just get your butt in here, Robie."

4

Jessica Reel could not sleep either. And the weather was as bad on the Eastern Shore as it was in D.C. She stared at where her home had once been before it had been destroyed. She had actually done the deed herself. Well, she had booby-trapped the place and Will Robie had triggered the explosion that had almost claimed his life. It was incredible how a partnership could have been born out of such grim circumstances.

She pulled her hood tighter against the rain and wind and continued to tramp over the muddy earth, while the waters of the Chesapeake Bay to the west continued to pound the little spit of land.

She had departed from Robie feeling both hopeful and lost, such an unsettling feeling that she was unsure from which end to work through it. If there was even a way to do so. For most of her adult life her work had been her entire world. Now Reel wasn't sure she really had a job or world left. Her agency despised her. Its leadership wanted her not merely out of the way but dead.

If she left her employment there she felt she would be giving them license to terminate her in that far more permanent way. Yet if she stayed, what would her future be like? How long could she reasonably survive? What was her exit strategy?

All troubling questions with no apparent answers.

The last few months had cost her all she had. Her three closest friends in the world. Her reputation at the agency. Perhaps her way of life.

But she had gained something. Or someone.

Will Robie, initially her foe, had become her friend, her ally, the one person she could count on, when Reel had never been able to do that easily or convincingly.

But Robie knew her way of life as well as she did. Her way was his way. They would forever share that experience. He had offered her friendship, a shoulder to lean on if it ever came to that.

Yet part of her still wanted to withdraw from such an offer, to keep going it alone. She had not figured out her response to that or him yet. Maybe she would never have one.

She looked up at the sky and let the pelting raindrops hit her in the face. She closed her eyes and a rush of images came to her. Each one a person and each one of them dead. Some were innocent. Others not. Two had been killed by someone else. All the rest had died by her hand. One, her mentor and friend, lay in a vegetative state from which she would never awaken.

It was all pointless. And it was all true. And Reel was powerless to change any of it.

She slipped the medal on its chain from her pocket and looked down at it. It was identical to the one Robie had been awarded. It had been given to her for the same mission. She had performed the kill shot—agency orders. Robie had helped her escape nearly certain death. They had made it back to the States to the chagrin of a powerful few.

It was a meaningless gesture, this medal.

What they really wanted to do was put a hole in her head.

She walked to the edge of the land and watched the waters of the bay spray over the dirt.

Reel hurled the medal out into the bay as far as she could. She turned away before it struck the surface of the water. Metal didn't float. It would vanish in a few moments.

But then she turned back around and used her middle finger to flip off the sinking medal, the CIA in general, and Evan Tucker specifically.

That was the main reason she'd come—to chuck her medal into the bay. And this place had been her home, to the extent any place was. She did not intend to come back here. She had come to take one last look, perhaps to gain some closure. Yet she wasn't finding any.

The next instant she pulled her gun and ducked down low.

Over the sounds of the water had come a new intrusion.

A vehicle was pulling to a stop near the ruins of her waterside cottage.

There was no reason for anyone to be visiting her here. The only reason anyone would appear here would be a violent one.

She raced over to the only cover there was: a pile of rotted wood stacked near the water's edge. She knelt down and used the top log as a gun rest. While she could see nothing clearly, they might have night optics that would reveal all, including her location.

She managed to follow them only by subtracting their darkened silhouettes from the darkness around them. She centered on one spot and waited for their movements to cross that point. By this method she counted four of them. She assumed they were all armed, all commed, and here for a specific purpose: her elimination.

They would try to outflank her, but her rear was not capable of being flanked, unless they wanted to jump into the bay's cold and storm-tossed waters. She focused on other spots and waited for them to cross. She did this again and again until they were within twenty meters of her location.

She wondered why they were staying packed together. Separating during an attack was standard tactics. She could not follow so easily multiple groups coming at her from different points of the compass. But so long as they stayed together her focus need not be diffused.

She was deciding whether to fire or not when her phone buzzed.

She was not inclined to answer, not with four bogies bearing down on her outgunned butt.

But it might be Robie. As corny as it sounded, this might give her an opportunity to say goodbye in a way that had not been possible before. And maybe he would go after her killers and slay them for her.

"Yes?" she said into the phone, keeping her shooting hand on her Glock and her eyes on the forces coming for her.

"Please hold for DD Amanda Marks," said the efficient voice.

"What the—" began Reel.

"Agent Reel, this is Amanda Marks, the new deputy director of Central Intelligence. We need you to come in to Langley immediately."

"I'm a little busy right now, DD Marks," replied Reel sarcastically. "But maybe you're already aware of that," she added in a harsh tone.

"There are four agents currently at your cottage on the Eastern Shore. Correction, where your cottage used to be. They are there simply to escort you to Langley. Please do not think of engaging with them and perhaps doing them harm."

"And are they planning to do me harm?" snapped Reel. "Because it's the middle of the night, I have no idea how they even knew I was here, and they're acting quite furtive."

"Your reputation precedes you. Hence they are acting with care. As to your location, we determined you were nowhere else."

"And why do you need me to come in ASAP?"

"That will all be explained when you get here."

"Is this about a new mission?"

"When you get here, Agent Reel. I can't trust that this line is secure."

"And if I choose not to come in?"

"As I told Agent Robie—"

"You called Robie in as well?"

"Yes. He's part of all this, Agent Reel."

"And you're really the new DD?"

"Yes."

"Do you know what happened to the last two?"

"The exact same question Agent Robie presented to me."

In spite of everything Reel smiled. "And your answer?"

"The same as yours will be. Just get your butt in here."

The line went dead.

5

Hours later Jessica Reel arrived at Langley. The sun was up, the rain had passed, but her mood had not improved.

She cleared security and entered a building she knew well.

In some ways too well.

She was escorted to a room where she found a familiar face already waiting.

"Robie," she said curtly before sitting down next to him.

"Jessica," said Robie, inclining his head slightly. "I take it you received the same invitation."

"It wasn't an invitation. It was an order. Did they send goons to bring you in?"

He shook his head.

"Then I guess they trust you more than they trust me."

"We trust you both the same," said a voice as the door opened and a woman in her early forties, with shoulder-length brown hair, walked in carrying an electronic tablet. She was petite, about five-four and maybe a hundred and ten pounds, but lean and fit, and her wiry physique suggested a strength that belied her small size.

DD Amanda Marks. She shook each of their hands while Robie and Reel exchanged bemused looks.

"Thank you both for coming in so promptly."

Reel said, "If I'd known I had a choice I wouldn't have. The four guys you sent after me didn't provide any options."

"Nevertheless, your cooperation is appreciated," said Marks in a brisk tone.

Robie said, "I thought after the last mission we had some stand-down time?"

"You did and now that's over."

"So a new mission?" Reel said wearily.

"Not yet," replied Marks. "First things first."

"Meaning what?" asked Reel.

"Meaning that you both need to be what I would term recalibrated."

Robie and Reel exchanged another glance. He said, "You recalibrate instruments."

"You are instruments. Of this agency."

"And we need recalibration why, exactly?" asked Reel.

Marks had not made eye contact with them before, even when shaking their hands. She had either looked down or over their shoulders. It was disconcerting, but the tactic was not unexpected by either Robie or Reel.

Now Marks stared directly at them. And to Robie she had the eyes of someone who had spent time behind a long-range scope at some point in her career.

"You really want to waste my time and yours asking crap like that?" she said in a low, even voice.

Before either of them could respond Marks said, "You both went rogue on us." She turned to look at Reel. "You killed one of our analysts and my predecessor."

She turned next to stare at Robie. "And you aided and abetted her after being sent out to terminate her. In the aftermath of that *situation,* we had the decision to terminate or rehabilitate. The decision to rehabilitate was made. I'm not saying I agree with it, but I am here to implement it."

"I guess so much for our being awarded the CIA's highest honor," said Robie.

"Congratulations," said Marks. "I have one in my closet too. But that's history. I'm concerned only with the present and the future. Yours. You've been given an unbelievable offer. There are some people here who desperately want you to screw up so other plans can be put into motion."

"I can guess who one of them is," said Reel. "Your boss, Evan Tucker."

"And there are others here who hope you succeed and become productive members of this organization once more."

"And what camp are you in?" Robie asked.

"Neither. I'm Switzerland. I will lead your rehab, but the outcome is entirely up to both of you. I don't really care which way it goes. Up, down, or sideways. It doesn't matter one iota to me."

Reel nodded. "Comforting. But you report directly to Evan Tucker."

"In a sense everyone here reports directly to him. But I can assure you that you will have a full and fair opportunity to be rehabilitated. Whether you are or not is up to you."

Robie said, "And exactly whose idea was this? If it was Tucker's I really can't see how the process will be fair in any way."

"Without going into details I can tell you that a compromise was reached at the very highest level. You have powerful friends, Mr. Robie. You know exactly who I'm talking about. But there are also powerful forces aligned against both of you." She looked at Reel. "Some who want nothing more than to see you executed for your past actions. If I'm not making myself crystal clear, please stop me."

Neither Robie nor Reel spoke.

She continued. "Those forces collided and the result was this compromise. Rehab. Do or die. Up to you. Pretty generous, actually, in my humble opinion."

"I didn't think anyone trumped the president," said Robie.

"Politics is a dirty, ruthless business, Agent Robie. It makes the intelligence sector look relatively honorable by comparison. While it's true that the president is the thousand-pound gorilla, there are lots of big beasts in this playground. And the president has an agenda he wants to push through, and that means he has to make concessions. In the grand scheme of things you and Agent Reel are not so important that you are above being traded as chits to further the man's agenda. Whether you got a medal or not. Do you follow?"

"What precisely does rehab mean in this context?" asked Robie.

"We start from square one. You both have to be evaluated in every possible way. Physically, psychologically, and intellectually. We're going to look pretty deep into your heads. We're going to see whether you have what it takes to cut it in the field."

"I thought we had proved that in Syria," interjected Reel.

"Not part of the compromise. That was a one-off and even then you didn't follow orders."

"Well, if we had followed orders we'd both be dead," Robie pointed out.

"Again, not something I care about. It was the not-following-orders part that helped trigger what will happen now."

She turned on her electronic tablet and tapped the screen. Robie noted that her fingernails were cut below the tips of her fingers and had not a speck of color on them. The image of her as a sniper entered his mind once more.

She looked up at him. "You sustained serious burns to your leg and arm." She glanced at Reel. "Her doing, not that anyone is keeping count. How are these injuries?"

"Coming along."

"Not good enough," said Marks. "Now, you both jumped off a moving train. I'm sure that was fun."

"More fun than the alternative," replied Reel.

Marks said, "You lost friends during this past, uh, *adventure*. I understand that you blame the agency for that."

"Well, their personnel were partially responsible. I'm not sure how else you can cut that."

"To have an effective rehab you will have to get over that," replied Marks sharply.

She looked once more at Robie. "You were sent out to find Reel. You did find her but did not bring her in. You ended up joining forces with her against the agency's orders."

"I went with my gut and it turned out to be right."

"Again, during rehab you will have to decide where your ultimate loyalties lie, Robie. The next time your gut may be wrong. And where does that leave you and the agency?"

She did not wait for an answer but continued.

"The rehab will be very hard on all of us. I will be with you both every step of the way. You may quit the process at any time."

"And if we do?" asked Reel quickly.

"Then all appropriate action will be taken against you."

"So I get habeas corpus and a fair trial?" Reel said.

Marks looked up. "I didn't say *legal* action, did I?"

"So it's do or die, then?" said Robie.

"You can label it however you wish. But ultimately the choice is completely up to you. So what will it be?"

Robie and Reel exchanged another glance. Then Reel nodded. Robie did the same.

"Excellent choice," said Marks.

"Where is this rehab going to take place?" asked Reel.

"Oh, I'm sorry, didn't I mention that?"

"No, you didn't," said Reel tersely.

"It will take place at a location I think you both know well."

She paused and took a moment to look at one and then the other.

"The Burner Box," she said with a slight smile. "We leave in twenty-four hours."

6

"How long will you be gone?" Julie Getty asked.

Robie looked down at his plate and didn't answer right away. They were at a hole-in-the-wall diner in D.C., not far from where fifteen-year-old Julie attended school. Robie had about eight hours to go before he and Reel would be headed to the Burner Box. Julie had been excited to hear from him; her excitement had diminished when she learned it was to say goodbye, at least for a while.

"I'm not sure," said Robie as he pushed his food around on his plate. "It wasn't specified," he clarified.

"And you can't tell me where you're going, of course," she said resignedly.

"It's . . . it's a training site."

"Why do you need to train? You're already, like, I mean, great at what you do, Will."

"It's like going back to school, you know, continuing education. Lots of professions do it." He hesitated. "Even mine."

She studied him critically and he just as resolutely avoided her gaze.

39

"Are you going alone on this?" she asked.

He shook his head. "No."

"Is that woman going with you? Jessica?"

Robie hesitated before answering. "Yes."

"So you're both in trouble?"

Robie glanced sharply at her. She stared back at him with an expression that said his look of surprise was unnecessary.

"I've spent a lot of time with you, Will. When people were trying to kill us. When you were moody. When you didn't have many options, but you still figured out how to get out of a jam."

"And your point?" he asked with genuine curiosity.

"You look to me like a guy who doesn't see a way out of this. And that's just not you. So it must be really bad."

Robie said nothing while Julie fiddled with the straw in her drink. She said, "I read in the papers a while back that Ferat Ahmadi, the crazy Syrian trying to gain power over there, was gunned down. They never found who killed him."

Robie remained silent.

"I'm not going to ask you if you and Jessica had something to do with that because I know all I'll get is a blank stare. But if you did, then it seems that your mission was successful. So it has to be something else. Is it connected to Jessica?"

"Why do you ask that?" Robie said abruptly.

"Because things were going good for you at your agency. Until she showed up."

"I can't get into that with you, Julie."

"Because, you see, I liked her. I think she's a good person."

"I think so too," said Robie before he could catch himself.

Julie smiled. "Cool."

"What?"

"You're letting your guard down around me. And you must really care for her," she added in a more serious tone.

"I can relate to her and what she's going through," Robie said diplomatically.

"So she's your friend?"

"Yes."

"You need to take care of your friends, Will."

"I'm trying, Julie, I really am."

"Are you ever going to be free of all this crap?"

"I wish I had the answer to that."

After they left the restaurant and Robie dropped Julie off, his phone buzzed. It was Reel.

"I think we need to talk."

"Okay."

"But you're being followed and I want some privacy."

Robie's gaze flicked to his rearview mirror. He noted the car on the street two back from his.

"Okay, let me see what I can do."

"No need. I'll take care of it."

"So you're back there too?"

"Did you really have to ask? How's Julie?"

"Concerned. Where do you want to meet?"

"In case someone is listening in, our place in the rain."

"Roger that."

"Take the next right. When you reach the alley, punch it."

Robie clicked off and sped up. He hung the right. The tail did the same.

He saw the alley and floored it, creating separation from the tail. In the rearview he watched as a semi pulled out of the alley, blocking the road.

He heard brakes screech and a horn blaring.

"Nice, Jessica," he said to himself.

He punched the gas, made a series of turns, and then glided onto Constitution and passed the Washington Monument, no longer shrouded in scaffolding after the earthquake and lit up like the Eiffel Tower. Some people thought they should have left it that way.

Five minutes and as many turns later he pulled to the curb, put the car in park, cut the engine, and got out. He walked to the car parked in front of him and slid into the passenger seat. Jessica Reel started the car and sped off.

"Where to?" he asked.

"Nowhere. Just want to move while we talk."

"Talk about what?"

"The Burner Box."

"We've both been there, Jessica."

"And you really want to go back?"

"I didn't think we had a choice."

"You have a choice, Will. It's me they really want. I'll go. You don't have to."

"I think it was a package deal."

She pulled off the street, stopped the car, and slammed it into park.

"Look, if you think you're doing me a favor by coming with me, you're not. It's just one more thing for me to worry about."

"When did I say you ever had to worry about me?"

"You know what I'm talking about. It's better if I go it alone."

"And what if they kill me for not going? How is that better for me?"

"I pulled the triggers on those two, Robie, not you. You can work out a deal. Go to your people. They'll provide you cover. POTUS is on your side, for God's sake."

"But what if I want to go to the Burner Box?"

"Why in the hell would you? And don't say for me, because that'll just piss me off even more."

"Then I'm doing it for me."

"You're making no sense now."

"I want to know if I can still cut it, Jessica. The Burner will tell me that."

"The Burner could end up killing you."

"Well, if I can't cut it there, I sure as hell can't cut it in the field."

"You heard Marks. She'll be gunning for both of us. It won't be a fair evaluation, despite what she said. Evan Tucker will have seen to that."

"I don't really care."

"Robie, how can you not care? You've only got one life."

"Now you're the one not making sense. Every time I walk out the door I'm risking my *one* life."

"Evan Tucker went after us once and missed. This is his follow-up act. I doubt he'll make the same mistake. Unlike in Syria, he can control all aspects of the Burner Box and what goes on in there. Take it from me, an 'accident' will happen that will tragically end our lives."

"Well, if we're both there he'll have to work twice as hard to nail us."

"But he'll still nail us."

"You need to be more optimistic."

"And you need to get your head out of your ass."

"I'm going, Jessica."

"What about Julie? You're just going to walk out on her?"

"No, I'll do my best to get through this and see

her again. But I have a job to do. And I'm good at it. And I'm going to keep doing it. And I'm going to have as normal a life as I possibly can *while* I'm doing it."

"That's impossible and you damn well know it."

He shook his head wearily. "You really have to work on having a more positive attitude. And the only thing I know for certain is that I'm leaving on a trip tomorrow. So just drive me back to my car. I need to pack my bag and get some shut-eye."

She dropped him back at his car. As he was getting out she broke the silence. "You are the most exasperating person I have ever met in my life."

"You need to get out more."

She snorted and then, despite her evident anger, she smiled. "Why are you really doing this?"

"Just remember the rain, Jessica. What I said then is what I mean now."

"That you'll always have my six?"

"Just so you know, it's not a freebie. I expect the same in return. Figure it's the only way we survive this."

Then he was gone.

7

Evan Tucker stared across at her. They were in a SCIF at Langley. Technically, Langley was one big SCIF, or Sensitive Compartmented Information Facility, but Tucker had become paranoid and had demanded an extra layer of protection from prying eyes and ears at keyholes.

Tucker's waist had thickened over the last month and his hair had turned whiter. In fact, he seemed to have aged even more since his meeting with the president in the Situation Room complex.

Amanda Marks looked back at him.

"So it's a go?" asked Tucker. "I told the president it was."

"They both agreed to it, so I'd say yes. It's a go."

"Like they had a choice," muttered Tucker.

"Well, they did. It just wasn't much of one."

"And you have eyes on them now, just in case? They're slippery, Marks, trust me. I speak from experience."

"I'm sure you do, sir. To tell the truth, we lost them

for a bit this evening. It seems they wanted a quiet word with one another."

Tucker came halfway out of his seat. "You lost them?" he exclaimed.

"Only temporarily, Director. They went their separate ways and we regained surveillance. Robie is at his apartment and Reel is staying at a hotel."

"Don't let that happen again. You have carte blanche in the way of assets to throw at this sucker, Marks. Do what you have to do. But do not lose them again."

"Understood. And now a question for you, Director?"

"I'm listening."

"What outcome do you want on this exactly?"

"They're going to the Burner Box."

Marks nodded, crossed her legs, and placed her hands in her lap. "I understand that. But what exactly is the endgame here?"

"You put them through their paces. You put them through their paces hard. I want to see if they still have it. And I'm not simply talking about shooting straight and kicking someone's ass. By what they just accomplished I have little doubt they're fully qualified there, but I don't want that personal assessment to cause you to let up on them one iota, Amanda."

"Rest assured, it will not. I was a trainer at the Burner for two years. I do not let up on anyone, most of all myself."

"What I'm most concerned about," began Tucker, "is what's going on up here." He tapped his head. "You know what Reel did?"

"I know the allegations."

"They're not allegations," he snapped. "They're *facts*. She's admitted to them."

"Yes, sir," she said quickly.

"And Robie was sent after her, disobeyed orders, and joined forces with her. Under any other scenario they would both be in prison right now. Hell, Reel should be executed for *treason.*"

"Granted that, sir. But the men she killed, weren't they also traitors?"

"That was never proven. *That* is an allegation, but from a less than trustworthy source."

"My apologies. I spoke with APNSA Potter and—"

"Potter just came on board and doesn't even know where the damn bathrooms are in the White House. He's the national security advisor, Marks. He works for the president. You, you work for me."

"Indisputably," she replied. "Which gets me back to what you want to accomplish here."

"If they pass the Burner they'll be deployed on a mission that is currently shaping up. It is a mission to end all missions, and I have to know that they're ready for it, because there is no margin for error."

She looked at him curiously. "We have lots of teams that can do those sorts of missions."

"I told the president we were vetting Robie and Reel for it. And that's what we're going to do."

"And do you want them to pass the Burner, sir?"

Tucker looked at her warily. "That's not up to me. Either they pass it or not. It's up to them."

"If you say so, sir."

Tucker took off his glasses, laid them on the table, and rubbed his eyes. "But just so we make this as clear as possible, you are to stretch them to their absolute limits. And then you are to keep going. If you can break them, break them. If you can, they're of no use to me in the field. They will not qualify for this mission. I have a Plan B standing by just in case."

"It's not a question of if. I can break anyone, Director."

"One reason I selected you for this task."

"And made me the DD?"

"Hand in hand." He tapped his head and then his hand dipped to his chest. "Those are what count, Amanda, the head and the heart. If they're not with us, with me, then they are against us. Against me. I cannot have agents going rogue, I don't give a shit what reasons or grievances they have. Rogues cause international incidents. International incidents can get this country embroiled in unnecessary conflicts. That will not happen on my watch."

"But it seems that they acted to avoid just such an international incident," said Marks. "And they succeeded. I think that's why they have such powerful allies, starting with the man in the Oval Office."

"I'm quite aware of that, thank you. But your friend today can be your foe tomorrow. It all depends on what happens on the ground."

"And conditions on the ground can be dictated, as I'm sure you are aware."

"You just do your job and see how it shakes out."

"And no preference?"

"If they pass they get the mission. It'll be the most difficult one they've ever attempted so they might die trying. And if they don't pass the Burner, well, that's their problem."

Marks rose. "Understood, sir."

"Do you really understand?"

She looked taken aback by this. "I'm on your side, Director."

"I thought others were on my side too, but it appears they weren't."

"I'm not sure who you're referring to. I just arrived on the scene and—"

"That will be all, Marks. I want hourly reports on how my protégés are doing. Make sure I get them."

"Consider it done, sir." She turned and left.

★

As soon as the door was closed Tucker rose and poured himself a drink from the small bar in a cabinet behind his desk. A bar behind a desk at CIA seemed very Cold War-ish. But he didn't care. With this job one needed a belt of booze every once in a while. Well, perhaps more often than that.

He envisioned having to stand up at an AA meeting one night and say, *I'm Evan Tucker. My job is to keep all Americans safe. And I'm a raging alcoholic.*

He sat back behind his desk.

There were forces aligned against him here, he was aware of that. Someone had tipped off Reel and Robie about the mission in Syria. Forewarned, they had taken advantage of that intelligence and escaped a fate that they shouldn't have. Someone here had done that. Tucker had suspicions of who that might be. But he needed more than suspicions. And he aimed to get it.

Along with two rogue agents.

He stared at the doorway that Amanda Marks had walked through a few minutes before.

He had brought her here principally because she had the reputation of being both a ball buster and a company person through and through. He hoped that she lived up to that rep. If not, she would be assigned to a place in the middle of nowhere, with no possibility of ever getting back.

But he didn't really care about her. His fixation was Robie and Reel. Jessica Reel was in his crosshairs.

She was the trigger woman on his former DD and an analyst whom she had shot in the back.

Illegal. Treasonous. Unforgivable.

Tucker didn't care what her reasons were. That was why they had courts and judges and juries. And executioners. Reel had taken it upon herself to be all of those things. Then she had jumped right to the execution part. For that she had been allowed to walk free and even given a medal.

That stark injustice made Tucker seethe.

Well, he was not without influence or resources. He would use both to make sure that the appropriate punishment was meted out to her. And Robie too, if he was idiotic enough to stick with her.

The fact was, Tucker knew that he would likely be resorting to his Plan B on the upcoming mission. The odds were very high that Robie and Reel were not going to make it out of the Burner Box. So if justice could not prevail in a court of law, it would still triumph somewhere in the wilderness of North Carolina.

Tucker knew that he was staking everything on this. The mission he was engaged in with General Pak would be the pinnacle of his career. Or the catalyst for his downfall. For what they were proposing to do was quite illegal, even if the president had signed off on it. Tucker had not believed that the current occupant of the Oval Office had the cojones to make that sort of call. But the president had surprised Tucker and done so. Now the die was cast. There was no going back.

In a perfect world, the mission would succeed and Robie and Reel would be history.

A perfect world. The only problem was, his world was about as imperfect as it could possibly be.

He cradled his drink, took a sip, and sat back. Another long day of keeping everyone safe. It was a dirty, filthy business, what he did. And no one involved in it was anything other than filthy.

Including me, thought Evan Tucker. *Most of all, me.*

8

Earl Fontaine sat back in his bed and let out a contented sigh.

The visit had been a successful one. The two men had been all that they had claimed to be when they had first contacted him. It was a little surprising to Earl that he was allowed visitors at this point, but perhaps the warden didn't think he was dangerous anymore since he was old and dying in a crappy prison hospital ward.

Well, the man could not have been more wrong. Maybe his stinger had been pulled, but Earl had other resources, starting with the two men in the black suits toting the Bibles. And they had others, lots of others, to work with them.

The Bibles were a nice touch, he thought. Bibles put people at ease, when they should be on the highest alert. Good for Earl. Bad for the law. In fact, what was bad for the law was always great for Earl Fontaine.

The men in black had done their part. They were all ready. Now it was time for Earl to do his part.

The Target

He grabbed at his belly and hacked up what felt like part of his left lung. That was really the only one he had left. They'd cut most of the other one out years ago in an effort to stem the cancer. They'd only done it to try to get him healthy so they could kill him. But he'd beaten them on that. He wasn't getting healthier. He was dying. Dying fast, but not too fast.

Ironically, the only thing keeping him going was the idea that if he could accomplish this last thing in his life, he could die easy. It was all he thought about. He was obsessed with it. It was the only thing keeping his good lung moving, his diseased heart pumping, and the pain relatively at bay.

He caught his breath, wiped the sweat from his face, and struggled to a sitting position. It was hot. It was always hot here. Apparently, Alabama didn't enjoy a winter season. For over twenty years the sweat had spilled off him day by day, hour by hour, minute by minute—but he had endured, eventually making clever jokes about the heat that had passed from one cell to the next, making Earl a bit of a celebrity in here.

He looked down at the tube. He got his basic nutrients through an IV right into his belly. Although he'd been a hearty eater all his life, food meant nothing to him now. And neither did the smokes, despite his giving the nurse a hard time about those.

He gathered his energy and eyed the woman making her rounds through the patients here. She was young and attractive, and the first time Earl had seen her, he had had thoughts that he hadn't had in a while. In his day, big, tall, handsome, what he could have done with a woman like that. *To* a woman like that. She would know who ruled the roost, that was for damn sure. She was a doctor, smart, educated, liberated no doubt. She probably had a bunch of ideas in that pretty head. Hell, she probably went and voted too, and not just the way her hubby told her to. He loathed women like that. But that didn't mean he didn't want to possess them.

He stared over at Junior, who had perked up when he too had eyed the young doctor making her rounds. Earl grinned at this. He could see Junior taking in the shoulder-length hair that smelled so good, the slender hips, the nicely rounded bottom that pushed against the fabric of her skirt, the glimpse of a soft bosom resting just beneath the white blouse. The stethoscope around the long neck. Her ears were pretty too, Earl had decided. He would like to nibble on them. He would like to nibble on all of her.

He imagined her naked and then in every sort of scanty lingerie. He imagined himself doing things to her. His breathing grew heavy, but that was all. His equipment downstairs no longer worked. The chemo and radiation had seen to that.

But Junior had no such problem. Earl could see his right hand under his sheet. Disgusting little shit. World would be better off when they killed the bastard. But part of Earl was jealous that Junior could still jack off and he couldn't.

Behind the doc was Albert, the largest and meanest guard here by far. He made Earl look small. He made everybody look small. His uniforms were always too tight because the Alabama correctional system apparently had none large enough to properly fit him. He surveyed the room, his gaze always moving, his baton held at his side. He was shadowing the doc, Earl knew, because of past incidents.

Inmates had tried to put hands on her, feel her up, snatch a kiss. Now Albert walked with her as she made her rounds. You tried to touch the skirt now, you got a baton rammed down your throat. Albert didn't care how sick you were or how much pain you were in. He'd just make you hurt more. Earl knew because he'd seen Junior try it once. And any thought Earl had had of doing the same had disappeared because of what had happened to Junior.

Albert had knocked three of his teeth out and the blood had flown so far that it had reached Earl's bed. That had been two months ago, when Junior had been in here for another ailment. The man was full of sick, it seemed. Although maybe it was just the thought of the poison needle heading his way that made him feel so poorly. Earl didn't know and really didn't care. He was simply biding his time until she got to him.

Twenty minutes later the doctor arrived.

Her scent reached him long before that, though—
honeysuckle and lily of the valley. They were smells
he knew well growing up in the backwoods of
Georgia. She was the only one who smelled like that
in the whole place. There were no female guards, and
the male guards reeked almost as bad as the inmates.
But the doc was a honeysuckle. She was fine. Earl
looked forward to her visits and got himself in a
temper when another doc substituted for her.

She took his records off the hook on the end of
the bed and read through them. She must know them
intimately by now, Earl thought, and they all pointed
relentlessly to his demise. But she had to see that his
meds and such had been properly given, he figured.

"How are we doing today, Mr. Fontaine?" she
asked. She never smiled, never frowned. Never looked
happy or sad. She was just . . . there. And for Earl, that
was enough, especially today.

He eyed Albert standing behind her. Albert glanced
down at Earl, and the smirk on his face was something that made Earl want to put a bullet in the
guard's brain.

"Fine, fine. No complaints. Mebbe a little more
morphine in the drip, Doc. Get me through the
night."

"I'll see if we can do something about that," she
said, her eyes flicking over his chart. She checked his
vitals on the monitor and then listened to his heart
pumping away. When her hand grazed his neck he

felt his skin burn with pleasure. He hadn't been touched by a woman in over . . . well, he couldn't exactly remember how long it'd been. Before the Clinton boy got to be president, probably.

She asked him a few questions and even sat on the edge of his bed as she checked him over. When she crossed her legs her skirt rose enough that Earl could see her rounded knee. It gave him the tingles. Her in his bed?

He looked up at Albert and gave the smirk right back, the big asshole.

"Anything else, Mr. Fontaine?" she asked as she rose off the bed and looked down at him.

This was the moment. This was what Earl had been waiting all this time for.

"I do got me something, Doc."

"What's that?" she said, but there was no interest behind her eyes. Inmates here probably had lots of special requests of her, most of them perverted, even with the massive Albert standing behind her. Lust often trumped good sense.

"Got me a daughter."

Now her eyes focused on him. "A daughter?"

He nodded and struggled to sit up. "Ain't seen her in forever. She's all growed now. Must be, let me see, well into her thirties sure enough."

"Okay?"

"See, thing is, hell, you know it, I'm dying. Ain't long for this world, right? She's all I got left. Like to see her, if I could. Say goodbye, all that. You unner-stand?"

She nodded. "I can see that, certainly. Where is she?"

"See, there's the thing. I don't know. Hell, for all I know she's changed her name. Well, I know she did for a fact."

"Why would she have done that?"

Earl could not lie here, though he wanted to. The doctor could check. And if she found out he was lying she would surely not do what he so desperately needed her to do.

"She went into Witness Protection. Her real name's Sally, named after my momma, God rest her soul. Last name Fontaine, o'course. Like mine. I'm her daddy. Ain't seen hide nor hair since she done that."

"Why did she go into Witness Protection?"

"Ain't nothing I done," he said quickly. And this was true. She had gone into the protection program for another reason unrelated to her murderous father. "It was because of what others done, over in Georgia. After her momma died and I went to prison she got put into foster care. Got mixed up with some bad eggs and then turned agin 'em. That's why she went in."

"Okay, but what do you want me to do?"

Earl shrugged and put on his most pathetic expression. He even forced tears to slide down his face. He had always been able to do that on command. The tactic had worked on many women. Too bad for them.

He said simply, "I'm dying. Want to see my only kid before I kick off."

"But if she's in Witness—"

He broke in, growing impatient. "You can call 'em. Tell 'em about me. They'll have a record of her. Maybe she's still in there, maybe she ain't. Maybe it's a long shot. Hell, probably is. But if they could get a message to her? Be up to her, o'course, if she wants to come see me or not."

"But will they let her?"

"Long time ago all that stuff happened. Folks after her, hell, they're all dead now. Or in prison. She's got nothing to be afraid of. And she don't have to come. Up to her, like I said." He paused and looked directly at the doctor, assuming the most sincere expression of his life. "My only chance to say goodbye, Doc. Ain't got much time left. Hell, you know that better'n anybody. Better'n me even. Why I decided to ask you. Don't think the warden gives a damn." He paused. "You got kids?"

She looked startled by this. "No, I mean not yet. But I hope to—"

"Best thing I ever did in my life. Royally screwed up the rest of it, no lie there, but my little girl? Now, I done good bringing her into this world, and I'll tell anyone who asks."

Earl heard Albert snort at this but he kept his gaze on the doctor. His eyes bored into hers. He had always been able to play to the sympathies of women. He hoped he had not lost this skill.

"My little girl," he said. "Last chance. If she wants to come and see me, so be it. If not, then that's okay too. But I just want to give her the chance to see her daddy one last time. That's all, Doc. Can't make you do it. You got to want to. All I can do is ask. Well, that's all I got to say. Up to you now. If you don't want to, I'll unnerstand. Shoot, just go to my grave wondering, I guess. Mebbe no mor'n I deserve. Don't know. Just don't know. My little girl. My little . . ."

He lay back against his pillow, out of breath, his frame sunken in, looking as pitiful as he possibly could.

He could see the conflict going on in the woman's mind. He had spent much of his life studying people in order to learn how to best exploit them. The eyes revealed the internal turmoil she was experiencing. She looked uncertain, confused, all good things for him.

At last she said, "I'll . . . I'll see what I can do, Mr. Fontaine."

He reached out his hand for her to shake. Albert quickly stepped up but the doctor motioned him back. She shook Earl's hand. Hers felt warm and soft inside his bony cold one.

"God bless you, Doc. God bless you from a dying old man."

She walked off to the next patient. But Earl had done his job.

He knew she was going to do exactly as he had asked.

9

The cargo plane bumped along at about ten thousand feet as they descended into what looked to be dense forest. Robie and Reel sat across from each other in jump seats in the cargo hold. As the plane shuddered and thrashed through the air Reel smiled.

"What?" asked Robie.

"For some reason I thought the agency would have sent one of the Gulf stream jets for us."

"Right. At least the trip wasn't long."

"Good old North Carolina. In the middle of nowhere, North Carolina," she amended.

"The agency does not encourage neighbors," replied Robie.

There were no windows for them to look out, but their ear pops told them the plane was in descent. And their watches confirmed this to be the case.

"What's your best guess for when we get there?" she asked.

Robie shrugged. "They said they were going to put us through the paces. I expect them to do nothing less than that."

"And afterward?"

"If there is an afterward."

"I don't think that's entirely up to us, Robie."

"Never thought anything different."

Five minutes later they heard the landing gear come down. A few minutes after that the plane touched down on the tarmac, then rolled for a bit as the thrust reversers and wheel brakes were engaged and the aircraft came to a clunky halt far down the runway.

The plane taxied and then the engines were killed. A door was opened and they were told by one of the aircraft's personnel to exit.

They walked down a set of portable stairs that had been rolled to the open door of the plane.

When they touched ground a Humvee pulled up with a skid. Inside was a driver and, next to him, Amanda Marks, dressed in cammie gear. She got out and faced them.

"Welcome to the Burner. We've made some changes since you were here last."

"What kind?" asked Reel.

"I don't want to spoil the surprise," replied Marks. She eyed them both and then looked at a sky full of clouds. The chilly wind whipped around them.

"Down to your skivvies. You can keep your shoes on."

"Excuse me?" said Reel.

"Strip down to your skivvies," Marks said again. Her tone now carried no pleasantness.

"And why would that be?" asked Robie.

"Either do it or get back on the plane and hire a lawyer," she retorted.

Robie and Reel looked at each other and then slowly started to undress on the tarmac.

Robie had on running shorts and a white thermal long-sleeved T. Reel had on bike shorts and a blue tight-fitting long-sleeved Under Armour workout shirt. Both had on running shoes.

This was not lost on Marks.

"I can see you anticipated something like this," she said, her tone somewhat disappointed.

Robie and Reel said nothing.

Marks pointed to her left. "The complex is down that way. Only a few miles, although it does get hilly the last mile. You will follow the Humvee. We will keep to a six-minute-a-mile pace. If you drop back from that for longer than five seconds, we will have an issue."

She climbed back into the Humvee and signaled for the driver to start up. He spun the vehicle around and headed off east.

Robie and Reel exchanged one more glance and then fell in behind the vehicle at a swift pace.

"Good thing we figured they'd start to kick our asses from the get-go," said Robie. "And dressed accordingly."

"Six-minute pace isn't a killer. But the hills might make it seem like a five-minute pace, maybe less." She eyed the Humvee, gauging distance and speed. "Figure fifty feet back will keep us from having an *issue.*"

"Right."

The run was not three miles, though. It was six. And the last mile wasn't hilly. The last *three* miles were. Exactly four seconds short of thirty-six minutes later they reached the sprawling complex set on a plateau surrounded by forests of mostly evergreens. The CIA loved putting facilities in the middle of nowhere, if only because they could see someone coming from miles away.

The Humvee stopped and Marks jumped out as Robie and Reel reached her. They kept running in place, letting their muscles, lungs, and hearts cool down.

"Now, that wasn't so bad was it?" said Marks.

"No. I'm sure your Hummer ride was very warm and comfortable," said Reel. "So when you said you'd be with us every step of the way I guess that was metaphorically speaking?"

Marks smiled. "You'll see far more of me than you ever wanted to."

"From behind a window? Or next to us?" said Reel. "I mean, why should we have all the fun? But if you can't cut it, no worries. Desk jockeys get out of shape really fast."

Marks's smile disappeared. "Your gear is in your room. But we won't be heading there just yet. After that little warm-up we wanted to let you get in a real workout."

She jogged up the steps into the complex. It was built of logs, had a metal roof, was covered with cammie netting, and had sensors arrayed all over it with jamming devices built into them. There were more surveillance cameras than in the city of London and armed guards patrolled with German shepherd attack dogs that would not be your friends if you didn't belong here. There were watchtowers with men wielding sniper rifles that could kill from over a mile away. The entire property was enclosed with electrified fencing.

There were also minefields located on the perimeter; several deer and a black bear had discovered this fact at the exact moment they had died.

There was only one road, full of switchbacks, in and out. The rest of the area was thick forest except for the runway, which had been carved out of the flattest spot on the mountain.

Marks parked her eye in front of a retina scanner and the steel door set in a bomb-resistant frame clicked open. She pulled it all the way open and motioned to Reel and Robie to hurry.

"We're on a tight schedule. So let's step it up."

"Stepping it up," said Reel as she passed by Marks and into the complex.

The halls were empty and smelled like someone had sprayed a chemical wash over them. The walls and ceiling were layered with surveillance devices mostly invisible to the naked eye.

There would be no such thing as privacy here. Reel wondered briefly if the agency had discovered how to read minds. She wouldn't put it past them.

Marks led them down the main corridor and then hung a left down another, narrower hall. The overhead lights were so bright that it was actually painful to look around. This was intended and both Robie and Reel kept their gazes down, following Marks's heels as she marched toward their destination.

The next four hours were challenging, even by Robie's and Reel's standards.

Swimming against machine-generated currents with weights on their ankles and wrists.

Rope climbing up six stories without benefit of a net while a wind machine did its best to blow them off two-inch-wide ledges.

The military functional fitness training done at triple speed until the sweat poured off them and muscles and tendons were pushed to their breaking points.

Next came push-ups and sit-ups and pull-ups in a sauna where the temperature soared well past a hundred degrees.

Then stair runs where the vertical comprised one hundred steps on a sixty-degree angle. They did it over and over until they were both gasping for air.

Then guns were tossed at them, they were shoved into a darkened room, and beams of light hit them from every angle. Then the shots started coming. And the fire was composed of rubber bullets, as evidenced by a slug ricocheting off a wall and nearly hitting Robie in the head.

Their moves were instinctive. Forgetting about their fatigue, they started advancing in seemingly choreographed steps, shooting target after target until the fire aimed at them stopped.

The lights came on and they blinked their eyes rapidly to adjust to the glare.

Two stories above them, an observation window made of polycarbonate glass slid open and Marks leaned out.

"Exit at the door over there. You'll be escorted to your room. I'll meet you there."

Robie and Reel looked at each other.

"Nice first day," he said.

"Who says it's over?" she shot back. "Not the bitch up there."

Their guns were taken at the door and a man in black cammies led them down a hall and pointed to a room at the end.

Robie opened the door and looked in. Reel stared over his shoulder.

It was about the size of a typical prison cell and just as inviting.

"Just the one room?" said Reel.

Robie shrugged. "Guess so."

"Well, this will be fun. Comfy-cozy. I just hope you don't snore."

"Thinking the same thing about you."

They walked in and shut the door behind them. There were two bunk beds with thin mattresses and a single sheet and flat pillow on each. There was a sink. There was no commode. There was nothing on the walls. There was a single metal desk. There was a single chair bolted to the floor. There was an overhead light. The walls were painted beige.

Robie sat on a bed.

Reel leaned against the wall.

The door opened and Marks stood there.

"You both did better than I thought you would. But it's only the first day. And it's not over yet, of course. Plenty of time."

Reel looked over at Robie and hiked her eyebrows as if to say, *I told you so.*

Marks shut the door behind her.

"So what's the deal here?" said Reel. "Did Tucker tell you to make sure we never left here alive? Are we going to end up maimed? Drugged out of our minds? Losing a limb?"

"Or all of the above?" added Robie.

Marks smiled. "What, from just those little exercises

you divine some sinister purpose? Regular recruits go through far worse."

"No, they don't," said Reel.

Marks focused on her. "Oh, really?"

"Yeah, really."

"And you know this how?"

"Tucker didn't brief you properly. I used to be an instructor here. Recruits didn't get hit with this much even on their last day. But it's your program to run, not ours. So just save the bullshit for somebody who has her head up her ass."

Robie looked from Marks to Reel and back to Marks. "What now?" he said.

Marks finally drew her gaze from Reel and looked at him.

"You get a little break. You're both going to have physicals. So strip down to skin and follow me."

"Strip down here?" said Reel.

"You have a problem getting naked in front of people, Reel?"

"No, but anyone that's not a doctor grabs my ass or my boobs, they won't wake up for a week. And that includes you."

She shucked her clothes and stood there naked while Robie peeled off his own.

Reel said, "You joining us, Marks? Or you sitting this one out too?"

"I don't have to have a physical," she shot back.

But as she looked over Reel's lean, muscled physique, it was obvious she was impressed by what she saw.

She turned her attention to Robie. There wasn't an ounce of fat on the man; he was in his early forties yet nearly as fit as an Olympian. But her attention was drawn to the burns on his arm and leg.

"I understand you have Reel to thank for those," said Marks in a mocking tone.

"If you're going to do something, do it well," said Robie matter-of-factly. "Now, if you're done eyeballing us, can we get our physicals?"

10

"You should probably get skin grafts," said the doctor who was examining Robie's burns.

"Thanks. I'll put that on my to-do list," Robie said.

The doctor was a man in his fifties with powdery white hair and not very much of it. He was beefy and sweaty, and he had a thin line of mustache over his top lip. Robie didn't know if it was by design or just inattention.

"Well, it should be sooner rather than later. The agency has an excellent person on staff."

"And how long would I be out of commission?"

"Well, several weeks at least."

"Yeah," said Robie.

"Got any vacation coming up?"

"No, can I have some of yours?"

The doctor straightened and put some of the examination instruments into a drawer next to the table.

"I take it you don't get much downtime."

"Well, it's been nice here so far. Started with a leisurely run. Then I went for a swim and then did some sauna time. And then a little target practice."

"With you as the target?"

"Didn't think the medicos were read in for details like that."

"I've been here a long time, Agent Robie. I'm surprised our paths never crossed. I presume you've been to the Burner before."

"I have," he said curtly.

"Otherwise you are in outstanding physical shape."

"Are you also examining Agent Reel?"

"No, we're running parallel courses today."

"You know her? She used to instruct here."

"I know her," he said. "Proud to call her a friend, actually."

"That's good to know, Doctor . . . ?"

"Halliday. But you can call me Frank."

Robie looked around for surveillance devices planted in the walls. Halliday followed his movement with understanding.

"Not in here, Agent Robie. One of the few places they're not. Doctor/patient confidentiality extends even to the CIA. The room where you'll be staying is not so configured."

"Yeah, that I knew."

"I'll give you some topical ointment for the burns, but you really should consider the skin grafts and some antibiotics. If left unrepaired, at some point the skin will tighten so much it will limit your mobility. And then of course there's always the possibility of infection."

"Thanks, Frank. I'll definitely consider that option."

"You can wear that robe hanging on the wall."

"Good. It wasn't my idea to come here in my birthday suit."

"I'm well aware of that."

Robie slipped off the table, crossed the room, and donned the robe. "Are you also aware of why we're here?"

Halliday stiffened just a bit. "No, not really."

"Two different answers, Frank."

"I'm just the doctor. As you know, my security clearances are limited."

"But you still have some or else you wouldn't be here. What do you know about Marks?"

"She's the DD, Clandestine."

"You know what happened to her predecessors?"

"Of course. It's sort of like the Defense Against the Dark Arts teachers. Bad things happen to them."

"Defense Against the Dark Arts?"

"You know, in *Harry Potter.*"

"Makes one wonder why Marks wanted the job."

"She's ambitious."

"Has she been here recently?"

"Yes."

"To get ready for us?"

"I don't know about that. Look, I'm very uncomfortable with this discussion."

"I'm very uncomfortable having to ask, but I have to. I'm in the intelligence business. It's second nature."

Halliday washed his hands in the sink. "I can see that."

"So you knew Reel when she instructed here? You said you were friends."

"Yes, well, as much as one can be in this place."

"I'm her friend too."

Halliday dried his hands and turned to look at Robie. "I am not unaware of what the two of you recently have been through."

"We're just trying to survive, Frank. Any assistance you can give on that will be much appreciated."

"I'm not sure I can do anything to help with that."

"You might surprise yourself. I'll tell your friend you said hello."

Robie left Halliday standing there lost in thought.

Robie was escorted back to their room. Reel had not yet returned.

Their duffels had been brought to the room and Robie quickly dressed. He had no idea what was next on the agenda, but he preferred clothes over being in the buff.

He looked around the room and his experienced gaze caught four different surveillance devices, two audio and the other pair video feeds. The video cams were strategically placed so that there was no hidden angle anywhere in the small space.

He wondered how Reel's exam was going.

It was not lost on Robie that Reel was really the

marked woman here. He was just along for the ride. She had killed two CIA agents. Tucker had his gunsights set on her. Robie was, at best, collateral damage.

He looked around the small space again. This might be the last place he ever saw. Training accidents happened at the CIA. They were just never publicized. Smart, dedicated people lost their lives all the time as they trained to be the best they could be to serve their country.

Celebrities broke a nail and they immediately took to Twitter, alerting their millions of followers to the "injury," which in turn elicited thousands of replies from people with apparently not enough going on in their lives.

And all the while brave men and women died in silence, forgotten by all except their families.

And I don't even have family to remember me.

"Agent Robie?"

Robie glanced up to see a woman in her thirties standing at the door. She was dressed in a black skirt, white blouse, and heels. Her hair was pinned back. Around her neck was a lanyard with her ID in a plastic case.

"Yeah?"

"Will you please come with me?"

Robie remained seated. "To where?"

The woman looked flustered. "Some more tests."

"I've already had my physical. I've already had my butt dragged all over this place. I've already been shot at, nearly drowned, nearly blown off a ledge six stories up. So exactly what tests are we talking about?"

"I'm not authorized to say."

"Then get someone in here who is."

The woman glanced up at one of the surveillance devices on the wall.

"Agent Robie, they're expecting you now."

"Well, they can expect me later."

"I'm not sure you have that latitude."

"Are you armed?"

She took a step back. "No."

"Then I *have* that latitude until they send people who *are* armed and who are prepared to shoot me."

The woman glanced nervously around the room once more. In a soft voice she said, "It's psychological testing."

Robie rose. "Then lead the way."

11

The doctor had finished examining Reel. She glanced over at her patient as she looked through some paperwork.

"How long ago was it?" she asked.

"How long ago was what?"

"The birth of your child."

Reel said nothing.

The doctor pointed to her flat belly.

"Low transverse abdominal incision. Technically, it's called the Pfannenstiel incision. Also known as the bikini cut because it's just over the pubic hairline. It's very faint but unmistakable to the trained eye. Did you have a go at removing traces by Fraxel laser? It works pretty well."

Reel said, "Can I put on a robe?"

"Yes, absolutely. Take that one on the wall over there. And I didn't mean to pry. It was just a medically based inquiry."

Reel slipped on the robe and cinched it tight. "Do you need a response from me for any reason related to why I'm here?"

"No."

"Good to know," said Reel curtly. "Not that I would have given you one if you'd answered yes."

"I'm sorry. I didn't mean to—"

Reel cut her off. "Look, I'm sure you're a very nice person and a highly competent doctor, but the odds of me even leaving this place alive are pretty slim, so I'm focusing on my future, not my past, okay?"

The doctor frowned. "I'm not sure I know what you mean about not leaving here alive. If you're sugges—"

Reel had already walked out the door.

A uniformed escort waiting outside the room accompanied Reel back to her quarters.

Robie was not there. She opened her duffel and quickly dressed, mindful of the eyes watching her from the devices on the wall.

Reel took out a Sharpie pen from her duffel and wrote on the wall:

Déjà vu Orwell's 1984.

Then she sat and waited for the footsteps to come. And for the door to open.

It wouldn't be long. She doubted Marks had built a refreshing nap into their itinerary.

Next, she wondered where Robie had gone. Had they split them up deliberately to try to turn one against the other?

Barely five minutes went by and then two things happened.

The footsteps came and the door opened.

It was the same young woman who had come for Robie. "Agent Reel, if you would accom—"

Before she could finish Reel was up and past her through the door.

"Let's get this over with," she called out over her shoulder as the surprised woman hurried to catch up with her.

Robie sat across from the man in an office lined with bookcases. The light was low. There were no windows. Soft music played in the background.

The man across from him had a beard, was bald on top, and fiddled with a pipe. He had black glasses that he let slide down near the tip of his nose. He pushed them back into place and held up his pipe.

"No-smoking policy extends even here," he said by way of explanation. "I'm addicted to it, I confess. Sorry state of affairs for a psychologist. I help others with their issues and I find I can't solve my own."

He held out a hand across the desk. "Alfred Bitterman. Psychologist. I'm like a psychiatrist, only without a medical license. I can't prescribe the big-gun drugs."

Robie shook his hand and then sat back. "I take it you know who I am." He eyed the thick file in front of Bitterman.

"I know what the file says. That is not the same as knowing the man himself."

"Enlightened statement," said Robie.

"You are a veteran of this agency. You have accomplished many things. Some would say impossible things. You have received the highest official commendations the agency can bestow on one of its own." Bitterman leaned across the desk and tapped his pipe against the wood. "Which raises the question of why you're even here."

Robie instantly started to glance around the room. Bitterman shook his head. "No surveillance," he said. "It's not allowed."

"Who says?" asked Robie.

"The highest authorities at the agency."

"And you trust that to be the case?"

"I've been here a long time. And in my work I have been privy to a lot of secrets, many from people high up in the agency."

Robie looked interested in this. "And this gives you protection how? Something happens to you those secrets get sent to the media?"

"Oh, it's not really that melodramatic. And it's far more self-serving. You see, none of these 'higher-ups' would ever want these secrets to be recorded and later come out. Thus great pains were taken and multiple eyes ensured that the psychologists' offices here are free from surveillance of any kind. You can speak freely."

"Why do you think I'm here, then?"

"You have undoubtedly pissed off upper management. Unless you have another explanation."

"No, I think that one covers it."

"Jessica Reel is here as well."

"She was an instructor at the Burner."

"I know she was. A damn good one too. But she's a complicated person. Far more complicated than most who come through here, and that's saying something, for they're all complicated, in a way."

"I know something of her history."

Bitterman nodded. "Did you know that I did her entry psych evaluation when she first came to us as a recruit?"

"No, I didn't know that."

"After reading her background file, but before meeting her, I was convinced that she could not pass the psych eval. There was no way. She was too screwed up by life's events."

"But she did pass, obviously."

"Of course she did. She literally amazed me in our first meeting. And she couldn't have been much more than nineteen. An unheard-of thing. I don't believe the agency bothers recruiting field agents that have not graduated college. And near the top of their classes. If 'the best and the brightest' sounds archaic, it's anything but. You can't be stupid and unmotivated and succeed at the CIA. The work is too demanding."

"You must have seen something special in her."

"Perhaps, perhaps not."

"What do you mean by that?"

"Despite all my experience with reading people I'm not convinced that I was ever able to see the real person inside her, Agent Robie. I don't think anyone ever has. Including probably you."

"Janet DiCarlo told me roughly the same thing."

Bitterman sat back, a frown creasing his features. "A tragedy. I understand that you are the only reason she's not dead."

"No, there was another reason. Jessica Reel. She's also the reason *I'm* not dead."

Bitterman tapped Robie's bulky file. "I take it you two make a good team."

"We have."

"You respect her?"

"I do."

"She has done questionable things in the past. Some have classified them as treasonous."

"And now we jump to management's side of things?" said Robie.

"I have to earn my paycheck, Agent Robie. I make no judgments. I don't take sides. I just try to . . . understand."

"But you're here to evaluate whether I'm still psychologically fit for field duty. Not to figure out Reel."

"I think those fields of inquiry may be interconnected. You made the decision to help her. Against

85

orders. That is a serious breach of agency protocols. Even you must admit that. So the question becomes why a highly professional agent like yourself would have done that. Now that, Agent Robie, that *does* speak directly to the question of fitness to perform."

"Well, if you're judging that on the basis of my ability to follow orders, then I guess I've already failed the test."

"Not at all. It goes deeper than that. Agents have not followed orders before. Some for reasons that later turned out to be indefensible. Others did so for reasons that later turned out to be justified. But even that is not definitive. Justified or not, not following orders is a very serious breach of duty. An army controlled by the whim of the lowest soldier is not an army at all. It is anarchy."

Robie shifted in his seat. "I wouldn't disagree with that."

"And this was not the first time you so acted," said Bitterman.

Now he opened the file and perused some pages. In fact, he took so long that Robie thought he had forgotten he was even there.

Finally, he looked up. "You didn't pull the trigger."

"The woman died anyway. And her very young son."

"But not by your hand."

"She was innocent. She was set up. The order for her death was not given by the agency. It was given for personal reasons by those who had infiltrated the agency. I did the right thing in not shooting her."

"Based on what?"

"My gut. Conditions on the ground. Things I saw in her apartment that did not add up. All those things told me that something was off. I had never not pulled the trigger before. It was justified that time."

"And then we come to Jessica Reel. You did not pull the trigger on her either. Based on what? Your instinct once more? Conditions on the ground?"

"A little of both. And I was proved right again."

"Some at the agency don't believe that."

"And I know who they are, trust me."

Bitterman pointed a stubby finger at him. "That's the gist of it, Agent Robie, isn't it? Can you be *trusted*? That's what they all want to know."

"I think I've proven that I can be. But if the agency wants me to be a robot and not exercise my judgment, then maybe we should part company."

Bitterman sat back and seemed to be considering this.

Robie looked over his shoulder. "Do you regret not having windows?"

Bitterman looked behind him. "Sometimes, yes."

"It's hard to see what's around you without windows. You tend to get cloistered, detached, and your judgment can be impaired."

Bitterman smiled. "Now who is testing whom?"

"I'm just being transparent, Doc."

"And I know better than that, don't I?"

"How well do you *know* Amanda Marks?"

"Not all that well. She's the new number two, of course. You don't get there without being an over-achiever. Her record is a brilliant one. Excelled at every level."

"And she can be trusted to follow orders under any circumstance?" asked Robie.

Bitterman didn't say anything for several long moments as a clock on a shelf ticked the seconds away.

"I have not performed a psych evaluation on her."

"Best guess based on your observations thus far."

"I would say that she is a good soldier," said Bitter-man slowly.

"Then you've answered my question."

"But you haven't answered mine, Agent Robie. Far from it."

"So I failed the eval?"

"This is just the preliminary. We'll meet again."

"And how long am I being kept here?"

"That's way above my pay grade."

"And if it's determined that I don't measure up?"

Bitterman clamped down on his unlit pipe's stem. "Same answer."

12

Your history is one of the most unusual I've ever encountered."

Reel sat across from another agency shrink, this one a woman in her fifties with dull brown hair with gray roots, spectacles on a chain, and a dour expression. Her name was Linda Spitzer. She wore a long skirt, a cotton vest over a white blouse, and boots. They were seated across from each other in the woman's office, a coffee table between them.

"So do I get a prize?" said Reel.

Spitzer closed the folder she was holding. "Why do you think you're here?"

"I don't think, I know. I'm here to be punished."

"For what?"

Reel closed her eyes and sighed. When she reopened them she said, "Do we really have to do this? I'm a little tired and I'm sure DD Marks has more fun planned for me today."

Spitzer shrugged. "We have an hour. It's up to you how we use it."

"Why don't you read a book, then? I can steal a catnap."

"You know, I'm not sure I would have recommended you for field duty given your history."

"Well, maybe I was unlucky I didn't run into you way back when. I could have skipped this part of my life."

Spitzer smiled benignly. "I know that you're very smart and cunning and you can talk circles around pretty much anyone, including me. But that doesn't get us far, does it?"

"It works for me, actually."

"Agent Reel, I think we can be more productive than this."

Reel sat forward. "Do you know why I'm here? I mean really why?"

"My job is not tied to that. My job is to evaluate you to determine if you are up to the task of field redeployment."

"Well, they didn't seem to have a problem with my field deployment on my last mission. They gave me a medal."

"Nevertheless, those are my instructions," countered Spitzer.

"And you always follow orders, I take it?" said Reel contemptuously.

"Do you?"

"Okay, so here we go." She sat back. "I pretty much always follow orders."

Spitzer said, "Does that mean nine times out of ten? And under what circumstances do you not follow orders?"

"Actually higher than nine times out of ten. And I don't follow orders when my gut tells me not to."

"Your gut? Can you elaborate?"

"Sure. My gut." She pointed to her belly. "That thing right here. It gives me tingly feelings when something is off. It's also useful in holding and then digesting food."

"And you listen to this instinct always?" asked Spitzer.

"Yes."

"What is it telling you now?"

This query seemed to catch Reel off guard. She quickly regrouped. "That both of us are wasting our time."

"Why?" Spitzer wanted to know.

"Because my being here is bullshit. I'm not being evaluated for redeployment. I'm damaged goods. I was sent here for another reason."

"To be punished, like you said."

"Or killed. Might be the same thing to some."

Spitzer looked at her skeptically. "You actually think the agency wants to kill you? Aren't you being a bit paranoid?"

"I'm not a bit paranoid. I'm *a lot* paranoid. I have been most of my life. The mind-set serves me well."

Spitzer looked down at the file she held. "I guess I can understand that given your background."

"I'm sick of people defining me by where I came from," snapped Reel. She rose and paced the small room while the other woman watched her closely. "Lots of people have shitty backgrounds and grow up normal and accomplish a great deal. Lots of people born with silver spoons turn out to be worthless, bad people."

"Yes, they do," said Spitzer. "We're all individuals. There are no hard-and-fast rules. You have accomplished much, Agent Reel. I think you would have done so whether you were born with a silver spoon or not. I believe it's just how you're wired."

Reel sat down and studied her. "Right," she scoffed. "You really think that?"

"You yourself just said that you were sick of people defining you by your upbringing. Or lack of one." She stared at Reel expectantly.

"If you're waiting for me to spill my guts, Doc, you're going to be disappointed."

"I wouldn't expect a field agent with your level of experience to be loose of lip."

"So what I am doing here?"

Spitzer said, "I've been instructed to perform a psych eval on you. I know you've had them done before. Nothing more, nothing less."

Reel sat back. "Okay."

"Do you agree that following orders is important if the agency is to be functional?"

"I do."

"And yet you chose not to follow orders."

"I did. Because the agency also expects me to exercise my judgment. Orders are handed out by humans. Humans make mistakes. They issue their orders from the safe confines of their offices. I'm in the field, where it is hardly ever safe. I have to make decisions on the fly. I have to execute the assignment in the best way I see fit."

"And does that sometimes include *not* executing the assignment?" asked Spitzer.

"It could."

"And what about creating your own assignments for your own purposes?"

Reel appraised the other woman from under half-closed eyes. "I see your briefing has been more complete than you let on."

"It is a very tight need to know. I have always felt that is the only way I can do my job. But I'm here to listen far more than talk."

"So you know what I did."

Spitzer nodded. "I do."

"Were you also told why I did it?"

"Yes. Although some of the facts seem to be in dispute."

"You mean the truth versus the lies?"

"I would like to hear your side," answered Spitzer.

"Why? Why does that possibly matter?"

"It's part of the eval. But if you don't want to go into it—"

Reel impatiently waved this away. "What the hell? If I don't, I suppose it'll just be another mark against me, not that they need one." She leaned forward, resting her elbows on her knees and clasping her hands. "You ever have a close friend of yours murdered?"

Spitzer shook her head. "Fortunately, no."

"The shock of it just takes hold of you. You go through all the stages of grief in what seems like a few seconds. It's not like an accident, or illness, or old age. It's like someone shot you as well as your friend. They took both your lives, just like that."

"I can see that."

"No, you really can't. Not unless it's happened to you. But when it does, all you want is revenge. You want to take the hurt you're feeling, this acid hole in your belly, and hurl it at the person responsible. You don't just want to make them suffer. You want them to die too. You want to take from them what they took from you."

Spitzer sat back, looking uncomfortable but curious. "Is that how you felt then?"

"Of course it's how I felt," said Reel quietly. "But unlike most people in that situation, I could do something about it. I took the pain and I hurled it right back where it belonged."

"And two people died. Two members of this agency, in fact."

"That's right."

"So you played the roles of judge, jury, and executioner?"

"Judge, jury, and executioner," repeated Reel, her eyes hooded again as she stared over at the other woman. "But I've been playing the executioner role for years. You people here have been handling the judge and jury parts. You decide who dies and you tell me. And then I do it. Sort of like playing God, isn't it? Who lives, who doesn't?" Before Spitzer could say anything Reel added, "Do you want to know how that makes me feel? You shrink types always like to know that, right? How we feel about every little thing?"

Spitzer slowly nodded. "I would like to know."

"It makes me feel great. The agency does the heavy lifting. They decide who bites the bullet. I just carry out the order. What could be better?"

"So how did it make you feel to play all three roles?"

The smile that had emerged on Reel's face slowly disappeared. She covered her eyes with her hands for a moment. "I didn't care for it as much."

"So not a role you can see yourself playing in the future?" asked Spitzer.

Reel glanced up. "Why don't we cut the bullshit and just face reality, shall we? It's not a role. This is not play-acting. The guy on the floor with the bullet in his head doesn't get back up when the curtain drops. My bullet. My kill. He stays quite dead."

"I take it you don't enjoy killing."

"I enjoy a job well done. But it's not like I'm a serial killer. Serial killers love it. They're obsessed with the opportunity for domination of another human being. The rituals, the details. The hunt. The strike. I'm not obsessed with any of it. It's my job. It's what I do as a profession. For me it's a means to an end. I build a wall around it, do it, and then move on. I don't care who the target is. I only care that it's *the* target. It's not a human to me. It is a mission. That's all. I don't read any more into it than that. If I did, I couldn't do it."

A minute of silence passed, punctuated only by Reel's accelerated breathing.

Finally Spitzer said, "You were recruited into the agency at a young age, with no college behind you. That is highly unusual."

"So they tell me. But I guess you don't need a degree to pull a trigger."

"Why did you choose to do so? You were a very young woman, barely at the age of majority. You could have done many other things in your life."

"Well, I didn't see many other options, actually."

"That is hard to believe," countered Spitzer.

"Well, *you* didn't have to believe it, did you? It was my choice," Reel said harshly.

The Target

Spitzer closed her notebook and capped her pen.

Reel noted this. "I don't think our hour is up."

"I think that's enough for today, Agent Reel."

Reel rose. "I think it's enough for the rest of my life."

She slammed the door on her way out.

13

The place had several different names: Bukchang, Pukchang, Pukch'ang.

It was officially known as Kwan-li-so Number 18. That meant Penal Labor Colony in Korean. It was a concentration camp. It was a gulag. It actually was hell, near the Taedong River in North Korea's P'yongan-namdo province.

The oldest of North Korean labor camps, Bukchang had been hosting dissidents and alleged enemies of the state since the fifties. Unlike the other labor camps, all of which were run by the *Bowibu*—also known as the State Security Department or the secret police—Bukchang was operated by the *inmin pohan seong*, the Interior Ministry. There were two parts to the camp. One zone was for reeducation. Inmates here would learn the teachings of the country's two great dead leaders and might be released, though they would be monitored for the rest of their lives. The other zone was for lifers who would never see outside the camp. The majority here were lifers.

Nearly the physical size of Los Angeles, Bukchang

housed fifty thousand prisoners who were kept in by, among many other things, a four-meter-high fence. If you were sent here, so was your entire family—the classic definition of guilt by association, which extended to infants, toddlers, teenagers, siblings, spouses, and grandparents. Babies born here shared the same guilt as their families. Unauthorized babies born here, because intercourse and pregnancies were strictly regulated, were killed. Age and personal culpability meant nothing, and a toddler and an ancient grandmother were treated the same—brutally.

At Bukchang everyone worked nearly all the time, in the coal mines, in the cement factories, and at other vocations. All of the work was dangerous. All of the workers were left totally unprotected. Many died from work accidents. Black lung disease alone had felled legions of forced coal miners. Food was largely unavailable. You were expected to scavenge for yourself, and families feasted on garbage, insects, weeds, and sometimes each other. Water came from the rain or the ground. It was dirty, and dysentery, among many other diseases, was rampant. These living conditions were used at Bukchang as highly effective population control.

It was not known precisely how many labor camps there were in North Korea, although the international consensus was six. The fact that they were numbered and those numbers reached at least as high as twenty-two was an indicator of their pervasiveness.

At least two hundred thousand North Koreans, or nearly one percent of the entire population, called these labor camps home.

There were allegations of corruption inside Bukchang. Things were not going smoothly. For one, there had been ten escapes in less than two months. That, by itself, was inexcusable. Two armed battalions guarded the camp. The four-meter-high fence was electrified, with booby traps everywhere. Five-meter-high guard towers ringed the fence, and guards on the ground remained both overt and hidden, looking for any signs of problems. Thus escape should have been impossible. But since it had happened, there had to be an explanation. There were rumors that the escapees had benefited from inside help. That was not only inexcusable, it was also treasonous.

The female prisoner was huddled in a corner of the stone room. She was a recent arrival here after being caught in China and repatriated. She was barely twenty-five but looked older. Her body was small, scarred but also hardened and sinewy; there was strength in her small footprint. The money that she had hidden inside an orifice had been discovered. The guards had pocketed it before beating her.

She now sat shivering with fear in the corner. Her clothes were rags, filthy from the trip out and now the forced journey back. She was bleeding, her hair matted and dirty. She was breathing heavily, her small chest pushing out and pulling in with each frantic breath.

The heavy door opened and four men came in: three guards in uniform and the administrator of Bukchang, who wore a gray tunic and pressed slacks. He was well fed, his hair neatly combed into a precise side part, his shoes shined, his skin smooth and healthy. He looked down at the mess of a human in front of him. She was like an animal found by the side of the road. He would treat her as such, which was how all prisoners here were treated. Any guard showing pity or kindness would in turn become a prisoner himself. Thus no guard ever showed compassion. From a totalitarian mind-set, it was a perfect arrangement.

He gave orders to his men, who finished stripping her down. The administrator stepped forward and nudged her exposed buttock with his glossy wingtip.

She bunched tighter, seemingly trying to melt into the wall. He smiled at this and then drew nearer still. He squatted down.

In Korean he said, "You have money, it seems."

She turned her face to his, her limbs trembling. She managed to nod.

"You have earned this while away?"

She nodded again.

"By taking Chinese filth into your bed?"

"Yes."

"You have more money?"

She started to shake her head but then stopped. She said, "I can get more."

The man nodded in satisfaction and looked up at the guards.

"How much more?" he asked.

"More," she said. "Much more."

"I want more. Much more," he answered. "When?"

"I will need to get a message out."

"How much more can you get?"

"Ten thousand wons."

He smiled and shook his head. "Not enough. And I don't want wons."

"Renminbis then?"

"Do I look like I want Chinese toilet paper?"

"What then?" she said fearfully.

"Euros. I want euros."

"Euros?" she said, shivering once more since it was freezing in here and she was naked. "What good are euros here?"

"I want euros, bitch," said the warden. "It is no concern of yours why."

"How much euros?" said the woman.

"Twenty thousand. Up front."

She looked shocked. "Twenty thousand euros?"

"That is my price."

"But how can I trust you?"

"You can't," he said, smiling. "But what choice do you have? The coal mine awaits." He paused. "Your record says you are from Kaechon," he said.

This was known as Camp 14 and located on the other side of the Taedong River, adjacent to Bukchang.

He continued. "They coddle their prisoners there. Even though we have a reeducation zone here, and Kaechon is only for sons of bitches that are irredeemable, we do not coddle at Bukchang. You will not leave here alive. You will be caught trying to escape. And you will be tied to a pole, your mouth stuffed with rocks, and you will be shot five times by each guard. And every minute you are here alive will feel like death."

He looked at his men. "Kaechon," he said, and laughed. "For shit coddlers."

They all laughed too, grinning at each other and slapping their thighs.

He stood. "Twenty thousand euros."

"When?"

"Five days."

"But that is impossible."

"Then I am sorry." He motioned to his guards, who moved forward.

"Wait, wait!" she screamed.

The men stopped and looked at her expectantly.

She rose on quivering legs. "I will get it. But I need to get a message out."

"Perhaps that can be arranged." He looked over her naked body. "You are not so scrawny. When you are cleaned up, you will be pretty, I think. Or at least not so disgusting."

He reached out and touched her hair. She flinched and he slapped her so violently he drew blood.

"You will never do that again," he ordered. "You will welcome my touch."

She nodded and rubbed the skin where he had struck her and tasted the blood on her lips.

"You will be cleaned up. And then you will be brought to me."

She looked at him and knew what that meant. "But the euros? I thought that was the payment."

"In *addition* to the euros. While we wait the five days. Or do you prefer the filthy, dangerous mines to my bed?"

She shook her head and looked down, defeated. "I . . . I do not want to go to the mines."

He smiled and cupped her trembling chin, lifting her gaze to his.

"You see, not so difficult. Food, clean water, warm bed. And I will have you as often as I want." He turned to his men. "As will they. Anytime we want. You understand? Anything we want, I don't care what it is. You are nothing but a dog, do you understand?"

She nodded tearfully. "I understand. But you will not hurt me? I . . . I have been hurt enough."

He slapped her again. "You make no demands, filth. You do not speak unless I ask you a question."

He put his hands around her throat and slammed her against the wall. "Do you understand?"

She nodded and said in a defeated voice, "I understand."

"You will call me *seu seung*," he added, using the Korean word for master. "You will call me this even after you leave here. *If* you leave here. I make no promises, even if you get me the euros. You may not safely escape. It is up to me and me only. Do you understand?"

She nodded. "I understand."

He shook her violently. "Say it. Give me my proper respect."

"Seu seung," she said in a tremulous voice.

He smiled and let her go. "See, that was not so bad."

A moment later he clutched at his throat where she had struck him. He staggered backward, colliding with one of his men.

She moved so fast it seemed that everyone else had slowed by comparison. She catapulted across the room, slipped one guard's gun from his holster, and shot him in the face with it. Another guard came at her. She turned and kicked so high her foot caught him in the eye. Her jagged toenails ripped his pupil, blinding him. He screamed and fell back as the third guard fired his gun. But she was no longer there. She had pushed backward off the wall and cartwheeled over him, taking the knife off his belt holder as she sailed past, landing a foot behind him. She slashed four times so fast no eye could follow. The guard clutched at his neck where his veins and arteries had been severed.

She never stopped moving. Using his falling body as a launch pad she leapt over him and caught the blinded guard in a leg lock around his head. She twisted her body in midair and hurled him forward, where his head struck the stone wall with such force that his skull cracked.

She picked up the pistol she had dropped, stood over each guard, and fired into their heads until they were all dead.

She had always loathed the camp guards. She had lived for years with them. They had left scars inside and outside of her that would never heal. She would never be a mother because of them. Because of them she had never even contemplated being a mother because that would mean she had come to accept herself as a human being, which she never could. Her name in the camp had been "Bitch." Every woman in the camp had had that name. "Bitch. Bitch." That was all she had ever heard from light to night for years on end. "Come, Bitch. Go, Bitch. Die, Bitch."

She turned to the administrator, who lay on the floor near the door. He was not yet dead. He was still clutching his throat and gasping for air, his eyes unfocused but panicked. She had planned it this way, hitting him just hard enough to incapacitate but not kill. She knew exactly what the difference was.

She knelt down next to him. He stared up with bulging eyes, his hands at his throat. She did not smile in triumph. She did not look sad. Her features were expressionless.

She knelt down closer.

"Say it," she said in a whisper.

He whimpered and clutched at his ruptured throat.

"Say it," she said again. "*Seu seung.*"

She cupped a hand under his neck and squeezed. "Say it."

He whimpered.

She placed her bony knee against his crotch and pressed. "Say it."

He screamed as she jammed her knee down harder against his privates.

"Say it. *Seu seung.* Say it and no more pain." She rammed her knee against him. He screamed louder. "Say it."

"S . . . *seu* . . . "

"Say it. Say it all." She ferociously ground her knee into him.

He screamed as loud as his damaged windpipe would allow. "*Seu seung.*"

She straightened. She did not smile in triumph. She did not look sad. She was expressionless. "See, that was not so bad," she said, parroting his earlier words.

As he stared helplessly up at her she leapt into the air and came down on top of him. Her elbow slammed into the man's nose with such force that she pushed the cartilage there right into his brain, like a fired bullet. This killed him instantly, whereas his crushed windpipe would have taken more time to finish him off.

She rose and looked around at the four dead men. "*Seu seung,*" she said. "Me, not you."

She searched the guards' pockets and found a walkie-talkie. She pulled it out, turned it to a different frequency, and said simply, "It is done."

She dropped the walkie-talkie, stepped over the dead men, and walked out of the room, still naked, covered in the men's blood.

Her name was Chung-Cha, and she and her family had been labor camp prisoners many years ago at Camp 15, also known as Yodok. She had been only one year old when the *Bowibu* had come for them in the night. They always came at night. Predators did not come during the light. She had survived Yodok. Her family had not.

Other guards passed her in the hall and rushed onward to the room where the dead men were.

They said nothing to her. They didn't look at her.

When they got there two of the guards vomited onto the stones after seeing the carnage.

When Chung-Cha reached the prearranged spot

two men who wore the markings of generals in the North Korean military greeted her with respect. One handed her a wet towel and soap with which to clean off. The other held fresh clothes for her. She cleaned and then dressed in front of them without a shade of embarrassment for her nudity. Both generals averted their gazes while she did so, although it did not matter to her. She had been naked and brutalized in front of many men. She had never had privacy and thus had no expectation of it. It simply meant nothing to her. Dogs did not require clothes.

She glanced at them only once. To her, they did not look like soldiers; with their broad-rimmed puffy caps they looked more like members of a band, ready to pick up musical instruments rather than weapons. They looked funny, weak, and incompetent, when she knew them to be cagey and paranoid and dangerous to everyone, including themselves.

One said, "Yie Chung-Cha, you are to be commended. His Supreme Leader Kim Jong Un has been informed and sends his personal thanks. You will be rewarded appropriately."

She handed back the soiled towel and soap.

"How appropriately?"

The generals glanced at each other, their features showing their amazement at this comment.

"The Supreme Leader will determine that," said the other. "And you will be grateful for whatever he decides."

His companion added, "There is no greater honor than to serve one's country."

She stared up at them both, her features unreadable. Then she turned and walked down the corridor and made her way out of the camp. As she passed, many watched her. None attempted to make eye contact. Not even the most brutal of all the guards there. Word of what she had done had already made its way through the camp. Thus none wanted to look Yie Chung-Cha in the eye because it might be the last thing they ever saw.

Her gaze never wavered. It pointed straight ahead.

Outside the four-meter fence a truck awaited. A door opened and she climbed in.

The truck immediately drove off, heading to the south, to Pyongyang, the capital. She had an apartment there. And a car. And food. And clean water. And some wons in a local bank. That was all she needed. It was far more than she had ever had. Far more than she had ever expected to have. She was grateful for this. Grateful to be alive.

Corruption could not be tolerated.

She knew that better than most.

Four men dead today by her hand.

The truck drove on.

Chung-Cha forgot about the corrupt administrator who had demanded euros and sex in payment for her escape. He was not worth any more of her thoughts.

She would return to her apartment. And she would await the next call.

It would come soon, she thought. It always did.

And she would be ready. It was the only life she had.

And for that too she was grateful.

No greater honor than to serve one's country?

She formed spit in her mouth and then swallowed it.

Chung-Cha looked out the window, seeing nothing as they drew nearer to Pyongyang. She spoke to none of the others in the vehicle.

She always kept her thoughts to herself. That was the only thing they couldn't take from her. And they had tried. They had tried mightily. They had taken everything else. But they had not taken that.

And they never would.

14

Her apartment. Until they took it away. It had a bedroom, a miniscule kitchen, a bathroom with a shower, and three small windows. About two hundred square feet total. To her, it was a magnificent castle.

Her car. Until they took it away. It was a two-door model made by the Sungri Motor Plant. It had four tires and a steering wheel and an engine and brakes that usually worked. Her possession of the vehicle made her a rare person in her country.

The vast majority of her fellow citizens traveled on bicycles, took the metro or the bus, or simply walked. For longer commutes there was the rail. But it could take up to six hours to go barely a hundred miles because the infrastructure and equipment were so poor. For the very elite there were commercial aircraft. Like with the rail service, there was only one airline—Air Koryo. And it flew mostly old, Russian-made aircraft. She did not like to ride on Russian wings. She did not like anything Russian.

But Chung-Cha had her own car and her own apartment. For now. That was stark proof of her worth to the Democratic People's Republic of Korea.

She walked into the kitchen and ran her hand over one of her most prized possessions. An electric rice cooker. This had been her reward from the Supreme Leader for her killing of the four men at Bukchang. That and an iPod loaded with country-and-western music. As she held the iPod she well knew that it was a device that most of her fellow North Koreans didn't even know existed. And she had also been given one thousand wons. That might not seem like much to some, but when you have nothing, anything seems like a fortune.

There were three classes of people in North Korea. There was the core, made up of loyalists to the country's leadership and, for lack of a better term, purebloods. There was the wavering class, whose total loyalty to the leadership was in doubt. It was this class that represented the majority of the country, and for whom many lucrative jobs and government positions were out of reach. And, lastly, there was the hostile class, made up of enemies of the leadership and their descendants. Only the most elite of the core group had rice cookers. And the elite numbered perhaps one hundred and fifty thousand in a country of twenty-three million. There were more people in the prison camps.

It was quite a feat for Chung-Cha to have attained what she had, because her family was of the hostile class. Rice in one's belly was a mark of wealthy, elite status. However, exclusive of the ruling Kim family—which lived like kings, with mansions and water parks and even their own train station—even the most elite of North Koreans existed at a level that would be looked upon as very near poverty in developed nations. There was no hot water; the electricity was totally unreliable, with only a few hours of it a day at best; and travel outside the country was nearly impossible. And a rice cooker and some songs was the reward given by one's enormously rich leadership for enduring torture and suffering and for killing four men and uncovering corruption and treason.

But still, for Chung-Cha, it was far more than she had ever expected to have. A roof over her head, a car to drive, a rice cooker; it was like all the wealth in the world was hers.

She moved to a window of her apartment and looked out. Her place overlooked the center of Pyongyang, with a nice view of the Taedong River. A city of nearly three and a half million souls, the capital was by far the largest metropolis in the country. Hamhung, the next most populous city, had barely a fifth of Pyongyang's people.

She liked to look out the window. She had spent a good part of her earlier life dearly wishing for a window that looked out onto anything. For over a decade at the labor camp her wish had not come true. Then things had changed. Dramatically.

And now look at me, she thought.

She put on her coat and boots with the four-inch heels that made her taller. She would never wear such footwear on a mission, but the women in Pyongyang were very much into their thin high heels. Even women in the military, working construction, and in the traffic police wore them. It was one of the few ways to feel, well, liberated, if that was even possible here.

The monsoon season, running from June to August, had passed. The cold, dry winter would begin in about a month. Yet now the air was mild, the breeze invigorating, and the skies clear. These were the days on which Chung-Cha liked to walk through her city. They were rare times, for her work carried her to many other parts of her country and the world. And there never was occasion for a leisurely walk during any of those times.

On the left breast of her jacket rode her Kim pin. All North Koreans wore this decoration, depicting either or both Kim Il Sung and his son Kim Jong Il, both dead, but both never to be forgotten. Chung-Cha did not want to always wear the pin, but if she did not her arrest would be imminent. Even she was not so important to the state that she could ever forgo this sign of respect.

As she walked she took in observations she had made long ago. In many ways the capital city was a twelve-hundred-square-mile tribute to the ruling

Kim family on the banks of the Taedong that flowed southward into Korea Bay. Pyongyang translated into "flat land" in Korean, and it was well named. It was only ninety feet above sea level and stretched outward smooth as a *bindaetteok,* or Korean pancake. The main boulevards were broad and largely devoid of cars. What passed by on the roads were mostly trolleys or buses.

The city did not seem like it had millions of residents. While the sidewalks were fairly full with pedestrians, in her work Chung-Cha had visited cities of comparable size in other countries where far more people were out and about. Perhaps it was all the surveillance cameras and police watching that made the citizens want to hide from view.

She walked down the steps to the metro. Pyongyang had the deepest subway system in the world, over a hundred meters in the ground. It ran only on the west side of the Taedong, while all foreign residents lived on the east side. Whether this was intentional or not she didn't know. But being North Korean, she assumed it was. Central planning combined with paranoia had been elevated to a high art here.

Citizens queuing up for the next train did so in precise straight lines. North Koreans were drilled from an early age to form pristine lines in under a minute. There were straight lines of humanity all over the capital city. It was part of the "single-hearted unity" for which the country was known.

The Target

Chung-Cha did not join the queue. She purposely waited apart from it until the train entered the station. She rode the train to another section of town and came back to the surface. The green spaces in Pyongyang were immense and many in number, but not as immense as the monuments.

There was the Arch of Triumph, a copy of the one in Paris, but far bigger. It commemorated the Korean resistance to Japan from the 1920s to the 1940s. There was the Washington Monument lookalike Juche Tower, which was one hundred and seventy meters tall and stood for the Korean philosophy of self-reliance.

As she passed it Chung-Cha nodded silently. She relied only on herself. She trusted only herself. No one here had to tell her that. She didn't need a monument shooting into the sky to make her believe *that*.

There was the also the Arch of Reunification, one of the few that featured Korean women. Dressed in traditional Korean garb, they held between them the map of a united Korea. The arch straddled the Reunification Highway, which went from the capital city all the way to the DMZ.

Symbolism again, she knew.

Chung-Cha had two notions on reunification. First, it would never happen, and second, she didn't care if it did or not. She would not be unified with anyone, north or south.

Later, she passed the Mansudae Grand Monument,

which was an enormous tribute to the memory of North Korea's founder, Il Sung, and also to his son, Jong Il.

Chung-Cha passed by this monolithic structure without looking at it. This was a bit dicey on her part. All North Koreans paid tribute here by standing and gazing lovingly at the statues of the two men. All brought flowers. Even foreign tourists were required to lay floral offerings here or else be arrested and/or deported.

Yet Chung-Cha walked on, almost daring a nearby policeman to stop her. There were limits to her patriotism.

Towering over the entire city was the white elephant of Pyongyang, the Ryugyong Hotel. It was begun in 1987, but construction funds ran out in 1992. Although construction had restarted in 2008, no one knew if it would ever be completed or whether even one guest would sleep there. For now it was a 330-meter-high monstrosity with nearly four million square feet of space in the shape of a pyramid.

Interesting central planning there, she thought.

Her belly grumbling, Chung-Cha entered a restaurant. North Koreans typically did not eat out because it was a luxury most could not afford. If a group did go out, it was usually on state business with the government footing the bill. At times like that the workers would eat and drink prodigious amounts, going home drunk on *soju*, or rice liquor.

The Target

She had passed other restaurants offering typical Korean fare like kimchi—spicy pickled vegetables that every Korean woman knew how to make—boiled chicken, fish, and squid, as well as the luxury of white rice. She kept going past all of these and entered the Samtaesung Hamburger Restaurant, which served burgers, fries, and shakes. Chung-Cha had often tried to reconcile in her mind how a restaurant serving what would be recognized around the world as American food could exist here when there was not even a U.S. embassy located in Pyongyang because the two countries did not have official diplomatic relations. An American citizen in trouble here had to go crawling to the Swedish embassy, and even then only for medical emergencies.

She was one of the few patrons here, and all the others were westerners.

She ordered a hamburger rare, fries, and a vanilla milk shake.

The waiter looked at her severely as though silently admonishing her for eating this Western garbage. When she showed him her government ID he bowed perfunctorily and hurried away to fill her order.

She had chosen a seat with her back against the wall. She knew where the entrances and exits were. She noted anyone moving in the space, whether it was toward or away from her. She didn't expect trouble, but she also anticipated that anything could happen at any time.

She ate her meal slowly, chewing her food thoroughly before swallowing. She had endured starvation for well over a decade. That hollow feeling in your belly never left you, even if you had ample food the rest of your life. Her diet at Yodok had consisted of whatever she could find to eat, but mostly corn, cabbage, salt, and rats. At least the rats had given her protein and helped to stave off diseases that had killed many other prisoners. She had become quite adept at catching the rodents. But she liked the taste of the burger better.

Chung-Cha was not fat and never would be. Not so long as she was working. Maybe as an aged woman living somewhere else she would allow herself to grow obese. But she did not dwell on this prospect for long. She doubted she would live long enough to grow old.

She finished her meal and paid her bill and left. She had one place she wanted to go. Something she wanted to see, although she had already seen it before. Everyone in North Korea probably had.

It had been recently moored on the Botong River in Pyongyang to become part of the Fatherland Liberation War Museum. This was so because it was a ship—a truly unique ship. It was the second oldest commissioned ship in the U.S. Navy, after the USS

Constitution. And it was the only U.S. naval vessel currently held by a foreign power.

The USS *Pueblo* had been in North Korean hands since 1968. Pyongyang said it had strayed into North Korean waters. The United States said it had not. The rest of the world used twelve nautical miles out to sea as the demarcation for international waters. However, Pyongyang did not follow what other countries did and claimed a fifty-nautical-mile boundary. The *Pueblo* was now a museum, a testament to the might and bravery of the homeland and a chilling reminder of the imperialist intentions of the evil America.

Chung-Cha had taken the guided tour, but she did so with a perspective different from other visitors. She had read an uncensored account of the sailors aboard the *Pueblo.* This was an unheard-of thing in her country, but Chung-Cha's work often carried her out of North Korea. The sailors had been forced to say and write things that they did not believe, like admitting to spying on North Korea and denouncing their own country. But in a famous photo of some of the seamen, they surreptitiously had been giving the finger to the North Korean cameraman and symbolically to their captors while seemingly just clasping their hands. The North Koreans did not know what a raised middle finger meant and asked the sailors about it. To a man they said it was a Hawaiian symbol of good luck. When *Time* magazine had run a story exposing the truth of the gesture, the sailors were reportedly severely beaten and tortured even more than they already had been.

When they were released in December 1968, eighty-two of them walked single file across the Bridge of No Return in the DMZ. One sailor had not walked across. He had died in the initial attack on the ship, the only fatality of the incident.

Chung-Cha finished the tour and made her way back to land. She looked back at the ship. She had been told that the Americans would not decommission the ship until it was returned to them.

Well, then it would never be decommissioned, she thought. North Korea had very little. And so they never gave anything back that they had taken. After the Soviets had left and North Korea had its independence it was as though it was this little country against the world. It had no friends. No one who truly understood it, not even the Chinese, whom Chung-Cha considered to be among the wiliest races on earth.

Chung-Cha was not a religious person. She knew no North Koreans who were. There were some Korean Shamanists, others who practiced Cheondoism, some Buddhists, and a relative handful of Christians. Religion was not encouraged since it could be a direct challenge to the country's leaders. Marx had had it right, she thought: Religion was the people's opium. Yet Pyongyang had once been known as the Jerusalem of the East because of the Protestant missionaries who had come in the 1800s, with the result that over a hundred churches had been erected on the "Flat Land." That was no more. It was simply not tolerated.

And to her it did not matter. She did not believe in a benign higher being. She could not. She had suffered too much to think of a heavenly force in the sky that would let such evil walk the earth without lifting a hand to stop it.

Self-reliance was the best policy. Then you alone were entitled to the rewards—and you alone bore responsibility for the losses.

She passed an open street market and stopped, tensing for a moment. There was a foreign tourist not five feet from her. It was a man. He looked German, but she could not be sure. He had his camera out and was about to take a picture of the marketplace and the vendors.

Chung-Cha looked around for the tour guide who must accompany all foreigners. She did not see any such person.

The German had his camera nearly up to his eye. She shot forward and snatched it from him. He looked at her, stunned.

"Give that back," he said in a language that she recognized as Dutch. She did not speak Dutch. She asked him if he spoke English.

He nodded.

She held up the camera. "If you take a picture of

the street market you will be arrested and deported. You might not be deported, actually. You might just stay here, which will be worse for you."

He paled and looked around to see several Korean vendors staring at him with malice.

He sputtered, "But why? It's just for my Facebook page."

"You do not need to know why. All you need to do is put your camera away and go and find your tour guide. Now. You will not receive another warning."

She handed him back the camera and he took it.

"Thank you," he said breathlessly.

But Chung-Cha had already turned away. She did not want his thanks. Maybe she should have just let the crowd attack him, let him be beaten, arrested, thrown in prison, and forgotten about. He was one person in a world of billions. Who would care? It was not her problem.

Yet as she walked down the street she thought of the man's question.

But why? he had asked.

The answer to that was both simple and complex. An open street market said to the world that North Korea's economy was weak, its traditional stores few in number, and thus the need for vendors in the street. That would be a slap in the face to a leadership acutely sensitive to world opinion. Conversely, an abundance of goods at a street market, if seen by the rest of the world, could result in international food aid being reduced. And since many North Koreans were barely surviving, that would not be a good thing. Pyongyang was not representative of the rest of the country. And yet even people here starved to death in their apartments. It was part of the so-called eating problem, which was very simple. There was not enough food. This was why North Koreans were shorter and lighter than their brethren to the south.

Chung-Cha did not know if either of these explanations was true. She only knew that these were the unofficial explanations for why the simple act of taking a picture could have such horrendous consequences, in addition to the fact that North Koreans did not like to have their pictures taken by foreigners. And things could get violent. The perpetrator would be arrested. That was reason enough never to leave your tour guide's side while in North Korea.

Our ways are just different because we are the most paranoid country on the face of the earth. And perhaps we have good reason to be. Or perhaps our leaders want to keep us united against an enemy that does not exist.

She didn't know how many other North Koreans had such thoughts. She did know that the ones who had publicly expressed them had all been sent to the penal colonies.

She knew this for a fact.

Because her parents had been sent to Yodok for doing that very thing. She had grown up there. She had nearly died there. But she had survived, the only one of her family to do so.

And her survival had come at a terrible price.

She had had to kill the rest of her family to be allowed to live.

15

Robie looked at Reel.

Reel studied the floor.

It was nearly midnight a week into their stay here. After their psychological vetting they had undergone more physical endurance tests, each more difficult than the last. They had been given a bit of food and water and then brought back here, sweaty and tired and increasingly depressed. Over the next days they had been worked relentlessly and had dropped exhausted into their bunks for a few hours of sleep before they were hustled from their beds and it all started up again.

Tonight, they had gotten off relatively early. And so this was the first real time they had been able to speak to each other since the first day.

"How did your shrink session go?" asked Robie, finally breaking the silence in their tiny shared room.

"Great, how about you?" she said sarcastically.

"We spent a good deal of the time talking about you, actually."

She looked up at him and then stared over at the nearest listening device.

She glanced back at him and mouthed, *Here? Now?*

He looked around the room and noted the video cameras that they both knew were embedded in the walls. He flipped up the mattress so that it leaned against his back, effectively shielding him from view. Then he motioned for her to sit on the other side of the bunk and face him. She did so, staring at him curiously.

Then he began using sign language. He had been taught this, as had Reel, he knew, because silent communication was often very useful in the field.

He said in sign, "Marks is Evan Tucker's person through and through. Can't believe we're intended to survive this place. Do we make a break for it?"

Reel thought about this and signed back, "Gives them a great excuse to kill us with no repercussions."

He signed, "So we sit tight?"

"I think we can survive this."

"What's your plan?"

"We recruit Marks to our side."

Robie's eyes widened. "How?"

"We suffer together."

"You've been bitchy to her so far. How can you turn that around?"

"I was bitchy to her for the very reason that it would allow me an opportunity to turn it around with credibility. If she thinks I hate her, it could work.

If I had started out nice, she would have been instantly suspicious."

Robie still looked dubious.

Reel signed, "What other option do we have?"

"None," he signed. "Except die."

At that moment the door burst open and a half
dozen armed men came in. Robie and Reel were
shackled and then hustled out of the room. They were
hurried down one long hall after another. They were
being moved so fast neither Reel nor Robie could get
a handle on which direction they were going.

A door was thrown open and they were pushed
inside. The door slammed shut behind them and
other hands grabbed them. Reel and Robie were
lifted off their feet and each was placed prone on a
long board.

The room was dimly lighted but they could still
see each other, being only inches apart. They both
knew what was coming. They were strapped to the
boards. Then the boards were tipped back. Their
heads were submerged in a large bucket of icy water.
They were held there nearly long enough to be
drowned.

When they were lifted free from the water, their
feet were kept elevated. Next, a thin cloth was placed
over their faces and icy water poured over it. The
liquid quickly saturated the cloth and then filled their
mouths and noses. The gag reflex was nearly immediate. They coughed and spit. More water was poured.

They coughed and gagged. More water was poured. They both retched.

The cloth was lifted and they were allowed to snatch three or four normal breaths before the cloth went back on. The water was poured again, with the same result. This process was repeated over the next twenty minutes.

Both Reel and Robie had vomited what little was in their stomachs. All that was coming out now was bile.

They were kept on the boards with the cloth over their faces. Neither knew when the water would start up again, which was all part of the technique. No training in the world could really insulate you from the terrors of waterboarding.

They both lay there gasping, their limbs pressing against the restraints, their chests heaving.

Normally, interrogation would start now. Both Robie and Reel knew this, but they each wondered what sort of interrogation they would be subjected to.

The lights dimmed even more and both of them braced for what might be coming next.

A voice said, "This can stop; it's up to you."

It was not Amanda Marks. It was a male voice neither of them recognized.

"What's the price?" gasped Reel.

"A signed confession," said the voice.

"Confessing what?" said Robie, spitting retch from his mouth.

"For Reel, the murders of two CIA operatives. For you, aiding and abetting her. And also to a count of treason."

"You a lawyer?" sputtered Reel.

"All I need is your answer."

Reel's next words made the man chuckle. He said, "I'm afraid that is physically impossible for me to do to myself. But that's an answer in itself, I suppose."

Twenty more minutes of waterboarding occurred.

When they came back up for air the same question was posed.

"This will stop," said the voice. "All you have to do is sign."

"Treason carries the death penalty," gasped Robie. Then he turned to the side and threw up more bile. His brain was about to explode and his lungs felt seared.

Reel interjected, "So what the hell does it matter?"

"It does matter. You'll be given lengthy prison terms, but you won't be executed. That's the deal. But you have to sign the confession. It's all prepared. You just have to sign."

Neither Robie nor Reel said anything.

The ordeal went on for twenty more minutes.

When it finished, neither of them was conscious. This was one drawback to this form of torture. The body just shut down. And there was no purpose in torturing an unconscious person.

The lights came on and the man stared down at the pair strapped to the long boards.

"An hour, impressive," he said.

His name was Andrew Viola. Up until the year before he had been the chief trainer at the Burner Box, and before that a legendary CIA field agent who'd had a hand in some of the most complex and dangerous missions of the past twenty-five years. He would be fifty on his next birthday. He was still fit and trim, although his hair was an iron gray and his face heavily lined. And scarred from one mission that had not gone according to plan.

He looked over at Amanda Marks, who had been observing the entire process with a look of slight revulsion. "Not for the weak of stomach, or heart," he said.

"And I didn't exactly understand the purpose. Did we really expect them to sign a confession?"

"Not my call. I was told to do this and I did it. CIA lawyers and upper management can figure out the rest."

"This was my mission to run," she said.

"And it still is, Amanda. I'm not stepping on toes here. But I had my orders. And"—he glanced down at Robie and then Reel—"unlike some, I always follow orders."

"So what now?"

"My work here is done until I'm called up again.

So I might see these two again before they leave here. *If* they leave here," he corrected himself.

"They both believe they were brought here to die," said Marks.

"And you don't think that's a possibility?" asked Viola, looking mildly surprised. "Recruits do die here. It's rare, but it happens. This is not summer camp, Amanda."

"That's different. *Accidents* happen. And Robie and Reel are not recruits. They are vets and battle-tested. But if the purpose from the start was—"

He cut her off. "Don't try to think too much about it. Just do your job. You'll be happy, and so will the higher-ups."

"And that doesn't bother you?"

He glanced sideways at her. "Maybe in the past. *Maybe*. But not anymore."

"What changed?"

"We were attacked. The Towers fell. The Pentagon was hit. Planes crashed. Americans died. Now I try to see the world only in black and white."

"The world is not black and white."

"That's why I said I *try* to do it."

He turned and left the room.

Marks came forward and stared down at the two unconscious agents. She thought back to her meeting with Evan Tucker before coming here. The director had been understandably clear on the outcome he wanted. On the surface it appeared fair and even-handed. If they passed the test, they passed. They would be redeployed. Simple and straightforward.

But then this had come—the order for the waterboarding to be conducted by Viola. The man was excellent at his job, Marks knew. But he had, well, a ruthlessness, a moral compass that did not seem to actually encompass any morals at all. That bothered her.

A signed confession admitting to murder and treason?

That had to have come from Evan Tucker. No one else in the agency would have dared issue such an order. So the rules had changed. Tucker was using the Burner Box not only to test and break Robie and Reel. He also wanted them to admit to acts that would result in their imprisonment. He had not told her this part of the plan. He had been wise not to, because Marks would have refused.

This seemingly simple thought stunned her. She had never before refused to carry out a direct order. It was just not something one did. Failing to do that had been the cause of both Robie's and Reel's current troubles.

Am I becoming like them?

She heard Robie and Reel moan and then they started to come around.

She turned to one of her men. "Take them back to their room. Let them sleep. I'll give directions for when their next testing will begin."

This order was carried out immediately. She

watched Robie and Reel being carried back to their room.

Their prison cell, more like it.

Maybe their death row.

16

Robie woke first. There were no windows in the room so he had no idea what time it was. Their watches had been taken from them upon arrival. He slowly sat up and rubbed his aching head. He leaned over from the top bunk and saw Reel still sleeping in the lower berth.

Robie swallowed with difficulty and cringed when he tasted the remnants of the vomit still in his mouth and throat.

"Sucks, doesn't it?"

He looked down again to see Reel staring up at him.

"Not something I'd want to go through every day."

He swung his legs over the edge, dropped to the floor, and sat down on her bunk. She curled up her legs to give him room.

"To what purpose?" she asked. "They couldn't really believe we'd sign a confession."

Robie looked up at the listening device, but Reel shook her head. "I don't care if they hear." She sat up and said in a loud voice, "Not confessing to jack shit!"

She looked back at Robie, who was smiling.

"What?" she demanded.

"Nothing. Well, I just like your subtle style, Jessica."

She started to snap something back, but then stopped. And laughed.

He joined in for a few seconds.

And then they both grew quiet as footsteps approached.

The door opened and both of them immediately drew back, balled tight, hands up, reflexes ready. Taking them again would require a fight.

However, only Evan Tucker stood there.

Robie shot Reel a glance. Her look was so ferocious that he was afraid she was about to attack the DCI. He was actually putting out his arm to forestall this when she said, "Good morning, Director. Did you have a nice sleep last night? We did. Best in years."

Tucker managed a tight smile at this comment and then sat down in the chair opposite them. His suit was wrinkled and the collar of his shirt was slightly grimy, as though his journey here had not exactly been at first-class levels.

"I know what happened to you last night. I ordered it."

"Good to know," said Robie. "So is that a confession? Because I thought the use of waterboarding was illegal."

"It is illegal for purposes of interrogation on

detainees. Neither of you are detainees and it was not done for interrogation purposes."

"We were asked to sign confessions," Reel pointed out.

"A subterfuge only. There were no confessions for you to sign."

"That's not what the guy said last night. And the terms of the confession he recited were pretty specific," noted Robie.

"He had his script and he stuck to it. But there was no confession."

"So what was the point of the thing, then?" demanded Reel.

"To see if you two can still cut it. The mission you're to be deployed on entails the risk of being caught. And the enemy is known to use waterboarding among other interrogation tools to break prisoners. It's not all about being able to shoot straight."

"And so this had nothing to do with the hard-on you have for me, Director?" said Reel. "You really expect us to believe that?"

"I don't care what you believe or don't believe. I've made my position on you very clear. You murdered two of my people and got off scot free. I think that stinks. I think you should be in jail, but it's not my call. I still have my job to do and so do you. My job is to keep this country safe against outside threats. You two are tools that I have at my disposal. I will deploy you as necessary. If I think it wise to push your butts to the wall and then through it, I will do so. If you feel you can't cut it, then you can tell me right now and we cut out all this bullshit."

He stopped talking and looked at them expectantly.

"And if we want out?" said Robie.

"Then that can be made to happen. But chances are very good that your partner will be prosecuted for murder. And you as an accessory."

"So if we stay in and maybe get killed, either by the other side or our own people, we don't end up in court?" said Reel.

"Did you really expect anything more generous than that?" said Tucker skeptically. "You want to begin to wipe the slate clean of what you did, then suck it up, finish up here, and successfully execute the upcoming mission. If you want to cut and run, then that's a whole other ball game. Your choice. But make it now. I don't have time to waste."

"Is that why you're here?" asked Robie. "To deliver the ultimatum?"

"No, I'm here to finally lay to rest any misconception you two might have about my motives. You were not sent here to be killed. I'm far too busy to even have time to think about something like that. The fact is, in the grand scheme of things none of us is that important. Now, we have an opportunity to do something that will make the world a far better, far safer place. I need to know that you're with me on this one thousand percent, or I have no use for you at all. Again, your decision. And again, I need it now."

He once more quieted and looked at them.

Robie was the first to speak. "I'm in."

Reel nodded. "Me too."

"Glad to hear it." Tucker rose, opened the door, and was gone.

Before Reel and Robie could even say a word they heard the sounds of someone else approaching.

A few moments later an orderly wheeled a cart in. It was loaded with breakfast foods and a carafe of coffee. Another orderly brought in two foldable chairs. They set up the table, laid out the food and coffee, and departed.

Reel and Robie had not moved the entire time. Finally, they looked at each other.

"You think there's cyanide in it?" he asked.

"I don't care. I'm starving."

They rose, sat down in the chairs, and attacked the food and drank down the hot coffee. They said nothing as they devoured the meal.

Then they sat back looking both satisfied and energized.

Reel said, "You can never overestimate the effect of a good meal on one's spirits."

"Yeah, but maybe it's just that they're fattening the calf before leading it to slaughter."

"So that was our last meal before execution?"

"Wish I could tell you one way or another," Robie

replied. "Before Tucker showed up, I was pretty sure we were done for. Now I'm not so sure."

"Strange he came all this way to tell us something we already knew."

"You think he was sincere?"

"Give me a break. He was lying his ass off."

"For what reason?" asked Robie.

"Spies lie. And he's probably covering his butt on the water-boarding thing."

"Did he need to? It's not like we belong to a union and can file a grievance."

Footsteps sounded again, and each of them instinctively gripped the knives next to their plates. However, it was merely the orderly retrieving the table. Another escort was with him. He led them to the showers, where they cleaned up and changed into fresh clothes.

As they were walked back to their room Reel whispered into Robie's ear, "This is freaking me out more than the waterboarding. Why are they being nice to us?"

Robie whispered back, "Maybe Tucker gave the word."

"Like I believe that."

Four hours passed before someone came for them again. They were told to change into running gear. Then they were taken by Jeep to a remote part of the facility, deep within the forest, and dropped off.

The weather wasn't bad. In the forties, a little

overcast, but the sun was high in the sky and warming. Robie calculated it was about two o'clock in the afternoon.

After the vehicle drove off, someone stepped onto the path from behind some trees. They turned to see who it was.

Amanda Marks stood there wearing a running suit and Nikes.

"I trust you're well fed and rested?" she said.

"And clean," said Reel. "Let's not forget that."

"Then let's take a run, shall we?" Without waiting for their answer, Marks turned and jogged off.

Robie and Reel glanced confusedly at one another before joining her, he on the right, she on the left.

"So did you know Tucker was coming down today?" asked Reel.

"At the last minute. What did he want to talk to you about?"

"You mean he didn't tell you?" asked Robie.

"If he had I wouldn't be asking you."

"He wanted to let us know our being here was not part of a personal vendetta. He said we were waterboarded not in order to facilitate a confession, because there was no such thing, but rather to make sure we could withstand it in case we were captured."

"And did you believe him?" asked Marks.

"Would you?" Reel shot back.

"I don't know. I really don't. He's a more complicated person than I initially thought."

"I don't trust him," said Reel.

"If I were in your position, I wouldn't trust him either," replied Marks.

Reel said, "I take it the food and rest and showers were your doing?"

"Well, they certainly weren't the DCI's, or Andrew Viola's initiative."

"Viola," said a surprised Reel. "He's involved in this?"

"I thought you would have recognized his voice at the little waterboarding session. You two overlapped here, right? And I know you were in the field with him on a couple of missions."

"That's right, but I didn't recognize the voice."

"Probably had your mind on other things," said Marks dryly. She looked at Robie. "Do you know Viola?"

"Only by reputation. He's really good."

"Rock-solid warrior who never wavers from the playbook," replied Marks.

Reel and Robie exchanged a quick glance. Reel said, "Is that why we're out here jogging in the middle of the forest? So we can talk candidly?"

"Let me put it this way. I already ran ten miles this morning. So from a physical fitness point of view there's no reason for me to be out here."

"So Viola is a team player," said Robie.

"And you're not?" added Reel.

"Didn't say that," replied Marks. "I *am* a team player."

"And the little near-drowning session last night?" noted Reel.

"Not my call. And I wasn't picked to run it. That's where Viola stepped in."

"Surprised I hadn't seen him at the facility before," said Reel inquiringly.

"He was just called back in from temp duty elsewhere," answered Marks.

"By Evan Tucker?" asked Robie, swinging his arms loosely and popping his neck as they ran along at a comfortable pace.

"Don't know for sure, but I certainly wouldn't be surprised if that were the case. Viola is a high-level asset. He wouldn't be called in by a midlevel grunt. And I certainly didn't do it as the DD."

"So why wouldn't Tucker rely on you to do the dirty work?" Robie wanted to know.

Reel added, "Did you refuse to waterboard us?"

Marks ran along for another thirty feet before answering. "He never asked me to."

"And if he had?" Reel persisted. "What would you have done?"

"I never agreed with torturing bad guys, much less our own agents."

"Well, undoubtedly Tucker was aware of that," said Robie. "And didn't bother to ask you to do it. Obviously, Viola had no issue with doing it."

"No, he didn't. He would never decline to execute a direct order. He's not wired that way."

"But how could Tucker ever expect us to sign a confession?" said Reel. "Even if we were tortured?"

"He's not really CIA," answered Robie. "He was never in the intelligence field. His appointment to head up CIA was a political payback. He probably thought waterboarding works on everyone."

"As if a coerced confession is valid," noted Reel. "And he wanted us to sign it, despite the bullshit he tried to feed us back there."

"I don't think he was going to use it in a court of law," said Marks.

Reel shot her a glance. "What, then?"

Robie answered. "Probably proof to the president that we were bad guys."

Marks added, "And maybe the president signs off on your official termination. Not the kind where you clear out your desk and are escorted to the exit."

"If Tucker thought that was going to happen and he's running CIA, America is in a world of trouble," observed Reel.

"I don't know," said Robie. "Maybe he just wanted to kill us."

"He might just want us to feel the pain," said Reel.

"Mission accomplished there," said Robie.

Reel stopped running and the others pulled up and looked at her.

"Which brings us back to the question of why

you're doing what you're doing, Deputy Director," she said.

Marks jogged in place, keeping her body warm and loose. "I'm a team player, Reel, make no mistake about that."

"But?"

"But I draw the line at certain things. Waterboarding our own is one of those things."

"Anything else?"

"Tucker said he wanted me to push you right to your limit and then beyond. He really wanted to see if you were fit for duty and redeployment. Either you could cut it or not. I assumed that was his goal. To find that out."

"And now?"

"And now I don't know. His instructions had undertones that maybe he didn't want you to see the outside of this place again."

"And you chose to, what, ignore them?" said Reel.

"I chose to think he couldn't mean that," said Marks.

"Or convinced yourself that he couldn't," said Robie.

Marks started to run again and the pair followed her.

"So where does all this leave us?" asked Reel.

"I don't know," admitted Marks. "But I can tell you that from now on I will train with you."

"Why?" asked Robie.

"To be our guardian?" suggested Reel.

"I'm just going to train with you."

"This is not your problem or your fight, DD," said Robie. "Don't hang your career on this. You don't deserve the possible fallout."

"I'm the DD, as you pointed out, Robie. And the DD is responsible for her assets in the field. Well, you two are part of those assets and it's my responsibility to look out for you."

"So you're setting yourself up for a pissing contest with Evan Tucker over this?" exclaimed Reel. "Number one against two has a predetermined outcome."

"Maybe," replied Marks cryptically. "But then number twos tend to try harder."

Reel said, "You looking to make an enemy of Tucker?"

"I'm not intentionally making an enemy of anyone. What I'm trying to do is my job."

"I thought your job was to follow orders," said Robie.

"My job is to perform my duties as a DD to the best of my abilities. I intend to do just that."

She picked up her pace, leaving the pair of them behind by about ten yards. This seemed to be intentional to allow them to discuss what she had just said.

"You think she's on the up-and-up, or is she pretending to be our friend for some ulterior reason?" said Reel.

"I don't know. She seems sincere. And why the need to be our friend? She's got us here. She can do what she wants with us."

"And it's not like she's asked us to do anything," said Reel thoughtfully.

"Not yet," corrected Robie.

"So what do we do?"

"We let it play out. I think that's all we can do."

"And if she *is* on the up-and-up?"

"Then I hope she doesn't end up being collateral damage. Because I don't think Evan Tucker cares who gets in the way or who gets hurt."

Reel slowed down and then stopped.

He came back to her. "What is it?"

"Robie, I'm putting everyone in danger. You, her, Julie, anyone associated with me."

"Don't be stupid."

"You just said it! Anyone who gets in his way. In his way to get to *me*. Because, let's face it, I'm the one he really wants."

"So what?"

"So I need to go this alone, Robie."

"Go it alone? Against the CIA?"

"I'm not putting you or anyone else in danger. Any *more* danger. I've nearly gotten you killed more times than I can count."

"Do you remember what I told you while we were standing in the rain, Jessica?"

"I know that, but—"

"I've never said that to anyone else. Ever."

At his words Reel's eyes glimmered, and she seemed taken aback, but quickly regrouped.

"But this is not survivable, Robie. They water-boarded us last night. What's next? A firing squad?"

"Whatever it is, we'll take it on together. That way we double our chances of survival."

"No, we just double the potential number of casualties."

"Let's go. Marks gets too far ahead she might hold back dessert tonight as punishment."

Robie ran off. Reel waited a few more seconds and then shook her head and ran hard to catch up. But the worried look in her eyes remained.

17

"Mr. Fontaine?"

Earl, who had been dozing in his prison hospital bed, roused, opened his eyes, and looked around.

"Mr. Fontaine?"

He focused on her, the young doctor. He sat up straighter. "Yeah, Doc?"

She pulled up a chair and sat next to him. Earl noted that a guard other than big Albert was with her. But the man was still keenly watching Earl. He probably knew Earl's crimes even if the young doctor didn't.

"I wanted to let you know that I made some calls."

"Calls?"

"About your request."

Earl knew what she was talking about, but he had decided to play to the hilt the doddering old man with not much time to live.

"'Bout my little girl, you mean?"

"Yes, exactly."

"Sweet Jesus, thank you so much, Doc."

"I spoke to some people up in Washington."

"Washington! Holy Lord! Thank you, thank you."

"They put me in contact with other people after I explained the situation. Now, there are no guarantees."

"'Course not, Doc, never expected none. But what you did, well, I don't know enough words to properly thank you. It just means the world. The world to me."

The doctor seemed embarrassed by this outpouring of gratitude. Her cheeks tinged with red, she continued. "These matters are very delicate, as I'm sure you can imagine."

Earl hastily said, "O'course I understand. All hush-hush, you mean?"

"Yes. Now, this isn't exactly my field of expertise, but I explained the situation as best I could. The U.S. Marshals—"

"The Marshals, Lordy, Lordy," exclaimed Earl. "My little girl is okay, ain't she?"

"The Marshals oversee the Witness Protection Program, Mr. Fontaine."

"Oh, hell, that's right." He pointed to his IV lines. "These drugs, Doc, these dang drugs mess up my head. Can't think straight. Half the time ain't even know my own name."

"I'm sure," she said, giving him a sympathetic smile. Then she hurried on. "They said that the request was very unusual and that they would have to check it out. I'm not sure how long it will take. But

I did tell them of your personal circumstances. That is—" Here she faltered.

"Meaning I ain't got much longer to live," Earl said helpfully.

"Yes, I told them that. I didn't go into specifics because that would be a violation of patient confidentiality."

"Course, course," said Earl encouragingly. "Hell, glad you did. Not like I care who knows. Dying is dying."

"But they said if it proved legitimate, they would take steps to contact your daughter and at least put her in possession of the facts."

"A damn dream come true and I say that right from here," said Earl, with tears sliding down his cheeks as he touched his chest.

"Now, Mr. Fontaine, please understand, simply because they might reach out to her in no way assures that she will accept your offer to come and visit."

"Hell, I know that, Doc, but at least she'll know she has a choice, right? Mor'n I had before." He put out a shaky hand for her to take. "I ain't know how to thank you properly, Doc. I just hope when it's your time to go, you remember back to this here moment. To how you made an old man happier than he's been in a long, long time."

The doctor took his hand and shook it lightly while the guard hovered nearby rolling his eyes.

★

After she moved off, Earl lay back on his bed. He could feel his heart beating madly. He breathed deeply, calming his weak chest.

Can't die now, old man. Got to keep going. Got to keep going.

He looked over at Junior, who was staring at him from his bed. There was something in the other man's look that Earl did not care for.

"Sumthin' on your mind, Junior?" said Earl.

"What you got going on, old man?" said Junior.

"Anything I got going on ain't any of your damn bizness, now is it?"

Junior eyed Earl with a smile. "Know you, Earl. I'm a damn killer. Killed bitches all over Alabama. Can't help myself, just got to do it." He tapped his head. "Up here. Wired funny, doctors say, not that the damn jury gave a crap about that."

"Only thing funny 'bout you, Junior, is your face. Like a hog's backside. That's why you had to cut them gals up. They ain't screwing somebody ugly as you without a knife to their throat."

Junior did not appear to have heard him. "But you, Earl, now you are one sick son of a bitch. You are an evil prick and you got something cooking. I can smell it."

"What I smell is a pile of crap, and it's coming from your damn bed. You shit your sheet again like a damn baby?"

But Earl's heart wasn't in his zingers back at Junior.

He didn't like it that Junior was suspecting something. What if he told somebody? Made up shit? What would it do to his plan?

"I can smell it, old man," Junior persisted. He smiled menacingly. "And I ain't got nothing else to do 'cept think on it. Mebbe I figure it out. And if I do, mebbe I tell somebody, like the doc."

"And mebbe they ain't going to execute your ass, Junior. But I wouldn't bet the farm on it."

He looked away from Junior and hollered for the nurse. When she came over he said in a low voice, "I got me a phone call to make. You set that up for me, honey?"

"Who are you calling?"

Earl glanced over at Junior, whose eyes were once more closed.

"Some friends of mine. Feeling lonely. They say I get one call a day. Ain't had none in four days. Can you do it for me, sugah?"

The nurse said, "I'll see what I can do."

Earl smiled at her and said, "Now, I'll be right here when you get back."

She snorted at his quip and moved off.

The smile faded from Earl's lips. He looked back over at Junior.

Not good. Not good at all.

18

I need to know unequivocally where you stand."

Evan Tucker stared across the width of a conference room table at the man sitting there.

If Andrew Viola was surprised by the question, he didn't show it. "I stand where you want me to, sir," he replied evenly.

"Words, Viola, are easy."

"I think I've done more than words, sir. I carried out your orders to the letter."

"No confession, though."

"We did three sessions on them, sir. One more and maybe they're dead. Didn't think you wanted it to go down like that. And they're tough, you have to give them that."

"I don't give them anything, particularly Reel."

"I understand you visited the Burner?"

"I did. I spoke to Robie and Reel."

"And did it go according to your plan?"

"Exactly what plan is that?" asked Tucker suspiciously.

"I meant did you accomplish your goal, whatever that is?"

"I told them I needed their assurance that they were totally committed to this mission. I told them the waterboarding was to see if they could withstand such torture if captured."

"Okay," said Viola evenly.

"And I was speaking the truth, if you care to know."

"I never assumed otherwise, sir."

"The fact is, they are the best we have in the field right now, and this mission needs them. I don't necessarily like it, but I have to put my personal feelings aside for the greater good."

"I understand."

Tucker drummed his fingers on the table. "Marks has been a disappointment."

"She's a first-rate agent," said Viola. "Can't say anything against her."

Tucker looked keenly at Viola. "If you play your cards right, you might find yourself as DD."

Viola looked uncomfortable with this. "With all due respect, Director, I'm not sure I'm cut out for that. I'm a tactical field guy, always have been. Politics and long-term strategies are not my strengths."

"A man who knows his weaknesses can turn them into strengths."

"We might want to see how this plays out, sir."

Tucker nodded. "The mission they're being vetted

for is the most important in the last fifty years. Perhaps the most important of all time for us."

Viola leaned back in his chair, his eyes widening slightly at this comment but his features also holding some skepticism.

Tucker must have noted this, because he said, "Not an exaggeration, Viola. Not at all."

Viola said nothing.

"Do you think they'll make it through?" asked Tucker.

"I wouldn't bet against them. Like you said, they're the best we have right now."

"In ability, not loyalty. And I need both."

Viola shifted uncomfortably in his seat. "I never knew what the bad blood was between you and Reel, sir."

"There's no need for you to know," said Tucker. "Suffice it to say that Reel did something extraordinarily heinous."

Viola looked thoughtful. "I guess it must be pretty bad if you want her dead."

"I never said I wanted her dead," snapped Tucker.

"Sorry, sir. I assumed something I guess I shouldn't have."

Tucker sat back and steepled his hands. "I just need to know, Viola, that I have their loyalty and they are up to snuff. Do you understand?"

"The up-to-snuff part, I can control easily enough.

Loyalty is more part of the brain, sir. The psychs need to get there."

"They are. They will."

"So what exactly do you want me to do?"

"Your job. Nothing more, nothing less. Have you spoken to Marks?"

"Only enough to get filled in on certain things."

"I want you to watch her as carefully as you're watching Robie and Reel."

"What exactly am I looking for?"

"Loyalty, Viola. I demand it from everyone at this agency."

"So you want me to spy on the DD?" Viola said incredulously.

"Just keep in mind that while she's the DD, I'm the DCI. The last time I looked at the organizational chart, I'm above her."

Viola shifted again in his seat. "No doubt about that."

"Then do what I say. Regular reports. That'll be all."

Viola rose and turned to the door. He turned back to look at Tucker.

"Yes?" said Tucker expectantly, though something in his tone seemed to be bracing for a fight.

"I joined CIA to serve my country, Director."

"As did I. Your point?"

"No point, sir. I just wanted to make sure you understood that."

The Target

After Viola left, Tucker continued to sit in his seat. He stared at his hands, which were dotted with sunspots, the result of too much time sailing the Chesapeake Bay on hot summer days. That was all before he became DCI. Now there was no time for sailing. There was only time for this. It was consuming his life. No, he had no more life. He was the DCI. That was his life. That was his identity now.

But his dilemma was fairly obvious. Who could he trust?

Marks? Viola? Any of his people?

He had the most important mission of his career coming up, perhaps the most important mission the agency had had in decades. And he had told the president of the United States that he had it covered. That his team was being vetted, and if they weren't ready to go, he had another team ready to step in.

But did he?

He knew what he wanted. He wanted Reel to pay for what she had done. And if Robie stood with her, he would get the same treatment. But the fact was he needed them to perform this mission. He had to send the best. And they were the best. By a wide margin.

He put his face in his hands. His stomach was full of cold dread. His skin was wet with sweat. He felt nauseated. He felt . . . dead.

Am I suicidal? Has it come to this? Am I really losing it?

The DCI needed to be at the top of his game. Right this very minute.

He rocked back and forth with his head bracketed by his hands.

And then with a spark of clarity, his reason cleared. He lifted his face from his hands.

He had his answer. In fact, it had been staring him in the face the whole time.

Andrew Viola drove to a private airport to hop on agency wings on the way back to the Burner.

But he made one stop along the way. He had a phone call that he needed to make. And he didn't trust his secure mobile phone to make it without someone listening in.

He stopped at a twenty-four-hour convenience store and stepped out of his car.

He didn't go inside. He went to the single pay phone that was affixed to the exterior wall. He didn't even know if it would work.

He dropped in his change and got a dial tone.

He punched in the number and the phone rang three times before it was answered.

Blue Man said, "Hello?"

Andrew Viola said in a low voice, "You need to hear something, but you didn't hear it from me."

"Is this about Robie and Reel?" asked Blue Man.

"Yes, it is," replied Viola.

Viola said his piece and then took some questions

from Blue Man, whose real name was Roger Walton. He was very high up at the agency, though not as high up as Amanda Marks and Evan Tucker.

He was also a friend and ally of Will Robie's. And of Jessica Reel's.

When Viola finished he hung up the pay phone and got back into his car.

Ironically, the old-fashioned pay phone might be the safest form of communication there was these days. NSA tended to focus more on mobile phone traffic and texts and emails. There were so few coin phones left that no one really bothered to monitor them anymore.

He started the engine and headed off. He would be back at the Burner in a few hours.

And maybe he had just realized that the world was not simply black and white, no matter how much he wanted it to be.

19

Spitzer and Bitterman were playing tag team.

Seated across from them were Robie and Reel.

"Long time no see," began Reel. "Lost the love?"

The two psychologists glanced at one another, looking a bit uneasy.

Spitzer said, "We don't make our own appointments."

Robie said, "I know, you follow orders like everybody else."

"So why the double team today?" said Reel. She gave an anxious sideways glance at Robie. "I thought these sessions were supposed to be one-on-one."

"They usually are," replied Bitterman. "But not today. Does this make you uncomfortable?"

"No," said Reel. "I love revealing my innermost thoughts on a public stage."

Spitzer smiled. "It's not the preferred way, Agent Reel, but it might actually be beneficial to you, and to Agent Robie."

"I can't possibly see how, but I'm not a shrink." Reel sat back against the chair, her eyes half closed.

"And at least while we're in here no one is trying to kill us."

Bitterman said, "You mean kill you when you're in the field?"

Robie said, "No, she meant kill us as in while we're here at the Burner."

"It's definitely not a walk in the park here," noted Spitzer, as she doodled with her pen on the pad she held.

Reel said, "Oh, the training part we can handle. It's the waterboarding in the middle of the night that gets me a little uptight. I like a full six hours of sleep uninterrupted by torture just like the next person."

Spitzer and Bitterman both gazed at her open-mouthed.

Bitterman said, "Are you saying that you were tortured? Here?"

"Don't get your boxers in a wad, Doc," said Reel. "It wasn't the first time and I doubt it will be the last. It's just usually not our own people that do it to us."

Spitzer said, "But that's illegal."

"Yes, it is," replied Robie. "But please don't think of filing any paperwork on it."

"Why?" asked Bitterman.

Robie stared at him. "You're a bright guy. I think you can see the endgame on that one."

Bitterman paled and glanced nervously at Spitzer, who kept her gaze squarely on Reel. Bitterman said, "Well, perhaps we should go ahead with our session."

"Perhaps we should," said Reel. "So fire away."

The two psychologists readied their notes and Spitzer spoke first.

"The last time we talked, we were discussing roles."

"Judge, jury, executioner," said Reel promptly while Robie looked on curiously.

"Yes. What role do you feel you're playing right now?"

"Victim."

"And how does that make you feel?" asked Bitterman.

"Shitty."

He next looked at Robie. "And you?"

"Not a victim. A scapegoat. And pissed, in case you were going to ask how I felt about it."

"So you consider all of this unfair?" asked Bitterman.

"I've served my country, risked my life for many years. I've certainly earned more respect than I'm getting now. So has Reel."

"But you understand why the circumstances have changed?" asked Spitzer.

"Because two traitors are dead?" said Robie. "No, I really don't."

"She wasn't ordered to kill them," pointed out Bitterman.

"So she took a shortcut. The orders would have been coming. Believe me."

"No, they would have been tried and perhaps convicted," said Bitterman. "Just as spies and traitors have been before."

Robie shook his head. "Do you know what those two were involved in? What they were planning?"

"It wasn't selling secrets," Reel added as the two psychologists shook their heads.

"It was something that the world could never know about," said Robie. "There would never have been a trial. Never. And they would never have gone to prison."

"They would have been executed and gone into a grave," said Reel. "And that's where I sent them."

"Be that as it may," said Bitterman. "There is the issue of following orders and not acting unilaterally."

"Otherwise, there is chaos," added Spitzer.

"The slippery slope," said Bitterman. "I know you can see the implications."

"This was a special case," retorted Reel.

"Exceptions not only disprove the rule, they destroy it," replied Spitzer. "Our job is to psychologically vet both of you. While I know that you have been physically challenged while here and will continue to be, we are focused not on your bodies but on your minds. Do you still have the mental discipline and brain wiring to do your job in the field?"

"Or will you create a new mission on your own instead of following orders?" added Bitterman.

"We improvise all the time in the field," protested Robie.

165

"I'm not talking about improvisation," said Bitterman. "All good field agents do that. I'm talking about going off grid, going rogue and creating entirely new missions to counter perceived wrongs. Do you still have the wherewithal to follow only the orders given to you?"

Reel was about to say something and then stopped. Robie, for the first time, looked unsure.

Neither of the psychologists said anything. They just stared at the other two, awaiting an answer from one of them.

"I don't know," said Reel at last.

Robie said nothing.

Both Bitterman and Spitzer wrote down some notes.

Robie said, "So if we can't say that unequivocally, then what? Unfit for deployment?"

Spitzer looked up. "That's not for us to decide. We simply make recommendations."

"And what would your recommendation be right now?" asked Reel.

Spitzer glanced at Bitterman, who said, "An answer now would be meaningless."

"Why?" said Reel. "We've been here awhile. It's not like they're going to give us a year to figure this out, not if we're being vetted for a mission."

"My answer is still the same," replied Bitterman, and Spitzer nodded.

Spitzer said, "Do you even want to be redeployed?" She looked from Reel to Robie for an answer.

Reel said, "This job has been my whole life."

"That's not an answer," pointed out Bitterman.

"It's the only one I've got right now," replied Reel firmly.

Robie said, "How long do we have?"

Spitzer said, "We're not the ones to take that up with. Try DD Marks."

"Do you report to her or Evan Tucker?" asked Reel.

"The chain of command is clearly defined," said Spitzer. "But eventually all things make their way to the DCI. Particularly something like this."

Robie nodded. "Are we done here?"

"Do you want to be done?" asked Spitzer with a knowing look. She was clearly not simply referring to this meeting.

Neither Robie nor Reel answered.

20

It was an obstacle course laden with things that could actually kill you. The Burner Box didn't do things halfway.

The only difference now was Amanda Marks was right there with them as they hung from a metal line a hundred feet up and made their way slowly over a swamp that had the reputation of being infested with water moccasins, because it was.

None of them looked down, because what would have been the point?

They reached the other side, found their cache of weapons, and kept moving.

Marks pointed ahead and motioned Reel to her right and Robie to her left.

The incoming fire started thirty seconds later.

It was live ammo. In Reel's and Robie's world there always came a time when there was no other kind.

As the rounds whizzed over their heads Robie and Reel moved forward as a team. They had a mission and a goal, and the sooner they got to it, the better, because the bullets would stop.

Marks hung back since the op was designed for a two-person team. But she watched the pair closely for more than one reason.

She marveled at how Reel and Robie moved as a unit. They each seemed to know what the other was thinking. In less than twenty minutes they had achieved their goal and Marks ordered the live fire to stand down.

On the Jeep ride back Marks told them that they had a visitor.

"Who is it?" asked Robie.

"Someone you know well."

The Jeep dropped them off about a mile from the facility and then drove on. A minute later Blue Man stepped from behind a tree to greet them.

"You're both looking fit," said Blue Man. He was, as ever, dressed in a suit and tie with polished shoes. He looked decidedly out of place in the forest. His hair was white, his features grizzled, but his eyes were light and alert and his handshake strong.

Reel gave him a hug and whispered, "Thank you," in his ear.

Robie stared expectantly at Blue Man.

"I got a phone call from someone you've been *interviewed* by here," he began.

Robie and Reel exchanged a glance. Reel said, "Male or female?"

Blue Man said, "Male. He apologized for how late your session went and for the degree of wetness involved."

"Nice of him," said Reel dryly.

"He also told me that there is a Plan B in place in the event that your vetting here does not go well."

"And what is Plan B?" asked Robie.

"The B Team, actually. For the upcoming mission. You two are the preferred unit, of course."

"How flattering," commented Reel. "And do we know what the mission is?"

"One person at the agency knows, and that person is not me."

"Only one?" said Robie, looking startled.

"So Evan Tucker, then?" suggested Reel.

Blue Man nodded. "Highly unusual. I'm used to small circles of need to know, but a circle of one is problematic."

"We've survived so far," said Reel. "Do you see something coming up that might change that?"

"I won't mince words, because that won't do either of you any good. The director is enormously conflicted at this point. Facts that I have gathered demonstrate a man perilously near the edge. He both needs you and wants to punish you. And it is unclear at this point which of these competing views will win out."

"He tried to waterboard us into a confession," said

Robie. "That might indicate the 'punishment' side is winning out."

Blue Man nodded. "First blush might indicate that. But it's unfortunately more complicated than that. He seems to be changing his mind not day by day but hour by hour."

"And how do you know this?" asked Robie.

"We *are* an intelligence-gathering agency," replied Blue Man with a smile. "And there is no law against turning that skill inward."

Robie looked at Reel. "That may be why Tucker came calling here."

"He came here to see you?" asked Blue Man.

Robie said, "He wanted to 'assure' us that he has no personal vendetta against us and that everything they're throwing at us here, including the water-boarding, is part of the vetting."

"And did you believe him?" asked Blue Man.

"Hell no," snapped Reel. "And there are no assets we can call on to stop his vendetta against us?"

"That has been tried and his heels dug in. Personnel at the agency are convinced of the culpability of the former DD and the analyst. They were traitors pure and simple and their deaths are not unduly troubling. Unfortunately, none of those people run the CIA."

"We understand that some deal has been struck with the president," said Reel.

"That's the rub. This mission runs all the way

to the White House. I've learned that there was a transmission at the Sit Room involving only the president, the DCI, and the APNSA."

Reel looked confused. "What about the Watch Command?"

"Walled off. First time in history, I believe. Literally no one other than the three men in that meeting was privy to who was on the other end of that satellite. Certainly a breach of normal protocol."

"So the VP wasn't there?" said Robie.

Blue Man shook his head. "Ominous, since the VP is normally part of the loop on something like that."

"Wait a minute, do you think they're worried about transition exposure?" said Reel.

"In case of impeachment?" Blue Man nodded. "Yes, that's exactly what I think."

"So they're walling off the VP so he could take over in case his boss gets the ax," said Robie. "That tells us something."

"High crimes and misdemeanors," said Reel. "That's what the Constitution says are impeachable offenses. But those words can be widely interpreted."

"But in the intelligence world something jumps out," said Robie.

"Assassination of a head of state," said Reel. She looked sharply at Blue Man. "Is that what we're being dialed up to do?"

"I wish I could tell you for certain, but I can't."

"We hit Ahmadi *before* he came to power in Syria for that very reason," said Robie. "He wasn't yet a head of state. Otherwise, it's illegal."

"And bin Laden was a terrorist, not a head of state," added Reel.

Blue Man considered all of this and then filled his chest with the invigorating mountain air. "And there are a limited number of such targets for which the president would stick out his political neck."

"*Very* limited," said Robie. "And it simply can't be some asshole dictator raping his country. Saddam Hussein's fellow countrymen hung him, not us. And Africa is not that important to us geopolitically. No basis to argue in the national interest."

"I can actually think of two possible targets," said Reel. "And both of them are suicide missions for the people pulling the trigger." She stared at Blue Man. "With no double cross needed. The target might go down, but so will the mission team. They might get in, but they won't get out. We're dead."

Blue Man said, "Ergo, I believe that the director has resolved his conflict. But then again, that's what he thought last time."

21

Chung-Cha had never met a westerner who could tell the difference between a Chinese and a Japanese, much less a North Korean and a South Korean. This had proven very valuable to her work. To the world North Koreans were evil, while South Koreans and Japanese roused no suspicions at all. And Chinese were tolerated because China made everything that everyone else used and had all the money, or so Chung-Cha had been told.

She had taken a flight to Istanbul and boarded the train there. She was now in Romania, heading west. She had been on a North Korean clunker, but never a train such as this. She had never seen anything so luxurious that moved!

She was listening to music on her headphones as the train wended its way along. Chung-Cha liked to listen to music because it allowed her mind to wander to other things. She could afford to let her mind drift now. Later, that would not be possible.

The countryside here was quite remarkable. She enjoyed traveling by train for several reasons, not the least of which was the lessened standard of security. For this particular journey, there was another reason.

That reason was residing in the same train car as she was, only four compartments down from her.

She had seen him, but he had not seen her because he was not trained to observe, at least not at the level she was. The train's destination was Venice. From Istanbul the trip took six days.

She waited until he went to the dining car that night. Her gaze followed him all the way out of the sleeping car.

She figured she had thirty minutes. She shouldn't need half that time.

Chung-Cha didn't simply kill people; she gathered intelligence. She looked like a shy young Asian woman who would pose a threat to no one. The fact that she could kill everyone on this train would not occur to any passenger.

The man's compartment was locked. A few seconds later it was no longer locked. Chung-Cha slipped inside and shut the door behind her. She did not expect to find much. The man was a British envoy lately attached to the embassy in Pyongyang. Those types did not leave classified documents lying around in their empty train compartments. What secrets they did have were confined to their minds or on encrypted devices that would take an army of computers years to break into.

But there were exceptions to that rule. And this man might prove to be one of those rare exceptions.

It took her barely fifteen minutes to efficiently search his compartment and leave no trace that she had done so. He had left, by her count, six subtle traps for those attempting to find something here. Tripping any of them would reveal said search. She either didn't disturb them or returned them to their original positions, down to the millimeter.

If he had a phone he had taken it with him. There was no computer here. There were no documents of any kind. He was traveling very light. It must all be in his head. If it was, she could gain access to that as well.

She knew many torture techniques, and for a very good reason. They had all been inflicted upon her at Yodok.

She had been trained to be a snitch on her family in return for a reward, or sometimes simply so she wouldn't be beaten as badly. She had stolen food from her family. She had beaten others, some of them children. Her family had beaten her, snitched on her, stolen food from her. Children had beaten her, snitched on her, stolen food from her. That was just the way it was. Again, with enough fear, humans were capable of anything.

She had always wanted to be one of the *Bowiwon* children, the offspring of the guards. Their bloodlines had been affirmed by the Great Leader, Il Sung. They had food to eat and something softer than a concrete floor to sleep on. In her dreams she had become a pureblood like them with a full belly and perhaps a chance to pass through the electrified fence one day.

And then one day she had.

The greatest day of her life. No prisoner had ever been released from Yodok's lifer zone. She had been the first. She was still the only one.

She returned to her compartment, but she had left something back in the man's room.

She heard him return a half hour later. The door opened and closed. She waited, listening through the wireless device mounted in her ear. In her mind she followed his movements based on these sounds. She was not guessing. She was highly trained to be able to see with something other than her eyes.

The movements were slow at first, routine, measured. Then they picked up a bit. Then they picked up even more.

She knew exactly what that meant.

There had been a seventh trap that she had overlooked.

He *knew* his compartment had been searched. Perhaps he had also spotted the listening device she had planted there.

She immediately checked the train schedule.

Forty-five minutes from here.

She had one small bag with her for the six-day

trip. Chung-Cha never carried much because she had never had much. No more than would fit in a small bag. The car wasn't hers. The apartment wasn't hers. They could take it from her whenever they wanted. But what was in the bag was hers.

Forty-two minutes later the train slowed. Then it slowed some more. The conductor came on the PA and announced the next stop. She listened to the device. The man's compartment door opened and closed and she could no longer hear anything from the device she'd planted in the room.

However, she believed he would be heading to the right, away from her. The closest exit door was there. She opened the door to her compartment and sprinted to the left. She was out a service door and onto the station platform before the train even stopped. She took up position behind a stack of boxes and waited, peering through a crack in one of them.

He got off and looked up and down the platform. He was waiting for someone else to get off, obviously the person who had searched his compartment. No one else did. He waited until the train started to pull away. Then he turned and hurried off without seeing her and entered the station.

Her Asian appearance would be problematic for her now, she knew. There could not be many Asians in this ancient town of white Europeans. However, a hat and glasses helped hide her face. She started after him, keeping a good distance in between.

He was already on his phone. Getting off the train had been an impromptu move, so he would need either lodging or ground transportation.

If he opted for a car she would have to strike fast. If lodging, she would have at least the night and morning to sort things out. She would prefer that.

Fortunately for her, he picked lodging. She walked past where he entered and observed him through a window arranging for a room. He was still on the phone, multitasking as he showed his passport and took the old-fashioned room key tied to what looked to be a large golden paperweight.

It might come in handy, she thought, that paperweight.

Chung-Cha sat in her room in the same hotel as the Brit. She sipped her hot tea and smacked her lips appreciatively. At Yodok her gums had turned black and all her teeth had fallen out. What she had there now was the work of an orthodontist in the employ of the government. The worst of her scars had been hidden with plastic surgery, but the doctor had been unable to correct all of them. She didn't have enough undamaged skin left with which to do so. The burns had been the most painful. Being hung over a fire and made to confess something, anything to make the pain stop, was not good for one's complexion.

So she sipped her tea, then touched her bed with the fat pillows and thick blanket. They felt nice to the touch, far better than what she had back in Pyongyang.

She wondered whom he had called.

Midnight passed to one.

She heard a clock strike somewhere in the center of this ancient city.

The sound of revelers died away a half hour later.

That was when she was on the move.

She did not walk down the hall. She went out the window.

His room was three floors above hers. Room 607, fourth over from the right. She had observed this through the hotel window when the key had been removed from its numbered cubby at the front desk. Finding small handholds, Chung-Cha climbed swiftly.

She opened the window to his room noiselessly and slipped inside. As soon as her foot hit the carpet he was on her.

Chung-Cha felt the muzzle of the gun against her head. But before he could fire, she had spun away, placing her finger behind the trigger so he couldn't pull it. While he struggled with this, she used him as a fulcrum, leapt off her feet, spun her body around his, and slammed her knee into his right kidney. He screamed and dropped to his knees, his grip on the gun lessening, and she ripped it free. He tried to rise but she whirled in front of him, rammed her foot into his crotch, and at the same time made a V with her elbow and crushed it against his temple.

And then as he was toppling she stabbed him in the shoulder with the knife she held in her left hand, his gun in her right.

He lay on the floor holding his bleeding shoulder and gasping for air, his knees tucked involuntarily upward as the pain shot through his privates. He started to cry out, but she pounced and the rag was in his mouth, his shout stifled.

He was a large man and she was a small woman. Though badly injured, he tried to rise. She struck him on the wound and he fell back, sobbing and holding his injured shoulder.

She put his gun to his temple and told him what he must do or he would die now.

He slowly rolled onto his belly. She tied him up securely, hands lashed to the ankles via a zip tie she had brought with her. She put him on his side and faced him, shining a light in his eyes. She spoke to him again in English. He nodded.

She took the gag out and studied him.

She asked him a question. He answered. She asked four more questions. He answered only three.

She put the gag back in his mouth and pushed her knife blade deeply into his wound.

Without the gag he would have woken the entire hotel with his cries of pain. She withdrew the blade and waited for him to calm.

He looked at her, tears clustered in his eyes.

She took out the gag and asked him the last

question again. He shook his head. He snapped at her hand when she started to put the gag back in.

He screamed.

Or tried to.

She had already knocked him unconscious with the paperweight key she had spied on a nearby table. Blood poured down his face.

She hurried to his nightstand and retrieved the phone there.

She held it in her hand and looked down at the screen. She knew it was protected not by a password but by a fingerprint scanner. She had seen him access his phone on the train once by doing this. She also reckoned that it would be sophisticated enough to recognize a living man's print versus a dead man's print.

That was why she had not simply killed him.

She pressed his pulsing thumb to the screen and unlocked the phone. She went into the phone's settings and disabled the auto lock and turned on the airplane mode. Now it was both open for good and also untraceable.

She stooped down.

The blade cut cleanly across his neck. She avoided the arterial spray when it came. She had become practiced at that. Back at Bukchang she had not avoided it. She had wanted their blood literally on her hands.

She waited for a few moments, listening for sounds

outside the room. She heard nothing. The walls in the ancient hotel must be very thick, she thought.

She wiped the blood off her blade, rose, and hung a Do Not Disturb sign on the door. After that she went through the various emails and contacts in the man's phone.

She had been taught by captured South Koreans how to find ways into computer files, and she made ample use of this training. However, she didn't find much. She looked at the list of most recent phone calls. He had made two more from his room in addition to the one she had seen him making. Two she recognized by the country code as calls to England.

The third was far more interesting.

850.

That was the country code for North Korea. But it was not the number for the British embassy there, which she knew well. She swiftly calculated the time difference between where she was and North Korea. It would be about 8:45 a.m. there. She turned off airplane mode and then hit the button to call this number.

The phone rang three times and then someone answered, not in Korean, but in English. The voice spoke again. She listened until it stopped, and then Chung-Cha hit the end call button.

She left the room the way she had come after quickly staging a robbery in the room. She took the phone, as well as the man's wallet, watch, passport, and ring. She had not unpacked her bag, so it was a simple thing to leave the hotel quickly and unnoticed, especially at that time of night.

She proceeded to the train station in time to catch the next train that was rolling through. Ten minutes later she was five miles from the town where she had just committed murder. Four hours later, long before the body would be discovered, she had left that train and boarded a plane back to Turkey.

Now she needed to decide what to do.

And *how* to do it.

22

Jessica Reel put down her weapon, slipped off her sound mufflers, and hit the button to draw the target toward her.

Twenty shots. Nineteen in the kill zone. One two centimeters outside. She frowned. Not good enough. She had lost her focus on the fourteenth trigger pull.

She looked at Robie next to her as his target sheet sailed toward him.

All of his shots were in the kill zone. He looked at her errant shot mark.

"I know," she said miserably.

She had easily passed the test on the firing range even by Burner Box standards. This was her first miss in over two thousand fired rounds since they'd been here.

Amanda Marks came to stand next to them.

"I think you've proved your marksmanship still holds," she said.

They left the firing range and walked back to the main facility. Their days here had been long and arduous, and Robie and Reel felt both exhausted and finely tuned.

"Two possible targets," said Reel suddenly.

Marks and Robie slowed.

Marks looked at her. "Blue Man?"

"His visit was timely," said Robie.

"It wasn't at my prompting," said Marks.

"We know," replied Reel. "It apparently was your colleague."

"Viola? Now there's a surprise."

"Not if he's feeling like a fish out of water. Word is he had a one-on-one with Tucker. And came away more than a little nervous."

"Hence the call to Blue Man," said Robie.

"If *Viola* is nervous something is off."

"Two targets," said Reel again. "Twin possibilities."

They stopped walking altogether and stood in a tight circle.

"Two heads of state," said Robie after glancing at Reel. They had talked at length about how to break this to Marks. They had finally concluded that the direct way was best.

Marks stared at him. "What the hell are you talking about?"

"The target will be a head of state. And the list of possibilities is pretty short."

The look of incredulity still in her eyes, Marks swallowed nervously and said, "Is that what Blue Man told you?"

Robie said, "Not directly. But circumstantially, the way this is stacking up, that's the only thing it could be. And he's in agreement with that assessment. That's what Tucker is putting together and it's apparently eating him alive. That and figuring out what to do with the two of us."

"But that's illegal. Tucker would never go out on a limb like that."

"He would with appropriate alliances."

"There are very few alliances that would justify that sort of mission," said Marks sharply.

"And not all presidents are built the same," noted Reel.

Marks stared at her for a long moment. "Are you saying what I think you're saying?"

"Yes, I am."

"But that's an im—"

"Impeachable offense," interjected Robie. "That's why the need to know is so tight it's almost non-existent."

"So Iran or North Korea," said Reel. "Place your bets. Our two badass enemies. The remaining two of the old axis of evil. Now that Iraq is all nice and peaceful and full of terrorists."

Marks looked around. The area was deserted, but she still did not look comfortable discussing this. She said, "Clandestine ops like this are my whole wheelhouse as the DD. They're mine to direct. Or not. And I know nothing about this."

"Apparently, Tucker is the only one at CIA to know."

Reel added, "And the president and Potter, the APNSA."

"This is crazy," said Marks in a low voice. "How did Blue Man find this out?"

"By doing what Blue Man does better than anyone else: working his sources and reading the tea leaves and the faces of his superiors in the organization," said Robie. "Tucker doesn't have the greatest poker face. And he didn't come up in the intelligence field. He's a politician. I'm sure Blue Man has ways to find out things at Langley that Tucker can't even imagine."

Reel said, "So Iran's president or the ayatollah. Or North Korea's Supreme Leader, Un."

"This is absolutely insane," said Marks firmly. "North Korea has nukes. Iran is close to having them. And they have death squads all over the world, including right here. If they're deployed in force with chemical or biological weapons?"

"Then we retaliate. And the Russians get involved. And then the Chinese. And Israel gets attacked. And we go to bat for them," said Robie.

"Then it's all over," said Reel. "As in apocalyptic over."

Marks put a shaky hand to her face. "This can't be happening."

"If it is one of them, which?" said Reel.

The Target

"In some ways it doesn't matter," said Robie. "We can get into Iran and North Korea, maybe. But we won't be able to get out. Syria was hard enough and Syria is not in the same league as those two. North Korea might as well be another planet."

Marks said, "North Korea *is* another planet. But to get to that target we have to have rock-solid inside people at the very top. How did that happen without my being aware of it? Intel like that doesn't occur overnight."

"You haven't been on the job that long," said Robie. "It might have happened before you got here. DiCarlo wasn't on the job long enough to see that through either."

"That's true," said Marks.

"But the DD before her, Jim Gelder, was," noted Robie, as he glanced at Reel.

Reel looked away. She said, "Gelder could have been involved in something like that. He didn't just push the edges, he obliterated them. Taking down one of those guys, he would've seen it as his crowning glory, even if it did lead to Armageddon." She paused and added, "He already tried something like that once. Guy's just full of surprises. Too bad he's dead. We might want to kill him all over again."

Robie looked at Marks. "So how exactly does this go down? We're tasked to commit a hit on a target that is clearly illegal? How do we do that? I'm not going to be left holding the bag on something like that."

Reel said, "We've sat through our psych evals and they keep pounding away at us on one thing: Will we follow orders or will we make up our own? So you tell us, DD, what do we do if that order comes down?"

Marks started to say something but then stopped. Finally, she blurted out, "God help me, Jessica, I don't know. I just don't know."

23

Evan Tucker stared down at the secure email he had read about a dozen times now. And still his mind could not process what it was seeing.

Lloyd Carson found murdered in hotel in Romania. Robbery believed to be motive.

Tucker looked down at his hands, which were shaking. He tried to type a response but couldn't manage it. He rose from his desk, crossed his office at Langley, poured himself a glass of water, and drank it down. He poured another and accidentally splashed some of it down his shirt and tie.

He sat back down and peered at the screen. Part of him was hoping that the email had somehow disappeared, or had never been there, only a delusional by-product of his overly stressed mind.

But there it was. Lloyd Carson, an envoy from Britain to North Korea, had been found murdered. Robbery suspected because his wallet, jewelry, passport, and cell phone had been taken.

His cell phone.

Tucker made a call and ordered that something be done immediately. It was.

Another email soon fell into his in-box and he clicked it open.

He thought he might be physically sick.

What he was looking at was a list of phone calls made and received by Carson in the hours leading up to his death.

The last one had been placed in the wee hours of the morning in Bucharest. It had been placed to a phone number in North Korea. A very special number that only a handful of people had. The question was, had Carson placed that call? Or had someone else? Like the person who had murdered him?

He sent a secure communication at the very top level of secrecy. He did not expect an answer back immediately, and he tried to focus on other work, but found that impossible. There was no other work that came close to this in terms of importance. He couldn't wall off his mind to think of other things.

Two hours later a reply came back, and it froze him to the bone.

A call was received at that time but no one spoke on the other end.

No one spoke on the other end.

Tucker played out in his mind what had possibly happened on the ground in Romania. Carson was spooked by something and changed his travel plans on the spot. He made phone calls, all but one to British telephone numbers. One, however, was to North Korea. Whoever had killed him had recognized the country code and simply redialed that number. The person had answered the phone, thinking it was Carson calling again.

Tucker leaned his head back against his chair.

Did that mean what he thought it meant? Did it matter? He couldn't take that chance. Their ultrasecret operation possibly had just been blown wide open.

He had to inform the president.

His mind knew he had to do this, but his hand did not move to the phone.

He began to rethink things.

That phone number was untraceable. Maybe he was okay. Just maybe.

It might be possible that he need not contact the president. What he needed was to first ensure that the op had not been compromised. And if it hadn't been he needed to get his team up to speed and into the field so they could execute the op.

They would not get a second chance.

He made a few more calls, setting in motion this process.

Right now he didn't care if Robie and Reel survived or not. He was not overwhelmed by a sense of injustice that demanded they be punished.

He simply wanted to survive this. The risk had

been huge. Too big, he now lamented, but it was clearly too late for such thinking.

He hurried off to a meeting and sat through a presentation that he neither listened to nor cared about. He rushed through a full day of such events, stopping only to eat a cup of soup that felt like acid dropping into his belly.

He was driven home and walked into the house. Ordering his aides to remain behind, he sidestepped his wife, who was coming out of the living room to greet him, and fled to the back of the house where his home office was. He engaged the room's SCIF features and checked his emails and voice messages.

Nothing yet. That might be good or that might be bad.

He called Marks at the Burner Box and told her to speed up the process. It would be Robie and Reel, he told her. And they would potentially be deployed very soon. He didn't wait for her to ask questions but simply hung up.

He poured himself a drink of something far stronger than water and then had another. His nerves were wound so tight the alcohol had no effect at all. It was like he was drinking a soda.

He slumped down in his chair and closed his eyes.

He opened them when an alert went off on his computer.

That was a very special alert that he had set up. And it demanded immediate attention.

The Target

His mouth dry and his heart pounding in his chest, Tucker opened the email, which contained the very highest encryption features. The message was brief, but each word was like a bullet fired directly into his skull.

He could only stare in disbelief, because whatever hope he had held just a few moments before was now gone.

Irreversibly gone. In fact, this surpassed the worst scenario he could have imagined after he'd been informed of Carson's murder. Lloyd Carson was the go-between, the linchpin to this whole thing. And he had been uncovered and targeted. And he had gone down.

Well, now they were all going down. But it was even worse than that. This, in fact, changed everything.

He picked up his phone and punched in a number.

APNSA Potter answered on the second ring.

Tucker said, "We're dead. And we're dead beyond belief."

24

Tick-tick-tick.

The old-fashioned wall clock's second hand made its way around the timepiece's face.

The office Chung-Cha sat in was utilitarian, badly maintained, and depressing. Well, it would have been depressing for most people. It had no effect on her. She sat there impassively waiting her turn.

As she stared at the clerk in military uniform who sat at the metal desk next to the door she would at some point pass through, Chung-Cha let her mind wander back, far back, but not that far really, to Yodok, where part of her would always be imprisoned, no matter how far away from it she got.

There were teachers there who taught the children basic grammar, a few numbers, and that was about it. As one got older the instruction became all about the life of labor to come. Chung-Cha had commenced work in the mines at age ten, clawing rock from other rock and being beaten for not making her quotas.

Every student in the class was encouraged to snitch on every other student, and Chung-Cha was no exception to this. The rewards were meager, though back then they seemed like a mountain of gold: fewer beatings, a bit more cabbage and salt, fewer self-censure meetings where students were forced to confess to imaginary sins that they would be beaten for. Chung-Cha had gotten to the point where she came to class every day with invented sins to present to the teacher, because if you had none, the thrashings were twice as painful. It seemed to delight the teachers when students spoke of their weaknesses and the things that made them small, insignificant, less than human. In the camps the teacher was also your guard. But the only things they taught were cruelty, deceit, and pain.

There had been a girl a little older than Chung-Cha who had been accused by her parents of stealing a portion of their food. The parents had turned her in, after beating her.

Chung-Cha had come forward because she had seen that it was the parents who had taken food from their child and then blamed her for the crime.

Chung-Cha's reward for that was to be led into the prison located underneath the camp and hung upside down in a cage where guards continually poked her hour after hour with sword tips heated by a fire. She could smell her skin burning, yet she did not bleed much because the hot metal cauterized the wounds.

It was never explained to her why she was punished for telling the truth. When she was finally released and sent back to camp, the girl she had helped snitched on her. For that Chung-Cha was beaten by three guards until she could not move but just lay on the floor praying to die.

They bandaged her wounds, and the next day she was sent into the fields to pick her allotment of crops. When she failed to do so, her father was brought in to beat her, and he did so energetically, for he would be beaten even harder by the guards if he did not. And the other workers spit on her, because the way things worked here was that everyone suffered when one person failed to do his or her job.

Every day for a week she was flogged by the guards in the middle of camp for all to see. Prisoners hurled spit and curses at her and added their own beatings when the floggings were done.

When Chung-Cha had staggered off after this latest session she had heard one guard say, "She's a tough little bitch."

Chung-Cha absently rubbed the scars on her arms where the flamed sword had punctured her. The girl who had snitched on her had died the next month. Chung-Cha had lured her to a lonely spot with the promise of a handful of corn and had pushed her off a cliff. They had not found her body, what was left of it, until that winter.

From that day forward Chung-Cha, the "tough little bitch," never told the truth again.

The door opened and the man looked at her. He

was also dressed in a military uniform. He was a high-ranking general. To Chung-Cha they all looked the same. Short, wiry, with small, beady eyes and cruel features. They could all be guards at Yodok. Perhaps they all had been.

He motioned her in.

She rose and followed him into the office.

He closed the door and indicated a chair. She took it. He sat behind his metal desk, put his palms together, and studied her.

"This is all quite extraordinary, Dongmu Yie," he said.

Dongmu. That meant comrade. She was his comrade, but not really. She was no one's comrade. Self-reliance. She was her own comrade; that was all. And he clearly did not want her as a comrade.

She said nothing in response. It *was* extraordinary. She could add no more to the statement. And the prison camp had taught her that it was better to say nothing than to say something that you could be beaten for.

"He is a respected man," said the general. "He is my great friend."

Again, she remained silent.

But she kept her gaze directly on him. Normally, a North Korean male would not like that, particularly when faced by a female. But her stare did not waver. She had long ago lost the capacity to fear men like this. She had been hurt physically and psychologically every way she could have been. There was nothing left. So there was no reason to fear.

The general pulled out the cell phone that she had taken from Lloyd Carson in Bucharest. When she had called the number last dialed by Carson, General Pak had answered.

General Pak was indeed a greatly respected man here. He was in the very inner circle of the Supreme Leader; some said he was his most trusted advisor.

Yet she had recognized the man's voice on the other end of the phone. She had heard him speak. She had met with him once in person, though it had been many years ago. But she would never forget that meeting. It had definitely been his voice on the phone.

She was snitching once more, Chung-Cha knew. But that was her job now. The Brit Lloyd Carson had attracted the attention of the North Korean security forces. He had been seen in the company of known American agents. It was well known in North Korea that the Brits and the Americans were joined at the hip. She had been assigned to track him, search his things, and, if necessary, kill him as he traveled on his train journey.

Well, she had tracked him, searched his things, and killed him. And she had the phone. And they had her testimony, that it was General Pak, the respected one. The great friend of the man seated opposite her. It was a delicate situation, she knew. It was a potentially deadly one for her.

"The phone number is not traceable. When we called the number no one answered," said the general. "So we only have your word, Dongmu Yie. Against that of a revered leader." He put the phone down and looked quizzically at her.

She finally decided to speak, but chose her words with great care. "I have made my report. I have told you what I know. I have no more than that to offer."

"And you could not be mistaken about this, about the voice you heard? Are you absolutely certain?"

Chung-Cha knew exactly what he wanted to hear. He was not, however, going to hear it from her. He was going to hear something else.

She reached into her pocket and pulled out her phone. She hit a few buttons and held it up. She had turned the speaker on.

A voice could be heard clearly speaking in English.

"Hello, hello. Mr. Carson, is that you? Hello? Are you calling back? Is something wrong?"

The general jerked forward in his seat, knocking over a jar of pens sitting on his desk. He looked first at the phone and then at Chung-Cha.

"That is General Pak's voice."

She nodded. "Yes."

"Where did you get this?"

"I recorded it when I called the North Korean number from Bucharest."

He banged the desk with his fists. "Why did you not show us this before?"

"I hoped that you would believe the word of a loyal agent of the Supreme Leader over that of a traitor."

The door opened and two more men came in. They were also generals. It seemed to Chung-Cha that North Korea had far too many generals.

These men were outranked by the one sitting across from her. But things like that could change swiftly in her country. Generals came, generals went. They were executed. She had already visited these two, let them listen to the phone recording, and then she had come here. The men behind her were too cowardly to face their higher-ranking comrade, so they had sent her in first.

The man at the desk rose slowly and stared at them. "What is the meaning of this intrusion?"

"The Supreme Leader must be told," said one of the other men.

They all well knew that the higher-ranking general was a personal friend of Pak's. This had all been orchestrated because of that fact. The truth in North Korea did not necessarily set one free or cause one to die. It was merely one factor of many that had to be taken into account if your goal was survival.

"Do you not agree, General?" asked the other man.

The general looked at the phone and then down at Chung-Cha's unreadable features. He knew he had just been badly outmaneuvered and there was absolutely nothing he could do about it.

He nodded, took his cap off a hook, and led the two other generals out the door.

They simply left Chung-Cha behind. She was not surprised by this. There was no gender equality here. She was not in the military and was thus a second-class citizen to those who were.

She wondered if they would send her to kill Pak. She thought the odds were against his simply being executed by firing squad, the normal way of dealing with traitors. It was a tricky balance, she knew, much like the street vendors and the Dutch tourist. Publicly executing Pak would require some explanation. They could lie, of course, but savvier folks would know that only an egregious transgression would justify such a high-ranking official's execution, and the speculation would undoubtedly come to rest on an attempted coup of the Supreme Leader. That such an inner-circle official could have participated in such a scheme would reflect badly on the Supreme Leader. Even though the traitor would have been caught, others might be emboldened to try as well. But traitors had to be dealt with, and execution was usually the only punishment deemed acceptable. So Chung-Cha might be called on to do it, but make it look like an accident, a task she had performed in the past. Thus the traitor would be dead, and any of his confederates would think twice before trying again. But the public and other potential enemies within the country would not necessarily know of the attempted coup at all. That way the Supreme Leader would not appear weakened.

She thought about all of this and then thought no more. The order would either come or it would not.

She slipped her phone back into her pocket, rose, and left.

A few moments later she walked out into the sunshine and looked to the sky, where there were no clouds visible.

At Yodok this was the time of year when prisoners knew the cold was coming. The first set of clothes Chung-Cha had received upon entering the camp had come from a dead child. The clothes were filthy and full of holes. She would not receive a "new" set of rags for three years. She labored in a gold mine, digging out the precious metal, unaware of what it was or that it was valuable. She also worked in a gypsum quarry, in a distillery, and in the fields. Her days started at four in the morning and ended at eleven at night. She had seen clearly insane people forced to dig holes and pull weeds. Dying prisoners were sometimes simply released so their deaths would not be officially reported, thereby making the mortality rates of the camps look better. Chung-Cha had not known this was the reason; she only remembered old and young prisoners dragging themselves through the open gates only to expire meters from the spot, their bodies left to decompose or be eaten by animals.

The Target

She had lived with thirty other prisoners in a mud hut not much bigger than her current apartment. The huts were unheated and the blankets threadbare. She had suffered frostbite while inside the hut. She had awoken to find the person next to her dead of the cold. There was one toilet for two hundred prisoners. To the outside world this probably seemed unimaginable. For Chung-Cha it was simply her life.

Ten.

Ten was the number of basic rules at all the camps.

The first and most important was, *You must not escape.*

The last and nearly as important was, *If you break any of the above rules you will be shot.*

All the rules in between—no stealing, obey all orders, spy on and betray other prisoners—were just filler, she believed. The fact was they could kill you for any reason or no reason at all.

Rule number nine had intrigued her, however. It said that one must truly be remorseful for one's mistakes. She knew this was an incentive for those who hoped one day to be free of the camps. She had never hoped this. She never believed she would be free. She was not remorseful for her mistakes. She was simply trying to survive. In that regard her life now was no different from her life in the camp.

I am simply trying to survive.

25

The three men were in the White House Situation Room again. And once more the NSC Watch teams had been walled off. There were no recordings being made. There were no other attendees. No official transcript would be kept.

Evan Tucker looked at the president, and the president stared back at him. The latter had not been told why this meeting had been called, only that it was urgent and needed to take place immediately. That was why they were sitting here now and why the president had canceled four meetings that he had been scheduled to attend.

"Care to take me out of the dark, Evan?" the president said in a clearly annoyed tone.

Josh Potter had already met with Tucker and thus knew what was coming. He had been uncomfortable not informing the president directly since he was the president's man, but Tucker had browbeaten him into letting the DCI make the briefing.

And, in truth, Potter did not want to be the messenger on this debacle.

Tucker cleared his throat, which lately had felt like mold was growing there. He clasped his hands together and rubbed his two thumbs against one another so hard they turned bright pink.

"There have been developments of a critical nature related to the mission and none of them are good."

All the color seemed to drain from the president's face. He barked, "Explain that."

Tucker said, "As you know, Lloyd Carson was the British envoy assigned to the embassy in Pyongyang. He has been our chief go-between with General Pak. Really our only go-between."

The president said, "And I was initially incredulous. He should've gone to his own government with this. Then my esteemed colleague at 10 Downing Street could have dealt with it."

"And as I explained, Carson was well aware that no one in his country would have the stomach to follow this through. So with his leader's blessing he presented the opportunity to us."

The president closed his eyes, his top row of teeth clamping onto his bottom lip. When he opened his eyes, his look was one of fury. "It always falls to us, doesn't it? The good old USA, the world's policeman. We'll do the dirty work while everyone else stays safely on the sidelines. And if things go to hell feel free to turn on us or simply run away."

Tucker nodded and said, "Superpower status carries great responsibility and much of it is unfair.

But the fact remains we did follow it up because we saw a tremendous opportunity to get rid of a regime that has been a thorn in the civilized world's side for decades. We knew there were risks, but we all felt that the benefits outweighed them."

"Save the cover-your-ass speech, Evan," snapped the president, "and tell me what happened."

Tucker sat back and composed himself. The president had read him exactly right. That *was* his CYA speech, but at least he had said it.

"Lloyd Carson apparently got on the radar of the North Korean's state security people."

"How?"

"The entire country is one huge pool of paranoia where everyone spies on everyone else, sir. That's built into their psyche from the cradle. It truly is like Orwell's novel."

"So he got on their radar. Then what?" said the president tersely.

"He was traveling outside the country. He had stops along the way, so he flew to Istanbul and boarded the Orient Express, which would take him first to eastern Europe and then on to western Europe, ending in Venice."

"But he didn't finish his ride?"

"He apparently felt compromised in Romania and got off. He went to a hotel. In his room there he was attacked. And killed."

"My God," exclaimed the president, and then he waited for Tucker to continue.

"Apparently he had called a number shortly before he was murdered."

"Whose number?"

"General Pak's. It was a special phone, untraceable."

"All right. So what exactly is the problem?" said the president, looking puzzled.

"Apparently, their agent called the number. General Pak, thinking it was Carson, answered. And the agent recognized his voice."

"Shit!" roared the president. "Are you serious, Tucker? That's how it went down?" He slumped back in his chair, his eyes closed once more.

Tucker and Potter exchanged anxious glances. Each man was probably thinking about what his next career might be. Certainly it would be outside government.

Without opening his eyes the president said, "And if Carson was murdered and no one other than us knew about this mission, how did we learn about all this?"

Tucker knew the question was coming and he had prepared many answers, some longer than others. He had decided the shortest response would be the best.

"General Pak. When he learned that Carson had been murdered, he immediately recognized his mistake in answering the phone and reported to us."

The president opened his eyes. "So what exactly does North Korea intend to do?"

"Well, this is only conjecture, but I imagine that they intend to tell the world what the plot was. That Western powers were planning to assassinate their Supreme Leader and install General Pak as the new leader. And even though Carson was a Brit, the term 'Western powers' would obviously include us."

"And who would believe that?"

"Well, we've done it before," pointed out Tucker. "In other countries."

"But not for a long time," replied the president. "That's why there's a law now that—" He broke off and muttered "Shit" again.

"Great Britain is our closest ally. No one would believe they would act without us on something like this," added Potter.

"They will torture Pak and his family until he tells all he knows," said Tucker. "He will have details, facts that will substantiate his position. He will tell them of the video conference here where you gave him your word—"

The president slammed his fist against the tabletop. "Don't throw that in my face, Tucker; this is your screwup and yours only."

"I absolutely agree with you, sir. Only—"

"Only what!" snapped the president.

Potter spoke, perhaps feeling that as the president's advisor he needed to, well, advise. "Only the ultimate blame will fall to you, sir," he said in an apologetic tone.

The president put a hand to his face and said, "Harry Truman, right? Buck stops here?"

Potter nodded and eyed Tucker severely. "Unfair, sir, but true. The DCI won't be the main target. You will."

The president opened his eyes and looked at Tucker.

"We certainly hoped for better, sir," said Tucker lamely.

The president sighed and said resignedly, "So they tell the world. All right. They torture Pak and he gives them ammo for it. All right. I guess we wait and counterpunch when the blow comes. Do we know what the timing will be? I assume they already have Pak in custody."

"He's not in North Korea," answered Tucker.

The president shot him a glance. "What?"

"He left North Korea both on official business and because of a medical condition that needed tending to and which he felt foreign doctors were better suited to treat. Because of his position within the leadership he was able to do that."

"Well, where the hell is he?" sputtered the president, evidently still trying to process all of this.

"He's in France."

"But with what the North Koreans know, won't he already be under arrest there?"

"He would have been, except he has unofficially left his entourage and is now in hiding."

"Why the hell didn't you tell me this before?"

"Because I needed you to fully understand the situation, sir, before I started to present possible solutions."

Potter spoke up. "If he's in hiding and not under North Korean arrest, why don't we simply go get him and put him in hiding permanently?"

"With what explanation?" asked Tucker.

The president said, "Why the need for explanation at all? They don't have to know that we have him."

"Then they'll simply release publicly that we attempted to use Pak to overthrow the government in violation of both international law and our own laws. And that we are now harboring him and granting him asylum in the United States."

"And they won't have a shred of proof."

"Sir, they do not deal in facts. But consider this. If they do make the allegations, it will stir up a lot of attention. As you've said, Carson was a Brit. That will entangle our allies in London. He goes missing in France. Our Paris colleagues will be targeted. No one will believe that they acted without the United States. The media will have a field day. They will leave no stone unturned. Questions will be asked. Answers will have to be given. And if the truth comes out?" He looked at both Potter and the president. "I personally do not want to go to prison over this."

The president jerked to his feet, put his hands in his pockets, and began to pace, agitation all over his features. "I can't believe this situation, I really cannot believe that I allowed myself to be put in this . . . in this untenable, *bullshit* position."

"I think that we must remain calm and think this through," said Potter, though his face was very pale.

The president stopped pacing and looked derisively at his aide. "Easy for you to say, Josh. Your participation in this will amount to no more than a stupid footnote in history. I'll take the major hit. I'll be the president in disgrace."

Potter's face turned bright red. "Of course, sir, I did not mean to imply otherwise. I—"

The president held up his hand and dropped into his seat. "Just . . . don't," he said wearily. He looked at Tucker. "So what are you proposing?"

Tucker took a moment to compose his reply while the president and Potter watched him closely. "I propose that we target and kill General Pak while he is in France and then blame it on the North Koreans."

The president gaped. "Kill him? But I gave the man my word. I— "

Tucker broke in. "That was then and this is now. And besides, I blame Pak for this. He must've known Carson was compromised. He never should have answered the damn phone. He screwed up. And when you screw up you pay the price." He looked at both men. "Well," he said breathlessly, "this is the price."

"His death? His murder?" said the president.

"How does that help us?" asked Potter.

"Power struggles occur in North Korea all the time. There was a recent assassination attempt on Un that failed. We can tie all that to Pak and wrap it up neatly. With that as an alternative explanation and with the help of our allies I believe we can effectively turn this around and throw it right in their faces. We can argue that they're blaming us for something they did. General and blanket denials without the need to get into specifics that might come back to haunt us, all based on Pak as the scapegoat."

The president was about to say something and then stopped as he continued to mull this over.

Neither Potter nor Tucker seemed inclined to break the silence.

"This is a choice that would befuddle Solomon," the president said at last. "A choice between awful and terrible."

"Yes, sir," agreed Tucker.

"If we do what you propose, it must be now."

"I have my team in place. They can be deployed at once."

The president cast him a sharp glance. "Robie and Reel?"

Tucker nodded. "Robie and Reel."

More silence passed.

Finally, Tucker said, "Sir, have you made a decision?"

The president didn't speak right away. When he did, his voice was weak and resigned. "I really can't believe this is happening. But it is. We've gone far enough down this road that there's no turning back."

"I'm afraid not."

"Well, at least we didn't start a war, right? No American has died." His face was ashen as he said this.

"Not yet," muttered Potter under his breath.

"No, sir," replied Tucker firmly.

The president rose and without looking at Tucker said, "Do what you have to do. And when this is all over, start thinking about a career outside of my administration, Tucker. You're done."

Then he walked out of the room.

26

They waited. They had been waiting for some time now.

Reel looked at Robie and he glanced back at her. Then both their gazes turned to the door, which was opening.

They had expected to see DD Marks standing there, and were startled when, instead, it was DCI Evan Tucker.

He strode briskly in with an air of calm and authority. He unbuttoned his suit coat, sat down, and opened the bottle of water waiting for him there. He turned to an aide who had walked in with him.

"Coffee." He looked at Robie and Reel. "You two want anything to drink?"

Reel shook her head, her lips pursed, her arms folded in front of her. Robie said, "No, thanks."

Tucker waited for the aide to bring the coffee and leave, closing the door behind her. Then he turned to them after taking a sip.

"I understand that you both made it through the

Burner Box with flying colors," he said pleasantly. "Congratulations."

"Does that mean we're done?" asked Reel.

Tucker seemed surprised by this. "Didn't the DD tell you?"

"She said a mission was coming and things had to be sped up," answered Robie while Reel simply stared at the DCI.

"Well, I might not have been entirely clear with her," conceded Tucker.

"And why isn't she in this meeting?" asked Robie. "She runs the ops."

"She doesn't run all the ops," corrected Tucker. "I'm the DCI."

"So what's the mission?" asked Robie.

"Yes, what *is* the mission, Director?" asked Reel pointedly.

Tucker took another swig of his coffee, uncapped the water, and took a drink from that too. Both Robie and Reel saw the beads of sweat on his forehead although the room was very chilly.

"I wanted to tell you personally," began Tucker. "Heightened rules of secrecy will apply to this."

"So high the DD isn't in the loop?" asked Reel.

Tucker licked his lips. "I didn't say that."

"So who *is* the *target*?" asked Robie.

Tucker indicated computer screen panels built into the table in front of them. He hit some keys on his panel, and the screens in front of Robie and Reel came to life. They looked down at them and saw a photo of a man there.

Tucker said, "His name is General Pak Chin-Hae. He is vice marshal, chief of the North Korean Army's general staff, and he helps to run the Central Military Committee, arguably the most powerful body in the country."

"And he's the target?" asked Robie. "Why?"

"You don't have to know why, Robie," snapped Tucker. "Have you learned nothing while you've been at the Burner? You follow orders. You don't do analysis. Your job is to pull the trigger, not question those who tell you to do so."

A few moments of silence passed before Tucker said, "I'm sorry. We're all under a lot of pressure. We need to work together. Just be assured that this target has to be eliminated. It's in the national security interests of this country."

Robie looked over at Reel. She said, "Okay, he has to die. Does this mean we go to North Korea? If so, how do we get in and how do we get out? Or is that not in the game plan, the 'getting out' part?"

Tucker cleared his throat. "I understand the concerns you might have after Syria."

"That's good to hear, sir," replied Robie.

"But I met with you before to assure you that this is not personal. This mission is for the greater good. Nothing gets in the way of that."

"So, where is the target?" asked Reel.

"The target will not be in North Korea."

"Where, then?"

"He's currently in France. He traveled there for a medical procedure. The hit will take place there."

"A medical issue and he went to France?" pondered Robie. "Why not China? Or Russia? They're buddies with Pyongyang."

"I really didn't bother to find out why," said Tucker curtly. "And hitting him in either of those places would have been far more problematic and perhaps resulted in dangerous international turmoil."

"We're taking out basically the number two guy in North Korea and you don't think there'll be international turmoil?" said Reel incredulously.

"We're not going to announce that it's us, for God's sake," said Tucker. "We're not the only enemies that North Korea has. There's a long list, actually. And that cover I think will be enough." He added, "We're going to lay the blame elsewhere. We might very well lay it at the feet of North Korea itself. Un has many internal enemies. It's not a stretch to think one of them could have plotted against him and he took his revenge. No one will find out we did it."

"When is all this taking place?" asked Robie.

Tucker took another sip of coffee and fiddled with the top to his bottled water.

"You leave tonight."

Robie and Reel both stared at him incredulously.

Tucker finally lifted his gaze to meet theirs. "I

understand that it's not the usual amount of time for an op like this."

"It's not even close, actually," said Robie.

"The SEALs did bin Laden on short notice," the DCI pointed out.

"The target site there had been under eyes for a long time. There were plans. The squad was 'coptered in. They hit hard and fast. There was no cover-up or finger pointing. We wanted the world to know we'd done it," Robie responded. "What you're asking from us is far more challenging."

"Yes, I admit that is a difference," said Tucker.

"What sort of support will we have from the locals?" asked Robie.

"None," said Tucker. "You're going in naked."

"And the exit plan?" said Reel. "You never really addressed that."

"There *is* an exit plan."

"You're sure about that?" asked Robie.

"And with no local help?" Reel added.

Tucker's features darkened. "You managed to get out of Syria and back home without the benefit of any local help," he barked, momentarily losing his temper. He took another gulp of water and wiped his face.

"And the margin for error there was so narrow as to be nonexistent," said Robie. "We hoped for better this time around."

"There will be assets there to help you. Our assets. We will get you out. That I promise."

Reel leaned forward and studied him. "And why the change of heart, Director? You go from waterboarding us to try and get a signed confession to being concerned for our personal welfare."

"I already explained that to you," Tucker said in an exasperated tone. More calmly he added, "Things have changed."

Reel sat back. "Yes, I think they have. This isn't the original mission you'd envisioned. Something happened and now we're being sent in to clean up a mess." She leaned forward again. "So what was the original mission?"

"I have no idea what you're talking about," replied Tucker.

"Sure you do. It's as plain as the spooked look in your eyes and the beads of sweat on your forehead." She paused and added, "Does the president know?"

Tucker rose and gripped his coffee. "You'll receive training briefs in a few minutes. Once you get to France you will do a practice scenario and come up to speed on every aspect of the op. You will do the hit and you will return home." He paused. "You do that," he said, staring directly at Reel, "and all will be forgiven."

Reel stood too and looked directly back at him.

"That's very nice, Director, only I don't remember asking for your forgiveness."

27

Earl Fontaine rolled over in his bed and looked at the man opposite him.

"Hey, Junior," he said. "Junior? Junior, wake your ass up."

Junior finally stirred and looked over at him. "What?" he said dully.

"Hear your butt's going back to death row today."

"Huh, where'd you hear that, old man?"

"Keep my ears open. Don't just sleep all day like you do. You got to enjoy life, boy, while you can. Pretty soon all you'll be doing is sleeping six feet under the ground with mold growing on you."

Junior snorted. "Being cremated, dumbass."

"They gonna sprinkle your ashes where you come from? Which outhouse is that, Junior?"

Junior rattled his chain ominously. "You lucky I'm over here and you're over there."

"Guess so. Don't want you to shit on me like you been doing on yourself."

Junior grinned. "Know me something, old man."

Earl returned the smile. "What's that? How to count to ten?"

"You know what I'm talking 'bout. The doc. And that load'a bullshit you laying on her."

"Don't know what you talking 'bout, boy."

"Your daughter, huh? Bet you ain't got no daughter."

"Sure I do, son. Sure I do."

"I'm thinking you got something up and I need to talk to somebody."

Earl sat up. "Is that right? You gonna talk to somebody? What you gonna say?"

Junior absently scratched his chin. "Now, I been thinkin' on that. Been thinkin' what could Earl Fontaine and his fat ass be up to?"

"And what your little pea brain say back to you, huh?"

"It says to me that Earl Fontaine got some scam going. He wants to get somebody down here to see him for some reason ain't nobody but him knows about."

"Damn, son, you good. You real good."

"Yes, I am," said Junior firmly.

"But who you gonna tell who'll believe your ass? They killing you pretty damn soon. You nothing to them but some statistic. One more asshole with a number they making leave this here world. So long, Alabama."

"I say my piece with the doc. Women? I can be pretty damn convincing."

"I bet you can." Earl rubbed his chin and looked thoughtful. "Yessir, I bet you damn sure can. Sure, I can see that. Hell, you like that movie star, what's his name? Brad Pitt? Gals throw their underwear at that boy."

"So soon as I see her again, she gonna hear from me."

"But you going back to death row before she comes back."

"So's I tell me somebody else. Or I tell her come see me in there."

"I believe you would. I do indeed."

Earl looked over and saw a man enter the ward. He gazed back at Junior. "Mebbe we can make some kinda deal, Junior."

"Mebbe you can go to hell, Earl."

"Is that your final word, son?"

"No. Go to hell *twice.*"

"Damn, son, what's that under your sheet?"

"What?"

"Under your sheet, boy. What's that thing I see there?"

Junior put his hand under his sheet and his fingers closed around it. He slowly withdrew it, looking stunned.

"He got a knife," screamed Earl. "He gonna kill somebody. Knife. Knife!"

Others in the ward looked over and started yelling.

A nurse overturned her tray. Another patient started yelling. Someone hit an alarm.

Junior said, "Wait. I ain't know where this—"

He looked up into the immense face of Albert the guard.

"Wait!" screamed Junior as he started to drop the knife.

Albert clamped his hand over Junior's, keeping the knife right where it was. He seemed to be struggling with Junior for the weapon. Then Albert's baton came down once, twice, and then a third time on Junior's head.

Each impact sounded like a melon being hit with a hammer.

The first blow knocked Junior out.

The second blow clearly killed him.

The third blow was just because Albert wanted to.

Albert let go and the knife clattered to the floor.

Junior slid halfway off his bed. His body was held there by the chain bolted to the wall. Albert took a step back and looked at the blood, hair, and brain matter on his baton. He used Junior's sheet to wipe it off.

He looked around and said, "It's okay. He's not going to hurt nobody no more." He looked back at Junior. "Dumb sonofabitch."

"Holy Lord, Albert, you done saved us all," said Earl. "No telling what that crazy man was gonna do with that there blade."

"All he's gonna do now is nothing," said Albert

with finality. He looked over at Earl and a glimmer of a smile crossed his lips. To everyone, he said, "I'll report this here incident. Everybody saw what happened, right?"

Earl nodded vigorously. "I sure as hell did. Maniac was trying to kill us with that there knife. Saw it clear as day. He knows his ass is gonna get lethal-injected. Probably wanted to take as many of us with him as he could. Bastard ain't got nothing to lose. Can't execute him twice, right?"

"Right," said Albert. He surveyed the room again. "Right?"

Everyone in the room, from the prisoners to the staff, nodded back.

Albert smiled and looked satisfied. "We good then. I'll get the boys come get this pile'a trash. Least now we don't have to spend the money to execute his sorry ass."

He turned and walked off.

Earl settled back against his pillow, trying hard to hide his smile as he stared over at the dead Junior. The same male nurse who had chastised him for wanting to smoke while hooked to oxygen came over to him.

"Damn," said the nurse. "Where the hell did Junior get that knife?"

Earl slowly shook his head. "No telling. You better count your scalpels and all that stuff. Sonofabitch probably took it from one of you."

"But he's chained to a wall. And what was he going to do with it?"

"Wait till somebody got close and take 'em hostage, I betcha," said Earl. "They gonna kill his ass. He wants outta here. Last chance, right?"

"Damn, talk about your evil scum."

"That's right," said Earl as he puffed up his pillow and lay back, still watching Junior's blood drip down the sheets. "Talk about your evil scum. Trying to beat the hangman, that sumbitch. After all the shit he done pulled in his sorry-ass life. Good riddance, I say."

"What is the world coming to?" said the nurse.

It's coming, thought Earl. *It's coming all right. It's coming right to me.*

An investigation crew came in and took some pictures and did some forensic analysis, but everyone in the ward could tell their hearts were hardly in it. A man who had committed vile murders and was scheduled to be executed for these crimes had tried to kill people with a stolen knife. Then he'd had his brains bashed in by a heroic prison guard for his troubles.

They couldn't have cared less.

Later, Earl watched as a prison crew came in and took Junior away and then cleaned up the area.

Earl kept his gaze on the black body bag until it disappeared out the door.

Then he closed his eyes and grinned.

Under his breath he said, "Nighty-night, Junior."

28

The dawn was breaking cool and clear when they landed at a private airstrip outside of Avignon in France. Clearing customs was not a problem; they simply bypassed it. When you arrived on clandestine wings on soil governed by an ally, conveniences like that tended to occur.

Robie and Reel carried duffels off the jet and dumped them in a truck waiting for them on the tarmac. Reel took the wheel while Robie rode shotgun.

After their meeting with Evan Tucker they had geared up and game-planned, as much as was possible in the few hours they had to do so. They had spent the flight time going over various scenarios.

As they drove along Reel rolled down her window and let the breeze wash over her face. Neither had slept the entire trip except for a forty-five-minute catnap right before landing.

"So," she said, breaking the silence.

Robie turned on the radio on the off chance that there was a bug somewhere in their vehicle.

"General Pak," said Robie.

"Tucker screwed up big-time somewhere. I could see it in his sweat, the chickenshit."

"North Korean general goes down in France. I wonder who the original target was?"

She glanced at him. "We both know that, don't we?"

Robie looked out the window. The countryside in the south of France was beautiful much of the year. While the lavender wasn't as vibrant right now as it was in the summer, it was still something to look at. But for Robie, it might as well have been dead cacti.

He said, "Blue Man thought it was a head of state, and Blue Man is almost always right."

"So for North Korea that means the Supreme Leader, Kim Jong Un."

"But he's no longer the target."

"And General Pak is," she noted. "So what changed?"

"General Pak is the second in command over there. You think he was behind a coup orchestrated by us?"

She nodded, tapping her fingers on the steering wheel as she did so. "It certainly happens. Military wants to take over. We work with them and turn an enemy into an ally."

"Coups work when they're a surprise. My take is something happened to blow the surprise."

Reel said, "You think the president signed off on the hit on Pak?"

Robie nodded. "Not even Evan Tucker has the balls to authorize this alone."

She said, "Mission got screwed, blowback could be a tsunami, and all thanks to Evan Tucker and his megalomaniac plans. And we get called in to clean up his mess. And he walks in to meet us with a smile on his face like he didn't try to drown a confession out of us and we're suddenly best friends. I knew the guy was an asshole. This just confirms it."

Robie slipped the gun from his holster and examined it. The pistol was his old reliable. He'd used it in dozens of missions. It was lightweight, compact, had perfectly aligned iron sights, and fit his hand precisely. It was a beautiful piece of customized engineering.

With a ton of blood symbolically coated on its metal-and-polymer skin.

Reel glanced at him again. "Having second thoughts?"

He looked at her. "And you're not?"

Reel didn't respond to this. She just stared down the road and kept driving.

Robie and Reel spent the day preparing for the targeted hit, including a reconnaissance visit to the cottage Pak was renting. They ate a late lunch in their hotel room overlooking a valley steeped in the colors of fall. Reel went to the window with her cup of coffee and looked out. Robie remained at the table going over the details one more time.

He said, "You got it down?"

"Every millimeter and microsecond," she replied. Reel added, "You ever think of living in a place like this when all is said and done?"

He rose and joined her at the window, following her gaze.

She turned to him. "Have you?"

"I told you once before, I don't look that far down the road."

"And I told you once before, you should start."

He glanced over her shoulder. "Peaceful. Pretty."

"Go to the market with your basket and get your food fresh for that day. Take walks. Ride bicycles. Sit outside at a café and just . . . do . . . nothing."

"You sound like an ad for a travel magazine," he said, smiling.

"Why shouldn't I have something like that?"

"No reason in the world," he said, turning serious at her response. "You *can* have it."

She looked wistfully out the window for a few seconds more and then turned to him with a resigned smile. "The hell I can. Let's get back to work."

Night came. And then the deepest dark of night arrived hours later.

They set out from their hotel and made a circuitous journey to their final destination.

It was a cottage on the outskirts of a cliff-hugging village about twenty miles south of Avignon. The property was wooded and isolated. There was no car in front when Robie and Reel reached the edge of

231

the tree line and peered at the structure through their night optics.

"You think this is a setup?" he said.

"I've been thinking that ever since we went wheels up stateside."

"Me too."

He went to the rear. She started toward the front. During their earlier recon of the target site they had left behind motion-triggered cameras on all sides of the property and also pointed at the front and rear of the house.

They had checked all these images on their tablet on the drive over. The cameras had captured nothing other than the occasional squirrel and bird. No humans. No movement from anyone into or out of the cottage.

Robie cleared the back door at the same time Reel cleared the front window. He wasn't guessing about this. They were commed and kept each other informed of their movements and locations. The last thing they wanted was to kill each other by mistake.

They cleared the few rooms of the cottage and met in the back hall. There was only one room left to go. Probably a bedroom.

They both could hear movement, slight move-ment, in that room.

They raised their guns, fingers slipped to triggers.

Reel touched Robie. "I'll do the kill shot," she whispered.

"Why?" he whispered back.

"Because I'm the only reason you're in this mess," she replied.

They silently made their way to the door. Robie covered her while Reel nudged it open with her foot.

The light inside the room came on. They were ready for this. Their optics automatically adjusted to the increased level of illumination.

The old man sat in his undershorts and white T-shirt on the edge of the bed. His feet were in slippers with white socks on them. His hair was perfectly combed and his manner calm.

His uniform with the stars was neatly draped over the arm of a chair next to the bed. His cap was on the seat of the chair.

These observations were quickly forgotten.

Both Robie's and Reel's attention was drawn to the gun in his hand.

They both took aim.

But firing became unnecessary.

He said in clearly articulated English, "Don't let them hurt my family. And tell your president to go to hell."

Then the old man stuffed the gun in his mouth and pulled the trigger.

29

Robie sipped on a cup of lukewarm coffee and studied the other people in the small room. They were in a CIA safe house twelve miles outside of Paris.

Reel was there, leaning against a wall and staring at nothing.

DD Amanda Marks was reading something on her phone.

Andrew Viola sat in a chair, his gaze on the floor.

Evan Tucker was in another chair and staring at the ceiling.

Marks finished with her phone and looked at Robie and Reel.

"Anything to add to your debrief?"

Robie shook his head and Reel said, "No. He obviously knew we were coming and he shot himself before we could. He said not to let them hurt his family and he told the president to go to hell."

Evan Tucker seemed to shudder with every word she spoke. Reel looked at him with disgust but said nothing.

Robie put down the coffee and rose. "You want to tell us what's really going on now?"

His question was directed not at Marks but at Tucker.

The DCI slowly seemed to realize this by the silence that persisted. He looked down to see Robie staring at him.

"And what the hell do you mean by that?" Tucker said slowly.

"I mean I'd like to hear the truth."

Robie took a few steps toward the man. Reel did the same.

Viola rose and stood between the DCI and them. "I think we all need to take a breath and calm down."

Marks said, "Robie and Reel, you need to stand down on this. The mission is over."

Reel glanced at her. "I highly doubt that."

"What do you mean?" snapped Tucker.

"The second in command in North Korea just offs himself in France and you think it ends here?"

"The whole scene has been cleansed," said Tucker. "There's nothing tying us to this. He killed himself. That's clear. When the body is found that's what the verdict will be. Because it's the truth."

"You're joking, right?" said Reel. "You think the North Koreans, the paranoid North Koreans who desperately want to be taken seriously by the rest of the world, will let this drop?"

235

"Why do you think they care about this?" yelled Tucker.

"Because your lip is sweating," retorted Reel. "You are up to your ass in this, Tucker. The general's last words were telling our president to go to hell. Do you want us to report directly to him what we were told? Since it concerns him, he might want to know."

Marks held up a warning hand. "Reel, I get where you're coming from, I really do, but don't go there. Stand down. Now! This is not helping."

Reel started to say something and then turned away, obviously furious.

Robie said, "So what now?"

Tucker looked at him. "We let sleeping dogs lie."

"That's it? *That's* your strategy?"

Marks said, "I think we need to go wheels up and back to the States. None of what we're doing here is productive." She looked at Robie and Reel. "Pack up your gear and let's roll."

Robie kept his gaze on Tucker. "Sir, with all due respect, this is not going away, no matter how much you and the president want it to. So I would respectfully suggest that you have a backup strategy to be deployed when the North Koreans come back at us. And they will."

"What do you know about anything, Robie?" said Tucker, but his voice cracked when he said it.

"I know enough to know that this is a potential powder keg and North Korea has nukes. And it seems like their only goal in life is to kick sand in our face every chance they get. Well, I think we just handed them a great opportunity to nail us right in the balls. And they will. The only question is how."

Marks said, "How do you think they will?"

Tucker looked at her and then back at Robie. He seemed to be waiting for an answer too.

Reel spoke up. "They either go big or small. Going big means they launch a missile. Going small means they send out their own team of assassins against a specific target or targets."

Robie nodded in agreement at this.

Marks said, "And which do you think it will be, best guess?"

Robie answered. "A missile does nothing. They can't reach us or any of our allies, and they've never shown they can deliver a payload."

"So, small then. A team sent out against a target," said Marks slowly. "But what target?"

"Targets, maybe," corrected Robie. "And if our plan was to take out their leader?"

"There is no way they can do that, Robie," said Tucker. "The president is too well protected."

"Maybe he is and maybe he isn't. But as all of us know, he almost bought it recently inside the White House."

Reel added, "And the North Koreans are known for having some of the most ruthless assassins in the world. And like the suicide bombers in the Middle East, they don't mind if they die."

"I can't believe they would pull that trigger," said Marks. "We would annihilate them."

Tucker rose. "We'll cross that bridge when and if we have to."

Reel stepped forward. "Fine, but let's get one thing straight. You try and lay any of this at our feet, it won't just be the North Koreans coming for you."

Tucker got in her face. "How dare you threaten me."

"It's not a threat. It's more than a threat, Director. And as you know very well, when someone hurts me or someone I care about, I hurt them back. I don't care what flag they're carrying."

She turned and left the room.

30

"Don't ever let me in a room with that man again, because only one of us will come out alive," said Reel. "And it won't be him."

They were back in the States and in Robie's apartment.

"I don't want to be in the same building as the guy, much less the same room," said Robie as he moved around the kitchen making them a meal.

Reel poured a fresh cup of coffee and leaned against the sink, watching him maneuver pots, pans, and dishes.

"You get domestic much?" she asked.

"I live alone. I can't eat out all the time. My repertoire is limited, but it fills the bill." He held up two boxes. "Pasta or rice?"

"I'm not hungry."

"I haven't seen any food go down your throat for about forty-eight hours. How can you not be hungry? It wasn't like they overfed us at the Burner."

Reel sighed resignedly. "Pasta."

Robie heated some water in a large pot.

Reel said, "You know this is going to blow up into some huge international incident."

"Probably," said Robie as he looked in the pantry for some marinara sauce.

"And they'll probably send us out again to clean it all up."

Robie found the sauce and then tossed her a loaf of hard bread. "Get a knife, cut this loaf into small sizes, and take out your frustrations. Pretend Evan Tucker has been magically transformed into olive bread."

While she was cutting, Reel said, "To hell with it. If they ask, I'm not going to do it. Are you?"

"Depends on what they ask and who's doing the asking."

He poured the noodles into the boiling water and then cracked open a bottle of wine and pulled two glasses from a cabinet. He poured the wine and handed one glass to Reel while he took a sip from the other and started cutting up some vegetables.

"What I know," began Robie, "is that DD Marks told us to stand down and gave us time off. And I, for one, can use it. I'm too old for the Burner Box crap they pulled. And you're not that much younger than me."

"In dog years I'm far older," pointed out Reel. "And that's what I feel like, a dog. An old, washed-up dog."

Robie finished cutting the vegetables and then began to sauté them in a heated pan that was on the cooktop. He took a sip of wine and glanced toward the window where outside the rain was bucketing down.

"General Pak said don't let them hurt his family."

Reel nodded. "Right. In North Korea it's guilt by association. The labor camps over there are all based on that. If Mom and Dad get arrested and sent there, so do the kids. That way they cleanse the generations of 'undesirables' or whatever bullshit term they use."

"I know that. But I checked Pak out. His wife is dead. He's over seventy, so I assume his parents are probably dead. And he has no kids."

"Brothers and sisters?"

"Not that I could find. The briefing said he was an only child."

Reel drank her wine down and poured another glass. "I don't know, Robie. That is odd. Speaking of family, what about Julie?"

"She's not my family."

"Close as you've got, I'm thinking."

"I haven't talked to her since before we left for the Burner Box."

"Time off, like you said. You should hook up with her."

"And why do you care?"

"I like to live vicariously through people more normal than I. Which is basically everyone on the planet, present company excluded."

Robie checked his watch. "How about we invite her for dinner? You watch the food, I go get her."

"You're serious?"

"Why not? She really seemed to like you."

Reel took a sip of her wine and studied him. "You think?"

"Actually, I know. She told me she thought you were cool."

Reel considered this and then glanced at the cooking food. "I suck in the kitchen. How about you call and I go get her while you play domesticated?"

Robie smiled and tossed her his car keys. "You're on."

Julie was available and Reel picked her up outside her town house in Robie's car.

She slipped into the passenger seat and looked at Reel. "So you guys survived wherever it was you went?"

"Actually the jury's still out on that."

Julie put on her seat belt as Reel drove off fast. "Any fresh wounds?" she asked.

Reel said, "Only on the inside."

"Those hurt the worst."

"Believe me, I know."

"So how is Robie?"

"He's glad to be back," replied Reel.

"I've been watching the news for any global catastrophe so I might find out where you were."

"And?"

Julie shrugged. "And none seemed to match you

two." She gazed out the windshield at the pouring rain. "You and Robie seem tight."

"We are. Or as tight as someone can be with him."

"Do you have anyone else you're tight with?" asked Julie.

"Used to. Not anymore."

"Because they're not around anymore?" asked Julie.

"Something like that."

"Robie really respects you. I can tell."

"I would imagine there aren't many who he does respect," replied Reel.

"I bet you're the same."

"We trained together, Robie and me," said Reel. "He was the best, Julie. I always thought I was, but I have to admit, he's better."

"Why?"

"The intangibles. On the big stuff we're equal. Even he would agree with that. It's the small stuff, though, where I fall behind. Sometimes I let my emotions get the better of me."

"That only means you're human. I wish Robie would let that happen to him more often. He keeps it all inside."

"Which is exactly what we're trained to do," Reel pointed out.

"A job isn't everything, is it? It's not your whole life."

"Some jobs are. Our jobs are; at least mine used to be."

"And now?" asked Julie.

Reel glanced at her as she steered the car through the wet streets and over a bridge into D.C.

"Maybe I'm starting a transition phase."

"Into another job, or retiring?"

"Retiring? How old do you think I am?" Reel chuckled, but Julie's expression remained serious.

"Robie told me you don't retire from the sort of work you two do."

Reel glanced at her again. "He did?"

Julie nodded.

"Well, then it must be true. I've never known Will Robie to bullshit."

Julie put a hand on Reel's arm. "But you can make it true. You can be the first to do it."

Reel stared out the window at the storm that had come in from the Ohio Valley earlier and looked like it wanted to stay a while.

"I'm not sure I'm a good candidate to be a trend-setter."

"Really? I think you might be the perfect choice."

"You don't know me that well," said Reel.

"So why did you come and pick me up and not Robie?"

This question caught Reel off guard. "He . . . he was making dinner and I'm a crappy cook."

"So it was his idea for you to come get me?"

"No. I mean, yes. I might have suggested—"

Julie continued to study her. "So you wanted to talk to me alone? There's no crime in that."

A few moments of silence passed.

Reel said, "Robie told me about you. How you . . ."

"Made a transition to a new life?"

"You're way too perceptive for your age."

"I'm a lot older than I look." Julie tapped her chest. "In here. You get that. I know you do. You've had shit in your life. And I'm not just talking with your job. I mean when you were my age, younger. I can tell. I just can. It was like me, right?"

Reel turned down a side street, pulled to the curb, and put the car in park. "Robie told me you were super smart and had been through hell, but still, how can you tell?" she asked quietly. "I play my cards close."

"It's in your eyes. It's in your skin. It's in how you walk. It's in how you talk. I see it all over you. And I bet you see it all over me."

Reel slowly nodded. "You see, Julie, it's just that . . ." She couldn't seem to make the words come out. It was like a hand was around her throat.

Julie gripped her arm and squeezed. "It's just that you're scared. I know you're brave and can probably take down twelve guys at one time." She paused. "But you're still scared because you're wondering if this is all there is for you."

Reel was nodding before she finished.

Julie said, "I can't answer that for you. But you can, Jessica Reel. *You* can."

31

After dinner was over, Robie drove Julie back home.

Reel sat down in a chair in his living room and looked around. It was growing late, but she really had nowhere to go. Her cottage on the Eastern Shore was destroyed. Her property in the Keystone State was gone from her too. Because of what had happened up there she could never go back. She could go to a hotel. She probably would have to. But right now, right now she just wanted to sit in this chair, close her eyes, and not think about anything.

That was not to be.

Her phone buzzed. She looked down at it and then sat bolt upright. She recognized the number.

She had not had a call from this person in years. Many, many years.

Every other time she had answered. She was programmed to do so.

Apparently, she was still programmed to do so.

She said, "Hello?"

A man's voice said, "Did you remember the phone number?"

"Yes. Surprised you still have the same one after all these years."

"Federal bureaucracy moves slowly, if at all. I've gotten a few promotions over the years, but the main number is still the same. And when the request came through I told them I wanted to handle it. You were and still are a very special case."

"What request?" said Reel.

He didn't respond right away. "Your father," he finally said.

Reel said nothing at first. It was like a hand from the grave had just closed over her mouth.

"I don't have a father."

"I know in every sense of the word except bio-logically, you don't. But the biological one has asked to see you, before he dies."

"I have no interest in seeing him ever again."

"I thought that would be your answer and I sure as hell can't blame you."

"He's still in prison?"

"Absolutely. Same place. Alabama. And he's not going anywhere. He's currently in the prison hospital ward. Cancer. They can't execute him because of his medical condition. He's terminal. I was assured of that. The man will not be leaving prison alive."

"Good. Lethal injection is fast. Cancer is slow. The more pain the better. Hell is too good for him. Any-thing that happens to him is too good for him. He was born a son of a bitch and he'll die a son of a

bitch and he won't have one person to mourn him."
Reel's voice had risen as she spoke.

"I know, but I'm just the messenger, Sally."

"That's not my name anymore."

"They wouldn't tell me what you'd changed it to.
So Sally is the only one I know."

"Okay."

"Look, I debated whether to even bother you with
this. But I decided it was ultimately your decision,
not mine. I made a few calls. I sort of knew where
you ended up. Pulled a few strings and they gave me
your current number but not your name. Said I could
make one call. It was up to you to answer it or not.
They wouldn't have even done that, but I am a fellow
fed. It probably freaked you out when you saw the
number."

"It did. You know I'm no longer in Witness Protection. Haven't been for a long time."

"I know, but this was the only way he could think
to reach out to you. Apparently he knew you were in
the program. It must have come out all those years
ago."

"It doesn't matter. I'm not going."

"No argument here."

"How much longer does he have to live?"

"What? Oh, um, they didn't really say. The doc I
talked to said he was bad off. Cancer all over him. She
wasn't sure what was keeping him alive. Any day now,
I guess. And then you can really lay that ghost to rest."

Reel nodded to herself, thinking about things. "I appreciate the call."

"Well, I wish it were over something better than this. You were very memorable, Sa—I mean, whatever name you go by now."

"Jessica. It's Jessica."

"Okay, Jessica. It's been a long time, but I've never come close to forgetting you. And with all the hoops I had to jump through to get to even talk to you, I imagine you're a pretty big deal now. I'm happy for you. Always knew you'd do something special with your life."

"I wouldn't characterize my life as being 'special.'"

"Well, whatever the case, I wish you the best of luck. And if you ever need anything, please call. I know you're not in WITSEC anymore, but, well, I still care about what happens to you."

"I appreciate that, I really do."

"And your old man can go to hell."

Reel clicked off and stared down at the phone in her hand.

She was still staring at it when Robie came back.

"What's up?" he asked, taking off his coat and coming over to sit next to her.

"Nothing. How's Julie?"

"She's fine. She said you two had a nice talk on the drive over, but she wouldn't tell me anything about it."

"I like that kid more and more."

Robie looked at the phone and then up at her. "What is it, Jessica?"

"I got a call."

"From who?"

"WITSEC."

"You're not in the program anymore."

"They reached out to me because someone reached out to them."

"Who?"

"My father. Earl Fontaine."

32

Robie went into the kitchen and made a pot of coffee. He carried two cups back into the other room and handed one to Reel. The rain continued to pour down outside as he sat across from her and took a sip, letting the warmth of the beverage battle the chill in his bones.

"Your father?"

Reel nodded.

"Want to talk about it?"

"Not really."

"Okay." He started to get up, but she said, "Wait. Just wait."

Robie settled back in his chair as Reel took a drink and then clasped her hands around the cup. Robie could see that her hands were shaking slightly, something he had never witnessed in her before.

She didn't say anything, so Robie said, "In the interest of full disclosure, DiCarlo told me some about your past. I know why you were in WITSEC. I know some things about your old man. And what he did."

Without looking at him she said, "And my mother?"

Robie replied, "Yes." He added, "I'm sorry, Jessica."

She shrugged and sat back, almost burrowing into the cushion of the chair. She drank her coffee and they both listened to the rain.

"He wants to see me."

"Your father?"

She nodded. "He's dying, in prison, of course. He was supposed to be executed but he has terminal cancer."

"And they can't execute a dying inmate," said Robie. "A bit ironic."

"He wants to see me," she said again.

"It doesn't matter what *he* wants," replied Robie. "The choice is yours, not his." He leaned forward and tapped her knee. "I know that you understand that."

She nodded again. "I understand that. The choice *is* mine."

He cocked his head and studied her. "And it should be an easy choice." He paused and added, "But it's not?"

She let out a long breath that she seemed to have been holding in, because she gave a little gasp of discomfort. "Easy choices are among the most difficult of all," she said in a husky voice.

"I take it you never got to face him back then?"

She shook her head, drank more coffee down, and

retreated into a shell seemingly as thick as the armored hide of an Abrams tank.

"And you want that shot now, before it's too late? Hence the easy becomes difficult."

"It's irrational."

"Half the things people feel are irrational. It doesn't make it easier to deal with. It actually makes it harder, because logic doesn't come into it. That's one of the downsides of being 'merely' human."

Reel rubbed at one of her eyes. "He was an evil man. No conscience, Robie. His greatest thrill in life was to . . . was to hurt other people."

"And he hurt you?"

"Yes."

"And he killed your mother."

A tear formed at the corner of Reel's right eye. She flicked it away fiercely, even angrily, her hand moving like she was blocking a punishing blow about to be delivered against her.

She looked up at him, dry-eyed now. "He was the principal reason I do what I do." She paused, seemed to consider her own statement, and added, "He's the only reason I do what I do."

"Normal people don't grow up to do the sorts of jobs we do, Jessica," said Robie.

They listened to the rain a bit more before Robie said, "So what are you going to do? Just let it go?"

"Is that what you think I should do?" she said quickly, seizing on his words.

"The only thing I'm sure of is that you're the only one who can answer that question."

"And if it were you, what would you do?" she asked pointedly.

"But I'm not you," he said evenly.

"You're not helping much."

"I'm listening. I can't make up your mind for you. Not that you'd let anyone do that anyway."

"With this I might."

He drank his coffee and said nothing in response. He watched her as she closed her eyes and took several long breaths. When she opened them she said, "Why do you think he wants to see me?"

Robie sat back and put his cup on the coffee table that sat between them. "He's dying. Redemption? Say goodbye? Tell you to go to hell? All of the above?" He leaned forward. "I think the more important question is, what would you say to him?"

She looked at him and Robie suddenly saw a fragility that he had never thought could possibly dwell inside her.

She said, "There is no forgiveness. I don't care if he is a dead man."

"I can see that. But it doesn't answer the question."

"And if I don't have an answer?"

"Then you don't have an answer."

"Then I shouldn't go?"

He said nothing to this, just continued to watch her.

She said, "I feel like I'm back in the shrink session."

"I don't have the qualifications. But whatever you decide to do, you'll have regrets either way, you know that, right?"

"No, I don't know that," she said sharply. In a softer voice she said, "Why do you say that?"

"Maybe you're not the only one who's tried to come to grips with their past."

Her lips parted slightly. "You?"

"Again, I don't matter in this discussion. Just know that one answer over the other does not equal a solution. It's only a decision. And decisions have ramifications either way."

"You actually sound very qualified to be a shrink."

Robie shrugged. "You want more coffee?"

She shook her head but he rose and got another cup for himself. When he settled back down across from her she said, "So does it come down to a decision of lesser regrets, then?"

"It might very well. But that's only one set of factors."

"What's the most important one? In your opinion?" she quickly added.

"Like I said before. If you have something you want to say to him, then okay. If you have nothing in your heart that you want this man to hear before he croaks, then . . ."

"But not forgiveness," said Reel. "I can never forgive him."

"No, not forgiveness. And you don't have to make a decision now."

"They told me he could die anytime."

Robie took a swallow of coffee. "Not really your problem, Jessica."

"Can I ask you something, Robie?"

"Yes."

"If I decide to see him." She stopped. It seemed she was searching for either the words or possibly the courage to go on.

"Just say it, Jessica."

"If I decide to go, will you go with me?" She added in a rush, "Look, I know it's stupid. I'm a big girl. I can take care of myself and—"

He reached over and gripped her hand. "Yes, I'll go with you."

33

The airport was small and the car rental options stood at one. Robie got the car while Reel retrieved the hard-sided bag containing their weapons.

She handed Robie his pistol while she slid into the seat next to him. He holstered the weapon and said, "What are the gun laws like in Alabama?"

"You're kidding, right?"

"No, I'm being serious."

"Basically, in Alabama if you have a pulse you can have a gun, as many of them as you want."

She thunked the door closed and Robie started the car. "Thanks for the clarification," he said curtly.

"You're welcome."

The ride to the prison would take an hour. Reel had called ahead and they were on the visitors' list.

He gave her a sideways glance. "You ready for this?"

"No."

"When was the last time you saw him?"

"When I was a little girl."

"Then he's changed a lot. I mean physically."

"I've changed a lot more. And not just physically."

"Decided what you're going to say yet?"

"Maybe."

"I won't ask any more questions."

She reached over and gripped his arm. "I really appreciate you coming with me, Robie. It . . . it means a lot to me."

"Well, we've been through a lot together. If we don't watch each other's six, who will?"

She smiled at this comment and sat back against the seat. "I haven't been back to this part of the country for a long time."

"DiCarlo said you were a teenager when you went undercover and busted that neo-Nazi gang. Pretty remarkable. And the CIA found out about it when you were in WITSEC and recruited you."

Reel was silent for a few moments. "My father believed in all that shit too. White supremacy. There're many things to love in this country. The skinheads are not one of them."

"So your father was a skinhead too?"

"I'm not sure he was that specific, actually. He basically hated everybody."

"So the gang you busted all went to prison?"

"Not all of them. The head guy, Leon Dikes, had a good lawyer and only spent a few years in prison. When I was in foster care the 'dad' was related to some-one in Dikes's hate group."

"A guy like that is eligible to be a foster parent?" said Robie.

"It wasn't like he advertised it, Robie. And it was a perfect way to get teens in there to basically be slaves to their cause. Cooking, cleaning, delivering messages, sewing their ugly uniforms, xeroxing their hate pamphlets. It was like being in prison. Every time I tried to get away they caught me, beat me, terrorized me. Dikes was the worst of them by far. I hated him even more than I hated my father."

"But you finally turned the tables on them, Jessica. And brought it all down."

"Not all of it, Robie. Not all of it."

She looked down, her eyes closing and her face wrinkling in pain.

"You okay?"

She opened her eyes. "I'm fine. You want to pick up your speed? Let's just get this over with."

They left their guns in the rental and cleared the security checkpoint into the prison. The place looked like it had been built about a hundred years ago. Its outer walls were stained black and part of the front entrance was crumbling, with rebar exposed under the masonry. There was only one road in. The land was flat, leaving nowhere to hide.

Robie eyed the guard towers set on all sides. Inside, men in uniforms paced back and forth with long-range rifles in hand.

"Don't see many escapes happening from here," said Robie.

"Well, if my father had tried, they could have shot him. Saved us all a lot of grief."

They were escorted not to a visitors' area, but directly to the hospital ward.

When they reached the doorway Robie said, "Okay, we're here. You sure you're ready to do this?"

She took a deep breath but still shook slightly. "This is crazy. I've stared down scum five times worse than his ass."

"Those scum weren't your father."

She marched into the ward with Robie in her wake. The entrance to the area the patients were in was blocked by a guard stand. Robie and Reel went through this checkpoint. Robie eyed the name tag on the guard's shirt.

Albert.

Albert was a big man, he observed. And he looked meaner than he was big.

Albert eyed Reel with great interest. Robie saw her gaze sweep over Albert, but he knew she was merely sizing him up in case she had to kick his ass later.

Albert said, "What you want with old Earl?"

"Visit," said Reel curtly.

"I know that. You're on the list."

"Okay," said Reel. "I'm on the list."

"You know Earl?"

"You said I'm on the list. Do I get to visit him or not? If I have to answer twenty questions with you, I'll just turn around and go back to where I came from."

"Hey, hey, just asking, lady. You can go on and see him. Fourth bed on the left."

"Thanks," said Reel as she breezed by him with Robie next to her.

"Asshole," she said under her breath.

She took more steps, counting down beds until she reached the fourth on the left. Then she stopped and looked down, her face a mask of stone.

Earl Fontaine was obviously expecting her. He was sitting up in his bed, his hair washed and neatly combed and his face shaved.

"Hello there, baby girl," he said. "My, my, how you done grown. Is that really you, Sally?"

34

Chung-Cha was finishing her first cup of morning tea when there came a knock on her door. She rose, padded across the room, and looked through the peephole. She opened the door and stepped back.

Three men walked past her and into the room of her apartment. Two were in uniform. One wore a black tunic and slacks of the same color.

Chung-Cha closed the door behind her and joined them in the center of the tiny room.

"Good morning, Comrade Yie," said the man in the tunic.

Chung-Cha nodded slightly and waited. Her gaze darted to the uniforms and she counted the stars on their shoulders. As many as General Pak had possessed.

She indicated chairs for them to take and they all sat down. She offered tea but this was declined.

"Pak," said the black tunic.

"Yes?" replied Chung-Cha.

"He is dead. Apparently he killed himself while in

France. At least that is what preliminary reports are saying."

"He was feeling great guilt," said one of the generals. "For his treachery."

The other general shook his head. "It is difficult to believe. His family is an honored one."

"No longer," said the black tunic, who was a direct representative of the Supreme Leader. "His family is dishonored and will be appropriately punished. Indeed, that punishment is being meted out as we speak."

Chung-Cha knew this meant they were being sent to the labor camps. She did not know any of Pak's family, but she felt empathy for them nonetheless. She knew this order would include even young children. And what possible culpability could they have?

Three generations. The cleansing must happen.

But then she remembered something.

"What family does he have?" asked Chung-Cha. "I understand that his wife was dead and that he had no children."

"He has an adopted daughter and son. It was not well known. He adopted them later in life. They are both grown."

"But if they are adopted there is no traitor blood issue," said Chung-Cha.

The black tunic seemed to swell with indignation. "That is no concern of yours. He was a traitor, which means *they* are traitors. They will be appropriately dealt with."

"Which camp?" asked Chung-Cha, before she could stop herself.

The black tunic looked incredulous. "If I were you, Comrade, I would focus on things that concern you. I am well aware of your past. Do not give me occasion to revisit it."

Chung-Cha bowed her head. "I apologize for my foolishness. I will never again speak of it. You are right, it is no concern of mine."

"I'm glad that you understand that," said the black tunic, though his eyes remained suspicious.

"I was sad to have to report General Pak's treachery to you," said Chung-Cha. "But it was imperative that you knew. An enemy of the state is an enemy of the state, regardless of his exalted position."

Her underlying intent was probably missed by the three men. She was not of exalted position. She had never been of exalted position. And yet she was loyal. To a point. And she would never go back to the camps.

"Precisely," said the black tunic. "You have done well, Comrade Yie. You will be appropriately rewarded."

Chung-Cha wondered if this meant another electric rice cooker. Or perhaps another set of tires for her car. Actually, she would prefer a South Korean-made Kia. She had heard such things were possible if the Supreme Leader willed them to happen.

"Thank you."

"But there is yet another dilemma."

She inclined her head. She had wondered from the moment they had knocked on her thin door and entered her humble apartment what it was they actually wanted of her. They did not have to come here to thank her. They were busy, important men. To come merely to thank her was out of the question.

That could only mean one thing.

The black tunic said, "We require your services, Comrade Yie, for a very delicate mission."

"Yes?" she said inquiringly.

"General Pak was not alone at his death."

She sat there, her hands in her lap, and waited for what he would say next.

"We believe that two American agents were with him at the end."

"Did they kill him? Was it not suicide?"

One general exclaimed, "We are not sure. We cannot be sure of that. They could have made it look like Pak took his own life. They are as cunning as they are evil. You know that."

Chung-Cha nodded and said, "Yes. I know this."

There was no other possible response a North Korean could make to such a statement and hope to live or remain free.

"Pak must have known we would discover his treachery," said the same general. "That is why he immediately fled to France on the pretext of a health issue."

"Why France?" asked Chung-Cha.

The black tunic shrugged. "He had been there before. It was a quirk of his personality that he seemed to like French things. He did not always appreciate the glory and beauty that is his own country."

One of the generals said, "While the man you killed, this Lloyd Carson, was British, we believe he was secretly working with the Americans. We had tracked General Pak to the cottage where he died and had it under observation. We were about to take him when those two agents showed up. They had surveillance cameras up, but our people were able to avoid them. A single shot was fired. Then, very soon, people came and cleansed the area—more Americans. They were obviously behind all of this, the evil devils."

"And what is the delicate mission you wish me to perform?" she asked.

The generals looked at each other and then both turned to the black tunic. He, it seemed, had been chosen to deliver the instruction.

"We believe that the cowardly Americans sought to actually kill our Supreme Leader and replace him with the traitorous General Pak. We cannot allow that to stand without a response. A very forceful response. It is imperative."

"And what shape will this forceful response take?" asked Chung-Cha.

"An eye for an eye, Comrade Yie."

She blinked. "You wish the death of the American president?"

Now the black tunic blinked as well. "No. We must humbly admit to ourselves that such a goal is unrealistic. He is too well guarded. But there is another target that will deliver our response just as forcefully."

"And what is that?"

"He has a wife and two children. They must pay the price for their husband and father's evil work. They must die, because they are just as guilty as he is."

Chung-Cha looked at the two generals and found their features impassive. She looked back at the black tunic.

"You wish me to travel to America and kill them?" she asked.

"You must do so all at one time, while they are together, as they frequently are. We cannot eliminate them singly, because the survivors will be forewarned."

"And when I do so and the Americans retaliate?"

"They are a weak bully. They have nuclear weapons? Well, so do we. And unlike them we have the courage to use them. They have much to lose. We have relatively little. And because of that, they will turn tail and run away like the cowards they are. You must understand, Comrade Yie, that we desire this confrontation. After all that has come before, we will prove to the

267

world once and for all which country is mightier. The Supreme Leader is adamant on that point."

Chung-Cha attempted to process all of this. Once she did she could see a result that did not mirror the man's words at all. She could see her country literally wiped off the face of the earth. But it was not her place to question such things.

She said, "If this is to be accomplished a plan must be put into place, intelligence gathered, useful people recruited."

The black tunic smiled. "All of what you say is true. And we have begun all of this. We will not strike right away. But when we do, the world will never forget." He added in a patronizing tone, "And I know that you are honored beyond words, Comrade Yie, that you have been chosen by the Supreme Leader for such an important mission. I know that if you die in carrying it out, you will die with a heart full of pride that the Supreme Leader had such confidence in you. I cannot imagine a greater feeling when the end appears."

Chung-Cha nodded, but what she really knew was that if she were to die for her country, she would not be thinking any of those things.

It was easy enough for the black tunic and the generals to send her out on what seemed a suicide mission. But then to expect her to gladly give her life for a mission that might well lead to the destruction of her homeland, well, that was asking too much.

The black tunic said, "We will be in touch as things develop. And I will convey to the Supreme Leader your heartfelt thanks at being selected to fight on behalf of your country."

Chung-Cha respectfully nodded again but said nothing.

After the men left she went to her window and watched them pile into a small military van parked at the curb and speed off.

Once they were out of sight she glanced toward the sky and saw a storm approaching from the direction of the Taedong.

It could not be any darker than her current thoughts.

She turned away from the window and went to finish her now-cold tea.

35

Reel stared down at the man who had been a very "small" part of bringing her into the world. As Robie looked around he saw that everyone in the ward was focused on the pair. He wondered if Earl Fontaine had earlier announced to all here that his only child was coming to see him off to eternity.

He had changed a lot. But not enough to be unrecognizable to Reel. Within the wrinkles and damaged skin and bloated features was clearly the man who had abused her beyond all reckoning. And the man who had killed her mother. And so many others.

She decided to let him keep talking before she said anything.

"I'm so glad you done come, baby girl," he finally gushed.

"I'm not a baby. And I'm not a girl."

"Course not, course not, but you was the last time I seen you, Sally."

"Not my name anymore. And the reason that was the last time you saw me was your own choice. Being murderous scum sort of leaves you with few options. And since you killed my mother there wasn't really anyone left for me, was there?"

Earl grinned widely at this harsh rebuke. "Still got the sass, that's for damn sure. Good to see. Choices is right. I made 'em. Now I got to live with 'em. But sure glad you come 'round. Can go easier now."

"Why?"

"Why? Hell, girl, you the only family I got left. Want to say goodbye right and proper."

"Is that why you think I'm here? To say goodbye right and proper? Are you that stupid? Or egotistical? Or both?"

Earl waved these remarks off and his grin broadened. "You got every right in the world to hate my guts. I know that. And way back when, you'd be exactly right—I was a bastard. Evil and scum, like you said. But I made my peace. Got nothing left. Except to say goodbye. So you can hate me, got no defense to that. And you got your piece to say to me, I 'spect. So be good for you to get it off your chest. See, that was the other reason I wanted you to come. What I done to you? Despicable. Wrong as wrong can be. You can tell me to go to hell. Where I'm headed anyway. Thought it might help you, you know, to move on."

"And why would you want that?" asked Reel.

"Never done nothing for you in your whole damn life 'cept cause you pain. You think I don't know that? This is my one shot to do something other'n that. That's all."

"Why? To make you feel better about *yourself*?" barked Reel.

"No, it's to make you feel better 'bout yourself. So whale away, Sally, or whatever your name is. It's your turn. Go on, girl."

"You think me screaming at you will come close to making things even?"

"Ain't no doubt about it. It won't." He paused to wave his hand around the prison ward and then over himself. "But it's all I done got to give you."

Reel took a long breath and looked around. Everyone in the ward was staring at her and her father. She glanced at Robie to find his gaze on her. The expression in his eyes was unreadable. She looked back at Earl.

"I thought a lot about what I would say to you."

Earl grinned expectantly. "I bet you did. Yessiree."

"And even now I'm not sure what is right or what is wrong."

"Just wanted to give you a chance to make a choice about it, that's all. Ain't no more thinkin' I done put to it than that. Never even finished high school. I'm a dumb shit."

"They tell me you're dying."

Earl waggled the end of one of his IV lines at her. "Just been hanging on to see you, sweetie."

"Well, you can stop hanging on."

She turned to leave.

"Hey, ain't you want to say your piece to me?"

She looked back. "You're not worth the time it would cost me, Earl. See, to get mad at you would mean I have to think about you." She paused. "And I don't."

She walked out, leaving Earl looking bemused. He glanced at Robie.

"You her friend?"

"Yes."

"She's complicated."

"Yes."

"You want to say something to me, you know, like you taking her place?"

"No."

"No?"

"Just die and get it over with. Let the world have a laugh, Earl. Let 'em have a laugh. You were a badass when you were killing people who couldn't defend themselves. Even in your prime you couldn't take down your daughter. You were never in her league."

"See, that's what I'm talking 'bout. Tell me off."

"Yeah, whatever. If I see you on the other side at some point, I'll kill you all over again. If I want to take the time on a small fry like you."

Robie turned and followed Reel out.

With a deeply self-satisfied smile Earl dropped back onto his pillow, closed his eyes, and went to sleep.

★

Reel was already at the car when Robie showed up.

She said, "Well, that was anticlimactic."

"The important thing was you did it. You saw him. You said what you said and now he's out of your life. Forever."

"Thanks for coming with me."

"On your six, like I said."

"Did you say anything to him after I left?"

"A few things. Like you said, he's not worth the breath."

"He was a monster to me as a little girl. Now he's just pitiful. I can't believe I was ever afraid of that pathetic bastard."

"That's what growing up does for you. Destroys a lot of monsters."

"I guess you're right about that." She looked off.

"Let's get out of this hellhole."

"Sounds good."

Robie climbed into the car and they drove off.

They didn't see anyone on the drive back to the airport.

They couldn't have.

The long-range cameras were too far away. But they took shot after shot of the pair, more than enough, in fact.

And now it had truly begun.

36

Are you still going to be doing your job?" Julie asked.

Robie and Reel sat across from her. They had been back from Alabama for several days now and Reel had suggested taking Julie out to dinner to celebrate leaving that part of her past behind. Finally.

They were at the back of a restaurant in Georgetown. There were few patrons in the place, but they still talked in low voices.

"At some point," said Reel.

"But right now we're taking a break," said Robie. "An authorized one this time."

"Does that mean your last mission went okay?" Julie wanted to know.

Reel and Robie exchanged glances. Reel said, "As well as those sorts of missions go."

Julie focused on her. "Are you going to take the time to figure some things out?"

"I think I've got some of them figured out; at least I'm getting there."

Robie looked between them. "Am I missing out on something here?"

Julie kept her gaze on Reel. "Just girl stuff."

Reel cracked a smile at this but then said, "I understand you were in foster care."

Julie nodded.

"Me too," said Reel. "Didn't really work out for me."

"Me either."

Reel looked at Robie. "Can you give us a minute?"

Robie slowly nodded. "More girl stuff?"

"Something like that."

"I'll take my time in the men's room. You know, *guy* stuff."

After he left Reel moved over next to Julie. "I went to see my father in Alabama. Robie went with me."

"Where does he live in Alabama?"

"Max-security prison. He was supposed to be executed but he got cancer so they couldn't carry out the death sentence."

Julie accepted this matter-of-factly and asked, "What did he do?"

"Among other things, he murdered my mother."

Julie reached out and gripped Reel's shoulder.

Reel said shakily, "I can't believe I'm talking to you about this, Julie. One, I don't really know you that well. And, two, it's a lot to dump on a kid."

"I'm old for my age, like I said." She waited for a few seconds and added, "Why did you go see him?"

"He got a message to me that he wanted to see me before he died."

"Why?"

"To try and make amends, or so he said. I didn't believe him. He's evil, Julie, and evil never changes. It just is."

Julie had started nodding before Reel finished. "So he didn't want to make amends. What, then?"

"I'm not sure. Maybe to taunt me. He just grinned and was spewing this simpering crap. I think it was his last shot at me before he croaked."

"An evil man killed my parents," said Julie. "Robie knows about it. He stopped the man from killing me."

"I'm glad he was there for you, Julie."

"I'm glad he was there for you too."

"I guess we're both lucky to have him."

"But watch out for super agent Nicole Vance. She's got a thing for him. He won't believe me when I tell him, but that's because, despite all the cool stuff he can do, he's just a clueless guy when it comes to women."

Reel smiled and then laughed.

"I've never heard you laugh before," said Julie.

"I don't do it very often," replied Reel. "But it felt really good."

"Which logically means you should try and do it more often."

"I'm not sure logic has much to do with it."

The two sat in silence for a minute.

"So you went into foster care after what happened to your mom?" asked Julie.

Reel nodded. "But not for long. I got mixed up with some really bad people. Not my fault. They were involved with my foster parents. I didn't want to be part of it so I worked with the FBI to bring them down."

"The FBI? How old were you?"

"Not much older than you."

"Weren't you scared?"

"Every minute of every day, but there was no alternative. The FBI finally busted them and I got put in Witness Protection. From there I went to CIA. That's my whole life in a nutshell. And for the record, only a handful of people know."

"Then I'm flattered you trust me enough to tell me."

"I don't trust easily."

"Neither do I," said Julie. "But I trust you."

A minute later Robie returned to the table and sat down. He found both women looking at him so intently that he finally said, "What?"

"Nothing," they both said together, though Julie giggled and Reel snorted.

They drove Julie home and watched her go inside. When the door closed behind her, Reel said, "That is one special young woman."

"I got that a long time ago. You two really seem to have hit it off."

"We're a lot alike in many ways. When I first saw her you know what I thought?"

"What?"

"That she could be me, only twenty-some years younger." Reel gazed out the window. "And I thought something else."

"What was that?"

"That she might make a great recruit for the agency."

"Not what we do?"

Reel glanced at him and then shrugged. "Maybe not. But she's got the brains and the intuition to excel as an analyst. She could serve her country well."

"Maybe. But that's up to her."

"What, like it was up to us?"

"We had choices."

"We had bad choices, Robie. And we picked one. Or at least I did. You know far more about my past than I know about yours. In fact, I know nothing of your past."

"You know some of it," he corrected.

"Some," she agreed. "But far from all."

"There's not much to tell. Hardly worth listening to."

"And how much of that was a lie? All of it or just most?"

"I don't look back. I look forward."

"I looked back in Alabama."

"But not for long. Now you can look forward."

"And it's scaring the crap out of me. *My* future."

When they got back to Robie's apartment, Robie made some tea for himself and, at her request, poured out a tumbler of Scotch for Reel. They sat and talked until it grew quite late.

"I need to find a place to live," Reel said as she took a last sip of her drink.

"You're welcome to stay here until you do."

"I'm not sure how well that would work."

"Why not? We just bunked together at the Burner for way too long."

"There were cameras there, people watching."

He looked at her curiously. "Not getting your point."

"I propositioned you on a flight one time, Robie. And got turned down. I don't like getting turned down. It hurts my pride. I'll try again. It's just how I'm wired."

Robie stared at her. "The refusal had nothing to do with you. I explained that."

"Exactly. That's looking in the past. You said we needed to look to the future."

She rose and held out her hand. "How about we try this again?"

"Are you sure about this?"

"No, but I want to do it anyway."

Robie was about to stand when his phone buzzed.

"Shit," exclaimed Reel. "I don't care if that's Marks, Tucker, or the president himself. Don't answer it."

Robie looked at the phone screen. "It's Nicole Vance."

"Then *really* don't answer it."

Robie clicked a key and said, "What's up?"

He grinned at Reel, who was making a slicing motion with her finger across her neck. Then Robie's grin disappeared.

"On my way."

He clicked off and looked at Reel, who was now looking deadly serious.

"What?"

"It's Julie."

Reel's mouth sagged. "Julie? What happened?"

"She's been taken."

37

Nicole Vance met them outside the town house where only hours before Robie and Reel had dropped off Julie. Police cars lined the street and Robie could see FBI wheels parked along the curb. Yellow tape was up everywhere and police officers were holding back curious folks who craned their necks and jostled their neighbors trying to see.

"What happened?" Robie asked.

Vance looked at Reel and then at Robie. "Were you two together when I called you?"

"Yes," said Robie. "We had taken Julie to dinner and dropped her off. We watched her go inside. Everything seemed fine."

"Well, it wasn't," replied Vance, with another sharp glance at Reel. "Jerome Cassidy managed to call the police."

"Managed?" said Robie.

"They nearly killed him. I wonder now why they didn't. The cops in turn called us because it was a kidnapping. We have an Amber Alert out but nothing so far."

"How did they get to her?" asked Reel.

"Apparently they were waiting for her when she got home. Cassidy was already unconscious."

"So they broke into the house after we picked Julie up?" said Robie slowly.

"Apparently so," replied Vance. "They subdued Cassidy and then waited for her to return."

Reel added, "That means they were watching Julie's house."

"Looks to be the case," said Vance. "We know she might have some enemies," she added, looking at Robie.

Robie briefly returned the stare and then looked away, his gut suddenly full of acid.

"Any clues to who might have taken her?" asked Reel.

"Forensics team is going over everything right now. Cassidy might be some help once the docs sort him out. But I'm not holding out much hope. Cops say he was pretty garbled when he called 911. And I doubt they left a business card with helpful contact information."

Reel nodded and glanced at Robie. But her gaze shot back to Vance with the woman's next words.

"Julie's phone was left behind. She didn't drop it. It was on the table in the foyer, like they meant for us to find it. There was a text on it. From the time stamp it had to have been sent about the time she was taken. They'd turned off the auto lock on the phone so we could access it when we got here. It wasn't addressed to Julie, but to somebody called Sally Fontaine."

Reel and Robie exchanged a significant glance that Vance did not see because at that moment one of her men came up to her to deliver a report.

Vance finished with him and turned back to the pair. "You said you had dinner with her. Did she say anything that would make you believe she was nervous or scared?"

"No," said Robie in a distracted tone. "Quite the opposite."

"Did you see anybody following you?"

"Not that we noticed," said Reel. "But they wouldn't have to follow us if they knew where we'd picked Julie up from. They just had to wait for us to bring her back."

"That's true," said Vance wearily. "Poor kid. She's been through so much hell already. You'd think she'd catch a break."

Robie said, "Any leads on this Sally Fontaine person? Can you trace where the text came from?"

"Nothing so far, but we're working on both right now."

"Why did you call me?" asked Robie.

"It was Julie. I thought you'd want to know. And we looked at her phone calendar. You were listed on there for tonight. Didn't know it was dinner. But I figured if you had seen her you might have something useful."

"I'm sorry that I don't," replied Robie. He eyed Vance warily. "You want some help on this?"

"Official or unofficial?"

"I think it's going to have to be the latter."

She considered this. "I'm okay with that so long as you are completely up front with me about anything you find. I'll do my utmost to respond in kind."

Reel said, "Didn't know the Bureau was so cooperative."

"Oh, we can be," retorted Vance. "So long as we're accorded respect."

Reel nodded at this but said nothing. Her mind was evidently elsewhere. Then she said, "The text to this Sally Fontaine. What did it say?"

Vance shrugged. "Don't know."

"Why not?"

"It's apparently written in code. At least it made no sense to any of us."

"Can we see it?" asked Robie after Reel gave him a sharp look.

"Why, are you guys codebreakers?"

"I've got some experience with it," said Robie.

"Well, I guess it can't hurt."

Vance made a call and about fifteen minutes later one of her agents brought her a written copy of the text. The phone itself was already tagged and bagged and in the Bureau's evidence truck.

Reel glanced at the paper but showed no reaction.

Robie said, "We'll take a look at this and get back to you with anything we might have."

"So, you two are a team again?" asked Vance.

"Of sorts," answered Reel.

"How about that," said Vance without a trace of enthusiasm.

Robie said hurriedly, "We'll be in touch."

He took Reel by the elbow and turned her away from Vance, ushering her down the street. He looked back once to see Vance staring at them.

Reel did not speak until they got back to the car.

They climbed in and she held up the paper.

"Sally Fontaine," said Robie.

"They took her because of me," said Reel, and her voice trembled as she said this.

"You couldn't have known, Jessica."

"The hell I couldn't. It was a setup, Robie, clear and simple."

"Your father?"

"Wanting me to come and see him so he could say goodbye? What bullshit. Was I a damn idiot?" She slammed her fist against the dashboard. "Shit!" she screamed in fury.

"He was dying all alone in a prison he'd been in for twenty years. Not the sort of guy you worry about."

She held up the page again. "He wasn't alone,

Robie. He got me down there for a reason." She added dully, "And this tells me why."

"You can read that code?"

"I helped *invent* this code."

He looked at her, stunned. "What?"

"When I was a teenager and working undercover for the FBI."

"You mean when you'd infiltrated the neo-Nazi group?"

She nodded. "The neo-Nazis needed a safe way to communicate. I helped them come up with this communication protocol. Only they didn't know I was feeding it to the Bureau at the same time."

"So this is the same group? I thought they'd been arrested."

"That was almost twenty years ago, Robie. Many of them are out now."

"So they used your old man to get to you."

She gave a hollow laugh. "It was probably his idea, not theirs."

"So what does it say?"

Reel placed her hand over her eyes.

"Jessica, what does it say?"

She removed her hand and looked at him. "It's a choice, Robie. It's an ultimatum."

"What ultimatum?"

"They'll release Julie unharmed."

"And what do they want in return? You? As revenge all these years later?"

"Partly."

"Partly? What else, then?"

Reel gave a little gasp and Robie saw tears flicker across her eyes.

She composed herself and said, "They want my child."

38

Robie pulled the car to the curb and cut the engine. He turned sideways in his seat to look at her.

"Your *child*? You have a kid?"

"She's grown now. I was only seventeen when I had her."

"I didn't know about that."

"It's not part of my 'official' file. But the doctor who examined me back at the Burner knew."

"How?"

"I had to have a caesarean. She could tell by the scar."

"But how would these Nazi wannabes know anything about this?"

Reel wiped her eyes. "Because their leader is the father of my child."

Robie's features betrayed his astonishment at this admission.

She looked at him and noted this. "He raped me, Robie. It was not consensual. I was only sixteen. I carried the child and gave birth to her three days after the FBI came down on the group. They went to prison. I went into WITSEC."

"And the baby?"

"I had to give her up. They said I had to."

"Who did?"

"The powers that be, Robie. I was seventeen. I was in Witness Protection. I was moved around six times in less than a year. I had to testify against these scum. And I did." She snapped, "You can't exactly raise a kid with all that going on, can you? I could take care of myself. What I couldn't take care of was an infant."

"So it was your choice, to give her up?"

"I told you, I didn't *have* a choice."

"But if you'd had one?"

"What does it matter? I gave her up."

"You said the leader of the neo-Nazi group is the father. He raped you."

She nodded. "Leon Dikes."

"You said he had a good lawyer and didn't go to prison for all that long."

"Even though I knew he'd ordered the murders of at least six people."

"But he never knew where you were?"

"Not until I walked into that damn prison in Alabama. They must have been waiting. Followed us. And now they have Julie."

"Do you even know where your daughter is now?"

Reel didn't answer.

Robie said, "Do you know—"

"I heard you! But do you really think I'm going to bring her into something like this? Why do you think Dikes wants her, Robie? To tell her how much he loves her? To shower her with money and a wonderful life?"

"I don't know what he wants with her. I would imagine he wants to kill you."

"Not nearly as much as I want to kill *him*."

"He probably doesn't know *what* you are, though." She glanced at him. "What do you mean?"

"He knew you were in WITSEC. He doesn't know who you are now. Or he never would have done what he did."

She nodded slowly. "But how does that help Julie?"

"I don't know. And if they had followed us, why not just try to take you? Why go after Julie?"

"Because he may know where I am, but not where my daughter is. And he knows I'd never tell him."

"So Julie is the bait. Put your daughter in danger or Julie dies."

Reel put her face in her hands and started to weep, her body shuddering painfully.

Robie reached over and put his arm around her shoulders.

She finally calmed and wiped her eyes clear.

"There is no way out of this, Robie. The only thing I can do is offer myself for Julie. That's it."

"And if he won't let Julie go?"

"I don't know. I just don't know."

She closed her eyes and looked down.

He said, "They have to have a way for you to contact them somehow."

Reel straightened. "That was in the code too. There's a number to call."

"There are no numbers on the paper," said Robie.

"We didn't use numbers in the code. Too obvious. We had letters represent numbers."

"How would you know whether they were numbers or the actual letters, then?"

Reel pointed at the paper. "When a line begins with 'TNF,' that means 'the numbers follow.' That's how we distinguished them."

"The number's probably a burner phone, untraceable."

"I'm sure it is."

"So they want you to call? When?"

Reel held up her phone. "Now."

"So what are you going to say?"

"That I'll trade myself for Julie."

"And if they don't agree to that? And they probably won't."

"What else can I do, Robie? The fact is, I don't know where my daughter is now. It's been over twenty years. I wouldn't even know what she looks like," she added miserably.

"But you'd recognize this Leon Dikes?"

"I'll never forget him," she said coldly. "If it's possible, he's even worse than my father."

"Well, that is saying something."

Reel ran her fingers along the edge of the dash. "So what do we do, Robie? We have to get Julie back. I'll give my life for that to happen."

"I know you would," he replied quietly. "And so would I. But maybe it doesn't have to come to that."

She glanced at him. "Do you have a plan?"

"I have something. I'm not sure it qualifies as a plan just yet."

"We have to get her back," said Reel. "We have to. She's an innocent."

"She *is* an innocent. I've known that for a long time. And we will get her back. So let's go to my apartment, you make the call, and we'll see what these bastards say."

39

The old plane bumped along the runway before coming to a stop with its wheel brakes grinding, the fuselage shuddering, and the dual turboprops spinning slower until they too ceased.

The cabin door opened and steps came down.

A man in a black uniform stepped out first, followed by the only unwilling passenger on this flight from hell.

Julie was bound and gagged and a hood was over her head. Since she couldn't see where to go, the man behind her, also dressed in the same black uniform, lifted her down the stairs. When her feet hit the tarmac he pulled her roughly over to a white van with no windows. Julie was loaded in and the van drove off along roads that quickly went from asphalt to macadam and, finally, to plain dirt.

She slumped against her seatback. She made no attempt to look around since the hood prevented her from seeing anything or anyone. Two minutes after she'd walked into her house she had been attacked. They had been quick and effective. A wet cloth over her face, fumes that made her head spin, and then nothing. The next thing she knew she was coming to as the plane she was in was taking off. And now she was in a van.

She didn't even know if her guardian, Jerome Cassidy, was alive or dead. She didn't know why she'd been taken.

Well, she had a guess. It might have to do with Will Robie. Or Jessica Reel. It seemed to her far too coincidental that as soon as she had been dropped off by them she had been kidnapped.

The van drove for another half hour and then stopped. She was jerked out of the vehicle and led through a doorway, down a set of stairs, and through another doorway. It closed behind her. She was pushed into a seat, and through the hood she could sense a light being turned on.

The hood was abruptly pulled off and she blinked rapidly to adjust her eyes to the brightness. She was in a small room with stone walls and a dirt floor. She was seated at a rickety wooden table. On the walls were swastika banners. An overhead bulb crackled and blinked.

These observations were really afterthoughts.

Seated across from her was a thin man of medium height with dyed black hair carefully parted and sharp, angular features. His eyes did not match his hair color. They were pinpoints of shocking blue. Like the other men in the room, he wore a black uniform, but his was different from theirs. It had more stuff on it, Julie noted. Stars and medals and the armbands were a brilliant red, with the black swastika in the middle and three white stripes around it. A military-style officer's cap lay on the table within the man's reach.

The man flicked a hand at Julie, and her gag and bindings were quickly removed. He put his hands on the table in front of him.

"Welcome," he said, a smile flitting across his lips but never coming close to reaching the blue eyes.

Julie simply stared at him.

"I'm sure you are wondering where you are and why you are here."

"Did you hurt Jerome?" she said.

"Jerome?"

"My guardian. I live with him. Did you hurt him?"

"Not to the extent that he will not recover. Now, getting back to the matter at hand, I'm sure you have no idea where you are or why you're here."

She looked him over. "Well, we're not in Germany. The plane was a turboprop. No transatlantic range. And no plane can take you back in time to, say, the 1930s." She said this last part with a disgusted look at the swastikas on the walls. She continued, "We were in the air about two and a half hours. So I'd say we're somewhere in the Deep South."

He looked bemused by this statement. "Why not

the North? You don't think our brethren dwell there?"

"Your accent is southern." She glanced down. "And the dirt floor is red clay. Georgia. Alabama, maybe."

The man's bemusement receded and he looked stonily at her. "You would make a good detective."

"Yeah, I've heard that before. What do you want?"

"I want nothing from you."

"So it has to do with someone connected to me, then?"

The man nodded.

"Do you want me to guess?"

"You're good at deductions. Continue making them."

"Your hair doesn't match your eyes, and your face is way too old for the hair, which means you dye it. With all those age spots on your hands I'd say you're probably in your late fifties or even sixties. And the type of uniform you have on was worn by Himmler, who headed the SS. He was also the asshole behind the concentration camps. Congratulations. Something really to be proud of."

Julie heard the breathing of the men behind her accelerate, but the man across from her didn't change expressions. He said, "No, I was speaking of who you might be connected to. Please elaborate on that."

"And give you intel you might not otherwise have? No, I think I'll pass."

"You are a most unusual young woman, not at all like I expected."

"What, did you expect some timid pre-feminist girly-girl quaking in her boots at the sight of you? Sure, I'm scared. You guys kidnapped me. You have me outnumbered. You have guns. I'm completely in your power here." She looked at the swastikas again. "And you're all obviously full of hate and seriously demented. I'd be an idiot not to be afraid. But that doesn't mean I'll help you, because I won't."

"I actually have no need for you to do anything, Miss Getty."

"I'm not impressed that you know my name. Easy enough to find out."

"Do you know the name Sally Fontaine?"

"No."

"How about the name Jessica?"

Julie said nothing.

"Tall, lean woman with blonde hair?"

Julie still said nothing.

"Your silence speaks volumes."

"Okay," said Julie. "So what's the plan? Me for her? Won't be happening."

"Well, for your sake, you should hope that it does happen."

"It's not up to me. It's not up to you. It's actually not up to her."

"So you do admit knowing Jessica?"

"I admit to nothing. But let me ask you something, if I may?"

She waited until he nodded.

"You think this Sally Fontaine is the same person as this Jessica?"

"I know that she is, beyond doubt."

"And how do you know Sally Fontaine?"

"She used to be one of my most loyal followers."

"Okay, that's bullshit."

The man hiked his eyebrows. "And how do you know that? A guess with no factual foundation?"

Julie shook her head but said nothing.

"You don't seem intimidated by your surroundings. Most people, even adults, would be very distressed at being kidnapped and held at gunpoint."

"It's not my first time being kidnapped and held at gunpoint."

"Really?" he said in a skeptical tone.

"Yeah. The last time was a Saudi prince with serious jihadist tendencies. He nearly killed me."

"And why didn't he?"

"My friends came and rescued me."

"That won't be happening in this case."

"Never say never. And you have no intention of letting me go."

"And why is that?"

"You let me see your face. I can identify you. So, you can't let me go."

"We'll see. As you said, never say never."

"What is Sally Fontaine to you?"

"As I told you, she was one of my loyal followers."
Julie snorted at this.

The man pulled out a picture from his pocket. "Perhaps you will recognize your friend." He showed it to Julie.

It was of a teenage girl standing next to a younger version of the man across from Julie. He was dressed in a similar black SS uniform. As Julie looked closer she could see that the girl was Jessica Reel. And there was something else.

"She's pregnant," exclaimed Julie.

"Yes, she was carrying my child. Our love child, as I liked to say."

"But she looks my age and you were a grown man. Are you a pedophile too?"

The blow knocked Julie out of her chair and she landed on the hard clay. An instant later she was jerked up and thrown back into the chair by the men behind her. The man across from her was rubbing his hand where he had struck her.

"Forgive my outburst of anger. But your words struck a chord deeply in me."

Julie rubbed the blood off her mouth and stared across at him.

"We were very much in love," he said. "Despite our age difference."

She said, "But no longer in love, then." He cocked

his head at her. "If you have to kidnap me to get to her."

"Time passes and things change, it is true. But my feelings are still there."

"And the child?"

"Another empty hole in my heart. I wish to rectify that."

"Did you know Sally's father?"

"Earl? Yes, a good friend of mine."

"I'm sure he is. Is that how you got on to her and to me?"

"You really are extraordinarily precocious. I could use someone like you in our effort."

Julie didn't bother to respond to this. "So what's the next step?" she said.

"We have made contact. We expect her to do the same shortly."

There was a buzzing sound. Julie looked around for a moment before realizing it was coming from the man's pocket.

He took out the phone and looked at the screen. "Speak of the devil."

He turned and left the room.

40

"So tell me, do you prefer Sally or Jessica?"

Reel said, "How are you, Leon? Still playing behind closed doors with your little swastika?"

Leon Dikes smiled and looked toward the doorway to the room where Julie was being held. "It's so wonderful to hear your voice, Sally."

"Let's live in the present. The name is Jessica."

"All right, Jessica."

"Next time you see Earl, tell him I said hello. It's heartwarming to see that you two have remained close."

"The truth is, I never really cared for your father, Jessica. He's uncouth and uneducated. I have a PhD."

"Yeah, in the I Love Hitler program at the University of the Demented."

"Actually, it was political science and it was at Berkeley."

"Now, that's something I never knew about you, Leon."

"But your father did prove useful. He was dying, but he was dying unfulfilled."

"Let me guess. I was the last item on his bucket list?"

"It was a mutual goal. You cost me several years of my life in prison."

"What you did should have *cost* you your life. You got a ridiculously short sentence because I was prevented from coming back and testifying against you."

"But you decimated my organization. It took me a long time to rebuild it."

"Goody for you. Let's talk about the future."

"Julie is a very intelligent girl. She could go far in any field she chooses. Will she get the chance?"

"Let her go and the answer is yes."

"I would like to let her go. If my price is met."

"I've got a few bucks in my 401(k)."

"You and my daughter are the price."

"She's not your daughter."

"I am her biological father."

"You raped me."

"Your words. But in any case it does not take away my status."

"It most certainly does. And it did. The court already ruled on that."

"American courts do not have jurisdiction over me."

"Not really sure how you figure that one. But I don't want to get into that. You take me in return for Julie. It's me you really want, after all."

"I said you and my child."

"It's called compromise, Leon. You never get all you want."

"I do. Because if I don't I will impregnate Julie, hold her for the term of the baby. And then kill her. That way I will have my child. Those are my terms. They are not negotiable. You know me well enough to understand that."

Reel didn't say anything for several moments. "It will take me some time to get hold of Laura."

"Laura? You named her after—"

"My mother, yes."

"I told you her name was Eva."

"I was not naming my daughter after Adolf Hitler's mistress."

"They were lawfully married. Eva Braun was Der Führer's great love."

"Yeah, he married her and then killed her. Some love."

"I will not argue political philosophies with you. His mind was too advanced for someone like you to understand."

"And thank God for that."

"I will give you two days to locate 'Laura.' Then I will call and give you instructions on the exchange."

"Look, Leon, I can't just take Laura from the life she has and give her to you."

"Then I will get to you another way. And I will have my new child with Julie. And I will send you Julie's head nine months from now. It is simple. Do not worry yourself over it, Sally. You are female. Know your limits. Remember, I often counseled you about that."

"Well, this female brought you and your horror act down."

"You were lucky beyond all reasoning."

"I was smarter than you!"

"Do you want me to send you the girl's head now?" barked Dikes.

Reel calmed. "Call me in two days."

"You can count on it."

"And if you harm Julie in any way you will seriously regret it."

"I have already struck her once. She was disrespectful. You know I do not tolerate that. Two days, Sally. Please be ready to deliver what I ask."

He clicked off.

Reel put the phone down on the table. She didn't look at Robie, who had listened to every word of the conversation.

"He sounds as sick as you said," Robie noted.

"He's a monster, Robie."

"You said you were prevented from testifying against him again?"

"I was at CIA by then. They wouldn't let me. I tried everything I could think of, but I wasn't even twenty. They intimidated me into just ignoring it. I'll never forgive myself for that, Robie. Never."

"I get that, Jessica. I really do."

305

"And Dikes is a pathological liar and he has no intention of letting Julie go regardless of what I do."

"I never thought he would voluntarily let her go."

"Well, then what do we do?"

"We get Julie back safe. You walk away alive. And we nail this scum to the wall."

"That sounds like a plan. How exactly do you propose doing that?"

"I bet he still thinks you're in WITSEC."

"He may."

"Jessica, this guy has no idea *what* you are, does he?"

"You mean a stone cold killer?" she said grimly. "No, he doesn't."

"No, I mean a highly skilled government operative who knows how to take care of herself."

"Okay."

"And he doesn't know about me, does he?"

"No. Well, we were undoubtedly spotted at the prison. So he knows you were with me."

"But he has no idea what I do, and I sincerely doubt he can find out in two days."

"Agreed."

"Well, you know what I think?"

"What?"

"That *he* should be the one who's afraid."

Reel took this all in and nodded. "I'm an idiot, I really am."

"No, you're not. You're stressed beyond belief and

feeling incredible guilt. Most humans aren't equipped to deal well with that combination."

"But I'm not most humans, am I? I forgot that for a bit. I guess it seemed to me that I was still a teenager dealing with this piece of filth. But I'm not." She stood. "I'm not." She paused, choosing her words with care. "This actually might be a blessing in disguise, Robie. He used my old man to get to me. But he never looked at it the other way around."

"Meaning?"

"Meaning he never thought that this was the only way *I* was ever going to get to *him*. And trust me, I've wanted to for two decades. And now he's given me a shot. I'm going to make him regret the day he ever thought about coming at me or hurting someone I care about."

"Now that's the Jessica Reel I know. And this time the guy is going to prison for good."

"If he ever makes it to trial," replied Reel quietly. "And I wouldn't bet the farm that he does, Robie. I really wouldn't. Because this son of a bitch . . . is mine."

As she left the room, Robie had one overriding thought.

He was very glad he was not Leon Dikes.

41

Leon Dikes sat down across from Julie, who was just finishing up a plate of food. She wiped her mouth, took a drink of water, and sat back watching him. Her face was swollen from where he had struck her.

"You want something?" she asked.

"How did you meet Jessica?"

"Why do you want to know?"

"Because it is better to know things than to not know things."

"She's just a friend I met through another friend."

"The names they gave at the prison were Jessica Reel and Will Robie. I have had them checked out. There is very little known about them. Very little. In fact, really nothing."

"I don't know anything about that."

"But I think that you do. Did you know that Sally, or Jessica, was in Witness Protection?"

"Because of you, right?"

"Now, I believe that this Will Robie might also be in Witness Protection, or else he might be a U.S. marshal assigned to protect her."

"Maybe he is."

"That answer is really not good enough."

"Like I said, we're just friends."

"Simple friends do not risk their lives for one another. Jessica offered to give herself up to me in exchange for your safe release. Why would she do that, I wonder?"

"Because she's a good person," replied Julie in a casual tone. "That must be hard for you to relate to. Probably why you find the concept so puzzling."

"Your arrogance in the face of imminent harm is really deserving of both admiration and puzzlement, a most unusual combination."

"I'm a complicated person."

"I want you to tell me everything you know about Jessica Reel and this Will Robie."

"I've told you what I know about Jessica. I don't really know Will Robie. Tonight was the first time I'd met him."

Dikes did not appear to be listening. "Are you yourself perhaps in Witness Protection? Is that how you met?"

"Why do you think that?"

"Because I have also made inquiries about you, and the results have been, shall we say, scant, which is problematic to me."

"Well, I'm not in Witness Protection, and even if I were I don't think they make a habit of putting different people in the program together or letting people in the program know the identities of others in the program."

"You are too young to have been placed in the program when Sally was."

"Jessica."

"To me she will always be Sally Fontaine."

"Whatever floats your boat," replied Julie curtly.

"Her father was able to reach her through Witness Protection. Whether she is still in the program or that was merely a conduit to deliver a message to her, wherever she is now, I do not know."

"Well, neither do I," said Julie.

"I think that you're lying."

"Think what you want."

"I will ask my questions and if I receive no answers I will have to ask more persuasively. It will not be pleasant for you, but if I have no choice . . . ?"

Dikes clapped his hands together. The door opened at once. The person now in the doorway must have been waiting there for this command, Julie thought.

He was huge, but his uniform fit him. Apparently, Dikes's group had more money to spend on uniforms than the Alabama correctional system did.

The prison guard Albert stared down at her. In one hand he held a fireplace poker, which was glowing red at one end. In his other hand was a whip that looked well used.

Dikes said, "This is my chief interrogator. I will

allow him to take charge of you for a while, unless there is something you wished to tell me."

Julie looked from Albert and his poker back to Dikes.

"What do you want to know?" she said fearfully.

"What I want to know is everything."

Julie said, "Then I'll tell you what I know."

42

"I want to talk to her," said Reel.

"No, I don't think so," said Dikes.

"Then you can forget it. Knowing you like I do, she's probably already dead. And so I'm not putting myself or Laura in danger if she is."

"You are so tiresome," said Dikes with an exaggerated sigh. "It was one of your least attractive features."

"I want to talk to her. Now!"

A few moments later Reel heard Julie's voice.

"I'm okay," Julie said.

"I'm so sorry about all this, Julie. Have they hurt you?"

"Nothing I can't handle. And they're standing right next to me in case I say something wrong."

"I know. I just want you to know that things will turn out okay, Julie. No matter what happens, you're going to be safe, okay?"

"Okay," Julie said in a small voice.

Reel heard a gasp from Julie, and Dikes said, "All right, you've confirmed that she's just fine."

"And she better remain that way," warned Reel.

"You are in no position to make demands. And don't attempt to employ your U.S. Marshal friends in WITSEC."

"What?"

"Your little friend told me all about you. That you're still in WITSEC. And that you are engaged to marry her guardian, Jerome, who is a very rich man."

"You bastard," snarled Reel. "Did you torture her to get her to tell you that?"

"The mere threat was enough. She's only a child. A precocious one, but still only a child. And she apparently lives in a fantasy world. She tried to feed me a cock-and-bull story about her being kidnapped by a Saudi prince, as if I'd believe that. But the mere sight of my, uh, chief interrogator, and she confessed all. It was rather pathetic."

"She's just a kid, Leon," barked Reel.

"Then she should act her age rather than wasting my time with stupid stories. And she also informed me about your friend, Mr. Robie. Or should I say Marshal Robie? Do not think of bringing him along. We will be able to see you coming from a long way off. And all you'll find when you get here is Julie's body."

"How do you want to do this, then?"

"Did you contact Laura?"

"I wouldn't be talking to you unless I had," retorted Reel.

"She will come with you. No tracking devices. No weapons. I recall that you were adept with a knife."

"Where am I going?"

"You mean where are you and Laura going," corrected Dikes.

"Just tell me, Leon."

"Don't let your nerves run away with you, Sally. It's unbecoming. How you were able to keep them in check when you were so young, I can't imagine. Luck, like I said before."

"Give me the instructions," Reel said flatly.

They were elaborate and well thought out, she had to admit.

They would first take a commercial aircraft to Atlanta and then a puddle jumper to Tuscaloosa. There they would board a Greyhound bus that would take them to an even smaller town. A car would be waiting in a parking lot next to the only grocery store in the town. The keys would be on the front seat. Directions going forward would be in the glove compartment. They would drive to a pre-arranged spot and they would be picked up from there. After that they would be driven to their final destination.

Dikes added, "Keep in mind that this is my country down here. I know every nook and cranny of it. I have the local police both in my back pocket and in my ranks. I own the town."

"I highly doubt that."

"People in bad economic times look to any savior possible," replied Dikes. "I can give them what they want. Order, safety, jobs. We're even venturing into other parts of the country. Some of our groups are buying up entire towns in the Midwest and the Dakotas. It is a good platform for growth and the spread of our unique ways."

"You mean your sickness?"

"They obviously do not see it that way, do they?"

"You may think so. But you'd be wrong."

"Nevertheless, when you come here you will be in my power, lock, stock, and barrel."

"Which means you have no intention of letting Julie go."

"I give you my word, Sally."

"Your word means nothing to me."

"Then why come at all?"

Reel fumed for a few moments, trying to regain her composure. "Because you're not going to do to her what you did to me."

"Well, we'll see, won't we? And we'll see very soon." He told Reel when she would be expected and hung up.

Reel clicked off and looked at the notes she had written down with the travel directions. Then she looked up at Robie, who had, again, listened to the entire conversation.

"This complicates things," said Reel, tapping the paper.

"But it's not unexpected," noted Robie. "It's not his job to make it easy."

"Yeah, it's his job to make it impossible."

"But it's not impossible," observed Robie.

Reel looked down at her notes and suddenly smiled. "No, it's not. You remember Jalalabad?"

"How could I ever forget? Is that how you want to play it?"

"Yes, I do," said Reel firmly. She looked at the notes again. "I see two, maybe three possibilities."

Robie nodded. "Same here. I'll head out early."

Reel nodded thoughtfully at this. "Recon will be important. Like he said, the area is under his control. You'll need cover."

"Two birds with one stone, Jessica."

She looked excited. "I can see that. I can absolutely see that."

"Once they pick you up you'll be cut off from communications."

"You lose me, we're lost."

"So I don't plan on losing you." He tapped the table. "And Laura?"

"I got that covered, Robie."

"Really?"

"Really."

43

Two days later Reel and a young woman boarded a Delta flight that would take them to Atlanta. The plane landed about an hour and forty minutes later. They had a brief layover and then boarded a turboprop for the short flight to Tuscaloosa, home to the University of Alabama. From there they took a Greyhound bus another fifty miles in a southwesterly direction and got off in a town that had one street and a handful of stores. In the parking lot next to a grocery store was a rusted-out Plymouth Fury with the keys on the front seat and a map in the glove compartment.

Following the directions on the map, they drove another hour to a crossroads where a black van was waiting, its engine idling.

The two women climbed out of the Plymouth carrying small knapsacks. As soon as they did the rear doors of the van opened and five men climbed out. Weapons were pointed at Reel's and the other woman's heads.

They were ordered into the back of the van, which had a cargo area but no seats. Their knapsacks were gone through and then discarded. They were stripped down and searched.

Sewn into the lining of the other woman's shirt was a thin metal wire with a sharpened end. One of the men pulled it free and held it up for her to see. With a smile he threw it out of the van.

Their clothes were thrown away and they were given orange jumpsuits and tennis shoes to wear. The scrunchie that Reel had in her hair was taken off and examined before being thrown back at her.

One of the men ran a handheld wand over them. It started clicking when it reached Reel's watch. The man smiled, ripped it off her, dropped it to the floor, and crushed it with his foot.

"Not good enough," he said.

Reel could not hide her unhappiness at this as she put her hair up and retied it with the scrunchie. She glanced balefully at the other woman.

"Did you think we were hicks who can't be professional?" said the largest of their captors. "You're about to find out just how good we are," he added menacingly.

Reel and the other woman were bound with plasti-cuffs and forced to lie in the back of the van. Before the doors thunked closed Reel could see the head-lights of two other vehicles come on and she heard their engines start. The van was apparently part of a motorcade.

They got back on the road and the van picked up

speed. The roads were not in good shape, and Reel and her companion were bounced all over the place. The men sitting next to them took the opportunity to kick and punch them as their bodies collided with them.

"Know your place, bitches," yelled one of them as his friends laughed. "Groveling in the dirt."

Reel calculated that they drove for about an hour before the van began to slow. There had been many turns involved, so she assumed the driver had been back-tracking so as to make it nearly impossible for anyone to follow without being seen.

She heard the roar of what sounded like a group of motorcycles pass by them. Horns blared, and it seemed that a biker gang was saying hello to their Nazi buddies. Another minute passed and she heard the roar of a semi as it blasted past them, its wake buffeting the van.

Ten minutes later the van pulled off and eventually came to a stop after bouncing over what seemed to be a series of potholes. The doors were jerked open and they were pulled to their feet. They stumbled out.

Reel kicked at one man who grabbed her butt. He pushed her away and with her hands bound she lost her balance and fell. The man laughed and pulled her up by her ponytail. He stopped laughing when her knee found his crotch, and he dropped to the dirt, his face turning gray.

Another of the men pulled his gun and pointed it at Reel's head.

"Enough," called out the voice.

Reel looked over to see Leon Dikes staring at her.

He was dressed in his full black SS uniform, nearly invisible in the darkness. His red armbands stood out, though, making it seem like both his arms had been gashed open.

"Bring our guests in," said Dikes.

As Reel was led past him, he smiled.

"It is good to see you, Sally."

And then he looked at the other woman.

"And is this Eva?"

"Laura," barked Reel.

"Is it? I wonder?" asked Dikes. "Still, it can always be confirmed. With absolute certainty."

They were led into a small room and the door closed behind them. A man came forward holding something. Reel's and the other woman's mouths were forced open and swabs taken from inside their cheeks.

Dikes held up a small glass tube with a cap on it. "My DNA sample has already been collected," he said as the man with the cotton swabs put the sample from Reel and the woman in similar glass tubes and capped them. "In twenty-four hours we will know with absolute certainty. Is she mine or not?"

He drew close and gripped Reel by the shoulder. "Is she my child or isn't she? That is the question. If she is, wonderful." Dikes slid his hand along the other woman's cheek. She pulled back but his men forced her to her original position.

"If she is not," continued Dikes, "then you die, Sally. And this imposter becomes my concubine. And Julie will become the mother of my child. It really is a win-win."

"And if she is your child?" snapped Reel.

"Then I still win. Because you will die, as horribly as I can make you. I have my child here, who will provide me other children. And I will have Julie as a replacement when I grow bored with this one."

Dikes gave the woman a little slap on her cheek. "And I easily grow bored. You could never command my attention, Sally. Never. It was one of your chief weaknesses."

"So your word means nothing?" yelled Reel.

"No, my word is inviolate. When I give it to people who are my equals. You are not and will never be my equal. You are nothing. You might as well be a Jew. Or a Negro. Or heaven help us, a Mexican."

"Well, you're right about one thing, you're not *my* equal," said Reel. "Now, where is Julie?"

"Why should I let you see her?"

"Because you can. Because you want me to see her. You want me to know you have her and me in your power. Just admit it and get it over with."

Dikes smiled. "You're not stupid, I'll give you that."

He nodded at two of his men, who pulled Reel and the other woman from the room. They were led down a hall, another door was unlocked, and they were pushed inside so roughly that they both fell to the floor.

"Jessica?" Julie raced over to help them up.

"Julie, are you okay?" said Reel, looking at the girl's puffy face.

"I'm okay," she said quickly, staring at the other woman.

"Julie, this . . . this is my daughter, Laura."

"Oh my God," said Julie. "I . . . I . . . Jessica, why are you here? They're going to kill you."

"It'll be okay," said Reel as her eyes searched the walls for a listening device and found two of them within twenty seconds. "We'll be okay."

Julie said, "Hi, Laura, I'm Julie Getty."

Laura tried to smile but she was clearly afraid.

Julie looked at Reel reproachfully. "Why did you bring her here?"

"I had to, Julie, otherwise they would have killed you."

"So now they kill all three of us?"

"They won't kill you two. Just me."

"Correct."

Dikes was standing in the doorway. He held out his hand. "But now it is time to get to know you."

"No," snapped Reel, stepping in front of Laura.

"I wasn't talking about her," said Dikes, smiling. "I was talking about you, Sally. Perhaps I should have said get *reacquainted* with you."

44

"Yie Chung-Cha?"

Chung-Cha looked up from her seat and studied the man who was speaking to her. He was short and lightly built with dark hair and eyes behind square lenses.

"Yes?"

"Will you follow me, please?"

She rose and did as he had so politely asked.

As they walked the long corridor he slowed his pace so that she was walking beside him. "We all know of you, of course, Comrade Yie. You are legendary in our circle. A national hero."

"I am not a hero, Comrade. I am simply one person who does what her country asks of her. Our Supreme Leader and his father and grandfather are the heroes. The only true heroes of our people."

"Of course, of course," he said hurriedly. "I did not mean to say anything that might—"

"And I do not say that you have. We will leave it at that."

He nodded curtly, his face reddening and his eyes downcast.

She was led to a small room with wooden walls and a dull tube of fluorescent light overhead. It flickered so badly that if she were not accustomed to her country's difficulty with maintaining a consistent flow of electricity, it would have given her a migraine.

She sat at the scarred table and placed her hands in her lap. She looked at the concrete floor beneath her feet and wondered if the cement came from one of the camps. Prisoners were good at making things like this. Hard, dangerous, unhealthy work was better performed by slaves than those who were free. Or who thought themselves so.

The door opened and two men came in. One was the same general to whom Chung-Cha had demonstrated concrete evidence of Pak's guilt by letting him hear the man's voice on her phone recording. She knew he had been one of Pak's biggest supporters, which meant that suspicion had instantly focused on him. He would now do everything in his power to show his loyalty. And, Chung-Cha was aware, he would also try to punish her for bringing down his comrade. The other wore a dark suit and white shirt but no tie. The shirt was buttoned to the top button. He carried a bulky briefcase.

They sat down and spoke words of greeting.

She nodded respectfully and waited expectantly. She had long since learned to offer nothing except in response to something else. Otherwise, they might realize what she was actually thinking. And she did not want that.

The general said, "Plans are going well, Comrade Yie, for your deployment in this grand mission on behalf of your country."

She nodded again but said nothing.

The suit took up the conversation with a nod of encouragement from the uniform.

For one second Chung-Cha allowed her mind to wander. How many meetings had she sat in with suits and uniforms? They all talked a lot but essentially said nothing she did not already know. She refocused as the suit took from his pocket three photos.

One was of a woman. She was dark-haired and pretty. Her eyes were blue and stood in considerable contrast to the color of her hair. The effect was to soften the hair and highlight the eyes and the warmth behind them.

"The First Lady of the United States of America," said the suit.

The general added, "The evil empire which seeks to destroy us."

Chung-Cha nodded. She knew who the woman was. She had seen her photo before while traveling overseas.

The suit continued. "Her name is Eleanor Cassion."

She also knew this but simply nodded.

The suit pointed to the next photo. The girl in it was about fifteen or so, gauged Chung-Cha. She did not know who this was, but had a good guess. She had dirty blonde hair and her face closely resembled the woman's.

The suit said, "The First Lady's daughter, Claire Cassion."

Chung-Cha nodded. She had been correct.

He then indicated the third photo. This was of a boy, about ten, who had the woman's hair but the girl's soft brown eyes.

"Thomas Cassion Junior, named after his father, Thomas Cassion, the president of the United States," said the suit.

"These are the targets," added the general unnecessarily.

"I understand that they are to be killed simultaneously," said Chung-Cha.

The men nodded. The suit said, "Absolutely."

"By you, Comrade Yie," added the general.

Chung-Cha noted the barely veiled hostility behind the man's words. She thought that he should be more subtle.

"Is it feasible to expect one person to be able to kill all three at the same time?" she said.

"You have been presented to me as a great warrior, Chung-Cha; do you not live up to your reputation?" asked the general in a taunting tone.

She bowed humbly and said, "I am flattered by

such words, sir, but I will not allow my vanity to interfere with the success of the mission. I look at it only logically as someone who has done these types of actions before."

"Explain," said the suit.

"There will be Secret Service agents accompanying these three people at all times. The children have their own details, as does the First Lady. When they are traveling together, these details will be merged and will therefore be more formidable than if each target is taken separately but simultaneously."

The suit nodded thoughtfully, but the general cut the air with his hand and gave a derisive snort. "Impossible." He glared at Chung-Cha. "To send three separate teams of agents into the United States and target three separate people?" He shook his head emphatically. "All that does is divide your forces and exponentially increase the odds that something will go awry. And if one attack fails, they all almost certainly will fail." He collected all three photos and held them up, splayed out like playing cards.

"It will be all together. There is no question of an alternative." He pointed his finger at her again. "And it will be you who pulls the trigger, Comrade Yie. You bring down mighty generals in North Korea with ease, it seems. This will be child's play by comparison."

"I only bring down generals who are *traitors*," replied Chung-Cha evenly.

The general started to grin at this statement, but then his expression changed. "Are you accusing me of—"

"I accuse no one," she said, breaking in.

The suit held up a hand. "We fight amongst ourselves without purpose. The Supreme Leader would not be pleased. And what Comrade Yie said is quite correct. She did her duty and was richly rewarded by our Supreme Leader."

This statement instantly wiped the anger off the general's face and he calmed. "My colleague is quite correct. And so are you, Comrade Yie. You exposed a traitor. That is as it should be."

"But I will still go in alone?"

"You will not go in alone," said the general, and the suit nodded. "There will be a team to accompany you. But the Americans will die by your hand alone." The general now managed a smile. "You are a woman, Comrade Yie. The Americans have a soft spot for your gender. They will not believe that a woman can harm them."

Chung-Cha simply stared at him until he looked away.

The suit slipped a file folder from the briefcase he had carried in and handed it to her. "This is our preliminary report about the three targets. You will read and memorize and then there will be more."

"Have any plans been formulated as to when and

where the targets will be attacked?" asked Chung-Cha.

"They are being processed and vetted now," said the suit. "The best one will be chosen. In the meantime you will read these materials, practice your English, and return to your rigorous training. We will build the necessary background documents for you and your team to enter the United States. You must be ready to be activated for this mission at a minute's notice."

She rose, took the folder, and slid it into her bag.

The general scooped up the photos and handed them to her. "You will need these, Comrade Yie. You will study these faces until the very moment before you kill them." He looked at her patronizingly.

Chung-Cha took the photos and put them in her bag. She did not look at either of the men as she left the room.

She took the metro home, walking the last few blocks. She passed a few people and looked at none of them. She did, however, note the man following her. She arrived at her apartment and walked the few flights up. She made tea and put rice in her cooker, sat by the window with her cup, and opened her bag.

She glanced up and down the street. The man was nowhere in sight. But he was down there. She could sense his presence.

She pulled out the photos and the file.

She set aside the mother's picture and focused on

the girl. Claire Cassion. She looked at the file. She was fifteen, born in March. She attended something called Sidwell Friends. As Chung-Cha read more, she learned that Sidwell was a school that both boys and girls attended. She looked at pictures of the school and thought it very handsome and peaceful. The school had been founded by Quakers. The report helpfully provided that Quakers are a religious group that pride themselves on their nonviolent beliefs. That was a stupid principle on which to found a religion, Chung-Cha thought. One could not rule out violence, because violence was often necessary. And since other religions routinely employed violence, those that did not were in constant danger of being rendered extinct.

She read on as she sipped the strong, hot tea, occasionally looking out her window as she contemplated the facts she was accumulating in her mind. But she found herself again wandering to other things.

It seemed that this Sidwell Friends was a very prestigious place and many of the students there were the children of very prominent families. They received a rigorous education. She read that many graduated and went on to other elite schools with names like Harvard, which she had heard of, and Stanford, which she had not, and some place called Notre Dame. She had visited the Middle East and ventured into countries where girls were not educated at all. Apparently they didn't think girls were worth the trouble. Chung-Cha thought they were actually worth more than the boys.

Girls were educated in North Korea, but not if they were in the camps. At Yodok Chung-Cha had never been in class to really learn, only to fix a few numbers and letters in her head and acknowledge her sins. Then she had gone on to the mine and the factory.

She looked at the pretty buildings of Sidwell Friends with just a bit of wistfulness.

She turned to the boy, Thomas Junior. He went to a place called St. Albans. The file said it was named after the first British martyr, Saint Alban. The buildings were made of stone and they looked almost castle-like to her. Fine old buildings where boys—it was only boys who attended St. Albans—went to learn. It seemed to be as highly regarded as Sidwell Friends.

The mascot of St. Albans was a bulldog. Chung-Cha had never had a dog. There had never been an opportunity. She wouldn't have known what to do with one anyway.

Yet there had been a hound, on the other side of the fence at Yodok. She had glimpsed it one day. She thought it rather ugly and dirty and thus just like her. That had been the bond that formed for her. When they were let outside the fence to collect wood the dog had followed her, licked her hand. She drew back and struck it because a touch to her meant an attack was imminent. The beast yipped and sat down on its haunches, its tongue out and what looked to be a smile on its snout, a smile that reached to its wide eyes.

The dog had been there when she was next let through the gate to gather wood. This time, when it approached, she held out her hand and it licked it. She had nothing to give the thing, no food. She would never give food away. Never. No one in the camp would. It would be like giving away your blood or your heart. But she let it lick her hand. And she rubbed its head, which it seemed to like.

She never heard the bolt on the rifle being slammed back. She heard the shot. She heard the yip. She tasted the beast's blood on her. She heard the guard laugh as she cried out and fell away.

She saw the dog twitch once and then it lay still, the bloody wound on its chest widening, its tongue hanging lopsided out of its mouth. She ran away. She heard the guard laugh again. If she had known how to kill a guard and live she would have.

She put the papers back into the folder, spooned the rice into a bowl, and ate it as she drank her tea. Like the burger at the American-style restaurant, she ate her rice slowly, almost a grain at a time it seemed. She looked out the window.

She finally saw the man, lurking near the corner. He was not dressed in a uniform, but he was military. He had forgotten to change his shoes. They were distinctive. And his hair was matted down where the cap would usually sit.

They were having her followed. That was clear. What was not as clear was why. Chung-Cha had a few ideas that might answer that query. None of them were good for her. Not a single one.

It was just the way it was here.

45

"You will see that we are not disturbed."

Dikes said this to the large man in a black uniform who was stationed at the end of the hall. Along this hall was only one doorway and behind it a bedroom.

The guard saluted, and as Dikes turned away, shoving Reel in front of him, the man let a small smile escape his lips.

Dikes unlocked the door and pushed Reel, her hands still bound behind her, through the opening. He walked in, closed the door, and locked it.

He took off his gloves. She turned to face him.

"It has been a long time, Sally. Too long."

"I feel the same. I've been wanting to come back and kill you for a long time. Thanks for giving me the chance."

He laughed, a cold, mirthless sound.

"Kill me? You obviously know nothing of the situation. You are entirely within my power here. You are a woman. I am a man. You are tied up. I have a gun. This place is heavily guarded by my men. I will decide when you die. Only me. It is just like the concentration camps. Run with absolute authority and perfect order. Things of beauty. But I don't expect you to understand."

"What I understand and what you don't could fill a library, Leon."

His smug look faded. "You know I do not permit anyone to call me by that name. I am Der Führer to all."

"Really? My nickname for you was always Little Dicky Dikes. Descriptive and accurate. I still don't know how you got me pregnant. I never felt a thing. Didn't even know you were inside me. But you do have small hands and feet, and you know what they say."

"If it makes you feel better to speak such nonsense, please, go right ahead. It will not change anything that will happen here tonight."

"I agree. It won't."

He took off his cap and undid the buttons of his shirt. He smiled. "So, did you miss me?" He took off his gun belt and put it on the table.

"Probably not as much as you missed me."

He removed his boots and undid his trousers and stepped out of them.

She looked down. "I hope you took a Viagra pill. Otherwise, there's probably not going to be an appearance of the equipment you're going to need. You are an old man, after all."

"I intend to show you that I am a *man*, all over

again. You remember last time, how you screamed? In joy, I am sure." He pointed to the bed. "Lie down. Now."

"I'm not in the mood."

He pulled his pistol from its holster and pointed the muzzle at her head. "Now, Sally. I am growing impatient."

Reel lay on the bed.

He pulled off her sneakers and then her socks.

He rubbed her feet. "Your skin is still soft." With a violent jerk he ripped her jumpsuit down to her ankles and threw the garment against the wall. "I forget if you like it rough or not. I have had so many women since you."

"How many did you have to pay? And how many did you have to kidnap?"

"You never really saw my virtues, did you?"

"Why would I waste my time in a pointless exercise?"

He was bending over her when she spit in his face. He straightened and took a moment to wipe his face with the back of his hand before turning to pick up his pistol.

Reel sprang off the bed and swung her bound hands under her feet so they were in front of her. She ripped the scrunchie out of her hair and held it like a garrote. Before Dikes could turn back around, the garrote was around his throat. She jumped off the floor and clamped her legs around his torso, pinning his arms to his sides. She lurched backward and they fell onto the bed.

They bounced up and down as he struggled to free himself. The mattress springs started to squeak noisily. Reel heard footsteps grow closer to the door.

She started to pant and then moan loudly as the mattress kept squeaking. Saliva was coming out of Dikes's mouth as he was slowly being strangled.

As he tried to cry out for help, Reel started yelling. "Do me! Oh, God, do me, Der Führer! Do me!" she shrieked. "Yes, yes!" She bounced up and down on the mattress until she thought the bed would collapse.

Then she heard the footsteps tiptoeing away from the door. She could imagine the guard smiling to himself, imagining his boss screwing her brains out. Maybe he thought he would get the leftovers.

She felt Dikes growing weaker. She clamped her legs like a vise around him. The garrote was cutting into his neck, so fiercely was she pulling on it. He started gurgling.

"Yes, yes!" she screamed, covering the sounds he was making.

And then she started to turn his head slowly to the side even as she kept increasing the pressure on his neck.

"Give it to me," she called out. "Give it all to me."

He was facing her now. His eyes were bulging and blood-filled from the hemorrhaging her stranglehold was causing. Foam was pouring out of his mouth.

337

He exerted his last bit of strength to try to throw her off. That did topple them off the bed, but Reel's grip never failed. She swung her right leg up and placed her foot against the top of his head.

She whispered, "Goodbye, Leon. And tell Der Führer to kiss my ass when you see him in hell."

She screamed, "Yes, you son of a bitch!" She jerked his neck to the right with her hands at the same time she slammed his head to the left with her foot. Dikes's neck snapped cleanly.

As he grew limp she relaxed her legs around his torso, pushed away from him, and then gripped his lifeless hand and took off his watch. She rose from the floor breathless.

With her hands still bound, she picked up his gun, strode to the door, checked the time on the watch, counted to five, and then fired the weapon three quick times into the ceiling.

And then all hell truly broke loose.

46

The extra-long semi that had passed the van earlier had doubled back and parked. From the trailer had emerged three black SUVs. There were eight men in each vehicle. Each man was armored, had night-vision optics, and was loaded with weaponry.

They headed toward the front of the neo-Nazi complex.

From the rear came ten more men who had parked their motorcycles a quarter mile away and made the last part of the trek on foot. They were armored and had night optics too, and were also loaded for bear. Or at least for neo-Nazis.

Robie was leading this group. They crossed a rise and then swiftly made their way down it. Three hundred feet away was the cluster of buildings with a fence around it. Robie checked his watch and waited five minutes. Then he signaled his men forward.

A hundred feet away they stopped. Their optics revealed clear green images of the perimeter patrol. There were only three of them. Robie's group moved forward again to within fifty feet. Rifles were aimed and red dots appeared on the chests of each of the perimeter uniforms.

Robie checked his watch again. He followed the second hand as it made its way around the clock face.

Then the three shots rang out and Robie started to run.

Instantly, three rifles fired and the three perimeter men dropped where they stood. They weren't dead, merely tranquilized. Robie and his team didn't want to deprive the men of a long prison sentence.

Robie was over the fence in a few seconds, followed by five of his men. They dropped down inside the compound and immediately received fire. They took cover and returned it, this time with live rounds.

Meanwhile, in the front, the electric-powered SUVs had moved so silently with lights out that they were nearly at the gate before the guards there could react. By then it was too late. The gates crashed inward and the SUVs hurtled into the inner yard. The men sprang out of the vehicles and raced straight toward the main building.

The two guards there were quickly surrounded and trussed up.

Reel had shot the guard in the hall who had been eavesdropping on her and Dikes's "lovemaking." She hurried on and shot another neo-Nazi who appeared in front of her with his weapon out.

A moment later she was slammed against the wall and the gun fell from her bound hands. A foot kicked it away. She recovered her balance and stared up into the face of the huge Albert, dressed in his black SS uniform. He smiled down at her still in her underwear as he slid his tongue along his mouth.

"I'm gonna have some fun with you, sweet thing."

Reel struck so fast Albert had no time to react. She slammed her foot into his crotch, doubling him over, and then whipsawed around and struck him in the right kidney with her elbow. He screamed in fury, but only for a second. Using the wall opposite as both a launch point and for leverage, she pushed off and slammed both feet into his buttocks. Bent over as he was, Albert crashed headfirst into the wall opposite. The top of his skull hit first, driving his neck upward to an impossible degree and his head back so far that his neck broke.

Dead Albert dropped to his knees. Reel was already racing onward and never saw him slump to the concrete floor.

She heard a scream to her left and raced down that hall.

One man stumbled out of a doorway, a knife sticking out of his chest. He slumped to the floor, dead, his cap falling off his head on the way down.

Laura appeared in the doorway, saw Reel, and said, "They separated me from Julie. I think she's down this way. Hurry."

The two women raced down the hall and toward the room at the end. There was a crashing of glass, screams, and then gunshots.

Reel shouted, "That's Julie!"

She and Laura sprinted forward.

"Julie!" screamed Reel.

The door was bolted, but she shot the lock off and burst into the room.

And stopped.

Two men lay on the floor, their bodies covered by shattered glass. Julie was flattened against one wall.

There was movement at the window.

Reel pointed her gun that way and then caught a breath.

Robie clambered through the empty window and dropped to the floor. He put his pistol back into his holster and looked at Julie.

"Are you hurt?"

She shook her head and stepped toward Robie, her feet crunching over the glass that littered the floor. Robie put his arm around her and then looked down at the men.

"I think they had orders to kill Julie in the event of an attack."

"So you shot them through the window," deduced Reel.

"So I shot them through the window," confirmed Robie.

His walkie-talkie squawked and he spoke into it and then listened.

"We're secure. No casualties on our side. Most of the assholes just gave up."

"Well, not the one who really counted," said Reel.

"No prison for Mr. Dikes?" said Robie.

"Not in this life," replied Reel. "Let's hope in his next one. For all eternity."

Robie pulled his knife and severed the bindings on Reel's hands. He took off his jacket and draped it around her.

Julie looked from Reel to Laura. "Is she your daughter?"

Reel rubbed her wrists and shook her head slowly. "I'd like you to meet FBI Special Agent Lesley Shepherd, Julie."

Shepherd nodded at Julie and gave her a shy smile. "I just look really young for my age."

Robie said, "The FBI doesn't like people being kidnapped. They provided all the ground assets we needed."

Julie said, "FBI? So, super agent Vance?"

"She cares about you a great deal, Julie. She's the reason we were able to put this all-out effort together."

Reel looked at Robie. "Any problems finding us?"

He shook his head.

"How did you track them?" asked Julie. "I heard

Dikes and his men talking about the steps they'd taken to make sure you couldn't do that."

"Our friends at National Geospatial," answered Robie. "They sort of run the spy satellite network."

"The DD of the CIA spoke with her counterpart at Geospatial," added Reel. "And they dialed up several satellites. They tracked us all the way to our rendezvous with Dikes's men. They placed an electronic marker on us at that point. There was no way to lose us. They simply followed using multiple eyes up in the sky. The actual technology has a specific name, but it's classified. I'm just glad it worked."

"Very hard to lose a bunch of satellites," said Robie. "They fed us the location on the ground. We passed by the van carrying Reel and Shepherd. We were on motorcycles and in a semi. We surrounded the place and waited for the signal."

"Signal?" asked Julie.

"Gun fired three times in a row by Jessica," said Robie.

"But how did you know she'd be able to get to a gun?"

Robie smiled. "That's where the element of trust comes in."

"I did what I needed to do," said Reel. "And then fired the gun."

"And that's when we came charging in," said Robie.

"And saved me again," finished Julie.

Reel went over to her and knelt down. "You wouldn't have needed saving but for me. I was the reason you were taken."

"I told them a false story about you. That you were still in WITSEC. I wanted him to be surprised when he found out what you really could do."

"He *was* surprised."

"And I was never really afraid."

"Why not?" asked Reel.

"I knew you'd come and save me."

"How could you be so sure?"

Now Julie smiled. "That's where the element of trust comes in."

47

Nicole Vance sipped a mug of hot coffee as her team processed the scene.

She glanced over at Robie and Reel and Agent Lesley Shepherd, who were sitting in chairs inside one of the rooms of the neo-Nazi facility. Sitting between Robie and Reel was Julie, huddled in a blanket and drinking hot chocolate.

Vance walked over to them and said, "We've had our eyes on this group for a while. Domestic terrorism in addition to just being scumbags. They were smart how they went about it. Never left any evidence or witnesses behind. They had their hands in lots of things, though, we believe. Including human trafficking and arms dealing."

"Nice people, just like the assholes they were emulating," said Robie.

"And with so many of them in custody it might lead us to other places and more arrests."

"I wish you nothing but the best on that."

She glanced at Julie. "You need anything else, Julie?"

The girl shook her head. "I'm just glad Jerome is okay."

"He was lucky. His skull is apparently a lot harder than they thought. He's still in the hospital, but the docs have assured me he's going to be okay. We'll get you home on a pair of Bureau wings as soon as we can."

"I've got a lot of homework to catch up on," admitted Julie.

Vance glanced at Robie. "How jaded youth becomes."

Julie shot a glance at Shepherd and then looked over at Reel. "So where is your real daughter?"

Reel looked down at her hands. She said quietly, "I don't know. I had to give her up for adoption a long time ago."

"Why?" Julie wanted to know.

"Because I was really still just a kid myself and I had no job. And then the job that was offered to me didn't provide for a baby in tow."

"Right," said Julie, both looking and sounding disappointed.

Reel got to her feet and turned to Shepherd. "Lesley, I owe you more than I can ever repay."

Shepherd took Reel's offered hand and shook it. "Are you kidding? My honor."

Reel turned to Vance. "Can I ask a favor?"

"How can I say no?" said Vance.

"Can I take a couple of photos?"

"Of what?"

"I'll show you."

The two women left. Robie turned to Julie.

"You sure you're okay? They didn't . . . you know, do anything to you?"

"Other than smacking me around, the creeps left me alone. But that wouldn't have lasted. The head guy was a psycho."

She drew closer to Robie. "Did you know that Jessica didn't know where her daughter was?"

"No. I just recently found out she *had* a daughter. She'd never talked about it before."

"Do you think she regrets it? I mean, giving up her kid?"

"I don't know. I guess most mothers regret it, don't they?"

Julie shrugged and looked somber. "Some don't have a choice. Like my mom. But she always wanted me back." She thought for a few seconds. "I think Jessica regrets it."

"I think you're right." Robie put an arm around her shoulders. "And I know Jerome will be glad to get you back."

"Are you going to make this, like, a habit?"

"What?"

"Saving me."

She was joking, but Robie frowned. "I hope I never have to again, Julie. Considering it was our screwup that got you involved in the first place."

"We got out okay."

"No one can count on that to keep happening." He was about to say something else when a woman appeared in the doorway.

Robie looked at her in surprise.

It was DD Amanda Marks. She smiled and came forward.

"You must be Julie. I've heard quite a bit about you from a friend of yours."

"Jessica?" asked Julie.

Marks nodded. "I've been told that everything turned out all right."

"It did," said Robie. "And thanks for the assist."

"I almost never get an opportunity to give back. It actually felt good."

Reel came back into the room, trailed by Vance. Reel looked relieved about something. Vance actually looked pleased. Reel shook her hand.

"Thanks, this means a lot."

"I truly hope it works out for you."

"Oh, I think it'll work out just fine now." She looked over and saw Marks. "I'd like to finish this now, ma'am, if that's okay."

"With my blessing, Agent Reel. With my blessing."

Julie glanced sharply at Robie. "What are they talking about?"

"I'm not sure," admitted Robie.

Reel called out to him. "Hey, Robie? You want to be in on the end of this thing?"

"And what would that be?"

"I'd prefer to show rather than tell."

Julie whispered to him, "You better go. And you better tell me everything that happens."

Robie rose and headed toward Reel. "Where to?" he asked.

"Not that far away, actually. We can take a car. But I need to make a phone call first and get things set up."

"Just one phone call?"

"One is all it takes, if you call the right person."

48

It was raining. Even in here Earl Fontaine could hear the drops colliding against the roof of the prison. He could hear the wind howling too. He snuggled more comfortably in his hospital bed. Now that it was over, he knew he could die a happy man. But then again, he might just hang on a little longer. He had a bed, a roof over his head, meds for the pain, three squares a day, even if they were in the form of liquid shot into his gut via a tube, and a good-looking personal doctor to look after him. Not a bad life, actually.

He glanced over at the bed once occupied by Junior. He smiled. He had no idea how such a moron had been able to kill so many people and elude capture for as long as Junior had. Earl had only had to call his "friend" and big Albert had been put on the case, first to hide the knife in Junior's bed. Then it had been up to Earl to get the idiot to pull it out. Well, that had been easy enough. When Junior's fingers had touched the knife, his fate had been sealed. Albert had been instructed on exactly what to do. Grab Junior, keep the knife clamped in his hand,

351

pretend to struggle and then kill the little son of a bitch, and kill him good.

And if there was one thing Albert was good at, it was killing. Earl wondered if he had been the one designated to kill Sally. He hoped so. She would be dead as dead could be.

He sighed contentedly and closed his eyes as the rain continued to pound down. He slept for a while, figuring that a nap before his last round of meds would be good.

"Earl?" A hand grasped his shoulder. "Earl?" the voice said more urgently.

Earl slowly opened his eyes. He had been dreaming about the female doctor. It had been a damn fine dream. She had been naked and tied up and he was about to—

"What?" He blinked and slowly rolled over on his back to stare up into the face of the same male nurse he'd talked to before. "What is it? Time for my meds?"

He looked at the big clock on the wall. He'd only been asleep an hour. It wasn't time for his medication. The rain was still falling outside and the wind made the old prison shudder under its assault.

Earl grimaced. "What'd you wake me up for? Ain't time for my meds, boy, not by a long shot." He was upset that his dream had been interrupted. He started to close his eyes once more.

The nurse shook him once more. "It's not about your meds, Earl. You got a visitor. Well, visitors."

Earl blinked more rapidly. "Visitors? It's nighttime, boy. Ain't no visitors allowed after dark. You know that."

"Well, they're here."

"Who is?"

The nurse pointed to his left. "Them."

Earl looked over, and when he saw them his heart almost stopped.

Jessica Reel and Will Robie stood there, their hair slicked down and their clothes dripping from the inclement weather they had just come through.

Earl sat up so fast one of his IV lines became tangled in his bed-sheets.

The nurse disentangled it and stepped back. He looked at the expression on Earl's features and then at the one on Reel's and he said quickly, "I'll . . . I'll just let you folks visit, then."

He turned and hurried off.

Reel stepped forward, with Robie right behind her.

"Sally?" said Earl. He attempted a grin, but it failed about halfway to his mouth. "What you be doing here, girl?"

"Just coming to say goodbye, Earl."

"Hell, you already done that. Not that I ain't glad to see you again."

Reel ignored this as she stepped closer. "And I

have something to show you too." She slipped from her pocket a picture and held it out to him. "I think you'll recognize him even if he looks a little pale."

Earl put out a shaky hand and took the photo from her. When he gazed down at the picture he immediately gasped.

"Albert, I think, is his name," said Reel. "He's dead, of course, but you should still be able to tell it's him."

"How did he die?" said Earl in a croaky voice.

"Oh, I guess I forgot to mention that. I killed him. Broke his neck. For such a big guy he went fast. Which was good for me. I had other pretend-Nazis to deal with."

Gaping, Earl looked up at her, his eyes wide. "You done killed him? Him!"

"I don't think I ever told you what I do now, Earl. On behalf of the American people I take scum like Albert and make sure they never hurt anyone ever again. Like this bastard."

She pulled another picture from her jacket and dropped it on Earl's belly. He took it with a trembling hand, his face the color of ash.

"This is one of your buddies too. Leon Dikes. I knew him a long time ago. We recently got together. At his insistence. Apparently he was hanging around the prison and coincidentally saw me when I came to visit you. Talk about a small world."

Earl looked up into her face. "Did you kill him too?"

Reel made a rough oval with her hands and then ripped them apart. "Highly effective move. Death is instant. Before he died Leon sent his regards and told you he was sorry your plan didn't work."

Earl dropped the photo like it was a snake about to bite him. "Ain't know what you talkin' 'bout."

"Sure you do, Earl. Don't back away from the credit for all this now. It really was very clever, and I don't give compliments easily, I can assure you."

"You making no sense. Now, you got nothing else, I'm going back to sleep."

"Well, I think your nap will have to wait."

"Why's that?" snapped Earl, his confidence returning. "You got nothing or else you woulda done brought the cops with you. What they gonna do to me anyway? Arrest me? Put me in jail? Shit!" He laughed until he choked.

"No, no police. No new charges. The old ones will suffice."

"So like I said, get your ass gone. I need my rest."

"But you're doing great. A lot healthier than you were."

He sat up straighter. "What the hell you talking 'bout? I got terminal cancer. I ain't getting better."

"Yeah, but there's more to it than that."

She pointed to her right. Earl looked that way and saw the female prison doctor striding toward them.

"Dr. Andrews, thank you for coming in tonight," said Reel.

Andrews gave a forced smile. "My pleasure. Wouldn't have missed it, actually."

Reel said to Earl, "I explained to Dr. Andrews her role in getting you and me back together. And also how that led to a very nice visit with your good friend Leon Dikes and his group of merry neo-Nazi freaks."

"Yes, it was fascinating, Mr. Fontaine," said Dr. Andrews, who looked like she wanted to pull a gun and fire a round right into Earl's brain.

"I ain't got no idea what you two gals are jabbering 'bout," said Earl. "No idea a'tall."

"Well, let's see if I can make it crystal-clear for you," said Reel. "First, Dr. Andrews has some terrific news for you."

Earl looked at Andrews. "What news?"

"While your cancer is still terminal, it's been determined that your condition has stabilized."

"What the hell does that mean?"

"That means that you can leave the hospital ward and this prison. You're being sent back to solitary confinement on death row."

Earl's face collapsed. "But they can't execute me."

Andrews smiled. "Unfortunately, that's true, but you can be cared for there, although I have to say it won't be nearly as pleasant as here. And you will have no human contact with anyone other than the prison personnel."

"You . . . you can't do that," Earl protested.

"Well, actually we can," said another voice.

A man in a suit walked in with four beefy guards behind him.

"What the hell is he doing here?" exclaimed Earl.

Reel looked behind her. "The warden of this fine facility and his men are here to take care of your transfer back to death row at the Holman Correctional Facility."

There was a flash of lightning at the barred window, followed by a vicious crack of thunder.

The warden waved his men forward. "Just roll the bed and all right out. The transport vehicle is waiting."

"You can't do this," sputtered Earl. "You can't."

"Get him out of here," ordered the warden. "Now!"

The guards unhooked Earl's shackles from the wall and rolled his bed, with him screaming his head off, out of the room. They heard his shouts for another minute before a heavy door clanged shut and then Earl Fontaine was heard no more.

Reel turned to the warden and Andrews. "Thank you," she said.

"No, thank *you*," said Andrews. "To think that bastard used me to . . . to try and accomplish all these horrific things."

"Damn right," said the warden. "We might not be able to execute him. But we can make whatever time he has left as unpleasant as legally possible. And we will." He marched off.

Andrews said, "When I got your call I really couldn't believe it. I thought I was helping a father find his daughter. I should have known that Earl Fontaine was a man who didn't care about that."

"He took a lot of people in, Doc," said Reel.

"But never again," said Robie.

"No, never again," added Reel.

After thanking Andrews again for her help, they turned and left the prison.

"Feel better?" asked Robie when they climbed into the car after running across the parking lot as the rain continued to pour.

"Actually, Robie, I don't feel anything. And maybe that's for the best."

Robie put the car in gear and they left the Alabama prison, and with it Earl Fontaine, behind forever.

49

The North Koreans had no facility like the Burner Box. They didn't have the budget for it. No country spent what the Americans did on defense or internal security. But Chung-Cha felt like they made up with effort and dedication what they lacked in funding.

She ran through the streets of Pyongyang until she could run no more. And then she kept going. The State Security Department had a generic gymnasium facility where she built up her strength. They had shooting ranges deep underground where she worked on her aim, reaction time, and motor skills in the use of all sorts of firearms and other weapons. There, against only men who were far larger and stronger than she was, she drilled on certain close-quarter combat techniques, some of which she had employed to subdue Lloyd Carson in Romania.

Her training wasn't only physical. She could speak fluent English as well as three other languages.

But what she really excelled at, in addition to remaining calm under the most extreme circumstances, was martial arts. There had never been a man to beat her. Not even several of them. She attributed this to her time at the camp. To survive the camp took herculean toughness. But that was not enough. To survive the camp and keep your human spirit, your belly fire, was nearly impossible. She had accomplished the impossible. And to survive the camp one had to think ten moves ahead. She had become adept at that. The same held true for the martial arts. She not only outfought her opponents, she outthought them as well.

Her department had spent much time and money in developing her ability to attack superior numbers and come away victorious. It was a combination of original tactics, superlative fighting skills, and the ability to assess and take risks, often turning a disadvantage into an advantage. She had shown that when confronted with the administrator and the prison guards. She had turned the strengths of her opponents into weaknesses and she had never stopped moving or fighting. It was as if her mind and her body were a single unit.

She returned to her apartment tired, but satisfied that her skill level remained undiminished. She was aware that with the upcoming mission she would be pitted against the best security detail in the world. She knew that the U.S. Secret Service was widely regarded as invincible, all agents willing to die to protect whomever they were guarding. But they had lost protectees in the past, so they weren't infallible. Still, it would probably be her greatest challenge.

She ate her rice and drank her tea and listened to country music on the iPod that the Supreme Leader had given her. She looked out the window for the man who had been there every day. He was still there. It was as though he didn't care now if she knew he was there or not. That actually said a lot to her.

In North Korea it was said that alliances were as fragile as ice on a hot day.

She left her apartment and got into her car. It was ten years old but still serviceable. And it was hers. Until they took it away, which they could at any time. And depending on how the next mission turned out, that time might soon be coming.

She drove out of Pyongyang. She checked her rearview mirror and was not surprised to see a black sedan following her. She drove slowly, well under the speed limit. She was in no hurry. She had no intention of losing whoever was back there.

Her trip would take her roughly seventy miles northeast of the capital into a mountainous part of South Hamgyong province, bisected by the Ipsok River valley.

The official name of where she was heading was Kwan-li-so Number 15. But most people simply called it Yodok. It was a labor camp or concentration camp or penal colony; Chung-Cha did not care which term was used. It all amounted to the same thing.

People taking away the freedom of other people.

For years she had had another name for it: home.

Like other labor camps, Yodok was comprised of two parts: the total control zone from which prisoners were never released, and the revolutionary zone, where prisoners were punished, reeducated, and eventually released. The camp was about one hundred and fifty square miles in size and had about fifty thousand prisoners. Electric fences and over a thousand guards made sure that no one left of their own volition.

Chung-Cha did not believe there was corruption at Yodok. The guards there seemed to do their duty with barbaric joy. At least they had when she was there. And she was still the only prisoner from the total control zone ever voluntarily released. But that release had come with a heavy price, perhaps heavier than if she had tried to escape.

That was why she was here today, to relive this part of her life. Well, that was only partly true. It took special permission to do this, which she had requested and received. Those granting that permission understood her to be coming here to pay homage to those who had allowed her freedom, in exchange for her lifelong commitment to serve her country. At least that had been the original intent. Then she had convinced those more powerful than her that there should be another reason. And that she was the ideal person to implement this plan. She had had no guarantee that permission would be granted, but it had been. The necessary papers documenting this rode in her inner pocket. The august signatures on the papers would brook no opposition.

She parked near the gate and was met there by two guards and the administrator. Chung-Cha knew this man well. He had been the administrator when she was a prisoner there.

He bowed to her with respect and she returned the bow. Her gaze never left his face as they each straightened. In his burnt, wrinkled countenance she saw the one man she had dreamt of killing for most of her life. She knew that he knew this. But now he was powerless to harm her anymore. Yet there was the way his lip curled back, exposing one misshapen tooth, that made Chung-Cha understand quite clearly that he would dearly love to have her back here and in his power.

"It is an honor to have you here, Comrade Yie," he said.

"The Supreme Leader sends his best wishes to you, Comrade Doh," replied Chung-Cha, making the point of exactly where she was at this stage in her life.

Doh blinked rapidly behind his thick glasses and his smile was as false as his next words. "It does my heart good to see how far you have risen, Comrade Yie."

He escorted her through the gate and into the prison compound.

Although Chung-Cha had been gone from this

place for many years now, much of it had not
changed at all. The huts where the prisoners lived
were still made of mud with straw roofs. As she
peered inside one she saw the boards with blankets
on them representing a prisoner's bed. There were
forty of them in a room that was only about five
hundred square feet in size. The huts were not heated
and they were not clean, thus disease was rampant.
She had heard the administrator say once when she
was here that such widespread fatal epidemics saved
them the price of bullets.

She stopped in front of one hut. She did so for a
particular reason. This had been "her" hut, where she
had lived for years. She glanced over at Doh and saw
that he too remembered this.

"You have indeed risen far," he said, his fake smile
broadening across his tanned features.

He was a pureblood, she knew, a member of the
very elite core group. His grandfather had been one
of Kim Il Sung's earliest and most ardent supporters.
For that he and his family had been forever rewarded
greatly. For the grandson it meant he got to play God
with the lives of hundreds of thousands of his fellow
citizens over the years, determining who got to live
and, far more often, who died.

"I am still the only one," she said back.

"Still," he conceded snidely, "it must have seemed a
miracle for you."

"For you too," she shot back.

He bowed again.

She waited for him to straighten before adding, "The Supreme Leader believes that this is a shame. He wants to know why more are not capable of being converted."

This had been the other reward that Chung-Cha had requested and been given for her part in exposing the treachery of General Pak. The power to come here and make these sorts of inquiries. And she had been granted something else.

She looked expectantly at Doh, who had obviously not been anticipating this. She saw a vein in his temple begin to throb, and his hand shook as he raised it to his face to adjust his glasses.

"The Supreme Leader believes?" he said, his voice shaking. The guards with him took a few steps backward, as though to distance themselves from whatever repercussions might befall the man.

Chung-Cha reached into her pocket and produced the authorizing documents. Doh took them, adjusted his glasses again, and read through them before meekly handing them back.

"I understand. The Supreme Leader is wise beyond his years. It is an honor to do his bidding."

"I'm sure. But let us get down to it. I was in the total control zone. I was not core, or wavering. I was in the hostile class, Comrade Doh. And now I am acknowledged as one of the most valuable assets we have. Perhaps there are other such assets here, but going to waste. The Supreme Leader does not like waste."

"No, no, of course not. I . . . what would you have me do, Comrade Yie? Please, you have but to name it and it shall be done."

Chung-Cha looked the man over. He was far smaller and weaker-looking than she remembered. To a little girl whose very life or death depended on the daily mood of this person and his underlings, he might as well have been a giant. Now, though, he was nothing to her.

"I want to look over some of the hostiles. The girls in particular."

"Girls?" he repeated in a bewildered tone that matched his expression.

"Yes. The Supreme Leader understands quite clearly how useful females can be in certain areas of service. Much more so than males, who are more easily identified and targeted as potential enemies of other countries. Do you understand?"

He nodded quickly. "Yes, yes, of course, I can see that."

Chung-Cha added, "And I want you to show me some of the more interesting prospects."

He nodded again. "Yes, yes. I will take you myself."

"I'm sure you will," she said without smiling.

He did not seem to grasp the significance of what she had said. He was a cruel, cagey, and evil man; that she knew. But he was also petty, vain, and shallow.

And such a person could never attain brilliance or even acuity no matter how hard he tried.

"And I will be sure to communicate your excellent level of cooperation."

"Oh, thank you, Comrade Yie. Thank you, you have no idea what that means to me."

"On the contrary, I have *every* idea."

He looked a bit put off by this statement but regained his composure and said, "Um, by *interesting* you mean . . . ?"

"By that, Comrade, I mean someone like *me*."

50

She had examined over a hundred children aged four to fourteen. They all looked alike in many respects: malnourished, filthy, and blank-eyed. She spoke a few words to each of them. Their answers, when they came, were halting, inelegant, and simple. None of this was their fault, she knew.

She turned to the guard accompanying her. "How many were born here?"

He looked at her with some insolence, but had no doubt been told to cooperate fully or feel the Supreme Leader's wrath. He gazed over the ranks of young prisoners with a lazy eye. They might as well have been chickens lined up for slaughter.

"About half," he answered in a casual tone and then rubbed a smudge of dirt off his gun. "There were more, but they were unauthorized births, so they were of course killed along with their mothers."

Chung-Cha knew that the children's education, what there was of it, was totally inadequate. They had been raised as simpletons and they would perish as simpletons despite whatever belly fire they might have for something more in life. At some point, no matter the rage that dwelled within, the beatings and starvation and brainwashing that were all prevalent here would douse all hope until there was nothing left inside. She felt if she had stayed one more day in Yodok she never would have left it alive.

In the distance Chung-Cha saw a group of children laboring along under the weight of either logs or buckets she knew were filled with dung. One child stumbled and fell, dislodging the contents of her bucket. The guard accompanying the group hit her with both a stick and then the butt of his rifle, and then encouraged the other children to attack her, which they did. They had been taught that when one worker failed they would all be punished, directing their anger away from the guards, where it rightfully should be, onto one of their own.

Chung-Cha watched the beating until it stopped. She made no move to halt the attack herself. Even with the authority of the Supreme Leader riding in her pocket, she could never do such a thing and hope to avoid punishment. The rules of the camps were inviolate and certainly no one like her could intervene and break them without consequences.

But she had no desire to stop the beating. She *wanted* to see the result of it, because even from this distance she had noticed something that intrigued her.

The beaten child rose, wiped the blood off her

face, grabbed the bucket off the ground, scooped the dung into the bucket with her bare hands, and marched past the guard and the other children who had beaten her. Her head was held high and her gaze was fixed determinedly ahead.

"Who is that prisoner?" Chung-Cha asked the guard.

He squinted in the distance and then blanched. "Her name is Min."

"How old is she?"

The guard shrugged. "Maybe ten. Maybe younger. She is trouble."

"Why?"

He turned and grinned at her. "She is a tough little bitch. She gets beaten and then gets up and walks off like she won a great victory. She is stupid."

"You will bring her to me."

The guard's grin faded and he glanced at his watch. "She still has six hours of work to perform."

"You will bring her to me," said Chung-Cha again, more firmly, her gaze never leaving the man's face.

"We heard about you here. What you did at Buk-chang." The guard said this in a surly manner, but Chung-Cha, who could sense fear from almost anyone, could see that the man was afraid of her.

"About my killing the corrupt *men*? Yes, I did. I killed them all. The Supreme Leader was most grateful. He gave me an electric rice cooker in reward."

The guard gazed at her in astonishment, as though

she had just informed him that a mountain of gold had been delivered to her door.

"Is that why you are here?" he asked. "They suspect corruption?"

"*Is* there corruption here?" asked Chung-Cha aggressively.

"No, no. None. I promise it."

"A promise is a strong thing, Comrade. I will hold you to it. Now bring me Min."

He bowed quickly and hurriedly set off to fetch the child.

Twenty minutes later Chung-Cha sat in a small room with two chairs and one table. She stared over at the little girl. She had asked Min to sit down but Min had refused, preferring, she said, to stand.

And stand she did, with her hands balled into fists as she stared back at Chung-Cha with open defiance. With that look Chung-Cha knew it was a miracle the girl was even still alive at this place.

"My name is Yie Chung-Cha," she said. "I have been told that your name is Min. What is your other name?"

Min said nothing.

"Do you have family here?"

Min said nothing.

Chung-Cha looked over the girl's arms and legs. They were scarred and dirty and heavily bruised. There were open, festering wounds. Everything about the child was an open, festering wound. But in the eyes, yes, in the eyes Chung-Cha saw a fire that she did not believe any beatings or disease could extinguish.

"I ate rats," said Chung-Cha. "As many as I could. The meat, it staves off the sickness that others here get. It is the protein that does it. I did not know that when I was here. I only learned of it later. I was lucky in that way."

She watched as Min's fists uncurled. Yet Min still looked wary. Chung-Cha could understand this. The official first rule of the camp might be, *You must not escape.* But the unofficial and far more important first rule for any prisoner was, *You must trust no one.*

"I lived in the first hut by the path to the left of the inner gate," said Chung-Cha. "This was some years ago."

"You were a hostile, then," Min blurted out. "So why are you no longer here?" she asked, anger and resentment pronounced in each of the words.

"Because I was useful to others outside this place."

"How?" demanded Min, now forgetting her caution.

In that question Chung-Cha could see what she had hoped to see. The girl wanted out, when so many prisoners, even younger than she, were totally resigned to living here forever. The fire in their lives, and with it their courage, was gone. It was sad, but it was a fact. They were lost.

"I was a tough little bitch," replied Chung-Cha.

"I am a tough little bitch too."

"I could see that. It's the only reason you're here talking to me."

Min blinked and relaxed just a bit more. "How can I be useful to *you*?"

Defiance yes, but intelligence, and its first cousin cleverness, thought Chung-Cha. Well, after all, in Korean that's what Min meant: cleverness and intelligence.

"How do you think you can be?" asked Chung-Cha, turning the query around and flinging it back at her.

Min pondered this for a few moments. Chung-Cha could almost see the mental churnings going on inside the girl's head.

"How were you useful to others?" asked Min. "That allowed you to leave here?"

Chung-Cha managed to hide her smile, and her satisfaction. Min was proving to be up to the challenge.

"I was trained to do a specific job."

"Then I can too," said Min.

"Even though you don't know what the job is?"

"I can do anything," declared Min. "I *will* do anything to leave here."

"And your family?"

"I have no family."

"They're dead?"

"I have no family," repeated Min.

Chung-Cha nodded slowly and rose. "I will be back here in one week. You will be ready to go."

"Why one week?"

Chung-Cha was surprised by this question. "These things take time. There are arrangements, paperwork."

Min looked doubtfully at her.

"I will be back."

"But I may not be alive."

Chung-Cha cocked her head. "Why?"

"They will know what you are going to do."

"And?"

"And they will not let me go."

"I come with the highest authority. The guards will not harm you."

"There are accidents. And it's not just the guards."

Chung-Cha nodded thoughtfully. "The other prisoners?"

"They do not care about the highest authority. And what do they have to lose?"

"Their lives?"

Min screwed up her face. "Why would they care? That would be a good thing for them."

Chung-Cha knew that she was absolutely right about this.

"Then we will leave here today."

For the first time probably in her life, Min smiled.

51

Chung-Cha had patiently filled out the paperwork necessary for Min's release into her custody. They had driven back to Pyongyang in the Sungri with the windows down. Chung-Cha did not tell Min that she was doing this because she did not want to smell the girl's stench for the next seventy miles. Instead, she told her it was good to breathe free air.

And Min seemed to suck in each breath with delight.

She had been reluctant at first to get into the Sungri. Chung-Cha knew immediately why. The girl had never ridden in a car before. She had probably never even seen a car, just the old trucks used at the camp.

However, when Chung-Cha had told Min that it was the fastest way to get away from the camp, she had climbed in immediately. After she sat down her hand reached out and touched all the dials and other items of interest.

That was good, thought Chung-Cha. She still had her curiosity. Her wonderment. It meant that the child's mind was intact.

As they drove away, Chung-Cha looked twice in the rearview mirror at the camp. She had seen prisoners staring at them through the fence, perhaps wondering why they could not also be free.

When she looked over at Min the girl's gaze was pointed straight ahead. She did not look back once.

Chung-Cha had done the exact same thing when she had left the camp. She had been afraid that if she looked behind her, they would take her back. Or, more likely, that she would awaken from her dream and return to her nightmare.

They had arrived back in Pyongyang very late at night. Chung-Cha had parked her car and led Min up to her apartment. The girl had stared at everything as they had driven along. From asphalt streets to tall buildings, to something as simple as a traffic light, or a neon sign, or a bus, or someone walking along the sidewalk, she looked at it all in complete amazement. It was like she was just now being born, ten years late.

When Min looked up at the apartment building she wanted to know what this place was.

"It's where I live," answered Chung-Cha.

"How many people live with you?"

"I live alone. Well, I did. Now you live with me."

"This is allowed?" asked Min.

"It is allowed everywhere except in the camps," Chung-Cha answered.

The first order of business had been to prepare Min some food. Not too much and not too rich—

not that Chung-Cha possessed any rich food. But even too much white rice could make Min sick. Chung-Cha knew all of this because it was what those who had freed her had done. So the meals would be simple and small, to start.

The next order of business was a shower, a very long, hot shower with plenty of soap and elbow grease.

Chung-Cha did not let Min do this alone, because the girl did not know how to properly clean herself, so Chung-Cha had scrubbed her down. The filth that poured from her skin, hair, and orifices would have made most people sick. It did not faze Chung-Cha. She had been expecting it. And Min exhibited no shame as she watched the dirty water going down the drain. She knew no better. She just wanted to know where the water went.

"Into the river," answered Chung-Cha, because that response, she knew, would suffice for now. It would take many more cleanings for the girl to be truly free from her years of filth.

She laid out sheets and a pillow on the small sofa, which would be where Min would sleep for now. Chung-Cha had already purchased clothes and shoes for her, correctly assuming that a camp girl would be smallish. They fit very well, far better than the rags she had come here in. Those went into the trash.

Chung-Cha showed Min how to brush her teeth, cautioning her against swallowing the paste. Then she cleaned her nails, which were caked with years' worth of grime and crud. Next, she combed out Min's long hair, untangling knots and trimming errant strands with scissors. Min sat patiently while this was done, staring the whole time in the mirror Chung-Cha had seated her in front of in the small bathroom.

She well knew why the girl was studying herself so closely. She had never been in front of a mirror before. Thus she had no idea what she looked like. Chung-Cha could remember herself slipping out of bed at night and going to the bathroom, not because she had to relieve herself but because she wanted to see what she looked like again.

She fed Min another small meal and then attended to her multiple cuts and scabs with peroxide, salve, and bandages. Then she put Min in her makeshift bed under her clean sheets and wearing a new pair of shorts and a top. Even though she had tended to the girl's many injuries, healing cuts and scabbed-over old wounds as best she could, Chung-Cha had scheduled a visit to a doctor the next day. She wanted all of these seen to. Infections were rife in the camps and had killed many prisoners. She had not freed Min to watch her die. And ordinarily before prisoners were released from the camps they had to show that they were free from infection or disease. Since this was nearly impossible they almost never achieved their liberty. Chung-Cha had thus pledged in her signed paperwork to have a doctor thoroughly examine and treat Min within one day of leaving the camp.

After settling Min on the sofa, Chung-Cha turned the light off.

She heard Min gasp and then say, "Can you make it light again, Chung-Cha?"

She turned the light switch back on, then went over to Min, perching on the edge of the sofa.

"Does the darkness cause you fear?" She knew that the prison huts had no electricity, and that while Min had probably seen electric lights, she was not accustomed to them.

Min said, "I am not afraid."

"Then why do you want the light on?"

"So I can see where I live now."

Chung-Cha left the light on and went into her bedroom. She kept the door partly open and told Min if she needed anything to come wake her.

Chung-Cha got into bed but did not go to sleep. Not much scared her anymore; it simply wasn't possible after all she had experienced. But what she had just done frightened her more than beatings or fear of death possibly could. Her whole life had been spent alone, and now she had assumed responsibility for another human being.

She listened to Min's even breathing, which, because of the tiny size of the apartment, was happening only a few feet away. She wondered if the girl was sleeping, or was simply gazing around at a world that she could not believe even existed and, for her, had not existed until a few hours ago.

Chung-Cha knew exactly how she felt. She had gone through the same emotional spectrum. But her release and what happened to her afterward were far different from Min's situation.

The guards had come for her one morning. At first she thought they were coming to punish her because of a snitch. But that was not the reason. She had met with the prison administrator, Doh, the same man she had seen today. They had an offer for her. It came from high up in the government. She had no idea what had been the catalyst for it.

Would she like to be free? That's what they had asked her.

At first she had not understood what they meant. She instinctively thought it was a trick of some kind and was unable to answer, fearing she would say something that would lead to even more pain or perhaps her death.

But she was led into another room where there was a group of men and, startlingly enough, a woman who was not a prisoner. Chung-Cha had never seen a woman who was not a prisoner. The woman told Chung-Cha she was with the government and that the leadership was looking for offspring of wrongdoers who wanted to serve their country. They would have to prove their loyalty first, she said. And if they did that, they would be taken to another place, fed, clothed, and educated. They would then be trained, over many years, to serve North Korea.

Would Chung-Cha want that? the woman had asked.

Chung-Cha could still remember gazing around at the men in the room staring at her. They had on uniforms, not of the prison, but of something else. They had shiny things on their chests, all sorts of colors.

She had been dumbstruck, paralyzed, unable to answer.

One of the men who had more shiny things than anyone else finally said, "Get us another and take this bitch back to where she came from. And however hard you are working her, triple it. And cut her food too. She has wasted our time."

Hands had reached for Chung-Cha, but then she suddenly found her voice.

"What do I have to do?" she screamed out so loudly that one of the guards reached for his weapon, perhaps afraid she was going berserk and would attack them.

A minute of silence passed as all in the room looked at her. The man who had called her a bitch was scrutinizing her in a different way now.

He said, "You have been described as a tough little bitch. How tough are you?"

He backhanded her across the face, knocking her to the floor. Chung-Cha, all of ten years old, quickly got back on her feet and wiped the blood away from her mouth.

"That is nothing," said the man. "Do not think that makes you tough, because it does not."

Chung-Cha gathered her courage and stared back at him. "Tell me what it is I have to do to be free of this place, and I will do it."

The general looked back at her with amusement, and then his features went cold. "I do not discuss things with filth. Others will tell you. If you fail, you will never leave this place. I will instruct them to keep you just barely alive so that you will have many more decades here. Do you understand?"

Chung-Cha kept staring at the man, her mind as clear as it had ever been. It was as though a life of darkness had just been suddenly filled with light. She knew this was the only chance she would ever have to leave here. And she meant to seize it.

"If you will not discuss it with filth like me, then who here will tell me what I have to do to be free of this place?" she said firmly.

The man seemed surprised by her audacity. He turned to the woman and said, "She will."

Then he turned and left.

And that was the first and last time that Chung-Cha had personally laid eyes on General Pak.

Chung-Cha was stirred from her musings by her door slowly swinging open. Min stood in the doorway.

Chung-Cha sat up in her bed and looked at her. The two females did not say anything. Chung-Cha motioned with her hand and Min hurried over and climbed into bed with her.

She lay back and immediately went to sleep.

But Chung-Cha did not go to sleep. She just lay there looking at Min and thinking about events from what seemed like another life.

But it truly had once been hers.

52

She's back home and safe," Robie pointed out.

He and Reel were sitting outside at a café in D.C. having an early breakfast.

"By a miracle, Robie."

"Miracles happen by chance. This didn't."

She put her coffee down and stared at him. "You know what I mean. You know how many things could have gone wrong. Any one of them could have cratered the mission and Julie would be dead."

"But she's not dead."

Reel put her shades on, sat back, and stared off.

"And Earl?" he said.

She smiled grimly. "Back on death row and talking to himself. They don't expect him to last a week."

Robie's phone buzzed. He looked at it and then sat up straighter.

"Blue Man."

"At least it's not Evan Tucker. I couldn't take him, not today."

"He wants us to come in."

"Something up, you think?"

"He doesn't usually call to chitchat."

Reel rose and threw her cup of coffee into a trash can. "Then let's not keep the man waiting."

"Rumblings," said Blue Man. "But distinct ones."

They were seated in Blue Man's office at Langley. The skies had darkened on the ride over and rain was starting to fall.

Reel and Robie glanced at each other.

Reel said, "Distinct how?"

"We have numerous contacts in South Korea, China, and Taiwan. These contacts in turn have a smaller number of resources planted in North Korea, mostly in Pyongyang."

"And adding them all up, what do these rumblings say?" asked Robie.

"That the North Koreans are planning something."

"Retaliation, you mean," said Reel.

"I doubt it's anything else," said Blue Man. "The North Koreans are not known for either their tact or their compassion."

"But they can keep secrets," Robie pointed out. "Do we have any clue what form this retaliation might take?"

"It seems clear that they have discovered the level of Pak's actions. And now his family has disappeared."

"I didn't think he had any family," said Reel.

"So they've either been killed or sent to the labor camps," said Robie with a resigned sigh.

Blue Man nodded. "Appears to be the case."

Robie added, "If so, they're beyond help."

"I would have to agree with that. Any attempt to free them would create an international incident that we cannot afford at present."

"He said to protect his family," observed Reel quietly. "Well, we failed him on that."

"We were talking retaliation?" said Robie quickly, noting Reel's depressed look.

Blue Man nodded and opened a file on his desk. "It's why I called you two in really. Now the DCI—"

"Is he still in denial?" Reel interrupted.

"Apparently so. Head in the sand, hoping the other shoe does not drop."

"Great plan," said Reel with disgust.

"Perhaps. But options are limited."

"Surely we can take some defensive measures," said Robie.

"We can and are," replied Blue Man. "We feel that since our target was at the highest level in North Korea, any retaliatory action on their part will be aimed at the same level here."

Robie looked doubtful. "The president? They have to realize they can't get close to him."

"The Secret Service has been made aware of the need for heightened protection, although the president already enjoys the best protection in the world."

"So if not the president, what then?" asked Reel.

"The vice president? The Speaker of the House? A

prominent cabinet secretary? A Supreme Court justice perhaps? Maybe even a dirty bomb in a populous
area. And the target would be largely symbolic and
the message would be, 'We can get to your leaders
or people anytime we want.' It would definitely be a
blow to this country should they succeed."

"But what's the endgame on this?" asked Robie.

"After they strike back Pyongyang may release to
the world whatever evidence they have about a plot
led by this country to assassinate their leader."

"The world won't believe the North Koreans.
They hardly have credibility," Robie pointed out.

"But in this case they would be telling the truth,
wouldn't they? And we don't know what they might
have discovered. From Pak. Or from Lloyd Carson.
The DCI doesn't think there is anything there. But
his judgment has not been infallible."

"Quite the opposite," said Reel icily.

Robie said, "You didn't call us in here to tell us to
do nothing."

"No, I wanted to warn you," said Blue Man.

"About what?" asked Reel.

"At the cottage where you saw Pak kill himself?"

"Yeah?" said Robie warily.

"You may have been seen."

"That's impossible," said Reel. "We didn't see
anyone and our surveillance cameras showed no
activity."

"Nevertheless, the rumblings we're hearing indicate you may have been seen. And if so, you may become targets as well."

Robie looked over at Reel. "Well, it won't be the first time. Although I think I'd take the neo-Nazis over the North Koreans."

53

President Tom Cassion sat at the breakfast table in his family's private quarters in the White House. He'd already been given his daily briefing and was fortifying himself with an extra cup of coffee before truly beginning his day, which was mapped out to the minute.

He looked across the table at his wife, Eleanor, or Ellie, as he and her closest friends called her.

"I saw your schedule for the next couple of days," he said, folding up a copy of the *Washington Post* and setting it next to his largely uneaten breakfast. "Pretty busy."

She looked over her teacup at him. "Right. And I saw yours. Pretty empty. What a slacker."

He smiled resignedly. "It's not that bad."

She glanced at all the food left on his plate. "You haven't been eating lately, Tom."

"Stomach's been a little unsettled. Just under the weather."

"Go see the doctor, then. You have your own private one."

He nodded. "I will," he said, vaguely staring off.

"When do you get back?" she said.

"Four stops. Seattle, San Francisco, Houston, and Miami. Air Force One wheels down tomorrow afternoon at two."

"Sort of like the campaign."

"Not nearly as busy. How many times did we travel to eight or ten cities in a single day?"

"Too many times," she said dryly.

"And these days politicians never stop campaigning. With the changes in the laws any amount of money can be thrown into the ring. You have to make certain you get your share of it, because the other side certainly will take up any slack."

She said, "I miss the days of printing our own campaign flyers and collecting checks in a coffee can at backyard barbecues."

"Sometimes I do too."

He ran his gaze over Eleanor as she went back to studying her schedule for the day. She was still young, forty-six, four years younger than he was. They had two kids, Claire and Tommy Junior. Claire was fifteen going on forty. She had adapted extremely well to the life they now had. She'd made many friends at school and was active and popular at Sidwell Friends, and a very good student. Tommy was still very much a little boy who had at first loved living in the White House but had quickly grown to hate it. Neither the president nor his wife really knew what to do about it, and their son's unhappiness was weighing heavily on both of them.

Eleanor's voice broke through these thoughts. "The kids have a week off from school soon. I was thinking about taking them out of town. Maybe Nantucket. The Donovans have offered the house again."

He gaped at her. "Nantucket? At this time of year? It'll be cold and rainy."

"Actually, the average high is nearly seventy degrees and the average low is over fifty. And long-range weather forecasts say precipitation levels will be well below average, although the skies will probably be overcast. The Atlantic Ocean helps moderate the climate. It'll be warmer there than in Boston."

"As usual, I see you've done your homework, Ellie," said the president grudgingly.

She smiled. "And the tourists are all gone. It will be private and we can regroup as a family. Toasty fires, curling up with a good book. Playing board games. Taking walks together on the beach. Just recharging. Getting to spend time with the kids."

"You mean spending time with *Tommy*. Claire is doing just fine."

"I mean as a family," she said firmly. "And while I know your schedule is packed, it would be wonderful if you could come for at least a day."

The president looked at her strangely. Their lives were all governed by phone-book-thick itineraries with travel mapped out well in advance.

"Is this on the schedule? I didn't see it."

"No, I just was thinking about doing it."

"Well, I seriously doubt I'll be able to come for even a day. My schedule is packed for the next two months. And besides, the voters don't like presidents to just pop off to vacations. You'll have to check with the Secret Service. They'll need time to prepare. It might be too difficult on such short notice."

"I've already got them working on it."

"Okay, hope it works out. But I think you're over-reacting to Tommy's issues. He just needs more time to settle in, that's all." He picked up his newspaper.

Eleanor sighed, started to say something, and then returned to her tea and schedule, looking over notes for a speech she was set to deliver after a tour of the White House she was giving to a group of senators' spouses.

The president did not seem to notice his wife's disappointment. His stomach was unsettled for one simple reason.

Guilt. Massive, unrelenting guilt.

He had given his word to General Pak that he would carry through on all that they had planned. He had said this to Pak face-to-face. And now the man was dead. The president had actually sent agents out to kill him, but Pak had taken his own life. And had told the agents to be sure to tell him, "Go to hell." If the positions had been reversed the president would have done the same thing. He had betrayed the man, pure and simple. And now he had been told that Pak's adopted children had probably been sent to the labor camps, most likely for the rest of their lives.

I betrayed the man. I killed the man. I'm guilty of murder.

"Dad? Dad?"

The president shook his head and glanced around.

His daughter, Claire, had come down to breakfast. "I wanted you to look at the term paper I did for American Gov class."

"You think I know anything about government?" he said, attempting a weak smile.

"No, but Mom is obviously busy," she retorted with a broad smile.

He laughed while Eleanor looked on, amused. Then he continued to proudly watch as his daughter dug into her breakfast while scanning notes for what looked like her math class.

He watched warily as his son shuffled into the room wearing his school uniform. The boy had gone from a public school to one of the most elite institutions in the country. The transition had not been without some hiccups.

"Hey, big guy," said the president. "Sleep okay?"

"I'm not a big guy. I'm the smallest kid in my class. Even the girls are taller than me."

Claire put her spoonful of cereal down and cracked, "And smarter too."

"Shut up!" exclaimed Tommy.

"Claire!" said her mother sharply. "Leave it alone."

Claire smiled triumphantly and returned to her notes.

The president said, "Tommy, I'm six-two. Your mother is five-nine. You're going to be tall. Simple matter of genetics. I bet in a couple of years you'll shoot right past your sister. You just have to be patient."

Claire snorted and Tommy scowled.

"And we have three more years in this place," said Tommy. "Whoopee."

"*Seven* more when Dad wins reelection," pointed out Claire gleefully. "Right, Dad?"

The president was staring at his son and didn't answer her.

Eleanor quickly rose, did an inspection of Tommy's appearance, and went into full-scale mom mode, tidying his hair, tucking in his shirt, redoing his tie, and smoothing down his collar.

"You're running a little late," she said. "Better hurry with your breakfast."

Tommy plopped down and stared glumly at his plate.

Eleanor glanced quickly at her husband, but he had returned to gazing off. She had resigned herself, after a bit of kicking and screaming, that so long as they were in this house and he held his office, he was mostly gone from them. The problems he had to deal with were too immense, the vitriol too intense, the stakes too high. She felt like a single mother. But she had lots of help, and she was well aware that there were many women who were truly single struggling to raise families with far fewer resources than she had. Still, it wasn't easy. Family was hard, regardless of how much money one had.

But seeing his son had given the president something to think about.

Family.

He rose and dropped his napkin on his plate.

Eleanor looked up at him. "Are you okay?"

"Just forgot something I need to do before I fly out."

He rushed off.

Eleanor turned her attention back to Tommy and coaxed him into eating a few bites of his breakfast. Then she watched her children head off with their Secret Service protection details. They would drop Tommy off first and then Claire. A Secret Service agent would remain in the classroom with them throughout the day.

As the mini-motorcade pulled off, Eleanor did not notice the group of tourists congregating near the side gate to the White House. The place where the first family would leave and enter the White House was very private and not really visible to the public.

Most of the public.

A man and a woman held up their cameras and

were snapping pictures of everything they could see. They had sought positions that would give them the best view into this private area while the guards at this location were deliberately distracted by queries asked by others in their group.

As the motorcade turned onto the street, another member of the group took pictures of it, smiling and waving and looking excited as a tourist might. He kept snapping pictures of the motorcade until it disappeared from sight. Then the tail was taken up by a pair of sedans that were parked on Seventeenth Street. They worked in tandem, turning off and then coming back so as not to make the Secret Service grow suspicious.

Back at the White House, Eleanor had stopped to look at some plant beds being worked on by the grounds crew. As she stood there her secretary came up to her.

"Mrs. Cassion, I'm checking out the details for the trip to Nantucket for you. It'll just be you and the children, correct?"

"Yes. I talked to the president this morning. It doesn't look like he can make it."

"The Secret Service is working on the logistics and they'll have their preliminary report back later this week if that's okay."

Eleanor nodded and said, "I remember the day when we just jumped into the car with a couple of suitcases and our dog and drove off."

The secretary laughed. "Wish those days were back?"

"Only every minute of my life. But I really think it'll be good to get away. I only wish the president could join us."

"The house you've picked looks beautiful."

"Friends of ours. The Donovans. They're letting us use it. Very old, very rustic. We can walk to the beach. And we can ride bikes to town. Roaring fires. Books to read, chats to have. Just . . . just being together."

"Sounds idyllic."

"I'm hoping. I'm hoping that . . . Tommy will like it."

The secretary nodded knowingly. "It's hard for kids. I don't think I could do it."

"Well, we have to figure out a way that allows Tommy to deal with it. We have no other choice."

As the pair walked back inside a man in the uniform of the National Park Service rose from the planting bed he had been working on. Officially, he was from South Korea and had worked here for six years. In reality, he was North Korean and had been sent to the United States fifteen years ago with the sole task of being assigned to the White House in some capacity. Many occupations for him had been ruled out. But working the grounds had not. And after working far harder than anyone else around him, he had made it here.

He had been sending back regular reports to his

government of any details here that seemed worthwhile. Not that much had been worthwhile, however.

Until now. Now he might have just hit the mother
lode.

54

Robie and Reel had been heading back to Robie's apartment after their meeting with Blue Man when they received an urgent summons from him to come immediately to the White House.

They were escorted through security with record speed and led to the Situation Room complex's small conference room. It was unusual for people like them to be allowed in here, but they had been told that the president was going out of town that morning and needed to meet quickly and in relative secrecy.

Blue Man was already there when they arrived. He had phoned them on the way in.

"Care to brief us before the man arrives?" said Reel.

"I'm as much in the dark as you," admitted Blue Man. "I don't believe this went through official channels. I was surprised to get the call."

"Meaning spur of the moment?" observed Robie.

"I was told spur of the *breakfast*. At least that's when the president apparently had an epiphany that he now wants to discuss with us."

"And not Evan Tucker?" noted Reel. "He's still DCI, for better or worse. Well, worse, actually."

"I don't believe he is attending, no. In fact, it seems his days at CIA may be numbered."

"And the president asked for us specifically?" said Reel, taking a seat next to Blue Man while Robie hovered near the door.

Blue Man spread his hands. "You would not be here otherwise, nor would I. This is not a place you get to visit unless summoned."

Reel abruptly stood, as did Blue Man, when President Cassion strode into the room, alone. One of his aides shut the door behind him after a resentful look at the other occupants of the room. Apparently the president's team was not pleased about being cut out of this meeting.

Cassion said, "Thank you for coming. I don't have much time, so let's get down to it."

He sat and so did the others.

"To the point, we have learned that General Pak had an adopted son and daughter. They're now grown. They have been sent to a labor camp within North Korea in retaliation for what Pak did."

He stopped talking for a moment as the others stared pointedly at him.

Cassion looked first at Reel and then at Robie. "You were sent to France to kill Pak. I know this. You didn't have to carry out that assignment because he committed suicide, in your presence."

"That's correct, sir," said Robie.

"And his last words were to tell me to go to hell?"

Reel nodded but said nothing.

"And to save his family," added the president.

"Yes," said Robie. "It's all in our report."

The president sat back with a resigned air. "The fact of the matter is I'm thoroughly ashamed of myself for what happened. I sat in this very room and gave General Pak my word that I would not abandon him, no matter what happened. I did not keep my word. On the contrary, I authorized his death."

"Conditions change, Mr. President," said Blue Man. "Nothing is inviolate in the world anymore, unfortunately."

Cassion said heatedly, "Well, a person's word should be. A *president's* word should be." He bit down on his thumb and seemed lost in thought. None of the others interrupted this.

He finally said, "This may seem like a sudden inspiration on my part, but it's really not. It's something I've been kicking around in my head for some time now." He sat forward, his features filled with determination.

"I want a team to liberate Pak's family and bring them back here, where we will grant them full asylum."

A full minute of silence went by as Robie and Reel stared back at their commander in chief. When Robie glanced at Blue Man, he looked stunned.

Robie stared back at the president. "What sort of team?"

"I don't think I can send in the United States Army without doing more harm than good," replied Cassion, staring fixedly back at him. "So, a small team."

Blue Man said, "Do we even know which labor camp they're in? There are quite a few."

"That's why we have the best intelligence agencies in the world. I've asked for and been given a preliminary report. It seems likely that they would be sent to Bukchang, also known as Camp 18."

"Why is that?" asked Reel.

Blue Man answered. "Bukchang is operated by the Interior Ministry rather than the national security people. It's less brutal and prisoners there have more privileges. Some can even be reeducated and given their freedom."

Robie said, "But why do you think they would be sent there, then? Pak was a traitor. I'm sure they will want to take that out on his family. No second chances for them."

"Honor and loyalty run deep over there, especially in the military," replied Blue Man. "Pak undoubtedly had friends of high rank."

The president nodded. "I can see that."

"And it's not simply being kind to the children of a fallen friend," added Blue Man. "It's for their own sakes."

"How do you mean?" asked Reel.

"Some of the generals probably believe he was railroaded. They might worry that they might be next. Thus they want to establish a precedent that will allow their families, or themselves, to be sent to Bukchang if they find themselves on the wrong end of a treason charge. In North Korea you have to think five steps ahead if you want to survive, particularly at that level because alliances change swiftly."

Cassion mulled this over and nodded. "I think you're right. But we need to verify that they are indeed in this Bukchang place."

He glanced at Blue Man, who said, "That will be difficult, but we will get every resource on it, sir." He paused. "So you really want to extract Pak's children from the camp?"

Cassion drew a long breath and wouldn't meet Blue Man's eye. "I think that's what I said," he replied brusquely.

A minute of silence went by.

Finally, Blue Man said, "That has never been done before, sir. Never."

"I'm aware of that," replied Cassion, now looking directly at him. "Any ideas?"

Surprisingly, it was Reel who answered. "Well, I think we might turn to the handful of folks who have escaped from North Korean labor camps and who are in this country. I think one or more of them might have gotten out of Bukchang. If so, they can tell us how they did it. We don't want to reinvent the wheel if we don't have to."

Cassion looked impressed. "An excellent suggestion." He looked at Blue Man. "What sort of team would be required?"

Blue Man said, "Few in number and the best we have. But still, I don't see how it can be done. This is *North Korea*."

Robie said, "I thought our being here meant you wanted *us* involved, Mr. President."

Cassion looked at him guiltily. "I realize I'm your commander in chief, Agent Robie. But after what you've both been through, what with Syria and now Pak, I'm reluctant to call on you again."

Reel spoke up. "What if we volunteer?"

Blue Man looked at her oddly. Robie kept his gaze on the president.

Cassion said, "Are you volunteering?"

"Yes," said Reel, and Robie nodded.

"That is quite courageous of you," said Cassion.

"Actually," said Reel, "it's our job."

The president looked at Reel and then at Robie. "Thank you," he said. "You have no idea what this means to me."

"I think we do," said Reel.

After Cassion left the room for his flight on Air Force One, Robie looked at Blue Man. "*Can* we meet with someone who escaped from Bukchang?"

"I think we can arrange that, yes. But you realize this is a suicide mission, don't you?"

"A couple of American agents going into a North Korean labor camp and extracting two highly valued political prisoners?" said Reel, her eyebrows hiked. "Walk in the park."

"Capture equals death," said Blue Man.

"Or worse," said Robie.

"How?" said Reel.

"They could chuck us into the camp for the rest of our lives." He looked at Blue Man. "And I would assume that all knowledge of any connection to an official mission on behalf of the United States would be disavowed."

"I think we can safely assume that," said Blue Man.

"Well, it's nice to know where we all stand," said Reel dryly.

55

It had taken the better part of two weeks, but Chung-Cha rinsed Min off once more in the shower and beheld a girl devoid of dirt, even in her ears. And the stubborn grime under her fingernails and toenails was no more.

The medical visits had been conducted and Min's wounds and bruises had been attended to and were healing quickly. The girl's overall health had been pronounced sound and her immune system was functioning properly. That was truly a miracle, Chung-Cha knew, for a camp prisoner of any duration, because the conditions were so squalid. As on a battlefield, far more died from disease than wounds. Bacteria easily trumped bombs and bullets in lethality.

Min's teeth were in poor condition, but unlike Chung-Cha's they were capable of largely being saved. The girl had not flinched once at the dentist's office. She seemed to understand that all that was being done was for her own good.

Chung-Cha had increased the girl's meal intake slowly, giving Min more and diverse food each day until her stomach could handle it properly. The doctors had told her that Min had not reached her growth spurt yet and the additional food would help accelerate this event.

There was the matter of education, which for now Chung-Cha took on herself. Min was an eager if frustrated learner, and the hours of instruction went by quickly. She could read a bit and she knew her numbers to a point. She was well versed, as all prisoners were, in the philosophy and teachings of North Korea's great leaders. But she needed to know more than that.

This could not be accomplished in a week or even a year, Chung-Cha knew. And she was not a trained teacher. She would have to arrange for Min to attend school. But Min would be far behind other students her age and to place her there now would only serve to humiliate her. So Chung-Cha would work with her, and then she planned to arrange for a personal instructor. It would all take time and money. But Chung-Cha had requested and received special dispensation to accomplish this. It was a wonder to her that she had never asked for such things before. Apparently the leadership was willing to give her far more than a rice cooker and some wons.

As she spent time with Min, Chung-Cha waited for a phone call or a knock on the door that would summon her to work. She knew it would come at some point.

And when she had to go and train, as she did each day, Min was left with the family that managed the apartment building. At first Min wanted to stay with Chung-Cha, go wherever she was going. This was impossible, Chung-Cha had explained to the girl. The first time she had to go away, Min was very upset, and Chung-Cha knew why.

She doesn't believe I'm coming back.

Chung-Cha had taken off a ring that she wore and given it to Min. "You take care of this for me while I'm gone. You can give it back to me when I return. It is my prized possession."

"Did it belong to someone in your family?" Min asked.

Chung-Cha lied and said, "My mother."

The ring was actually of no significance to her. It was just a ring. But a lie was as good as the truth when it achieved one's goal.

One evening Chung-Cha dressed Min in her nicest clothes and they walked to the metro. At first Min was afraid to get on the train, but Chung-Cha told her it was a fun ride that would take them to a place where a great meal would be waiting. Min jumped on the train without further hesitation. She looked around in amazement both at all the people on the train and at how fast it moved. When they got off and ascended to street level she wanted to know if they would take "this train thing" back home.

Chung-Cha assured her that they would, which made Min smile.

They walked past a number of restaurants. While Min looked curiously at them, Chung-Cha kept her gaze straight ahead.

Then she led Min into the Samtaesung Hamburger Restaurant. They sat at a table. Chung-Cha kept her back to the wall.

She was surprised when Min noticed this and said, "You don't like people coming up behind you, do you?"

"Do you?"

"No. But they do anyway."

"Then you must do something about that."

They ate hamburgers and fries. Chung-Cha let Min have only a few sips of her vanilla milk shake because she was worried the richness might make her sick.

Min's eyes widened. "This is the best food I have ever had."

"It is not Korean food."

"Where, then?"

"Just not Korean."

They finished eating and left. Chung-Cha and Min walked around Pyongyang and she showed the young girl as many of the sights as possible in a few hours. Min had innumerable questions, and Chung-Cha tried to answer them all as best she could.

"Is the Supreme Leader really three meters tall?"

"I have never met him, so I do not know."

"They say he is the strongest person on earth and his mind is full of all the knowledge in the world."

"They said the same to me about his father."

They walked on in silence for a bit.

"You said you had no family at the camp," began Chung-Cha.

"I have no family."

"You were born in the camp, Min. You had to have a family."

"If I did, no one told me who they were."

"They separated you from your mother?"

Min shrugged. "I have always been alone there. That is just the way it was." She looked up at Chung-Cha. "What about your family?" She nudged the ring on Chung-Cha's finger. "Your mother gave you this?"

Chung-Cha did not answer. They walked on in silence.

After they returned on the train to the apartment, Chung-Cha settled Min into her bed on the sofa. Min studied her quietly. "Did I say something to make you sad, Chung-Cha?"

"You did nothing wrong. The wrong is all within me. Go to sleep."

Chung-Cha went to her room, undressed, and climbed into bed. She lay there staring at the ceiling.

And on that ceiling there appeared images she had forced from her mind seemingly forever.

The guards had come for her that day. General Pak had told her that she could be free. Then Pak had left. And the woman had taken Chung-Cha aside and told her what she must do to earn her freedom.

"Your mother and father are enemies of our country. Your brother's and sister's minds have been poisoned as well, Chung-Cha. You understand this, do you not?"

Chung-Cha had slowly nodded. She could not remember loving her parents. They regularly beat her, even when not instructed to by the guards. They snitched on her. Her brother and sister were competitors of hers for food, clothing. They too snitched on her. They too beat her. She did not love them. They were evil. She assumed they had always been evil. She was here because of her family. She had done nothing wrong. It was they who had committed the wrongs.

"Then you must act, Chung-Cha. You must rid your country of its enemies. Then you will be free."

"But how do I do this?" she had asked.

"I will show you. You must do it now."

She had been taken to a room underneath the prison. It was in the same area where she had lived for a while because of something her father had done while there. It was far worse than living in the hut. She had not believed that anything could be worse than that, but it was. During that time she had not seen the sun for what seemed like years. All of her

411

work was done underground, digging with a pickax, hauling rock, working her fingers down to the bone.

Inside this room were four people. They were tied to posts. Their heads were covered with hoods. Their mouths must have been gagged underneath, because all Chung-Cha could hear were grunts and moans.

There were two guards on either side of the four people.

The woman had taken a knife from her bag. It was long and curved and had a serrated edge. She handed it to Chung-Cha.

"Do you see the red circle drawn on their fronts?"

Chung-Cha looked over and indeed saw a red circle on the chest of each of the four people.

"You will stick this knife inside the red circle. You will then pull it out and stick it back in. This is for each of the people, do you understand?"

Chung-Cha said, "Is this my family?"

The woman said, "Do you want to be free of this place?"

Chung-Cha nodded vigorously.

"Then you do not question. You follow orders. This is your order. Do it now, or you will die here as an old woman."

Chung-Cha gripped the knife and walked hesitantly toward the bound figure on the far left, the one she assumed must be her father.

He was struggling against his binding, perhaps knowing what was coming. She heard his grunts increase in volume. He thrashed, but he could not really move because of the bindings and the stoutness of the wooden post.

Chung-Cha raised the knife as high as she could, over her head. She drew it back. The grunts increased. But for the gag her father would be screaming.

She screwed up her eyes until she could barely see out of them. Then she lunged forward and plunged the knife into the circle. His body went rigid and then he thrashed madly, nearly dislodging the knife from her grasp.

"Once more!" screamed the woman.

Chung-Cha withdrew the knife and stuck it in him again. Then he stopped moving as the blood poured down his front. A guard stepped forward and removed the hood. It was her father. His face hung down, the gag balled in his mouth. His eyes were open, lifeless. He seemed to be staring down at her.

"The next one, Chung-Cha. Do it or you are lost," screamed the woman.

Chung-Cha automatically turned to the next person and stabbed twice.

It was her sister.

"Do it now, Chung-Cha. Now. Or you are lost forever!"

The next. It was her brother.

The woman screamed the threat again and again. "Do it now, Chung-Cha. Now! Or you are lost forever."

The last two strikes. Metal thudded into flesh.

Chung-Cha no longer had any idea what she was doing. Her hand was moving of its own accord. She could have been stabbing a dead hog.

When the hood was taken off her dead mother looked down at her.

Chung-Cha dropped the knife, took a step back, and fell to the floor, crying, her body covered with the blood of her family. Then she picked up the knife and tried to kill herself with it, but the guards were too fast. They took it from her.

The woman pulled her up. "You have done well. Now you can leave here and serve your country. Forever. You have done well, Chung-Cha. You should be so proud."

Chung-Cha looked at the woman. She was smiling down at the little girl who had just slaughtered her family.

Chung-Cha did not know that she was crying in her bed now.

But she did know that Min had climbed in with her, wrapped her little body around her, and was hugging her tightly.

Chung-Cha could not hug her back. Not now.

On the ceiling was the image of her family.

Dead by her hand.

All dead.

The price of her freedom?

Chung-Cha's soul.

56

His name was Kim Sook. He had escaped from Buk-chang many years before. Sook had been extremely cooperative in helping Robie and Reel learn about his harrowing flight from the labor camp. He had escaped at age eighteen. He was now nearly thirty.

He had been imprisoned as a hostile with his family for his father's alleged crimes against the state. He and a friend, a young man a year older, had planned the escape for months. They had received information from two other prisoners who had escaped but been returned to the camp after their recapture in China.

They had come back from a work detail outside of the gates. They had dispersed to go back to their huts. The guards had been lackadaisical, Sook said. They had not counted correctly or paid enough attention to where the workers had gone off to. He and his friend had hurried away toward their respective huts. But it was a busy time of the day with many people moving about and few guards to watch over them.

Sook and his friend had gone to a place where

they had hidden old woolen sacks they had collected over time. They waited until dark. It would be madness to attempt escape during daylight, Sook said. Then they wrapped themselves in the woolen sacks, trying to cover their heads and their hands especially.

They crept toward an unguarded section of the fence. They had observed the patrols of the guards outside the gates and waited for a unit of them to pass by. Then they would have a half hour to make their escape.

They used a long board they had hidden near the fence to pry apart the electrified wires. Sook said he could feel the current moving through the board and into him, but the wraps around his hand seemed to be working. His friend slipped through the opening in the fence. Then Sook passed the board between the wires and the friend made a gap for him and he slipped through. One of the wires grazed his shoulder and he could feel the jolt of current and smell his skin burning.

He had opened his shirt and let Robie and Reel see the scar.

"I was lucky," he said. "One man who had attempted escape this way two years before got caught in the wires and was electrocuted."

Then both men had run. They ran for miles, following the road at first, then a path, and then they simply ran between trees in the surrounding forest.

That had been the beginning of their long journey,

a journey that included stealing clothes and food, bribing border guards with cigarettes, nearly being captured several times, and posing as workers in search of paying labor. Fortunately for them, there were millions of North Koreans looking for work and it was possible for them to become lost in such a multitude.

"It was still very difficult," said Sook. "We nearly starved. Were very nearly shot. We finally made it to China. I worked my way westward, into India. I saved my money for two years and then, with help, I flew to France. From there I came to America. I have been here ever since."

"And your friend?" Reel asked.

"I do not know. Once we were in China we parted ways. We thought if we stayed together it would invite suspicion. I hope that he made it to the West, but I do not know."

He looked at Robie and Reel. "So you propose to rescue these people from Bukchang?"

"Yes."

"You will not succeed."

"Why?" asked Robie.

"It may be easier than many believe to escape from the camp itself. There are far more prisoners than guards. It is like a handful of men trying to corral a small city. There are many holes, many ways out. They control the population through fear and the snitching of other prisoners. In that way they have many more eyes looking out for problems."

"Okay," said Reel. "And your point?"

"The real challenge begins *after* you escape the camp. You have to blend in. There are bribes that must be paid. You must show yourself to those who will have no loyalty. Now, they may look the other way if you are North Korean. After all, you are simply filth trying to get by. You can do no real harm. They will let you pass for a few packs of cigarettes. It is done. You may or may not be recaptured. But the border guards will not suffer because of it."

"But if we don't look like them?" said Robie.

"You obviously are American. When you open your mouths you will sound like Americans. You are the evil. They will never let you pass. I am sorry."

"We won't have to go through the border, Sook," said Reel. "We have other resources, ones you didn't have."

"But still, I will tell you, even with all your resources, they will not let you pass. They will capture you."

Robie looked at Reel. Reel turned back to Sook.

"Can you think of some way that we *could* manage it?"

Sook sat back in his chair and considered her question.

"Perhaps if you had a North Korean with you."

"I'm pretty sure we don't have any in our agency," said Robie.

"I will do it," said Sook.

Robie and Reel exchanged surprised glances.

She said, "You'd risk going back to a labor camp in North Korea to help people you don't even know?"

"I may not know them, but I know what will happen to them in there. That's enough for me. Let me help you."

"That's not our call, Sook, though we appreciate it," said Robie. "We'll have to run it by our superiors."

"Then do so," he replied. "Because without someone like me you don't stand a chance."

Blue Man was for it. Evan Tucker and Josh Potter were against it.

President Cassion approved it. That negated the two votes against. The president trumped everyone except the collective will of the voters at the ballot box every four years.

National Geospatial analysts had zeroed in on Bukchang with their satellite eyes, and what they reported back, coupled with the results of other intelligence assets, had confirmed that the adopted son and daughter of General Pak were there. They even knew which hut they were living in. And that four guards surrounded the hut.

There was also another intelligence success. General Pak had powerful friends in North Korea. One of them had managed to arrange for a coded message to be sent to the son and daughter in the camp. They would know that help would be coming.

It took another week to prep the mission. Every detail was gone over a hundred times. And every contingency as well in case something went wrong, which they knew was not unlikely.

North Korea was perhaps the toughest challenge Robie and Reel had yet faced. The country was hard to get into and even more difficult to get out of. It had millions of soldiers and a paranoid citizenry well versed in spying on each other. The terrain was difficult, the language and cultural barriers immense, and the country was located in a part of the world where, other than South Korea, the United States had few allies.

They spent a week at the Burner Box doing intense fieldwork in preparation. The rugged mountains of western North Carolina stood in for the ones they would face at Bukchang. A mockup of the prison and the targeted hut was constructed at the facility. During the first few exercises Robie, Reel, and Sook were "shot dead." They had made great strides since. But none of them knew if it would be enough when they tried it for real.

The route in and out of the target would be unusual. As Sook had told them, prisoners escaping from Bukchang invariably headed· north, toward China, whose long border with North Korea was not very far away. They would not be heading north. Too many things could go wrong, particularly with two obvious westerners in tow.

They all hoped that their out-of-the-box thinking would make it impossible for the North Koreans to follow them.

The night before they were to leave, Robie and Reel sat up late going over the plan one more time.

"Do you think Sook will hold up?" he asked.

"He's done it before, Robie."

"Many years ago. And it might have been part luck."

"It might have been. But we're probably going to need some luck too."

"I don't disagree with you. We have to keep our heads down, literally."

She said, "But we're the guardian angels. If we have to fight our way out, we're going to have to do it."

"I know."

"I wonder if the president has considered the long game on this?"

"You mean us snatching the traitor's family out from under the North Koreans?" Robie asked.

"Yep. If they were possibly going to come after us before, they're sure as hell going to come after us if we pull this off."

"He was pretty emotional about all this, so maybe

he didn't really think it through. But that's not our call, Jessica. We're just the muscle in the field."

"Yeah, well, maybe the 'brains' should follow the muscles' advice sometimes."

"I don't see that happening. Too many egos involved."

"Seriously though, Robie, the North Koreans have nukes. And they're crazy enough to use them. We pull this off they'll feel like they've lost all face. They are not going to turn the other cheek. A successful mission here might just prove to be the catalyst for Armageddon."

"Which means a lot of poor, innocent people will die because their leadership felt disrespected."

"Which pretty much happens in every war ever fought," she retorted.

"But this won't be war; it'll be annihilation."

"You want to refuse the mission?"

Robie shook his head. "No. I'll do the mission. I just want both of us to understand the possible outcomes."

"I understand them very clearly. And at least the president, with all his faulty logic, is trying to make things right after what happened with Pak. I have to admire that."

"So let's go do this thing," said Robie.

57

They flew to China and traveled to the coast by puddle jumper. From there they took a boat across Korea Bay at night and landed at the end of a small inlet that cut deeply into the North Korean coastline. The closest town was Anju. Bukchang was roughly thirty-five miles due east from their location.

There were just the three of them: Robie, Reel, and Kim Sook. They were all dressed in black, their faces also blackened. Robie and Reel were heavily armed and had state-of-the-art communication gear. They hoped to be able to use it at some point to later rendezvous with their support team.

Robie looked at Kim Sook as they tied down their high-performance rigid-hulled inflatable boat. The RIB could reach speeds of over fifty knots using relatively quiet engines.

"You ready?" Robie asked.

"Little late for that," said Sook.

"Just checking."

They had maps and directions loaded on electronic devices attached to their wrists like watches. Above them an American satellite was feeding them details about what lay ahead. In their earwigs a constant stream of intelligence info was being sent.

Stealth was critical here, but so was speed. They had a long distance to cover and they needed to get there and back while it was still dark. That would be impossible on foot. So they had something else— three small scooters, powered by batteries, which ran very quietly. There were also pedals that helped to recharge the batteries. With night-vision optics they could see in the dark. Robie went first, Sook took the middle, and Reel brought up the rear.

They stuck to the road as far as they dared, then went off road as they drew closer to the camp. Buk-chang was in the middle of nowhere, so they would not have to navigate a city or any sort of populated area before reaching it. You didn't build concentration camps among millions of people.

They encountered no problems on the trip in. The satellite gave them a clear line to the camp. The intelligence chatter updated them on recent developments.

Du-Ho and Eun Sun, Pak's adopted son and daughter, were being held in a hut near the back of the camp. Unlike other prisoners, who were lumped fifty to a hut, the Paks were being held by themselves with special guards. But having only two prisoners in the hut didn't make it easier for the rescue attempt; it made it more difficult. The other huts were not individually guarded. Apparently the North Koreans anticipated trouble securing Pak's children.

It had been confirmed that a coded message had been passed to Du-Ho and Eun Sun. They had not been told what night it would happen, because if that information had fallen into the wrong hands it would have been disastrous. But the two would know that a rescue attempt was being made and that they would have to be ready.

When Robie, Reel, and Sook drew close to the camp they dismounted from their scooters and hid them in a patch of trees. Sook changed his clothes, wiped off his face, and hoisted an old duffel bag over his shoulder. Now he looked like a typical North Korean peasant. He took to the road while Robie and Reel paralleled his movements through the trees.

The outer perimeter patrol of Bukchang lay dead ahead.

As Sook walked along three guards approached him. They told him to stop and identify himself. He did so, telling them that he was traveling east to Hamhung to see his family and take a job there he had been promised. He gave them his paperwork, which had been expertly prepared.

While two of them searched his duffel the lead guard examined the paperwork. He finally handed it back.

"You are near Bukchang camp." He pointed to the north. "You must head that way. There is a road that will take you around the camp and then you can head east." He suddenly eyed Sook suspiciously. "What sort of job are you going to do in Hamhung?"

"Farming."

"Let me see your hands."

Sook held them up. They were roughened and callused. He had spent a week making them so.

The guard nodded. "Then go work your ox and smell your horse shit," he said, and the other guards laughed.

They stopped laughing when three rounds from suppressed weapons entered their bodies, dropping them where they stood.

Robie and Reel emerged from the woods and dragged the bodies into the cover of the trees. Robie slipped off one of the guards' walkie-talkies and handed it to Sook so he could listen in on local communications.

They moved on and soon reached the rear outer fence of the camp. They had been given the patrol times of the guards and waited for four of them to pass by before moving closer to the fence. They knew it was electrified and had come prepared for that. Using a laser, Reel cut through enough strands to allow a good-sized hole that each of them could slip through.

Sook went first, followed by Reel and then Robie. The hut they wanted was at the very back of the camp. As they crept forward they saw a burst of light and then realized it was a guard lighting a cigarette. Reel and Robie circled the hut, counting off the number of guards surrounding it.

Four. Like the intel had said.

Then they separated. Reel went left and Robie and Sook went right.

Reel spoke into her headset to Robie. He listened and said, "Affirmative. Three count on second hand sweep at twelve."

He pulled two tranquilizer pistols from holsters and aimed each at a different guard. Now that they were inside the camp they didn't want to make any unnecessary noise. Based on the satellite reports and intelligence on the ground, they both carried two dart guns, for a total of four shots, equaling the number of anticipated guards. Fortunately, that number had not changed.

On the other side of the hut Reel was doing the same. It was more difficult than it looked, aiming two guns simultaneously at two different targets, but they had no choice. Dropping less than all four guards with the first volley would allow the others to react and shoot back. The entire camp would be alerted.

They each looked at their watches until the second hand hit twelve. Then they took double aim, counted "three Mississippi" in their heads, and fired both weapons.

Four men fell.

Sook rushed forward and into the hut.

Robie and Reel were right on his six.

Du-Ho and Eun Sun were not asleep and were dressed in their work clothes. Sook explained to them who their rescuers were and what they were about to do. They asked no questions, but merely nodded and followed them out.

They were through the hole in the fence and had fled down a path toward the woods when it happened.

A siren went off.

As they looked back, lights in the camp blazed on and they heard feet rushing and motors starting.

Robie pointed up an embankment. "This way. Now."

They ran up the embankment. Luckily, Du-Ho and Eun Sun were young and in good shape. They had no difficulty keeping up, also no doubt energized by the realization that if they were caught they would be executed.

As Robie and Reel rushed along she said, "Do you think we were set up?"

Sook answered. "I just heard on the walkie-talkie. The guards you shot on the perimeter were found."

"Great," said Robie. "Let's double-time it."

"This way," said Sook, pointing to his left. "It's a shortcut to where we left the scooters."

The five fled along the dark road. Robie kept a hand on Du-Ho and guided him along using his night optics while Reel did the same with Eun Sun.

They reached the scooters and Eun Sun climbed on with Reel while Du-Ho boarded Robie's. They hurtled down a path toward the road. Looking behind her, Reel saw headlights on the road. She spoke into her headset, telling Robie of the bogies coming.

Robie stopped his scooter and got Du-Ho to climb on with Sook.

"Good luck," Reel told him.

"If I'm not back in two minutes after you reach the RIB, go. Don't wait for me."

They set off and Robie doubled back, carrying a weapon over his shoulder. He knelt down on a knoll overlooking the road, took aim, and fired.

The RPG round hit the lead truck right in the radiator. It exploded, sending debris hundreds of feet into the air. It also did something else; it effectively blocked the road.

But the firing of the RPG had revealed his position, and bullets started flying at Robie from the other trucks. He loaded in another rocket, took aim, and fired at the second truck even as a round thudded into his chest and knocked him on his ass.

The second truck blew up and Robie heard the screams of men who were probably torn apart or burning to death.

He looked down at his chest where the round had nearly gone through his armored vest. He could feel the bruise on his sternum. It felt like he'd been hit by a car.

He rose and picked up his rifle.

There were two more trucks back there, but they couldn't get through the obstruction formed by the pair of destroyed vehicles. The troops were running past the flames and firing at his position.

Robie readied his auto rifle, set out the bipod support legs, got in a prone position, exhaled a long breath, nestled his chin against the weapon's stock, sighted through the night scope, took aim, and fired. And he kept firing. Acquiring a target and pulling the trigger. Acquiring another target and pulling the trigger.

He could have been on a firing range calmly mowing down paper targets. Except that here men were shooting back at him. Bullets whipped all around him. But he had the high ground and he kept firing. And with each shot a man died.

As he ran out of ammo the first mortar round exploded barely fifty feet from him, shaking the earth so violently that his rifle fell over and his face was driven into the dirt.

The next round fired, he knew, would be closer.

He couldn't stay here any longer. The only thing he could do in the face of superior fire and manpower was retreat.

He ran back to his scooter and climbed on.

With only one person on it the scooter's speed was much improved.

He zoomed down the path, then veered left and

down the embankment and onto the road. He wound the scooter up to its top speed while shots whizzed past him. He rode for about five minutes, putting as much distance between him and his pursuers as possible.

He realized he was not yet out of range of the mortar when a round struck ahead of him, lighting the night sky like a million candles. He had to cut the scooter sharply to the right and up an embankment to avoid being hit by debris.

He flung himself off the scooter as another mortar round hit less than twenty feet from him. The impact again shook the earth, and the concussive force of the explosion sent him tumbling painfully along the rough terrain.

When he rose, covered in dirt, a pain stabbed through his leg. He felt around his thigh and his hand came away wet and reddened.

When he hustled back and looked down at the scooter his spirits sank. The front wheel was shattered. He looked up ahead of him. Still miles and miles to go. It would take him forever on foot. The boat would be long gone.

He looked behind him. They were still coming.

Well, Robie thought, *this is it.* But he wouldn't go down without a fight.

He pulled his pistols from their holsters and made sure they were fully loaded. He started running, but his bad leg made it difficult. Still, everything about his job was difficult, so he forced the pain from his mind and just sucked it up.

He had covered about two painful miles when he heard it.

The *whump-whump* was a familiar sound to him.

The North Koreans had called in air support.

Well, that was smart. And also the end of the road for him.

He looked to the sky and saw the darkened silhouette of the chopper. There were no running lights on the bird and he wondered why. He expected a searchlight to start probing the ground for his location.

Instead, his earwig crackled.

"Agent Robie, this is Lieutenant Commander Jordan Nelson of the United States Navy in the chopper. We understand you might need some assistance."

"That's a roger."

"We've been tracking you via the electronic location signal you're wearing, but can you give us your precise coordinates, sir?"

Robie looked at the illuminated device on his wrist and reeled off his exact position to Nelson.

The chopper immediately circled and then came down closer to the ground in an opening among the trees.

Nelson's voice came on the earwig again. "Afraid

you're going to have to make a skid grab, sir. We can't land properly here."

"On my way."

Robie hustled across the open ground to where the chopper was hovering about six feet off the dirt.

Nelson's voice said warningly, "We've got bogies on your six and four at ten meters. We have to go, sir. Right now."

The North Koreans had made up a lot of ground. Maybe they had moved the trucks and gotten vehicles through. And now the chopper was acting like a beacon for them. None of it was good.

Bad wheel and all, Robie ran like he never had before. This was his absolute last chance.

Three feet from the chopper, with incoming fire slicing through the air, he jumped and his hands smacked against the left skid of the bird. He immediately wrapped his legs around the skid and held on with all his strength.

"*Go! Go!*" he screamed into his headset.

The chopper shot vertically with such speed that Robie's stomach felt like it had been left back on the ground.

With rifle rounds still pinging all around them, the chopper cleared the trees, banked hard to the left, shot across the sky, and righted itself, and then the pilot slammed the throttle forward.

As they raced west across the darkened sky, the chopper's side door slid open and a helmeted man peered down at him. He shouted, "Would you like to ride in the first-class section, sir?"

"If you've got room," Robie shouted back. "Coach kind of sucks."

The chopper's winch was deployed and a weighted cable was lowered down to the skid. The pilot cut back on the power so the wind forces on the cable would be reduced.

Robie grabbed the cable, which had a harness attached, and wrapped it around his middle, cinching the belt tight. He gave the helmeted man a thumbs-up and the chopper reduced speed and hovered in the air.

Robie let go of the skid and swung out into space. The cable motor was engaged and he slowly rose. When he reached the door, two men there, who were attached to cables so they couldn't fall to their deaths, maneuvered the winch closer to the chopper and then helped him inside. They took off the harness and the winch was retracted to its original position. The chopper's door slid shut and Robie managed to grab a seat right before the pilot pushed the bird to full throttle and they raced across the sky.

"Are you injured, sir?" asked one of the men.

"Nothing that'll kill me. But I need you to get a message to Agent Reel. I don't want her to—"

"Already done, sir. She was the one who sent for us to assist you. They have reached their RIB and are on their way back out to sea. We're from the same carrier that will be picking them up in Korea Bay. USS *George Washington*. We'll rendezvous there."

"Exactly what I wanted to hear," said a relieved Robie.

"Oh, and Agent Reel asked me to pass a message along to you."

"What's that?"

The helmet came off, revealing a sandy-haired young man of about twenty. He was grinning. "To quote, sir, you owe her a kickass dinner and a very expensive bottle of wine."

Robie smiled back. "Yes, I do."

58

USS *George Washington* was a floating city carrying thousands of personnel, nearly eighty aircraft, and a massive missile payload. Its bridge rose over seventy meters from the surface of the water. It displaced almost a hundred thousand tons and was longer than three football fields. When the chopper's skids landed on the carrier's deck, Robie breathed a final sigh of relief. He climbed out of the chopper under his own power but gripping his injured leg. The young airman on the chopper put an arm under his shoulder, supporting him.

"We'll get you down to sick bay, sir. They'll fix you right up."

"Can a guy get a cup of coffee on this boat?" asked Robie with a weary smile.

"Hell, sir, this tin can is nothing but a big coffee pot."

The ship's doctor was nearly done taping up Robie's wounds when Reel walked in.

He looked up at her. "So you didn't think I could get my ass out without help?"

She perched on the side of the bed and said, "No, I just figured the chopper guys needed some practice in land grabs on North Korean soil, and I know how accommodating you are."

The doctor smiled and said, "I'm pretty sure I'm not cleared for this."

"Then you better leave," said Reel. "I need to talk to this guy."

The doctor put one last strip of tape over the gauze on Robie's thigh. "All done. Have your chat." He walked off.

Reel held up a thermos she pulled from the pocket of her jumpsuit. "Thought you might need a refill." She topped off his cup of coffee and then drank directly from the thermos.

"How are the others?" Robie asked.

"Sook is fine. A real trouper. Du-Ho and Eun Sun are still a bit shell-shocked, I think. But pretty damn happy not to be where they were." She looked down at his bandaged leg. "I take it things got hairy back there."

"A little. Well, more than a little. The North Koreans regrouped a lot faster than we anticipated. But for the chopper?" He held up his mug of coffee. "Let's just say this ending was much preferred over what would have been."

"It's good to see you, Robie. It really is." There was a catch in her voice.

He sat back against his pillow and studied her. "So Du-Ho and Eun Sun will be relocated and put into what, Witness Protection of some sort?"

Reel nodded. "That's the gist of it. I think they're going to engage Sook to help them with the transition."

"Pyongyang will know exactly what happened."

"Yes, they will. If we weren't on the most powerful warship on earth right now, I'd be expecting incoming fire at us."

"So we won the tactical battle."

"But the strategic one is still out there."

"They're going to retaliate for sure. Pak was bad enough."

Reel sipped from her thermos and nodded. "We struck on their home turf. They'll feel they have to do the same."

"But where?"

"And what? Or who?" added Reel. She gazed off, her features tired, spent.

He said, "Is the plan still to airlift us to Seoul and a private wing ride home from there?"

She nodded. "That's the last I heard."

"And then what?"

She looked at him. "Then we stand down until they call us back up."

"Really?"

"What else?"

"You tell me."

"You thinking of hanging it up?"

Robie cracked a smile. "I know a certain DCI who would be just thrilled if we did."

"Isn't that reason enough *not* to retire, then?"

Robie's smile faded. "Is that what you want?"

"I don't know what I want, Robie. I just know what I'm *supposed* to want."

He lifted his hand and brushed a strand of hair from her face. "Well, you might want to take some time to figure out what it is you do want, Jessica. And leave 'supposed to' in the trash can. Because neither one of us is getting any younger."

"So are you saying fifteen years ago you wouldn't have needed the chopper ride to get away from the bad guys tonight?"

"Do you want the truth or what I'm *supposed* to say?"

"The fact is, Robie, we are highly trained and can do lots of amazing things, but we're still only flesh and bone." She tapped his chest. "And here we're as vulnerable as anybody else. I certainly found that out, didn't I?"

"Part of living. Part of dying."

"The good with the bad?" she asked. "It's hard to imagine we still live in a world where people live in concentration camps. Where they're treated like animals."

"You don't have to go to North Korea for that, Jessica. Happens all over the world. Some places just aren't as obvious. Which makes them even worse in my book."

"I know."

He reached out and took her hand, squeezed it, felt the strength there as she gripped him back.

She said, "I didn't want to leave you back there."

"But you did it right by the book. You don't leave the people we're guarding without coverage."

"But it's still going to stick with me, Robie."

"You need to let it go. I made the call. You did exactly what you were supposed to. And on top of it you had the foresight to save my ass. I owe you my life, Jess. But for you I'm gone. Forever."

She grazed his cheek with her hand and then leaned over and kissed him there. She settled against him as he wrapped his arm around her.

He didn't know if she was weeping. It was nearly impossible to tell with Jessica Reel. What was inside of her never seemed to truly make it to the outside.

So he just held her, as the big carrier made its way south where the free part of Korea would welcome them briefly before their journey home.

59

Chung-Cha watched as Min wrote out the symbols in the small lined notebook Chung-Cha had purchased for her. They were seated at the table by the window in Chung-Cha's apartment. Min was dutifully inking the marks as best she could. Chung-Cha's features did not betray what she was thinking.

At age ten Min could not really read and she could not really write. Her vocabulary was stunted, her breadth of thought constrained within the brutal limits of a concentration camp. She had seen more horrors than a soldier on a hellish battlefield. And for her, the war had been a decade long.

Min looked up after struggling with the alphabet. She searched Chung-Cha's face for approval or disappointment.

Chung-Cha smiled and said, "We will continue to work on this each day. A little at a time."

Min said, "I am not very smart."

"Why do you say that?"

"Because it is what they said back there."

She did not refer to the place as Yodok, or Camp 15,

or any of its myriad other names. She just called it "back there."

"Back there, they lie, Min. That is all they do. To them you are nothing. Why bother with the truth for nothing?"

"Could you read, or write your letters, when you were free?"

"No. And they called me stupid too. Now I have this place. I have a car. I have a job. And . . . I have you."

Min furrowed her brow as she thought about this. "What is it that you do?"

"I work for the Supreme Leader."

"But you said you had never met him."

"Most who serve him have never met him. He is a very important man. The most important of all. But we serve him well and he takes care of us like the father he is."

Min nodded slowly. "But he doesn't take care of people back there."

"To him they are his enemies."

"I did nothing to him," Min pointed out.

"No, you didn't. It is because of a philosophy."

"What is that word?"

"It means an idea."

"It was because of an idea that I was back there?"

Chung-Cha nodded and then worried that she was venturing into waters that would prove too deep for her. She looked at her watch. "It is time to eat."

This remark always served to make Min forget whatever else she was thinking.

"I will help you. Can we have the white rice again?"

Chung-Cha nodded and Min walked to the little kitchen to begin her tasks.

As the pair worked away in the tiny space, Chung-Cha glanced out the window and saw the same man out there. He was always out there, or else someone just like him was. He worked, she believed, for the black tunic. The tunic had a name, but it was unimportant to Chung-Cha, and she had decided not to add it to her memory. The black tunic was a suspicious, paranoid man, which was one of the major reasons he had risen so high in the government. In some ways he was more influential than the capped and medaled generals with their tight, weathered faces where the potential for violence percolated just below the surface.

He was both her savior and her enemy, Chung-Cha knew. She would always tread cautiously around him. The approval for taking Min from Yodok had come through his good offices. But he could take Min away at any moment and for any reason. She was well aware of that.

For now, Min was with her. That was what mattered. That was all, really, that mattered.

She glanced at Min, who was very carefully cutting a small tomato into precise slices. Her lips were pursed in concentration and her hands, Chung-Cha noted, were rock-steady.

They reminded her of her own hands. But Chung-Cha was more likely to be holding a knife for the purpose of killing someone than for cutting up a tomato.

Chung-Cha said, "My mother's name was Hea Woo."

Min stopped slicing and looked at her, but Chung-Cha was still staring out the window.

"She was tall, taller than my father. His name was Kwan. Yie Kwan. Do you know what *Kwan* means?"

Min said, "*Kwan* means strong. Was he strong?"

"He once was, yes. Perhaps all fathers are strong in the eyes of their daughters. He was a teacher. He taught at a university. So did my mother."

Min put down the knife. "But you said you could not read or write."

"I went to Yodok when I was very young. I do not remember my life before. I grew up there. That is all I knew. There was nothing else before Yodok."

"But didn't your parents teach you when—"

"They taught me nothing," said Chung-Cha sharply, as she closed the lid on the rice cooker and turned it on. She said more calmly, "They taught me nothing because it was forbidden. And by the time I could have learned . . . they could teach me nothing."

"Did you have brothers or sisters?"

Chung-Cha started to answer, but then the image

of the four hooded people tied to posts impacted her mind as suddenly as a rifle round.

Do you see the red circle drawn on their fronts? You will stick this knife inside the red circle . . . Do it now, or you will die here as an old woman.

Chung-Cha's hand moved involuntarily. She was gripping not a knife but a teaspoon. Min watched as the spoon made thrusts in the air. Then Min gripped her hand and said, "Are you okay, Chung-Cha?" Her voice was fearful.

Chung-Cha looked down at her and put aside the spoon. She readily interpreted the fear Min held: *Is my savior, the one person who stands between me and "back there," going mad?*

"Memories are sometimes as painful as wounds on the skin, Min. Do you see that?"

The girl nodded, the fear slowly receding from her eyes.

Chung-Cha said, "We cannot live without memories, but we cannot live within them either. Do you understand that?"

"I think that I do."

"Good. Now finish with that tomato. When the rice is done we will have our meal."

An hour later they set aside their bowls and utensils.

"Can I work on my writing now?" asked Min, and Chung-Cha nodded.

The girl rushed to get the tablet and the pen.

445

But before she returned there was a knock at the door.

They never summoned Chung-Cha by phone. They came and got her. She knew why this was. Just to show that they could do so at any time they wanted. And she would have to drop whatever it was she was doing and obey.

Min's face scrunched up as Chung-Cha rose to answer the knock.

The men there were not in military uniforms. They were in sleek slacks and jackets with white shirts buttoned up to the neck. They were young, nearly as young as she was, and their angular features were smug.

"Yes?" she said.

One of the men said, "You will come with us, Comrade Yie. Your presence is required."

She nodded and motioned to Min. "I will leave her with my landlord."

"You do what you must, but you will hurry," said the same one.

Chung-Cha put a jacket on Min and walked her down to her landlord's apartment. She spoke a few words, apologizing for the lack of notice, but the landlord observed the two men behind her and issued no protest. He simply took Min by the hand.

Min still held her tablet and pen. She looked up at Chung-Cha with wide, sad eyes.

Chung-Cha said to the landlord, "Can you work with her on her writing, please?"

The landlord looked down at Min and nodded. "My wife. She is good with that."

Chung-Cha nodded, took Min by the hand, and squeezed it. "I will be back for you, Min."

When the door closed behind Min the other man said sneeringly, "Your little bitch from Yodok, right? How can you stand the smell?"

Chung-Cha turned to the man and stared up at him. The look in her eyes caused the sneer to drain from his features. She could kill this man. She could kill them both with a teaspoon.

"Do you know what I am?" she said quietly.

"You are Yie Chung-Cha."

"I did not ask if you knew my name. I asked if you know *what* I am."

The man took a step back. "You . . . you are assigned—"

"I kill people who are enemies of this country, Comrade. That *little bitch* will one day do what I do now, for our country. For our Supreme Leader. Anyone who speaks ill of her I will treat as an enemy of this country." She took a quick step forward, closing the distance between them by half. "Does that include you, Comrade? I need to know. So you will tell me. Now."

These men were important, Chung-Cha knew.

And what she was doing right now was very danger-ous. But still, she had to do it. It was either that or her fury would cause her to kill them both.

"I am . . . not your enemy, Yie Chung-Cha," the man said, his voice quavering.

She turned away from him, her disgust ill-concealed. "Then let us go to our meeting."

She walked down the hall and the men hurried after her.

60

It was a dilapidated government building. The paint was cheap, the furnishings cheaper still. The bulbs overhead dimmed and brightened as the shaky electricity made its way through the corroded lines like blood through clogged arteries. The smell was sweat mixed with cigarettes. The packs of cigarettes available here carried the typical skulls and crossbones on them, but apparently no one in North Korea cared. They smoked. They died. What did it matter?

Chung-Cha stopped at the door indicated to her by one of the men who had come for her. The door was opened and she was ushered in. Then the two young men left her. She could hear their polished shoes tapping down the faded linoleum.

She turned to face the people in the room. There were three of them. Two men and one woman. The black tunic was one of the men. The general who had been Pak's good friend was the other man. The woman looked familiar to Chung-Cha. She blinked rapidly when she remembered her.

"It has been a long time, Yie Chung-Cha," she said,

rising from her seat. Her hair was white now instead of black. And her face was creased with age and worry. But it *had* been many years. Time did that to all. There was no escaping it.

Chung-Cha did not answer her. All she could think of was the woman's screaming at her all those years ago at Yodok.

You will stick this knife inside the red circle. You will then pull it out and stick it back in . . . Do it now, or you will die here as an old woman.

The woman resumed her seat and smiled at Chung-Cha. "My predictions of your rising far certainly came true. I can always tell. It was in your eyes, Chung-Cha. The eyes never lie. I saw that clearly enough at Yodok that day." She paused. "And you follow orders. You always follow orders. The sign of a good comrade."

Chung-Cha finally pulled her gaze from the woman and looked at the black tunic.

"You have summoned me?" she began.

"The Americans," said the black tunic. "They have struck."

"Struck how?" asked Chung-Cha as she took a seat directly opposite him. She did not look at the general. She did not look at the woman. She would not give either the satisfaction. She knew the black tunic was the de facto leader of this group. Her attention and perceived respect would flow only to him and to hell with the others.

"General Pak's adopted son and daughter, Pak Du-Ho and Pak Eun Sun, have escaped from Bukchang. They have done so with the help of the Americans."

"A man and a woman," added the general.

The black tunic added, "It may be the same pair that was sent to kill General Pak in France. But we cannot be sure. We are attempting to obtain a positive identification."

"Does it matter?" said the woman. "The Americans have legions of agents who do their evil bidding. The fact is, they came onto North Korean soil. They invaded this country and took from it two of our prisoners."

The general nodded. "Yes, Rim Yun is right. They are barbarians. They killed many North Koreans. It is an act of war."

"So we are going to war with the Americans?" asked Chung-Cha. Now she looked at all three, one at a time.

The black tunic said hesitantly, "Not precisely. They may want us to be so foolish. But we will counterattack in our way. In the way we had planned all along, Comrade."

"The American president's family?" said Chung-Cha.

Rim Yun said, "That is correct. We will kill them. *You* will kill them, Chung-Cha. Can you imagine the glory that the Supreme Leader will bestow upon you?"

451

"If I am alive," pointed out Chung-Cha.

"There is far more glory in death than in living," barked Rim Yun.

"I appreciate that fact one thousand times," replied Chung-Cha. "So would you like to accompany me to America where we both can share such glory after our deaths? What a wonderful thing, as you said."

The black tunic and the general said nothing. They glanced at each other and then at Rim Yun.

"You still have the defiant heart of Yodok in you, Chung-Cha," said Rim Yun coldly.

"I have many things from Yodok inside me. And I remember them all. Quite clearly."

The women locked gazes for a long moment before Rim Yun finally broke off and looked away.

She said in an oddly casual tone, "The administrator of Bukchang was shot this morning along with a half dozen guards for allowing this disgraceful escape to happen. I am sure that more will be shot as time goes on."

"I am sure that he deserved it," said Chung-Cha.

Rim Yun shot her a glance. "You killed the former administrator of Bukchang, did you not?"

"On orders, I did. He was corrupt. An enemy of this country."

"Did you know that he was recently replaced with the administrator from Yodok? Comrade Doh? You knew Doh, did you not? He was at Yodok when you were there, is that not so?"

Chung-Cha had to work hard to keep the smile off her lips. "Comrade Doh was executed?"

"That is what I said."

"I am sure that he deserved it," she said again.

Rim Yun gave her a piercing look before turning away and saying, "We waste time. Tell her what is needed."

The black tunic said, "Our timetable has been accelerated. You will leave for America within the week."

Chung-Cha hid the sudden panic she was feeling. "Within the week?"

"Is that a problem, Comrade?" said Rim Yun quickly.

"I have no problem serving the Supreme Leader with the sacrifice of my life."

"Then all is good."

"I do have a suggestion."

"How can that be? What nonsense," said Rim Yun dismissively.

Chung-Cha ignored her and said, "The Americans will be on the lookout for anyone who looks Asian, Korean; it does not matter. If they have our eyes, they will be suspect."

"We have a solid background for you," said the black tunic.

"Their scrutiny will be considerably heightened. They will be on the alert. We must be equal to the task. We must be better than they are."

"What do you suggest?" asked the general.

"The Muslims who blow themselves up?" began Chung-Cha politely.

"We are not Muslims," snapped Rim Yun. "We do not blow ourselves up."

"If I may be allowed to finish?" said Chung-Cha.

Rim Yun gave her a surly look followed by a curt nod.

"The Muslims use children as cover. It lowers suspicion. The Americans are often fooled by this, because they are softhearted. They do not like to think ill of the small ones."

Rim Yun tapped her long fingernails on the table. "Get to the point, Comrade."

"I have a young girl, Min—"

"I heard of your visit to Yodok," interrupted Rim Yun. "And you taking the little bitch home. I thought you must be insane to take on such a burden all by yourself. Explain to me how you are not."

Chung-Cha gazed directly at her. "I did so with the Supreme Leader's full knowledge and blessing. I am sure I do not interpret your words to suggest that the Supreme Leader is insane."

Rim Yun's face turned the color of blood and she sat up straighter, all of her casual disdain stricken clean from her. "I suggest no such thing. How dare you—"

"That is good," said Chung-Cha, interrupting her this time. "But we waste time, so let me explain. Min will accompany me to America. She will be my younger sister, or my daughter, whichever you think best. This will provide me excellent cover to fool the Americans. After the act is done, I will leave and travel back here with Min. If I die, then Min will go back with the others who will accompany us to the evil empire that is America."

"That is a foolish plan," said Rim Yun as soon as Chung-Cha had stopped talking. "Taking a child with you? And one from the camps? It's ridiculous. She would ruin everything."

Chung-Cha said calmly, "Because she was in the camp she knows nothing of the world. She will be very easy to control."

"Out of the question," snapped Rim Yun.

However, the general was looking thoughtful. "I am not so sure of that," he said. "In fact, I think it is a brilliant thought, Comrade, truly brilliant. You read the Americans just right. They are weak and sentimental. They assuredly will be fooled by the presence of the young one."

The black tunic nodded. "I agree."

All eyes turned to Rim Yun. She gave Chung-Cha a dark look but clearly knew she had been outmaneuvered and outvoted.

"I wish you good luck, then, Comrade Yie," she said, though her tone contained nothing "good."

"Whether I live or die, luck will have nothing to do with it," replied Chung-Cha.

61

President Cassion's handshake was strong and his face eager and filled with both happiness and gratitude.

Robie and Reel sat opposite him in the Oval Office. Across from them on a settee were Evan Tucker, Josh Potter, and Blue Man.

Cassion leaned back in his chair and surveyed them keenly.

"I have read the classified reports of your, um, adventure. I have to say it read like a thriller, only you two did it for real."

Robie said, "We had a lot of help, sir. And if Agent Reel hadn't called in air support for me, I would most certainly not be here today."

Cassion nodded and said, "Du-Ho and Eun Sun are transitioning to their new lives. And Kim Sook is helping in that transition."

"He's a good man," said Reel. "He did his job exceptionally well over there."

"And my conscience is far clearer," said Cassion. "Not that it makes up for what happened. But I have to think that General Pak would appreciate what we've done for his family."

"I would think so," said Tucker. "Without a doubt."

Cassion shot him a stern glance and Tucker immediately looked away.

Blue Man cleared his throat and said, "We do have to be prepared for the blowback, Mr. President."

"I understand that. It was part of my decision. I did not make it blindly."

"Of course not, sir," said Blue Man evenly. "But now we must address possible targets that the North Koreans will be after. As well as beefing up security and fine-tuning our surveillance networks."

Tucker broke in before Blue Man could continue. "We have taken all of that into account. Rest assured I'm doing all that can be done to defeat any actions by the North Koreans."

The president looked disdainfully at the CIA chief. "That makes me feel *so* much better," he said.

The president walked with Robie and Reel out of the Oval Office.

As they looked ahead of them, Eleanor Cassion was heading toward them with their son, Tommy, in tow. His head was down and his clothes looked dirty and ruffled. His braided blazer had a tear in the sleeve. His shirttail was completely out of his pants and his school tie was askew. Behind him was a burly Secret Service agent looking very uncomfortable.

As his wife and son stopped in front of him Cassion said, "What happened?"

Eleanor said sternly, "Tommy got into a fight at school. That's what happened."

"A fight?" said a stunned Cassion.

Robie and Reel exchanged glances. It seemed obvious to them that the president was swiftly calculating in his head how the story would play out in the media.

Cassion bent down. "Tommy, what happened?"

Tommy shook his head stubbornly and did not speak.

Cassion straightened and looked at the agent. "What happened, Agent Palmer?"

Palmer said, "It was right at the end of class, sir. They were heading outside. A group of students. Then there was yelling and a bunch of them got into sort of a scrum. By the time I pushed my way through the students Tommy and another boy were on the ground fighting. I pulled them apart, made sure the other kid was okay, and then brought Tommy directly here, sir."

Cassion put a hand through his hair. "What was the fight about, Tommy?"

When the boy didn't respond Cassion put a hand on his son's shoulder. "Tommy, I asked you a question, son. And I expect an answer."

"He called you a stupid, spineless shit," said Tommy, still looking down.

"Language, Thomas Michael Cassion," said Eleanor in a warning tone.

"He asked what the fight was about," retorted Tommy. "Well, that's what the kid called Dad and that's why I hit him."

Cassion cupped his son's chin and pointed it upward. Now they could all see that Tommy also had a black eye.

"Oh, Tommy," said Eleanor. "Fighting solves nothing. Name-calling is meaningless."

"You weren't there, Mom," Tommy retorted. Then he eyed Agent Palmer. "And if you hadn't pulled me off, I would've kicked his butt."

"He was doing his job, Tommy," said Eleanor. "Which is keeping you safe."

"I don't need anybody to keep me safe. I can take care of myself."

"Tommy, that is not the point," said Eleanor. "You could have hurt the other boy."

"I hope I did. I hate this place! I hate it! I want to go back home."

"Look, son," began the president, looking around nervously. "We'll discuss this later, in private."

"No, we won't. You're the president. You don't have time for your son."

"Tommy!" Eleanor exclaimed in a shocked tone.

"You were covering your dad's six," said Reel.

They all looked at her.

Tommy said, "What?"

"You were just covering your dad's six. Watching out for him. Sons do that for their dads. Daughters do that for their moms. Kids do that for their parents. You were protecting his honor. Covering his six. That's what we call it in my line of work."

Tommy rubbed his swollen eye. "I guess I did. Cover-his-six thing."

Cassion turned to Robie and Reel, obviously relieved that his son had calmed. "Tommy, these are two of the finest Americans you will ever meet. They just performed an important mission on behalf of our country. They're real heroes."

Tommy looked suitably impressed by this. His entire demeanor changed.

"Wow," he said.

Robie put out his hand. "Nice to meet you, Tommy. And for what it's worth, I got in fights at school too. But I figured something out."

"What? Better to turn the other cheek?" Tommy said in a sarcastic tone.

"No. I never really learned to do that. I figured out that if I talked to the other guy and tried to learn where his issues were coming from then maybe I could fix things that way instead of using my fists. Whether you win or lose, getting punched in the face still hurts."

Tommy did not look convinced by this but said, "Okay."

"You should get some ice on that eye," advised

Reel. "It really helps with the swelling. Just in case there's a round two."

Tommy flashed her a smile.

"Let's go get cleaned up, young man," said Eleanor quickly, pivoting him around. "And this is not over. I'm sure I'll be hearing from the school, and you're probably going to get a detention. I know you're getting one from me."

She glanced at her husband and said in a low voice, "Do you still think I'm overreacting? Nantucket here we come."

As his mother pulled him away, Tommy looked back at Robie and Reel. Robie winked at him, and Reel gave him an encouraging thumbs-up. Tommy smiled again before turning away.

Cassion said hurriedly, "Sorry about that."

"Kids are kids, Mr. President," said Robie. "And he has to live in the world's biggest fishbowl. Not easy."

"No, you're right. It's not easy. I doubt I could have done it when I was ten."

Cassion walked them to the outer door of the West Wing.

"I want to personally thank you both again. I know what I asked of you was truly unfair and really an impossible mission. And still you succeeded."

Robie said, "No problem, sir. It's what we do."

Cassion suddenly looked worried. "Have you any inkling what the North Koreans might do in retaliation?"

Reel said, "Unfortunately, Mr. President, we present a lot of soft targets for them. That's the downside to a free and open society."

The president nodded, turned, and walked back inside.

As Robie and Reel walked back to their parked vehicle, they passed a landscaping crew doing some work on a flowerbed and an adjacent bank of bushes. All but one stayed focused on their work.

This man looked up as the pair passed. He took off his cap and rubbed his brow.

This was not done because of the sweat on his face.

A group of tourists walking along the street on the other side of the fence included three men dressed in polo shirts and khaki pants. At this signal from the man inside the fence, all three started snapping photos of Robie and Reel. As the pair pulled out of a side entrance to the White House a few minutes later, this same group of tourists took photos of their license plate.

Robie and Reel drove on.

62

The jumbo jet flying in from Frankfurt, Germany, descended smoothly into the airspace around JFK. Min watched out the window from near the back of the plane. She had been nervous about boarding an airplane but had done so when reassured by Chung-Cha.

As Min looked out the window, Chung-Cha gazed over her shoulder at the impressive Manhattan skyline that appeared in her line of vision when the jet banked to come in for a landing.

Min looked at Chung-Cha in wonderment. "What is that?" she asked, pointing at the buildings down below.

"It is a city. New York City, they call it."

"I have never seen so many tall . . ." Here her limited vocabulary faltered.

"They are called skyscrapers," said Chung-Cha. "And they used to have two others that were the tallest of all."

"What happened to them?" asked Min.

"They fell down," replied Chung-Cha.

"How?" asked an astonished Min.

Since they were currently riding in a jet, Chung-Cha did not want to answer truthfully. "It was an accident."

They landed and taxied to the gate, where they deplaned. They went through customs. Chung-Cha steeled herself for any questions that might come her way. Her documents identified her as a South Korean here with her niece. South Korea was a staunch ally of America and thus they anticipated no problems. But such anticipation guaranteed nothing, Chung-Cha well knew.

However, the customs agent merely looked over her passport and smiled at Min, who clutched a doll that Chung-Cha had purchased for her, and welcomed them to America.

"You have a good time, honey," said the female customs agent. "The Big Apple is a great place for kids. Don't miss the zoo in Central Park."

Min smiled shyly and clutched Chung-Cha's hand.

Chung-Cha too smiled at the agent. Their plan had worked well. The child had caused all defenses, all natural caution to be abandoned. While she felt guilt for using Min in this way, she could not leave her back in North Korea.

They retrieved their luggage and were met by a car and driver in the area outside the international arrivals terminal.

They were driven to a hotel in lower Manhattan.

On the way Min spent the entire time staring out the window, her head constantly swiveling so she would miss nothing.

Chung-Cha was doing the same. She had never been to America either.

They arrived at the hotel and checked in. They had one room on the ninth floor. They took the elevator up and unpacked some of their clothes.

"Is this where we will live?" asked Min.

"Just for a little while," answered Chung-Cha.

Min looked around the room and then opened a small door in a cabinet.

"Chung-Cha, there is food in here. And things to drink."

Chung-Cha looked inside the minibar. "Would you like something?"

Min looked doubtful. "Can I?"

"Here is some candy."

"Candy?"

Chung-Cha withdrew a small package of M&M's and handed it to Min. "I think you will like these."

Min looked down at the package and then carefully opened it. She took one of the M&M's and looked up at Chung-Cha.

"Do I put it in my mouth?"

"Yes."

Min did so and her eyes widened at the taste. "This is very good."

"Just don't eat too many or you will get fat."

Min carefully shook out four more of the pieces and ate them slowly. Then she rolled up the package and started to put it back in the cabinet.

Chung-Cha said, "No, they are yours now, Min."

Min gaped at her. "Mine?"

"Just put them in your pocket for later."

In a flash Min had secreted the package in her jacket. She walked around the room touching everything and then stopped in front of the large TV set in another section of the cabinet.

"What is that?"

"It is a television." Like many North Koreans, Chung-Cha did not have a TV in her apartment. TV ownership was allowed in North Korea, but all sets had to be registered with the police. And all of the programming was heavily restricted and censored and mostly consisted of melodramatic praise of the country's leadership and the bashing of countries such as South Korea and the United States and organizations like the UN. Though she did not own one, Chung-Cha had seen and used TVs when traveling. She did own a radio, because they were far more widespread than TVs, but most of the programs were similarly censored.

Things were changing slowly, particularly with the advent of the Internet, but there was no one in North Korea who could be said to be connected with the rest of the world. It was simply not acceptable to the government. While North Korean law, like American law, provided for freedom of speech and the press, there could not be a greater contrast between the two countries in that regard.

Chung-Cha picked up the remote and turned the TV on. When a picture of a man came on and he seemingly started talking directly to her, Min drew back fearfully.

"Who is that man?" she whispered. "What does he want?"

Chung-Cha put a calming hand on her shoulder. "He is not here. He is in the little box. He cannot see or hear you. But you can see and hear him."

She clicked through the channels until she came to a cartoon. "Watch that, Min, while I check some things."

While Min was instantly intrigued by the cartoon, even going so far as to reach up and touch the screen, Chung-Cha took out the phone she had been given and accessed her texts. There were a number of them, all in Korean. And they were all in code. Yet even if someone broke the code they would seem nonsensical because behind that code was another code that only Chung-Cha and the sender knew, and it came from a book the identity of which only they knew. These one-time codes were virtually impossible to break, because unless you had the book, you would not be able to crack the code.

Using her copy of the book, she deciphered the messages. Now she had some free time. She looked over at Min, who was still engrossed in the TV show.

"Min, would you like to go for a walk and then get something to eat?"

"Will the TV be here when we get back?"

"Yes."

Min jumped up and put on her coat.

They walked many blocks until they reached the water. Across the harbor was the Statue of Liberty and Min asked what that was. Only this time Chung-Cha did not have an answer for her. She did not know what the thing was.

They later ate at a café. Min marveled at the odd assortment of people on the streets and in the shops.

"They have things on their skin and metal on their faces," observed Min as she dug into a hamburger and fries. "Have they been injured?"

"No, I think they did those things by their own choosing," said Chung-Cha as she glanced at the tattooed and skin-pierced people to whom Min was referring.

Min shook her head but could not tear her eyes away from a group of Asian girls who were giggling and carrying shopping bags and were dressed like typical college students. They clutched their phones and were endlessly texting.

In a low voice Min said, "They look like us."

Chung-Cha glanced over at the girls. One of them saw Min and waved.

Min hurriedly looked away and the girl laughed.

Chung-Cha said, "They do look like us. But they are not like us." She said this last part wistfully, but Min was too enthralled with all that was going on around her to notice.

Min said slowly, "People here, they laugh a lot." She looked at Chung-Cha. "At Yodok, only the guards laugh." She grew somber and continued to watch everything.

Chung-Cha observed the little girl and knew that it was as if she had been born in a cave and had now been whisked by a time machine into the present day and to a city that was a melting pot beyond all melting pots.

Where people laugh.

They stopped at Washington Square Park later and watched street artists perform: mimes and jugglers and magicians and unicyclists and musicians and dancers. Min stood there clutching Chung-Cha's hand, her face utterly amazed at what she was seeing. When a person dressed as a statue suddenly moved and plucked a coin from behind her ear, Min screamed but did not run away. When the person handed her the coin Min took it and smiled. The person smiled back and gave her an official salute.

Chung-Cha led her away after a while, but Min clutched the coin and kept looking back over her shoulder at the performers.

"What is this place?" she asked. "Where are we, Chung-Cha?"

"We are in America."

Min stopped so fast her fingers slipped from Chung-Cha's. She exclaimed, "But America is evil. I heard so at Yodok."

Chung-Cha quickly looked around and was relieved that no one had seemed to hear Min even though she was speaking Korean.

"You heard much at Yodok. It does not mean it is all true."

"So America is not evil?"

Chung-Cha knelt down and gripped Min by the shoulder. "Whether it is or not, you must not mention such things here, Min. There will be people who come to visit me. You will not talk when they are with us. It is very important."

Min slowly nodded, but there was fear in her eyes now.

Chung-Cha straightened and took Min's hand once more. They walked back to the hotel without breaking their silence.

And once more Chung-Cha second-guessed herself about bringing Min along.

But I could not leave her.

63

The train rolled along through the mid-Atlantic region. Min and Chung-Cha sat together in one of the train cars. Min was asleep. She had been so excited in New York that she had barely slept. Minutes after getting on the train, she had passed out.

Chung-Cha looked out the window as the train raced across a bridge over a river. She had no idea it was the Delaware River. She did not know what Delaware was, nor did she care. In a mission like this, one had to focus on what was important and rid one-self of all that was not important.

She dropped her gaze to Min. She moved a strand of hair from the girl's face. Min's skin was now clear of wounds. Her teeth were being repaired. She had gained weight. Her lessons were coming along nicely, but she had many years of work ahead of her before she would catch up to others her age.

Yet she could have a nice future. She could.

Chung-Cha looked away and studied the two passengers diagonally across from her. One man, one woman. Both Asian. They looked like a married couple, perhaps on holiday. They were not dressed as businesspeople like most of the passengers on the train.

But they were not married and they were not on holiday. They had already signaled her. They were her contacts. They would be getting off the train with her and Min at the last stop.

Washington, D.C.

The home of the American president. And his family.

When they pulled into Union Station, Chung-Cha woke Min. They left the train, and Chung-Cha steered Min until they were following in the wake of the young couple. They rode an escalator up to the parking garage and climbed into the back of a black SUV. The man drove and the woman sat next to him, while Chung-Cha and Min rode in the back.

"Where are we going?" Min asked in a whisper.

Chung-Cha shook her head once and Min lapsed into silence and stared fearfully ahead.

They drove to Springfield, Virginia, to a town house in a vast sea of them. As they pulled into a parking space in front of an end unit, Min looked out the truck window and saw children playing in a yard two units down. They looked up at her. One girl about Min's age held a ball. The other, a boy about seven, was calling to his sister to throw it to him. The girl did and then waved at Min. Min started to wave back, but then quickly looked away when Chung-Cha said something to her.

They went into the house carrying their small suit-cases.

The town house's interior was spacious, far larger than Chung-Cha's apartment, but it was barely furnished. They were shown to their room upstairs and set down their bags. The man and woman ignored Min but showed Chung-Cha the respect her position entailed.

"We brought the girl toys," said the woman. "They are in the basement. She can use them while we speak."

Chung-Cha led Min to the basement, a large, mostly empty room. There was a stuffed bear, a book that Chung-Cha knew the girl could not read but that had pictures, and a large red ball.

"I have some work to do upstairs, Min. You will stay and play with these things, all right?"

"How long will you be gone?" Min said uncertainly.

"I will just be upstairs."

"Can I stay with you?"

Chung-Cha said firmly, "I will just be upstairs. You will stay here and play."

Chung-Cha left the girl there, but as she walked up the stairs she could feel Min's gaze burning into her. And she felt a pang of guilt that was not easily swept away.

They met in the kitchen that was situated on the main floor at the rear of the town house. By now two more people had joined them, both men and both North Korean. One of them was the groundskeeper at the White House. They sat at the table, where pictures and files were laid out for Chung-Cha.

"There is a local team in place," the groundskeeper, whose name was Bae, informed her. "And it will be ready to go at a moment's notice, Comrade Yie. And it is an honor to have such an esteemed servant of the Supreme Leader here to assist us."

Chung-Cha looked at him over the file she was holding. Buried shallowly in his compliment was a complication.

Assist?

"Thank you, Comrade. It will most certainly take a team to accomplish this goal. I am grateful to have someone such as yourself *behind* me."

Bae's cocksure look quickly faded.

She could not blame him for trying such a thing. But she was relieved that he had backed down. Otherwise he was a liability and would have to be treated as such. There was no room for error here. The Americans were too good at what they did. It was said they caught every electronic message sent around the world from every phone or computer. Chung-Cha had even heard that they had invented some device that could read one's mind. She hoped that was not the case, or they might have already lost this fight.

The others guided Chung-Cha through the files and pictures over the next several hours. Chung-Cha's mind occasionally would drift to Min downstairs playing with her toys. But then it would snap back and focus on the matter at hand.

She studied the pictures of the three people: mother, daughter, and son. They were innocent, of course, but then not innocent because they were related to the American president, who was her enemy.

Then she was shown two other pictures.

Bae said, "This was taken outside of Bukchang."

The enhanced photo showed a man hanging on to the skid of a chopper. The image had been blown up such that his face was fairly clear despite the darkness.

"This scum killed our brethren at Bukchang," said Bae. "He stole the filth Pak's family from us. We are told he was wounded in his escape. And that the guards nearly brought the enemy's helicopter down with their gallant rifles."

Chung-Cha peered down at the image of Will Robie. Her immediate thought was that he was a capable man. Hanging on to the skid of a chopper fleeing enemy fire was not easy.

She was shown another photo. It was of a woman walking through an airport.

"In China," explained Bae. "Shortly before the attack on Bukchang. We believe she is an American agent. We believe that she arrived with the other man. There was a report of one being a female. And I saw these two together at the White House after Bukchang was attacked."

Chung-Cha stared at the picture of Jessica Reel. She was tall and lean and in her hardened physique Chung-Cha saw much strength.

"I understand there was a traitor with them?" she said.

Bae nodded. "He talked with one of the guards. He was North Korean. He was undoubtedly brought with them for his language skills and perhaps knowledge of Bukchang."

"He might have been a prisoner there," said Chung-Cha. "Some have escaped and fled to America."

Bae spit on the floor. "Filth!"

Chung-Cha looked at him. "And why am I being shown these people?"

Bae looked at the others and then back at her. "They must be killed too."

"But not by me?"

"That remains to be seen, Comrade Yie."

"I cannot be in two places at the same time."

"We will see," said Bae. "We will see. But whatever the course, I will be *behind* you all the way, Comrade Yie."

The two locked gazes until Chung-Cha again stared Bae down. As he looked aside, Chung-Cha returned to the files, but her mind was a long way away.

64

Chung-Cha and Min had eaten some dinner prepared by the woman who had come with them here. Then Bae had departed and the man and woman had gone upstairs to their rooms. That left Chung-Cha and Min. Min's eyes were droopy but she said, "Can we go for a walk?"

"I don't think that is a good idea," said Chung-Cha.

"Please, just for a few minutes?"

Chung-Cha looked out the window. It was dark, but that held no fear for her. It was true she had no weapons with her. Those would be provided later. But *she* was a weapon. She had heard that America was crime-ridden, with gangs on the streets attacking people, killing, raping, and robbing. She had seen no sign of this at all, either in New York City or here. Still, they might be out there.

"Just for a few minutes," she said to Min, and the girl smiled.

They walked hand in hand around the residential development, which was well lit by streetlamps. Min looked at all the parked cars and said, "Americans must have much money."

"I suppose," said Chung-Cha. She had been thinking the same thing. She looked at all the houses, where the lights burned bright and steady. In Pyongyang one was lucky to have an hour's worth of light at night. And there were more cars in this one parking lot than she had seen in all of North Korea.

They watched as a man and woman and their two small children came out of their house and headed to their car. The man smiled and said, "Hello."

Chung-Cha greeted him back.

"Are you moving into the neighborhood?" asked the woman.

"What?" asked Chung-Cha.

"We saw you arrive earlier. Are you moving in, or just visiting?"

"Just visiting," said Chung-Cha automatically.

The woman looked at Min. "What's your name?"

"Her name is Min," said Chung-Cha. She added in a more polite tone, "I'm sorry, she does not speak English."

The woman smiled and said, "I'm sure she'll pick it up right away. I wish they taught foreign languages here sooner, like they do overseas. Most kids don't get going on that here until middle school. Way too late in my opinion." She looked at Min again. "She looks to be about ten. Same age as Katie here. Katie, can you say hello?"

Katie, a small girl with blonde curls, was partially hiding behind her dad.

The woman said, "Katie's our shy one."

"Min too," said Chung-Cha.

"If you're doing the touristy thing and need any help or anything, let us know," said the man. "I work downtown. Take the Metro in. I know it like the back of my hand. Just give a shout. Glad to point you in the right direction. Definitely do the Air and Space and the National Archives. Pretty cool stuff."

"Thank you," replied Chung-Cha, though in truth she had no idea what he had just said.

The family got into their car and drove off while Chung-Cha and Min continued their walk.

"What did they want?" asked Min.

"Just to say hello. And see if we needed help."

"Were they pretending? So maybe they can try and hurt us later?"

"I do not know," said Chung-Cha. "They seemed nice."

"What was wrong with the girl's hair?"

"Wrong?"

"It was all bent."

It took Chung-Cha a moment to grasp what she was referring to. "Oh, some Americans' hair is like that. Or they use a tool to make it look like that."

"Why?"

"I do not know. I suppose they think it looks nice."

"I do not think it looks nice," said Min, although

her expression did not match her words. It was clear she not only thought it looked nice but was wondering how it would look on her.

They headed back to the town house and Chung-Cha put a sleepy Min to bed. Then she went back downstairs, made herself a cup of tea, and spread the documents out in front of her on the table in the kitchen. She went over every page, every note, and every photograph. These files would be her life for as long as it took.

After about three hours and two more cups of tea her eyes grew weary and she leaned back in her chair. She looked up to the ceiling where she knew Min was asleep in their room.

She rose and went to the window and stared out at all the houses. They were virtually all dark now at this late hour. She knew she should go to sleep. She was tired. She was still not acclimated to the time zone. She was under pressure like she had never been before. To do what was expected of her was nearly impossible. She might be able to succeed in the first part of the mission, but the second part, her escape, would be impossible.

And then what would become of Min?

It was two days later that Chung-Cha traveled to another place, far outside of the city. It was rural and the house she was driven to was isolated amid trees and old farm fields that had not seen a plow in a very long time.

There were a number of people waiting for her. Bae was not among them. He was embedded so deeply that care was taken not to expose his loyalties to North Korea. He had been in the United States a long time and was one of the most valuable operatives they had. His position at the White House allowed him to see and hear things that no one else could.

This was the team that Chung-Cha had been told about, composed entirely of men. They were all tough and hardened and could kill people in many different ways, Chung-Cha knew. She had read the files on all of them. Some had been here longer than others. Each was willing to die to achieve their goals. They knew that the people guarding their targets were excellent. They simply expected to be better.

They sat around an old table in what had once been the kitchen of the house, Chung-Cha observed, from the battered sink and rusty stove. They all spoke in swift, terse Korean, reporting what they had learned. The chief point was that a location for the attack had now been determined.

"They will be traveling to a place called Nantucket," said one of the men to Chung-Cha. "Our comrade Bae overheard this."

"He said nothing to me about it when we last met."

"It needed to be confirmed. Now it has been."

He showed her a map. "It is a small island just off the coast of their state of Massachusetts in the Atlantic Ocean. It is gotten to by plane or by ferry. They will be going there in two weeks. Just the wife and the two children with their guards and their staff. We know the house where they will be staying. It is near the small downtown area. It is old and historic and it provides for some opportunities."

"Do you have a schedule of events for them?" asked Chung-Cha.

"A preliminary one obtained through various sources. We are working hard to firm it up."

"We will need to get there before them," said Chung-Cha. "To allay suspicion."

"Undoubtedly. It is not the summer season when many tourists go. At that time the servant class comes from Africa and Russia and other eastern European countries to take care of the wealthy Americans who often have second homes there."

"Second homes?" asked Chung-Cha.

"These rich Americans often have more than one home. They travel between them and enjoy the fruits of their greed and exploitation of the poor."

"I see."

"During this time of year those servant people are gone. Fortunately, there are Asians who work there now, and Hispanics. Americans, as you know, cannot tell a Chinese from a Japanese, much less where we come from. They are ignorant and superior that way, as you well know. The world revolves around them, the filth. We have two operatives there right now. They will lay the groundwork for us. We will have jobs on different parts of the island. Not all of us. Some will be kept in reserve, such as yourself, Chung-Cha. You will come out when the moment to strike is upon us."

"And do we know when and where that moment is?"

"We will soon determine it," said the man, "and every detail will be gone over until we will see it in our dreams."

"How long will they be staying there?"

"It is a vacation of some sort for them. One week."

"And the children and their school? Are you sure they will be at this Nantucket?"

"Yes."

"And the president will not be coming?"

"He may, we cannot be sure that he will not. But we will know if he is. We will not strike when he is there. The security will be too tight. But for the others, while good, the strength is not nearly what it is when the president is there. He is important above all others. It is said the Secret Service will leave his wife and children behind in order to save his miserable life."

Chung-Cha nodded at all this and then studied the maps in front of her.

"I see how we will be able to get there," she said. "But after the mission is over, how do we escape from this little island in the ocean? Surely we cannot fly out or take the ferry to this"—she glanced quickly at a document—"this Massachusetts place."

They all looked at each other and then at her.

The same man said, "We do not expect to live through this, Chung-Cha."

She stared at him, her features impassive. She was, in truth, not surprised by this. It was a suicide mission. Her suicide. And she knew how she had come by it.

"Do you know Comrade Rim Yun?" she asked the man.

"I have that honor, yes."

"And was it she who told you this was so?"

"Yes."

Chung-Cha looked around at the others, who were all eyeing her both curiously and, in the case of two of them, with suspicion. "There is no greater honor than to serve our Supreme Leader," she said. "And to die in his service," she added.

She turned back to the documents. "Now, we have much work to do."

But as they went over elements of the plan, Chung-Cha could really see only one thing in her mind.

Min.

65

Robie's phone rang. He was sitting in his apartment with Reel, who was curled up in a chair, her eyes closed, but he knew she wasn't asleep. The rain was falling outside and it was chilly. Neither of them had anything to do, and though the break was nice, they were not wired to be idle.

"Yes?" said Robie into the phone. He sat up straighter. "Okay. When?" He nodded and said, "We'll be there."

He put the phone down and nudged Reel with his hand.

She opened her eyes. "Are we being deployed?"

"I'm not sure. What I do know is that we are being summoned to the White House."

"Again? Cassion already patted us on the head. What more does he have to do?"

"It's not Cassion who wants us."

"What?" she said, unfolding her long legs and sitting up in the chair.

"The request came from the First Lady. We're to

meet her in the private quarters at the White House in"—he checked his watch—"one hour."

"What could she want with us?"

"No clue. But I guess we'll find out."

They presented themselves at the White House at the time specified and were escorted to the first family's private quarters on the second floor after leaving their weapons behind with the Secret Service.

As they rode the elevator up, Reel whispered to Robie, "Ever been up here?"

He shook his head. "You?"

"Hell no."

They were led into a large sitting area with flowers displayed in large vases. Eleanor Cassion rose from a settee and greeted them. The attendant who had brought them here quietly left.

Eleanor motioned for them to sit on a large couch while she sat across from them. She was dressed in slacks, a short jacket with a white blouse underneath, and two-inch pumps. Her hair was swept back in a ponytail. Around her neck was a silver necklace with a Saint Christopher medal dangling from it.

"I'm sure you're wondering why I asked you here today," she began.

Robie said, "We were surprised."

"The fact is, well, you both made quite an impression on our son, Tommy. In fact, I think he's been researching you both."

"Not much to find," said Reel. "We don't do Facebook."

Eleanor smiled. "I know. And I also know that I'm not cleared for much of what you both do, but I have learned a few things." She added quickly, "And please let me add my thanks to that of my husband for your service to the country."

"Thank you," said Robie, while Reel nodded.

"I shared a few things with Tommy about you both. Nothing classified, just things. And that only heightened his regard for you both." She looked at Reel. "And I have been told something of your recent travails, Agent Reel. I'm relieved that you are, well, out of that situation."

Reel said nothing to this, but kept staring curiously at the woman.

The First Lady was nervously twisting her hands.

Robie said, "Ma'am, it might be better just to get it out."

Eleanor laughed. "I'm not usually so nervous and shy about a request. I used to be, but, married to a politician, you get really good at asking for things from people." She paused, collected her thoughts, and said, "The children and I are going to Nantucket for a week. It's to get away and recharge our batteries and to just spend some time together. Tommy, in particular, I think needs this."

"The fight at school?" said Reel.

"Among other things. He's had a hard time adjusting to life here. Very hard. The place where we came from is as different from here as it's possible to be."

"A truly unique city," commented Robie. "And not an easy one."

"You're absolutely right about that," said Eleanor emphatically.

"But what do you want from us?" said Reel.

"Well, let me just come out and say it. I would like you both to accompany us to Nantucket. The president can't make it and I just thought . . . well, I just thought that having the two of you there might . . . help things." She hurried on. "I know you must think this is crazy. I mean, we don't really know each other, but Tommy hasn't stopped talking about you two. I don't know what it was exactly. Well, I think I do know. You're heroes and Tommy's father obviously respects you greatly. And Tommy dearly wants his father's . . . well . . ." Her voice trailed off and she looked like someone who regretted saying too much.

"I've only met Tommy once," said Robie. "But I can tell he's a good kid. And the fight was because he was standing up for his dad."

"I know. I both admired what he did and was horrified by it. It hasn't been an easy time for either of us. I wasn't sure whether to ground him or give him a medal. The back-and-forth made my head hurt."

"I can see that," said Reel. "Not easy being a mom."

"I'm sorry I didn't ask before. Are you a mother, Agent Reel?"

Reel said unhesitatingly, "No, I'm not."

Eleanor sat back. "So will you do it?"

Reel looked at Robie. She said, "Are the president and the Secret Service okay with this?"

"Yes. My husband is fine with it. He thinks the added security you two will bring is a good thing, in fact. And my protection detail voiced no concerns. They obviously have researched you."

"And the kids?" said Reel.

"Tommy is over the moon about the possibility."

"And your daughter?"

"She was put out about going to Nantucket, especially at this time of year, I have to admit. She wanted to stay home and be with her friends. But now she's looking forward to going."

"What changed?" asked Robie.

Here, Eleanor blushed a bit. "Um, well, she saw a picture of you, Agent Robie."

Reel gave him a sideways glance, her eyes twinkling. "Not that that should go to your head," she said.

"Teenage girls can be quite impressionable," added Eleanor.

Robie said, "But this is really about Tommy, isn't it?"

"It really is, yes. But spending some time with my kids, away from this place, maybe it's about all three of us, Agent Robie."

"You can make it Will, ma'am."

"And I'm Jessica," said Reel.

"So you'll do it?"

Reel said, "Well, we're between deployments. I would imagine your request will take priority."

"So the short answer is, yes, we will. Just tell us where and when," added Robie.

"I can't tell you how grateful I am about this. I really am hoping for a good outcome from this trip. I think it could make a real difference, especially for Tommy."

"I'm sure it will," said Robie. "Anything in particular you want us to do while we're up there with you?"

"Since the president won't be joining us, I would hope that you could just spend time with Tommy. I could tell from your initial meeting that he looks up to you. Any words of wisdom you might have? Just being there? And a man for Tommy to . . . ?"

"I think I understand," said Robie.

Eleanor said, "Don't get me wrong. He loves his father. They had, I mean *have,* a great relationship. It's just that . . ."

"Not even Superman could do the job of a president," said Robie. "It doesn't leave time for a lot else. Even family."

"Something like that," said Eleanor. "The president tries, but everyone in the world, it seems, wants a piece of him."

"I'm sure."

As they rose to leave, Reel said, "Oh, one more thing."

"Yes?" said Eleanor expectantly.

"Remind your daughter that my partner here is old enough to be her father."

66

"This is really not helpful," said Evan Tucker.

He was sitting across from Robie and Reel in a conference room at Langley. To his left was Amanda Marks. To his right was Blue Man.

"We didn't have much choice," replied Robie.

"You always have a choice," snapped Tucker. "Going off vacationing in Nantucket when you're needed here?"

"Well, I think we need some downtime from when we were vacationing with the neo-Nazis and then the whole North Korea thing," said Reel sharply. "And they all begin with the letter N. Nazis, North Korea. And Nantucket. For what it's worth, I'll go with the last one as my preference."

"You know what I mean," said Tucker. "We still don't know what the Koreans are going to do. Between us, I tried to talk the president out of breaking Pak's family out of the camp, but he was dead set on it. Now I'm afraid we're going to pay the price for his inability to corral his guilt over what happened to Pak."

Reel looked at Marks. "Do we have any notion of where they might strike?"

Marks nodded. "We've gotten chatter that the North Koreans are positioning missiles to be fired at American bases in South Korea."

"Well, that would certainly start a war," said Blue Man.

"All indications are that they are pissed off beyond belief," said Marks. "First the planned coup against Un and now breaking Pak's family out. It was to be expected."

"Of course it was," interjected Tucker. "Just as I said. Was it worth two lives? We're going to pay the piper." He looked around, seemingly daring anyone to disagree with him.

"Any other potential target?" asked Robie.

"Too many, I'm afraid," said Blue Man.

"And you two will be whiling away your time in beautiful Nantucket, where all the jet-setters zip in during the summer," said Tucker.

"Really? I understand you have a place there," said Reel. "I checked."

"It's just a summer rental," groused Tucker.

Marks added, "It's actually a good thing that the First Lady and her kids will be out of town. And this trip is not on the official schedule, which is even better." She eyed Robie and Reel. "Are you part of the official protection detail?"

"Secret Service protocols won't allow for that,"

replied Reel. "But I don't think they're unhappy we're going. I think the First Lady wants us to spend some time with her son, who's going through a rocky time right now."

Marks nodded while Tucker just shook his head in exasperation. He said, "Well, while you're on your little holiday I want to hear from you every day. You don't work for the Secret Service or the First Lady. You work for me. Is that understood?"

"Never doubted it for a moment, sir," said Reel, with a slight edge to her voice. "So long as you're the DCI," she added.

As the meeting broke up, Tucker demanded that Reel remain behind. Robie glanced at her questioningly, but she nodded and he reluctantly left.

When the others had gone Tucker sat back down and motioned Reel to do the same.

"I'll stand if it's all the same to you."

"Do you want me to order you to sit? For Christ's sake, Reel, can't you just do what I say without making it an issue every damn time? You undercut my authority whenever you pull shit like this."

She gave him a stony look but sat.

"This won't take long," he said.

"Fine with me," she said.

He stared at her while she looked back at him impassively.

"You hate my guts, don't you?" he said.

"I don't think my feelings toward you have anything to do with my job."

"Of course they do. Without respect there's nothing."

"If you say so."

"I have never been confronted with a more complex problem than you. Never."

"Glad I could be there for you."

"I'm being serious, so cut the jokes."

She sat up a bit straighter but said nothing.

He held up two fingers. "My DD, James Gelder. And an analyst named Doug Jacobs."

Reel said nothing.

"You killed them both."

Reel folded her arms over her chest.

"They worked for this agency. Gelder was my friend. They're dead because of you."

Sensing where this was going, Reel started to speak, but Tucker held up his hand. "Just—just let me finish," he said. "It's taken me long enough to get to the point. Let me have my say and then you can respond."

Reel sat back, evidently put out by this request.

Tucker continued. "I've looked into every facet of the case, everything. And my conclusion is that, even though I don't want to believe it, Gelder, who I thought was my friend, and Doug Jacobs, who had sworn allegiance to this country, were traitors. They were planning an event that, if it had taken place, would have sent this world into an apocalypse."

He pointed a finger at her. "You prevented that from happening. You and Robie," he amended.

Reel's expression had softened. She was watching her boss closely now.

"I can't say that I agree with your method. Guilty until proven innocent. But I think I see now why you did what you did. They killed a man who meant a lot to you. There was no direct evidence against them. If you hadn't acted, the world as we know it would be gone." He gave a long, resigned sigh. "As much as I didn't want to admit it, I think you did the right thing, Reel."

Reel's lips parted and her eyes revealed her surprise.

Tucker looked away from her and studied the table. He said, "Your actions since then were nothing short of remarkable. You and Robie fought through every imaginable obstacle and put your lives on the line again and again. You stopped the coming global disaster while everyone else, myself included, had hands over our eyes and thumbs up our asses. And as reward for that, I sent you and Robie into Syria basically to die. I still can't believe that I did what I did, setting up two of my agents, my *best* agents, to get killed. There is no excuse and I'm ashamed of myself. I truly am. And yet you survived that. And you came back home and got your medals and I've been thinking of ways to nail you ever since those hunks of metal went around your necks, including trying to literally drown your asses at the Burner Box."

Tucker grew silent, but Reel seemed disinclined to say anything.

He said, "I have learned what went down with you and the scum who happened to be your father. I know what he tried to do. I know what you did to stop him and save Julie Getty's life. And I know the risk involved in going to North Korea and doing what you and Robie accomplished. It was nothing short of miraculous. Any other team would've been dead."

He grew quiet again, but for a shorter time now.

"So, I said all that to really say, thank you, Agent Reel, for your service. I was in the wrong and you were in the right."

He extended his hand, which she shook.

"I'm not sure what to say, Director," she said. "I think I understand how hard this was for you to do."

"The problem is, Reel, it shouldn't have been that hard. I'm just too damn stubborn. Look, I know people see me as an outsider. I didn't come up through the intelligence field. I'm a political appointee. Didn't know my ass from a hole in the ground. I get that. I worked hard to come up to speed, I really did. But I made mistakes. And you were the biggest one. So, my apologies again." He paused. "And when this threat from North Korea has been neutralized, I plan on stepping down and letting the president appoint my successor."

She looked shocked by this. "Are you sure about that, sir?"

"Even if I wanted to stay, I couldn't. A higher authority than me has made it very clear that my stint at the agency is coming to a close."

Reel knew exactly who the "higher authority" was, but only said, "I see."

"And I'm not a young guy, Reel. I've got other things I want to do in life. In truth, this job is a killer, it really is. You jump from crisis to crisis. Success to disaster. The highest peaks and the lowest valleys. My gut is one big acid burn. I think I've aged more in this job than I did in the previous thirty years of my life. But I don't want to leave until this thing is resolved. And I didn't want to leave without telling you what I just have." He paused again, glanced at her nervously, and said, "That's all I wanted to say. You can head out now."

As they rose, Reel said, "So why did you just bust our asses in the meeting?"

"For now at least I'm still the DCI. And I'm concerned that you will not be where I need you to be. That's why. But with that said, I hope you have a relaxing time in Nantucket."

"Thank you, sir. I hope I will too."

67

The seas were choppy, though in the twin-hulled high-speed catamaran it was hardly noticeable. Chung-Cha sat in her seat in the heated space while Min had her face glued to the window looking at the frothing water.

It had occurred to Chung-Cha that Min had never been on a boat of any kind before. Until recently she had never ridden in a car or a plane or a train. The young girl had come a long way in a short time.

As the island of Nantucket appeared out of the mist, Min resumed her seat next to Chung-Cha. The ferry was only about half full, mostly with older people returning to the island. Chung-Cha smiled occasionally at some of them but did not say anything.

The ferry passed by the man-made breakwater and headed into the harbor. A few minutes later they were docked and the passengers filed off the boat. Chung-Cha held Min's hand as they went down the gangplank. The ferry's captain tipped his hat and said, "Enjoy your visit."

Chung-Cha smiled. "We plan to."

They continued with their rolling bags to the car rental office, where Chung-Cha produced her license and her reservation and credit card. They drove off a bit later in a small white SUV. As the sun was setting to the west, burning the sky into reds and golds, Min stared out the car window and said, "What are we doing here, Chung-Cha?"

"I told you. Just a little trip."

"Who were those people at the other place?"

"Friends of mine."

"They didn't seem too friendly."

"Well, they are. They are good people."

"You work with them?" Min said, giving Chung-Cha a brief sideways glance.

"A little."

"What is this place called?"

"Nantucket. This is the Atlantic Ocean that you are seeing. Where Korea is, that's the Pacific Ocean."

"I know nothing about any of that."

Chung-Cha glanced at her as they drove along. "You will, Min. I promise. You will learn every day. Even—" Here she broke off.

"Even what?" said Min quickly, apparently sensing unease in the woman.

"Even when you are tired of learning," said Chung-Cha with a smile.

She had put her destination into the car's navigation system. The island was not large, but the roads

500

were not very well marked and she was glad of the assistance the computer provided. Min's eyes followed the little marker that represented their vehicle as it traveled along the navigation screen. She asked many questions about the device and Chung-Cha answered as best she could.

Their rental rumbled over the cobblestone streets of the village square. There were a number of people on the streets and many shops were still open. The weather was not cold, though as the sun fell it would grow chillier. The briny smell of the ocean was all around them.

Min sniffed. "That smell is not so nice."

"It's fishy. It's not bad. There are far worse smells."

Min looked at her and nodded. "There are far worse smells," she repeated.

Soon they turned down a winding lane with high grass on either side. The ocean was visible on three sides. The cottage they pulled into sat by itself off the road. Chung-Cha cut off the engine and opened the car door. She and Min pulled out their bags and they walked together up to the front door.

"Who lives here?" asked Min.

"We do, for now."

The inside of the cottage was quaint and neat, and when Min found that she had her own room and bed she was astonished.

"Just me?" she asked Chung-Cha.

"I will be in the room next to it. You will be fine.

But if you feel anxious, you will know where to find me."

They had not eaten since lunch, so Chung-Cha prepared a meal from the contents of the refrigerator, which had been filled for their visit. They ate and drank hot tea and watched the sun finish its fall to the horizon.

"It looks like the sun has dropped into the water," said Min as they watched out the window.

"Yes, it does."

Min spent the next hour going around the house and seeing what was there. The owners had left toys and board games in a closet. Min had pulled some things out and was playing with them, but she did not like it when Chung-Cha was out of her sight for very long.

Chung-Cha sat in a chair after hitting a switch, which caused the gas fireplace to turn on. When Min saw the flames spring out, she rushed over, her face filled with horror.

"We have to get water to put it out!"

"No, Min, it is all right. It is the way it works. It gives off heat. See, draw close, like this. It feels good."

She and Min stood in front of the fire and let it warm them.

An hour later Min fell asleep on the couch next to Chung-Cha. Now Chung-Cha could get to work.

Since she understood that the mission was not expected to produce any survivors, she had to think some things through. When she had, she pulled out her phone and studied the images on there. The three Cassions stared back at her. Mother, daughter, son.

Next she looked at images of Will Robie and Jessica Reel. She could just tell they were like her. They looked strong and capable and unafraid of anything.

As Min quietly snored next to her, Chung-Cha went through all the files and details once more.

The plan was still in progress because they did not yet have an exact itinerary for the first family. In fact, there might not be one, since this trip was apparently not really part of the official schedule but an impromptu decision.

They were all aware, from recent news stories, that the NSA and other American intelligence agencies listened to everyone in the world, so the use of their phones to communicate, even via text or email, was deemed to be too risky on the island, even if they used code. The thought was that any communications on the island, with the First Lady and her children here, would be given heightened scrutiny.

But it was not as though they could freely congregate and continue their planning. A group of Asians doing so would be a red flag and could sabotage their mission before it even began.

But they *had* to communicate. And they believed they had arrived at a plan to do so while staying below the Americans' radar. And Chung-Cha had devised a way for Min to play a part in that.

Over the next several days Chung-Cha and Min drove and walked through the town. They made treks along the beach. They collected shells and threw pebbles into the ocean. They watched seagulls glide across the sky and ferries race across the water.

Chung-Cha had her ears open for any snatches of conversation about the people who would soon be coming here. And details were learned, because Americans apparently liked to gossip.

While they were eating chowder in a local café several men came in. They wore jackets and khaki pants and had earwigs and looked quietly professional. They took a table near Chung-Cha and Min. While she pretended to listen to Min, Chung-Cha eavesdropped on the conversation the men were having. She learned some important details, including exactly when the party was arriving and how.

After they left the café she stopped to write some things down and then she and Min went to their car and drove off. She pulled into a gas station. Chung-Cha eyed the small windowed office where a clerk stood behind the cash register.

She folded up the paper she had written on and handed it to Min.

"Do you see the man in there?" she said, pointing. Min looked in that direction, saw the clerk, and nodded. "You will take him this note while I put fuel into the car."

"What does it say, the note?"

"It's unimportant. I'm just giving him some information he needs."

"How do you know him?"

"I know him from our country."

"Why is he here?"

"Just take him the note, Min. Do it now. And he will give you something in return for me."

Min opened the door, looked back once at Chung-Cha, and then hurried into the little office.

Chung-Cha pumped gas while she watched Min. She gave the man the note and he in turn gave her a piece of paper, along with some candy from the rack next to the register. He smiled and patted Min on the head.

When Min returned to the car, she handed Chung-Cha the note and held up the package of chocolates.

"Can I have these?"

"Just one. Save the rest for later."

Chung-Cha slipped the note into her pocket.

"You're not going to read what the note says?" asked Min as she popped the candy into her mouth.

"Later, not here."

They drove back to the cottage.

While Min went off to play, Chung-Cha looked at

the note. It was written in code, and not in Korean, just in case. They had used English instead.

She read through the contents twice to make sure she had missed nothing. Then she let out a small breath as she heard Min laugh. The TV was on and she must be watching her cartoons.

It must be good to laugh, thought Chung-Cha. *It must be very good.*

68

It looks like a baby's bib," observed Reel.

"Or a bikini bottom," replied Robie.

They were in a private jet descending into the airport on Nantucket. Looking at the island from this altitude had prompted their respective descriptions.

"Mars, Venus," said Reel wryly.

"Guess so."

Eleanor Cassion and her children were riding up front with their protection detail. Special motorcade cars were being ferried over. If the president had been coming, the logistics would have been far more daunting.

"Settled in 1641, about forty-eight square miles of land and about fifty-eight more of water. Fifty thousand people during the summer, about a fifth of that during the rest of the year," said Reel. "They call the island the 'little gray lady of the sea' when the place is fog-bound, which it apparently is a good deal of the time. But on that island is some of the most expensive land in the country. Highest point is Folger Hill, about one hundred and nine feet."

Robie stared at her. "Aren't you just the fount of information."

"Google makes everybody a genius."

The jet touched down and came to a stop. Reel and Robie grabbed their bags and headed for the exit.

Claire Cassion made a point of stepping directly in front of Robie in the aisle. Her mother and brother were just ahead of her. The Secret Service were already outside the plane making sure everything was okay before the family exited into the waiting SUV.

Claire had on skinny jeans, heels that made her much taller, and a Yale sweatshirt. She glanced back at Robie. "Enjoy the flight?"

"I enjoy every flight where the plane lands on its wheels."

She laughed. "That's really funny. Handsome *and* a sense of humor, pretty impressive."

Reel turned her head so Claire would not see her rolling her eyes. But she did poke Robie hard in the back and whispered, "God, it must be great to be so popular with *children*."

As they walked down the jet steps Claire tripped in her heels, but Robie caught her. She squeezed his arm, "Thanks, Mr. Robie."

"Just make it Will."

She flashed a toothy smile. "Okay, and you can make it Claire."

Robie was expecting another poke from Reel, but

it didn't come. He glanced over and saw Tommy staring, not at him, but at Reel, while Eleanor was watching her daughter with a look of resigned exasperation.

As they stepped onto the tarmac they saw the three-SUV motorcade waiting. Robie said to Reel, "I think you have your own fan club." His gaze led Reel's over to Tommy as the boy climbed into the middle SUV. Tommy was still staring at her.

"Great," said Reel wearily. "Just great."

They rode in the rear vehicle behind the SUV carrying the Cassions. Two Secret Service agents rode with them.

One of them said, "Welcome aboard. Understand you guys are with our intelligence community."

"State Department," said Reel, hiding her smile.

"Yeah," said the agent, grinning.

"Why Nantucket?" said Robie.

The agent shrugged. "First Lady went to school in Boston. Apparently she spent a lot of time here as a kid. Good memories."

"And must be nice to get away from D.C."

"Always nice to get away from that place," agreed the agent. He added, "You two being here, anything we need to know? Threats?"

"The only reason we're here," said Robie, "is because the First Lady asked us to be."

"I think she believes we can have a calming influence on her son," added Reel.

The agent nodded. "He's been having a rough time of it. Not easy for a kid."

"No, it's not," said Reel.

"You think you can help him?" asked the agent. "He's a good kid. Never gives us any problems, except when he gets in fights at school."

"I don't know if we can help him," said Reel. "But we can try."

"So you guys have experience with kids?"

Robie and Reel exchanged glances. Reel said, "We work in D.C., so we have lots of experience dealing with children."

The agent laughed as the motorcade drove on.

The place where they were staying was within easy walking distance of the downtown area. There were two buildings: a large main house and a four-bedroom guest cottage. The Cassions and their staff would be in the main house. The protection detail was in the guesthouse. Robie and Reel were given rooms in the main house.

After she'd unpacked, Reel came into Robie's bedroom, which was next to hers.

"Feeling privileged to be bunking with the Cassions?" she said as she perched on the bed.

Robie put the rest of his clothes away and said, "Jury's still out on that."

Reel looked out the window. "Never been here. Looks nice, if a little surreal. Like a Ralph Lauren ad."

Robie joined her at the window and looked out over the grounds. "Secret Service will have its work cut out for it. Lots of access points and that's a public thoroughfare right there. I bet they'd like more of a buffer."

"You thinking they're going to be attacked on dear old Nantucket?"

"Just saying."

"It's hard to turn it off, I guess."

"It's impossible to turn it off. Never look at the world any differently. Points of attack and counter-attack."

"Kind of sucks, doesn't it?"

"Not if it keeps you alive it doesn't."

Someone knocked on the door.

"Want to guess who?" said Reel.

"Come on in," said Robie.

The door opened and there stood Claire. Her smile faded when she saw Reel. "Will, my mom wanted to let you know that we're all planning to go get some lunch and then take a walk on the beach. She'd really like *you* to come." Claire did not look at Reel as she said this.

Reel put an arm around Robie's shoulders. "Tell your mom we'd be delighted."

Claire frowned and said, "Okay. Downstairs, five minutes." Then she spun around on her heels and stalked off.

"I'd be careful, Jessica," said Robie.

"Why?"

"Those are stilettos she's wearing."

At the restaurant Claire arranged things so she was sitting next to Robie while her brother and mom sat on either side of Reel.

She said to Robie, "Mom said you were, like, a hero."

"That was very kind of your mother. But all I did was my job, no more, no less."

She tapped him on the forearm. "I bet you have some great stories."

Eleanor said, "None of which he can tell you, Claire, so don't hound the poor man about them."

"I don't hound, Mom," said Claire, frowning. "I'm just interested, that's all."

"You thinking about going into public service?" asked Robie.

"Yes. And it won't be long. I'm practically in college."

"You just started your sophomore year, so you really have three more years of high school," her mother pointed out.

"Which will go by like that," said Claire, snapping her fingers.

"I'm afraid you're right about that," said her mother with a sigh and a glance at Tommy. She tousled his hair. "We're going to the beach after this, Tommy. You can add to your shell collection."

Tommy glanced awkwardly at Reel. "That's for kids, Mom."

"I actually like collecting seashells," said Reel.

Tommy immediately brightened. "I know a lot about them. I can show you stuff."

"Sounds good."

Eleanor gave Reel a grateful look and then they all turned to their menus.

The beach was deserted and rocky; it was low tide. Tendrils of sea foam and green algae coated the sand and the rocks. The day was overcast and the seas unstable. The breakers banged away, but far from where they walked.

Tommy and his mother had buckets in which they were collecting shells. Reel walked next to Tommy while Claire was glued to Robie. The protection detail, dressed in Windbreakers and jeans, formed a loose circle around them all.

"I'm really glad you came up here with us, Will," said Claire.

"You'd probably like to be back home with your friends," said Robie.

"Oh, no way," she said. "My friends are okay, but they're pretty immature. Especially the boys."

"Yeah," said Robie uncomfortably. He looked over at Reel for help, but she smiled and quickly looked away, focusing on Tommy and his bucket of shells.

Tommy held one up for her. "My dad said shells

can come from thousands of miles away. This one might have started off near China or something and then ended up here. Pretty cool."

"Pretty cool," said Reel.

"Are you married?" Tommy asked.

"No."

"Were you ever?"

"No. Why do you ask?"

"Well, I mean, most women your age are married, aren't they?"

"I don't know, Tommy. Maybe they are."

"Do you have kids?"

Reel looked past him, out to the ocean. "No, I don't."

Tommy looked disappointed. She added, "But I think I'd like to be a mother, one day. I guess I have to make up my mind before it's too late. I'm not getting any younger."

"Oh, you've got plenty of time," said Tommy encouragingly. "And I bet you'd make a great mom."

"Thank you, I appreciate that."

Tommy bent down and snagged another shell and then pointed to a horseshoe crab scuttling away. "Creepy things." He straightened and said, "Is what you do dangerous?"

"Why do you ask that?"

"My dad said you guys were heroes. Serving the country. That's usually dangerous."

"We try to make it as safe as possible," said Reel diplomatically.

"Have you ever killed anybody?"

"Tommy!" called out his mother, who apparently had overheard this. "I'm sure Agent Reel would prefer to talk about other things."

Tommy glanced up, looking embarrassed. "Sorry."

"No need to be," said Reel. "Asking questions is how you learn things. Can I ask you some?"

He looked at her nervously. "Like what?"

"Like what you like and don't like, living where you do?"

"I don't like any of it," said Tommy fiercely.

"None of it, really?"

He hesitated. "Well, I mean, riding in Air Force One is pretty cool."

"You're one of the few kids to ever do that."

"And the Secret Service guys are nice."

"I'm sure."

"I don't like people saying stuff about my dad."

"I wouldn't either."

"My sister thinks I'm a useless idiot."

"Well, I'm afraid that would be the case regardless of where you live. It's just this thing between big sisters and little brothers. When you're older you'll probably be really close."

"I doubt it."

"No, you will. Because what you're experiencing right now is so unique, Tommy, and you and your sister will always share that experience. She may not let on, but I would imagine this has been hard for her too."

"No, it hasn't! Everybody *loves* Claire."

"Really, everybody?"

Tommy looked at the shells in his bucket. "Well, there are a few girls at her school that give her a hard time. And she says one teacher hates her because she doesn't like Dad."

"So not everybody loves her, then."

"No."

"Your mother obviously loves you a lot."

"She's always bossing me. Fixing my clothes, my hair. Checking my homework, telling me to do stuff."

"Right. I guess it'd be a lot easier on you if she didn't care."

"What?"

"You know, she's the First Lady. She can do pretty much anything she wants. She could have come up here by herself. Maybe go to the spa, get her hair and nails done. Eat out all the time. See old friends. But here she is bringing you here, collecting seashells with you on the beach. And I heard her say later there's going to be a big Scrabble tournament."

"I'm good at Scrabble. I almost beat my mom once."

"Wow, that's pretty impressive."

Tommy looked over at his mom. To Reel he said, "Are you close to your mother?"

"She's not alive anymore."

Tommy looked shocked. "Oh, I'm sorry. And your dad?"

Reel pursed her lips and looked away. "He's been gone from my life for a long time."

"Were you ever close to him?"

"No. We didn't have a good relationship at all, Tommy. Which I guess is why I envy people like you. Because you obviously have parents who love you very much. Not all kids do. In fact, too many don't."

Tommy stood there for a bit fingering a shell. "I think I'm going to show my mom this one. I think she'll like it."

"Good idea."

Reel watched as he ran across the packed sand toward his mother.

Then she looked away, out to the ocean, as far as she could see.

When she turned back she looked upward toward the parking lot that bordered the beach.

A small, young Asian woman was walking hand in hand with a little girl about Tommy's age. She could see that the little girl was watching them curiously, although the woman didn't glance their way as they trudged along.

As Reel looked away she was thinking that life was quite odd. And families, in a way, were by far the most satisfying, and exasperating, parts of life.

69

"Who are they?" asked Min.

Chung-Cha glanced at the beach. "Just people. Tourists. They are picking up seashells like we did yesterday."

"Why are all those men around them? And what are those things in their ears?"

"I don't know," said Chung-Cha. "Perhaps they have bad hearing and it helps them."

In that one glance Chung-Cha had registered the fact that the two people who had been at Bukchang were also here. She did not know Robie's or Reel's names, but she wondered if they were here because the Americans had been warned about an attack against the first family. This was certainly a complication that needed to be addressed.

She pulled Min along as they left the parking lot. Chung-Cha sat on a bench and wrote out a note, folded it, and said to Min, "There is a man behind the counter in that store over there." She pointed. "He is short and bald and Korean. You will give him this note."

Min took the paper and looked down at it. "What does it say?"

"Just a note."

"You know this man too? Like at the other place?"

"Yes. Now please go and give it to him. He may ask you to wait while he writes a reply. Go now."

Min hurried across the street and into the shop. Chung-Cha could see the man through the window as Min walked up to the counter. There were no other customers in the shop. He had gotten this job very quickly, because after the summer season was over, many of the young people who performed these tasks went back to the mainland.

She watched as the man read the note and then wrote out a reply for Min to take back. He took a minute to put together some things for Min in a plastic bag, as though she had purchased them.

Min came back across the street with the bag in her hand. She gave Chung-Cha the note and they walked together back to their car. Chung-Cha sat in the driver's seat and read the coded note twice over while Min sat looking at her.

"Something is wrong, Chung-Cha," said Min as Chung-Cha folded up the note and put it in her pocket. "You do not look good."

"I am fine, Min. Just fine."

They drove back to the cottage in silence. When they got there Chung-Cha turned on the fireplace and made herself and Min some hot tea. They sat on the floor in front of the fire.

Finally Min said, "Why did you take me from Yodok?"

Chung-Cha kept her gaze on the flames. "Are you happy that I did so?"

"Yes. But why me?"

"Because you reminded me of . . . me." She glanced at Min to find her gaze full upon her. "Many years before you were there, Min, I was also at that place. I was not born at Yodok, as you were, but I went there at such a young age that I cannot remember my life before Yodok."

"Why did you go there?"

"I was sent there. Because my parents spoke out against our country's leaders."

"Why would they do that?" asked an astonished Min.

Chung-Cha started to shake her head and then said, "Because they once had courage."

Min's eyes widened, as though she could not believe what she had just heard. "Courage?" she asked.

Chung-Cha nodded. "It takes courage to speak your heart, when others do not want you to."

Min thought about this as she sipped her tea. "I guess it does."

"Like when you were defiant in the camp, Min. That took courage. You did not let the guards break you."

Min nodded. "I hated the guards. I hated everyone there."

"They made you hate everyone, even the ones who were like you. That is what they do, so the prisoners will not rise up against them. Instead, they would turn on each other. It makes the guards' job much easier."

Min nodded again. "Because people snitch on each other?"

"Yes," said Chung-Cha. "Yes," she said more emphatically.

"That boy on the beach?" began Min.

"What of him?"

"Do you think he would let me pick up shells with him?"

Chung-Cha froze at this suggestion. "I do not think that would be a good idea, Min," she said slowly.

"Why not?"

"Just not a good idea. I will be back in just a few minutes."

Chung-Cha went into her room and sat down in front of a small desk set against one wall. She took the note out and read through it once more.

The man had voiced his concerns about the presence of Robie and Reel with the first family. He had broached the idea of calling off the hit and waiting for another opportunity.

As the leader of this mission, Chung-Cha knew

that the assassination plan would go forward. They would not get another opportunity like this one. After the Americans were dead a note was to be left behind, written in English, that would detail the crimes that America had committed, crimes that had resulted in the North Koreans taking their revenge on the first family. This, it was believed, would hit the American public very hard. If nothing else, the American media would report anything, whether it made the government or country look bad or not. Such would be unheard of in North Korea.

She glanced toward the door. Min was in there, no doubt wondering what was going on.

Chung-Cha rose and walked into the other room. Min was still sitting in front of the fire, her teacup empty. Chung-Cha sat beside her.

"Would you like me to teach you a few words of English?" asked Chung-Cha.

Min looked surprised but then nodded eagerly.

Chung-Cha faced her and in English said, "I am Min." In Korean she added, "Now you say that."

Min's words came out garbled. But they kept working on it until the three words came out clear.

"Now say, 'I am ten.'"

Min accomplished this after five tries.

"Now put them together. 'I am Min. I am ten.'"

Min said this and waited for more from Chung-Cha, who apparently was deliberating with herself, her features perplexed.

"What next?" asked Min eagerly.

Chung-Cha seemed to reach a decision and faced Min again.

"Now say, 'Will you help me?'"

Min mouthed the words first and then struggled through them. But they kept working on it until she could say them fluently.

"See, now you can speak English," said Chung-Cha.

"What does that last part mean?" asked Min. "'Will you help me?'"

"It is simply a nice greeting. If anything happens to me—" Chung-Cha realized at once that she had made a mistake.

Min's face was instantly full of alarm. "What will happen to you?"

"Nothing, Min, nothing. But one never knows. So if something does, then those words will be good to say. Will you repeat it all again? I want to be sure you remember them."

They went through the words many more times. And as Chung-Cha put Min to bed that night, she heard the little girl saying them over and over.

"I am Min. I am ten. Will you help me?"

Chung-Cha closed her door, rested her forehead on the wood, and felt her chest and throat constrict and tears well up in her eyes.

She said under her breath, "I am Yie Chung-Cha. I am young but old. Will you help me too?"

70

After dinner that night, Eleanor Cassion met with Robie and Reel in the sitting room next to her bedroom.

"I want to thank you," she began.

"For what?" asked Reel.

"Whatever you said to Tommy really seemed to have made an impression. He told me this afternoon that he's going to control his anger at school and work more on developing friends."

"He's a really good kid, ma'am," said Reel. "He's just struggling with being part of the first family."

"I know this is only a small step and there will be challenges ahead, but it is something very positive, as far as I'm concerned."

"Glad we could help," said Reel.

"I hope you're enjoying yourselves. I don't know where your last mission was, but I doubt it was as bucolic and relaxing as it is here."

"It was most definitely not," said Robie.

She looked at him. "Now, if my daughter gets to be too much for you, please let me know. She can be quite headstrong and believes that she's already fully grown and knows everything."

"It'll be fine, Mrs. Cassion," said Robie. "She's, well, she's a very confident young woman."

"Yes, she is," said Eleanor. "A little *too* confident, if you ask me."

A bit later Robie was strolling through the rear grounds of the property and stopped in front of a faded flowerbed that would soon be turned under. The air was brisk and he zipped up his jacket.

He heard a door close behind him and turned around. Claire Cassion was advancing toward him. She had on another pair of skinny jeans and a long knitted sweater. In her front pocket he could see the outline of her smartphone. She had traded in the stilettos for clunky boots that were more suited to the wet grass. She gripped a mug of coffee with both hands as she walked up.

"Nice night," she said. She held the mug up to her face and then said, "Nothing like coffee on a crisp night in Nantucket."

"You like coffee?" said Robie.

"My mother doesn't like me to drink too much. But when I pull all-nighters studying, it helps. And when I go to college I'm sure it'll be part of my diet." She set the mug down on a table next to a swing and pulled out her phone. "Hey, would you mind taking a picture with me? I'd like to post it on my Facebook page."

"I'm afraid I can't do that," said Robie.

"My mom won't mind. Well, I'll explain it to her."

"It's not that. It's just that my work for the government requires me, well, to remain in the background."

She put her phone away and her casual look and tone vanished. "Oh, I didn't know that."

"It's not something either I or Agent Reel can talk about."

She sat on the swing and motioned for him to sit next to her. Robie reluctantly did. She picked up her mug and looked over at a Secret Service agent who was patrolling the perimeter of the property. "Nothing like having armed guards with you all the time."

"But think of the stories you'll have to tell. There really haven't been that many presidents, or that many first daughters. You're in pretty select company."

"I guess. It just doesn't seem so, well, great right now." She paused and studied him. "Have you known Agent Reel long?"

"Pretty long. We trained together way back when."

"Is she good?"

"She wouldn't have lasted all these years if she wasn't."

"Is she better than you?" Claire added playfully.

Robie looked at her with a serious expression. "In some ways, yes, she is. She's also saved my life. More than once."

Claire's features turned serious again and she took a nervous sip of her coffee.

He said, "So, you like your school?"

"Yeah, I do. I've made some good friends." She hesitated. "Mostly girls. The guys are—"

"You said immature? Sorry, that may not change much even when they get older."

"It's not so much that. But think about it. They have to come to the White House to pick me up for a date?"

"I can imagine your father can be pretty intimidating for a young man."

"My dad's a softie. It's my mom who's the tough one."

"I'm sure she's just looking out for you."

"Yeah, well, sometimes she looks out too much."

"What about your brother?"

"What about him?"

"You two get along?"

"He's ten. I don't have that much to do with him. He's still just a kid, Will."

"He's also going through a rough time. He ever try and talk to you about it?"

"He would never come to me with something like that."

"Why?"

"I mean, I'm almost six years older than he is. And he's a boy. And I'm, well, I'm a *woman*."

527

"I guess there is sort of a big gap in age between the two of you."

Now Claire looked pained. "My mom, um, she had a miscarriage when I was about three."

"I'm sorry to hear that."

Claire looked shocked that she had divulged this information. "Oh my God, please don't tell anyone I told you that. I mean, very few people know and it never came out during the campaign and I know my mom would—"

Robie said, "Claire, I don't repeat things people tell me to anyone. Ever."

She breathed a sigh of relief. "Thanks."

"But back to your brother. Did you two used to talk?"

"Sure, I mean, before Dad got elected. He was a governor before then. We lived in the executive mansion and everything, but it was nothing like this. Tommy was a sweet kid. He looked up to me."

"I think he still does."

She smiled. "There was this one year we went trick-or-treating? Dad went with us, on the sly so the camera crew wouldn't follow us. You know what he was dressed as?"

Robie shook his head. "What?"

"Maleficent. You know, the wicked character from Disney's *Sleeping Beauty*. Everybody thought it was my mom. But she was in really high heels and was dressed as Darth Vader. That's who they thought Dad was. It was really fun. It was like our own family secret. Something only we knew, when, you know . . ."

"Everybody knew everything about you?"

She looked at him. "Yeah," she said ruefully.

"I saw you had on a Yale sweatshirt. You thinking of going there in a few years?"

"If I get in."

"The president's daughter? I think you'll be fine."

"But that's not how it's supposed to work. I don't want to get in because of him. I want to get in because of me."

"That's a great way to look at things," said Robie.

"Besides, my dad went to Yale. My mom went to Columbia. I'm thinking of UVA. I went there a few times. Charlottesville is beautiful."

"Mr. Jefferson's university. The man who could not live without books."

"Not a bad guy to emulate."

Robie was about to say something when he heard the bang. In a second he had Claire down on the ground, shielding her with his body, and his gun was out, making sweeping arcs in front of him.

He heard feet running toward them and his finger slipped to the trigger guard as he crouched down, keeping his free hand on Claire's shoulder.

Claire said in a quavering voice, "What is it? What's happening, Will?"

In a low voice he said, "Just stay down, Claire. I won't let anything happen to you."

A Secret Service agent came running around the corner of the house and saw Robie. "Stand down, stand down, Agent Robie. There's no threat," he yelled.

Robie did not yet lower his weapon. The back door of the house opened and Reel and the First Lady came out, surrounded by agents.

Reel called out, "It was a backfire, Robie. Car passing the house."

Robie put his gun away and helped Claire up. "You okay?"

She was shaking but nodded. "Thanks, Will. I don't think I've ever seen anybody move that fast."

"Claire, honey?" said her mother anxiously.

Claire ran to her mom and the two women hugged.

Reel walked over to Robie. "Great, now you're really her hero."

"They sure it was just a backfire?"

"That's what they reported."

"Okay," he said, not looking convinced.

"Why, you think otherwise?"

"I always assume the worst. That way I'm rarely disappointed."

71

The team came to the cottage very late at night.

Min was in bed. Chung-Cha received them at the door and ushered them in. They sat at the table in the kitchen and spoke swiftly in Korean.

One of the men and the woman were the same ones who had ridden on the train to D.C. with Chung-Cha and Min. Another of the men was Kim Jing-Sang, a highly skilled operative from North Korea's Interior Ministry who had arrived two days ago. They all discussed and Chung-Cha quickly vetoed the idea of postponing the mission because of the presence of Robie and Reel. No one questioned her decision.

They spread out pictures and diagrams and maps and briefing papers on the table. They were calmly discussing it all as if it were a college midterm team project rather than the plans to assassinate a family.

Chung-Cha held up seven fingers. "That is the number of Secret Service agents. The staff is irrelevant. They are not armed."

The woman said, "But there is local police support."

Chung-Cha shook her head. "I have observed them the last few days. They are nothing. They will be no problem."

"And the man and woman?" said one of the men. "That helped free General Pak's children?"

"A good thing for us," said Chung-Cha. "Two birds with one stone, I think is what the Americans say. We will kill them at the same time." She looked at Jing-Sang. "My colleague will now discuss what will happen after the targets are eliminated. And his words come directly from the Supreme Leader."

Jing-Sang took from his pocket a small vial. "The Supreme Leader wants the world to know who did this. He wants them to understand that the United States cannot impose its will on our people without retribution. In order to ensure that such is the case, we will each be given a vial such as this. We will then take the contents of the vial after the mission is complete. It is fast-acting. We will be dead within a few minutes." He looked in the direction of the bedroom where Min was asleep.

"The little bitch must be taken care of too," he reminded her.

"I will deal with her myself," said Chung-Cha.

Jing-Sang nodded. "Of course, Comrade Yie. And it was good cover to bring her in the first place.

Americans never see evil in children. She is from Yodok, correct?"

"Yes."

Jing-Sang continued. "Then it hardly matters. It is not like anyone will miss her. It is not like she is one of the core and thus has value."

"Absolutely," said Chung-Cha.

But under the table her fingers curled into a fist. *I am also from Yodok,* she thought.

Out loud she said, "Now there only remains the details of the actual attack. We believe that we have it in place and that it will provide us the best opportunity for success."

She drew a paper from a file and unfolded it for all of them to see. "There is a holiday that the Americans celebrate where they dress in costumes," she said.

"Halloween," added Jing-Sang.

"Yes. It is a stupid thing that they spend much money on. There is a parade that begins in the downtown section in front of a church. It proceeds through the main streets."

"But there will be many people around," said one of the men. "That means distractions and obstructions and potential chaos. How can we be assured of our targets and reliable sight lines?"

Chung-Cha said, "For one simple reason. Our targets will be gathering at the town hall before the parade for a meeting with the person who is the mayor of this Nantucket and a few other important local people. The town hall will be otherwise empty. The parade does not start until two hours later. We will strike there and we will strike hard. We will pierce the outer circle of security and then the inner. And then we will complete our mission."

Jing-Sang said, "How did you come by this information? Is it reliable?"

"We have a person who helps to clean the mayor's office," Chung-Cha said. "He overheard them talking. And the itinerary for the town hall event was left on his desk last night. Our person photographed it. It is reliable. I have verified it myself."

Jing-Sang nodded. "Excellent."

"And now this holiday, Halloween, gives us the perfect way to breach their security wall," noted Chung-Cha.

She knew that the Secret Service was prepared to die to protect its charges. But then she was prepared to die in order to kill those same charges.

They finished their meeting and said their goodbyes. Before he left, Jing-Sang pressed two vials into Chung-Cha's hand.

"To the glory, Comrade Yie. To the glory."

She closed the door behind him and pocketed the vials.

Chung-Cha sat in front of the gas fire and finally fell asleep. She awoke with a start when she heard the noise. Her hand slipped to her pocket and closed around the knife. It was the same knife she had used to kill the British envoy.

The cottage was dark, the fire the only illumination. She heard cautious footsteps coming from the kitchen. She silently made her way to that spot and peered around the corner.

Min had poured out a glass of milk and was drinking it at the table.

Then Min stopped, put the glass down, and picked up the photo. The photo that Chung-Cha had foolishly left on the table; she had fallen asleep before picking everything up and hiding it.

Chung-Cha went into the kitchen and Min looked up at her.

"Why do you have this, Chung-Cha?" she asked, turning the photo around.

Looking back at her from the grainy photo were Eleanor, Claire, and Tommy Cassion.

Chung-Cha fingered the vials in her pocket and eyed the glass of milk. Death by cyanide was relatively quick but not painless. Would a bullet be better? Quick, no pain. Min would never know it was Chung-Cha who had done it.

She said, "A friend brought those by. He was just taking some different pictures of people and places here."

"These are the people from the beach. The boy picking seashells."

Chung-Cha came over to her, took the photo, and looked at it. "You're right. I had not noticed that."

"I did not hear anyone come tonight."

"It was late. You were already asleep." Chung-Cha ran a hand down Min's hair. "Now you should go back to sleep, Min."

The little girl was gazing down at the picture, and then she looked up at Chung-Cha. Her lip trembled and Chung-Cha recalled that the reason she had picked Min to take from the camp was her obvious spirit. And intelligence.

"Chung-Cha?" began Min.

"Not tonight, Min. We will talk about things tomorrow. But not tonight."

She put the girl back in bed and lay with her for a while until Min was breathing evenly and eventually fell asleep.

Then Chung-Cha did not go to bed, but went outside and sat in a wooden chair and stared at a sky that was filled with stars while a breeze lifted her hair and the smell of the nearby waters filled her nostrils.

She took the vials of poison from her pocket and held them in front of her. They were small, yet deadly.

Just as she was.

She envisioned herself lying among the dead at the town hall. The police and American agents swarming all over the scene. The world coming to understand what had happened. Perhaps the Americans and her country would go to war over this, with only one inevitable outcome.

Then she put the vials back in her pocket, laid her head back against the rough gray wood of the chair, closed her eyes, and thought of being in a place and a life that was as different from hers as it was possible to be.

72

"Omigod, Will, you can be Darth Vader," said Claire as they were finishing up lunch at the house.

She next looked fixedly at Reel. "And you could be Maleficent."

"Thanks," said Reel dryly.

Eleanor pretended to look hurt. "Hey, I thought I was Darth Vader."

Tommy put down his fork and said, "I don't care about the rest of you guys, I'm going as Wolverine. He's, like, the coolest."

"What will you go as?" Reel asked Claire.

"Oh, I'm really too old for that stuff. I might just put on a wig and pretend I'm a TV character from like way back in the early 2000s."

Eleanor looked at Reel comically. "Way back in the early 2000s? I have never felt so old."

"What time is the thing tonight?" asked Claire.

"We go to the town hall first. I have offered us up to be sort of the parade's grand marshals. So we're having a little pre-parade meeting followed by a reception at the town hall. The mayor will be there along with a few others."

"Meaning it will be really boring," said Claire.

"Meaning it will not take that long and it will mean a lot to the folks here," replied her mother briskly.

Robie looked at Reel. "You up for Maleficent?"

"I don't have the costume."

"I had them packed," said Eleanor. "I knew we'd be celebrating Halloween up here. I was hoping the president could make it, but that's apparently not going to happen."

"What are you going to be, Mom?" asked Tommy.

"I think this year I'll venture way, way back to the seventies and go as Cher." She confided to Reel, who was seated next to her, "I've always loved all her different looks over the years. Especially her hair."

"Share? Share what?" asked Tommy, looking confused. He had obviously never heard of the singer.

Eleanor said, "Need to know, and you don't."

After lunch was done Robie and Reel went outside.

"Town hall Halloween parade?"

"Yeah, sounds like a blast," said Reel, without a trace of enthusiasm.

"I take it you never went trick-or-treating?"

"You take it correctly."

"Well, you can make up for lost time."

"I'm glad we'll be leaving here soon; I'm starting to feel claustrophobic."

"So no islands in your future?"

"I'm more of a city girl."

"You had a cottage on the Eastern Shore in the middle of nowhere," Robie pointed out.

"That's why I'm a city girl now. I got sick of that."

"I guess the Secret Service will scope out the town hall and the parade route."

"Guess so. I'm sure they're not too happy about this. Lots of people, in costume. Easy to conceal stuff, weapons, explosives."

"No, they are not happy. At least the president's not here. If he were I'm not sure they'd be doing the parade."

"Are you really going to dress up?" she asked.

"Why not?"

"And I have to be Maleficent, huh?"

"Well, it does fit your personality," said Robie.

She punched him in the arm.

"So when we get back to the mainland, what then?" he asked.

"Wait for the next call-up."

"Doubtful it will be the both of us. They tend to send us out solo."

"I know that, Robie."

"I'm thinking I have about another year of doing this and then I'm calling it a career."

She looked surprised. "When did you decide that?"

"It seems like just now, but I've been thinking about it for a while." He stretched his arm where the burned skin was. "Your little booby-trap on the Eastern Shore made me think about my life, I guess." He smiled to show her he was kidding, but Reel did not return the look.

"I can't tell you how awful I feel about almost killing you."

"We were on opposite sides back then. It happened. I made it out. We're okay."

She looked at his arm and leg where she knew the burns were. "I'll make it up to you somehow, Robie."

"I think you already have."

"How?"

"Well, most recently, North Korea."

"Doesn't seem like enough."

"Trust me, it was," he replied.

"Are you really serious about getting out?"

"I am very serious."

"What will you do?"

He shrugged. "Who says I have to do anything? I've saved enough money. I live simply. I've seen the world, or at least the bad parts of it. I might just do . . . nothing."

"You don't believe that, Robie. Not for a second."

"I might do nothing, for a while. And then I'll figure it out." He studied her. "What about you? You were all fired up to call it a career."

"Yeah, but then you said we could continue our

careers *and* have a normal life. You made me believe that was possible."

"I still think it is."

"But now you're quitting," said Reel in a tone that indicated she felt he was betraying her.

"I said I'm leaving in a year. In our line of work a year can be a lifetime. What about you?"

"What about me?"

"I know Evan Tucker had a private discussion with you. What did he say? That no matter how long it takes he's going to bring you down?"

She let out a long breath and shook her head. "No, he basically apologized for all the stuff he'd done."

"What?" said Robie, looking stunned.

"He said I was right and he was wrong."

"Had he been drinking? Did his pupils look normal?"

"I think he knew exactly what he was saying, Robie."

"Well, how the hell do you like that? I wonder what happened for him to change his mind like that."

"He said he'd reviewed all the evidence and had given it a lot of thought. Plus you and I had almost gotten killed trying to stop the conspiracy Gelder and Jacobs were involved in. And you and I risked our lives in Syria and in North Korea. I guess it all added up for him."

"So does that change things for you?" he asked.

"How so?"

"You going to stay on for a while?"

"I don't know. Probably not. Especially if you're not going to be around."

He put an arm around her shoulders. "Well, you've got a year to think about that."

"Yeah, if I live that long."

73

Min had never heard of Halloween.

She had never worn a costume.

She still didn't understand what Halloween was, though Chung-Cha had tried to explain it to her. But she now had on a costume and she had been given Halloween candy. They were at a small café on the main street of the downtown area that had been turned into a kids' party room before the parade was to start.

Chung-Cha had taken Min, who was dressed as a frog, her face hidden behind the costume, only her eyes and mouth visible. Chung-Cha was in the costume of a pirate. The café was filled with children in a wide variety of outfits. At first Min had been terrified to have the frog costume on. But once Chung-Cha had shown her it was only plastic and cloth and couldn't hurt her, she allowed Chung-Cha to dress her up.

At the front of the café, giving out candy, were the Cassions. When Chung-Cha saw this she panicked slightly. She had seen security people roaming outside, but she never thought that meant the first family would be handing out candy.

She said to Min, "Go get your candy, I will be back." Then she hurried to the far corner of the café, quickly becoming lost among all the other costumed folks.

Min looked around frantically for her. With the frog costume covering her ears, she had barely heard what Chung-Cha had said, and then when she saw that she was gone, she started to panic. However, she was being herded with the rest of the kids to receive her candy from the Cassions.

As she got to the front of the line, Min was badly scared. She could not see Chung-Cha anywhere, and kids and their parents were crowding in on her from all sides.

When she looked up she was standing directly in front of Tommy Cassion, who was, as he had said, dressed as Wolverine. She looked at him and he looked at her.

"Nice frog," said Tommy as he held out a handful of candy.

Out of Min's panicked mind came one thought. She said, "My name is Min. I am ten. Will you help me?"

Tommy looked at her strangely as he dumped the candy into her pumpkin bucket.

Then Min said something else, but it wasn't in English. She had reverted to Korean.

"Are you okay?" asked Tommy.

"My name is Min. I am ten. Will you help me?"

Tommy started to say something, but a hand reached out and pulled Min away so that other kids could get their candy.

Min looked around the room and breathed a sigh of relief when Chung-Cha rushed over to her. Before she could say anything, Chung-Cha knelt down and hugged her.

"It's okay, Min. I'm right here. It's okay."

Chung-Cha led her outside and then down the street away from the crowds. They reached an alleyway where there was a little brick stoop. Chung-Cha perched next to Min on the bottom step. She had made certain that none of her team had seen them. They also didn't know that Min was dressed as a frog. Chung-Cha would carry out her mission, but Min would be safe. Min was not going to die. Not by Chung-Cha's hand.

"Min, you have to listen to me very carefully, okay?"

Min nodded, the frog head bobbing up and down.

"I have to go away for a little bit."

Min started to jump up, but Chung-Cha held her back.

"Just for a little bit."

From the alleyway she looked across the street where the town police station was located.

"Do you see that place over there?" She pointed.

Min looked past her and nodded.

"I want you to take my watch." She slipped it off her wrist and handed it to Min. "Now, when this little line gets here, I want you to go over to that place and tell them what I told you to say. You remember it? In English? Can you say it for me?"

"I am Min. I am ten. Will you help me?"

"That is perfect, Min. Perfect. Now, remember, when this line reaches this point, that is when you will go."

Chung-Cha was indicating an hour from now.

"But where will you be, Chung-Cha?"

"I have a few things to do. But I know those people over there will take care of you until I get back. They are good people, Min. They will help you."

"But you *are* coming back, aren't you?" said Min fearfully.

"I will be back," said Chung-Cha, forcing herself to smile. And then she thought to herself, *Please forgive me for that lie, Min. And please don't forget me. I only want your life to be a good one.*

Min reached out and wrapped her arms around her. Chung-Cha returned her hug, fighting back the tears.

"I love you, Chung-Cha."

"And I love you, Min."

Fifteen minutes later Chung-Cha joined her team near the target location. They were all dressed in costumes.

Jing-Sang came up to her. "Ready, Comrade?"

"Of course."

"And Min?"

"She is back at the cottage. She drank her milk . . . and went to sleep."

Jing-Sang smiled. "Then let us do this great deed. To the glory, Chung-Cha."

"To the glory," repeated Chung-Cha.

Out on the main street the elements of the parade were assembling. There were motorized vehicles with floats built on them, a high school band, dozens of costumed zombies, and a plethora of other colorfully clad Halloweeners.

There was also a long Chinese dragon that had emerged from an alley. Underneath its cover one could just make out a number of sneakered feet marching along.

"We ready to move to the town hall, Sam?" Eleanor Cassion was looking at her protection detail leader.

He spoke into his walkie-talkie and then gave her a thumbs-up. "We're ready to roll, ma'am. Side entrance over there. Two-minute walk to the left and up the front steps."

He and another of his men stood on either side of the Cassions as they filed toward the door.

Sam gave Robie and Reel a high sign. They nodded and fell into step behind the Cassions.

Claire was dressed in a poofed-out long blonde wig with a headband and skinny jeans. She turned and looked at Robie, who wasn't in costume. "Can you guess who I am?"

He shook his head while Reel, who had also decided against dressing up as Maleficent, looked on, a curious expression on her face.

"Stevie Nicks. She was a singer with some band way back."

"Uh, that *some* band would be Fleetwood Mac," said Reel.

"Yeah, them. They were apparently really popular at some point."

"I thought you were going as some TV character from way back in the early 2000s," said Robie.

"I was, but I couldn't think of any. My mom told me about this Stevie person and she had a blonde wig."

"Yay for Mom," said Reel.

The local police and the Secret Service detail surrounded the Cassions as they walked down the street toward the town hall. The sun was setting and the sky looked nearly molten. The wind was picking up and there was the threat of rain later that evening, something the parade organizers were desperately hoping would not happen.

74

They were nearly at the town hall when Robie spotted it. The Chinese dragon marched into place near the front doors of the building. He observed the great many feet under the dragon's skin.

He looked at Reel, whose gaze was also on the dragon.

"Better to be safe than sorry," he said, and Reel nodded in agreement.

He spoke into his walkie-talkie, and a minute later the Cassions were being hustled into the town hall. Several deputies raced over to the Chinese dragon and started pulling up the dragon's "skin."

Robie saw astonished faces revealed when they did so.

They were teenagers. American teenagers.

Robie smiled at Reel. "Okay, I'm officially paranoid."

"You think?" she replied.

They entered the town hall and Robie said to Sam, "Dragon was a false alarm. Sorry, kind of like the car backfire."

"No harm, no foul," replied Sam, though he looked a bit put off.

Eleanor came over to them. "What is going on?"

"False alarm, ma'am," said Sam. "We can proceed on schedule and—"

He didn't get a chance to finish as a round hit him in the head, spraying everyone with blood.

Robie grabbed Eleanor and jerked her downward as Reel turned and fired shots in the direction from which the round had come.

Making her stay low, Robie pushed Eleanor toward the others. He yelled to one Secret Service agent who was shielding the two children, "Get them through that door. Now!"

Another agent came up to help, and together they pushed the kids ahead of them.

Claire started crying as she saw Sam dead on the floor. Tommy looked too afraid to make a sound.

Eleanor called out to her children even as one of the agents with them was hit in the back of the head and went down, falling over a stack of chairs.

A body came tumbling down from the second-floor balcony and hit the floor hard. It was one of the deputies from the local police. He'd been shot in the forehead.

"They've got the high ground," yelled out Reel as she kept backing away, acting as the rear guard and firing widely angled shots at the balcony to provide cover.

"Move, move!" Robie urged Eleanor as more shots rang out.

The other agent with Claire and Tommy went down with a bullet in his spine.

"Reel!" yelled Robie.

Reel catapulted across the room and hit the man who had just appeared in the doorway. Her kick crushed his face and sent him flying backward, his weapon sailing away. Before he could try to get up, Reel had fired a bullet into his head.

The next instant she was falling backward as another man struck her low, driving his shoulder into her gut. She hit the floor and spun away on the smooth wood. She still had her gun and was preparing to fire when a shot rang out. The man who had hit Reel stood there stiffly for a second and then toppled forward, his face largely gone from the round Robie had fired into it.

Claire and Eleanor screamed as another man raced into the room brandishing an MP5 submachine gun. But before he could fire, Robie forced him to take cover when he emptied his clip at the man. Robie pulled Eleanor along and through a doorway as Reel sprinted across the room, hurdled a table, grabbed both kids, and propelled them into the same interior room, kicking the door shut behind her.

Back in the main room another Secret Service agent and a deputy raced in. The deputy was shot in the chest and went down before even firing his gun.

The agent fired three shots at the second floor and a yell indicated that he had struck someone. Then he went down in a hail of fire from the man toting the MP5. But he still managed to empty his clip and killed the man who had just ended his life.

Inside the other room Robie and Reel pulled the first family away from the doorway and flattened them to the floor just in time. MP5 rounds ripped through it, spraying metal and wood in all directions.

As soon as the shooting stopped, Robie and Reel led Eleanor and her kids through another interior doorway. Robie locked the door and then surveyed the room. It was small, windowless, and there was a set of stairs leading down.

Reel had already eyed it. "Probably the cellar," she said. "Curved staircase."

"Constrained fields of fire," he replied, understanding immediately. "Gives us an edge."

"Not much choice. Let's do it."

They propelled the first family down the steps. The cellar was even smaller than the room above and had no exit.

They were trapped.

There was a stout wooden table that they immediately overturned, putting Eleanor and her children behind it.

They could all hear the gun battle taking place around them. There were screams, and the zings of bullets missing, and then the thuds of bullets hitting and then bodies falling.

Claire was now hysterical.

Tommy simply seemed paralyzed.

Eleanor looked at Robie; she was scared, but when she spoke her voice was firm. "How do we get my children safely out of here, Agent Robie?"

Reel was surveying the staircase. She had already reloaded and she'd also taken pistols from the slain agents. She flipped a spare to Robie.

Robie said, "We're working on it, ma'am. We will do our best."

He tried the walkie-talkie three times but no one answered.

Eleanor looked at him in disbelief. "But that means . . ." she began, shooting a worried glance at her daughter, who was still sobbing uncontrollably.

Robie nodded and said quietly, "They're all gone."

He punched 911 on his phone. It just rang. "They must be swamped with calls," he concluded.

He looked at Claire and Tommy.

"Tommy?" The boy didn't look up.

"Wolverine! You with me?"

He looked at Robie and gave a small nod.

Reel said, "Claire? Claire? Hey, Stevie Nicks! Listen up."

Claire gulped, stopped sobbing, caught her breath, and finally looked at her.

Reel ran her gaze along the three of them. "We

can't sugarcoat this. The situation is bad. We've got some cover here. And we've got some weapons. We don't know how many there are out there. But there's got to be more of them than there are of us." She looked at Robie and then continued. "But we are here with you and we will stay with you the whole way. To get to you, they have to go through us. Okay?"

The three slowly nodded.

"Now stay down behind the table."

A few seconds later, three shots rang out and a man tumbled down the stairs and came to rest at the bottom.

Robie looked over to see Reel lowering her weapon, smoke still rising off the muzzle.

She said, "He was trying to be quiet, but didn't quite manage it."

Eleanor said, "I don't hear any sirens."

"The police force here consists of about thirty sworn officers," said Reel. "There were ten assigned to your detail. They might already all be dead. The other side has MP5s, which can do a lot of damage in a short period of time. And pistols are pretty much useless against them. The rest of the cops might not be here yet."

Robie looked around the room and was also listening for footfalls from above. The ceiling was thick. He didn't think the other side could fire through it. They would have to come down the stairs.

But they had already sent one man in and they knew how that had worked out. Robie and Reel had the advantage here because of the curved staircase. Their enemies couldn't attack them en masse or straight on. The curve allowed Robie and Reel to fire before the attackers could line up their shots.

They suddenly heard a loud bang from upstairs and then people screamed and then there was gunfire. And then more screams. And more gunfire.

And then silence.

And then they heard voices. But the words were not English.

"Shit," muttered Reel.

She looked at Robie. His gaze was on a shelf in the corner.

On the shelf was a stack of old clothes. She once more glanced at Robie, who nodded.

Reel ran and grabbed some of the clothes. She flipped out her knife and started cutting them up.

"What are you doing?" asked Eleanor.

"Getting us some protection," Robie answered.

"But those won't stop bullets," said Eleanor.

When Reel was done they worked the small strips of cloth into their ears and then tied other pieces that Reel had fashioned in the size and shape of kerchiefs around their necks. They helped Eleanor and the kids do the same.

"What are these for?" asked Tommy.

"Flash-bangs," answered Reel. "That's what we just

heard. They're really loud and the light flash is blind-ing. And there's a lot of smoke. The other side obviously has them."

"They're used to disorient," added Robie. "And they do that job well."

They heard more shots come from upstairs and then a number of footfalls.

Robie and Reel eyed each other and then pushed Eleanor and the kids flat to the floor. "Cover your eyes and nose with the cloth and put your hands over your ears. And stay down."

Robie and Reel took up their positions, each with one hand on their kerchiefs to pull them up quickly. Only they wouldn't have much time to recover and return the fire that was surely going to follow the flash-bangs. But then they didn't have any other options.

They heard the door open and then down they came.

Not one flash-bang or two.

There were three of them.

Robie and Reel hit the floor a second before the trio of explosives detonated. The combined sound was deafening, blowing right through the bits of cloth pushed into their ears, and the hands that covered those ears couldn't do much to deaden the noise. The smoke penetrated right through the flimsy cloth and into their mouths, noses, and lungs. And the flashes of light were like looking into the sun even though they were staring at the floor.

Eleanor and her children screamed and then all three passed out.

By the time Robie and Reel staggered to their feet, coughing and sickened by the blasts, smoke, and light, they were surrounded and outgunned.

MP5s against pistols.

North Koreans wanting bloody revenge.

It was over.

75

By the time Eleanor and her children came to, Robie and Reel had had their weapons taken from them and they stood with their hands behind their heads. Their faces were ashen and they swayed on their feet, looking nauseated and unbalanced.

"Oh my God," said Eleanor as she rose, pulling her children up with her and then putting them protectively behind her.

Composing himself, Robie said to the North Koreans, "This place is surrounded. You're not going to get away. If you surrender now, you will not be harmed." He knew as soon as the words were out of his mouth that the North Koreans didn't care about getting away. He could see it in all their faces.

Five men and one woman. The woman was dressed as a pirate. She looked vaguely familiar.

Chung-Cha stepped forward and said, "We are here to right the wrongs of your president."

Reel said, "Gotta tell you, this is not a great way to go about it."

Chung-Cha said, "You and he were in our country.

You took prisoners that belonged to us. Your country planned to kill our leader. For that you must and you will pay. All of you."

Eleanor said, "I have no idea what—"

Jing-Sang fired shots into the ceiling. "Do not interrupt, woman!" he roared, as Eleanor, Claire, and Tommy dropped to their knees, shaking with fear.

Chung-Cha continued. "You will all die right here. This will be a message to the world that the evil empire of America cannot and will not attack our great country without retribution that is fierce and swift and noble."

Robie said, "You'll need hostages to get out of here. Five is unmanageable. Take me and my partner. Like you said, we were the ones over there. We took your prisoners. These folks did nothing. Leave them here and use us to get out of here."

"We are not getting out of here," said Jing-Sang. He pointed his muzzle at the floor. "We die right here. After *you* do, that is."

"So this is a suicide mission," said Reel.

Jing-Sang smiled and shook his head. "It is death with great honor."

He looked at Chung-Cha. "Comrade Yie is the very best that we have. She has killed more enemies of our country than you could possibly imagine. Your deaths will at least be efficiently done, that I can guarantee."

Chung-Cha sliced the air with her hand and Jing-

Sang fell silent and took a respectful step back, bowing as he did so.

Chung-Cha slipped a pair of knives from sheaths riding on her belt. The blades were customized, serrated and slightly curved. She looked first at Robie and then at Reel.

Robie expected to see a face of pure hatred staring at him. Or perhaps he would only be looking at a blank face, all humanity long since driven from her.

But that was not what was staring back at him.

Jing-Sang said nervously, "Comrade Yie, we must hurry. We killed many of the enemy, but they will undoubtedly have more on the way."

Chung-Cha nodded, said a few words in Korean, and then looked at Robie and Reel.

She said, in English, "I am sorry for this."

Then she attacked.

She turned and gutted Jing-Sang with one of her knives, ripping upward. His gun fell from his grip but she snatched it before it hit the floor. She fired once, hitting the next man in the brain. With her free hand she threw her other knife and it plunged into the third man's chest.

The other two men were stunned by Chung-Cha's action but opened fire. However, she had gripped the third man, spun him around, and used his body as a shield, absorbing the fired rounds.

She then pushed him forward into the two men, dropped low, slid across the floor, and kicked the legs of the fourth man out from under him. As he fell, she pulled the knife free from the chest of the third man and raked it across the throat of the fourth man. Arterial spray covered her and the floor.

Chung-Cha never stopped moving. She somersaulted across the floor as the remaining man fired at her but missed.

Robie and Reel had grabbed the first family and thrown them behind the table again. Then the pair scrambled across the room to retrieve their weapons.

But they were not as fast as Chung-Cha. She had pushed off the far wall, flipping completely over the last man. As she went past him the thin razor line was revealed in her hands. She slipped the wire around the man's neck while she was in midair, hit the ground on both feet, and pulled with all her strength, at the same time crossing her arms and forming an X.

The man gurgled once and then dropped to the floor, bleeding out a few seconds later from his nearly severed head.

Chung-Cha straightened and then dropped the wire. She turned to look at the devastation she had wrought. Five men dead, all by her hand, all in less than a minute. She was breathing rapidly, her eyes focused and her limbs tensed.

She turned to face Robie and Reel, who had their weapons now. They were pointed at her, but neither agent had a finger on the trigger guard.

Robie said, "You want to explain why you just did what you did?"

Chung-Cha looked back at Eleanor and her children as they slowly rose from behind the table. Eleanor put her hands over Claire's and Tommy's faces so they wouldn't see the dead men.

"I hope that you are not hurt," said Chung-Cha.

Eleanor slowly shook her head, but her face betrayed her bewilderment.

"I'm okay," she said slowly. "We're okay. Thanks to you."

Chung-Cha turned back to Robie and Reel.

Reel took a cautious step forward. "That was the most amazing piece of close-quarter combat I've ever seen," she said admiringly. "But like my partner said, why?"

"We were sent here to kill them," said Chung-Cha, indicating Eleanor and her children. "The others always intended to do this."

"But not you?" asked Robie.

Chung-Cha did not answer right away. "I do not know," she said. "But in the end I could not kill this family," she added. "I just could not."

"Change of heart?" asked Reel with a skeptical look.

"I do not have a heart," said Chung-Cha firmly. "I am from Yodok. I will always be from Yodok. They took my heart many years ago. You cannot grow another back."

"Yodok," said Robie. "Then you were . . . ?"

"Yes."

Reel studied her more closely and said, "I've seen you before. Near the beach. You were with a little girl."

Chung-Cha nodded. "Her name is Min."

Tommy spoke up. "She was dressed as a frog. She told me she was ten. And that she needed help or something."

Robie looked at Chung-Cha with incredulity. "You brought a child on the mission?"

Chung-Cha said fiercely, "Min is not involved with any of this. She is innocent. She is just a little girl. From Yodok too. She still has her heart. Do not take it from her. Please do not. She is just a little girl who knows nothing."

Reel looked at her. "Why did you bring Min here?"

"I told my superiors it was for part of our cover. That Americans do not think badly of children."

"But the real reason?"

"To get her out of my country. To give her . . . a chance . . . elsewhere."

Chung-Cha reached into her pocket and slipped out one of the poison vials. "None of us were supposed to survive this," she said.

Robie said, "Death with great honor?"

"Including Min," said Chung-Cha slowly. "But I . . .

I could not let that happen. She has done nothing wrong. Min is just a child. An innocent child."

"Then I don't think you lost your heart at Yodok either," Reel said quietly.

Robie added, "But it was still extraordinary to turn on your own team."

"I . . . am . . . just . . . tired of it," said Chung-Cha simply, and her limbs relaxed as she said it. "Of it all."

Robie and Reel exchanged a knowing glance. He said, "What is your name? Other than Comrade Yie."

"Chung-Cha."

"Who were those men, Chung-Cha?" asked Reel, indicating the dead.

"From my country. Their identities do not matter. There are many just like them back home. There will always be many just like them back home."

"I won't lie to you, Chung-Cha," said Robie. "You're in a world of trouble. Even with what you did here."

Eleanor said, "But surely saving our lives will count for a great deal."

"You'll have to cooperate and give a full debriefing," said Reel. "Exactly how you were able to get here undetected, how you knew of their itinerary, how you breached security—"

The shot rang out and the bullet pierced Chung-Cha's neck.

Robie and Reel looked over at the curved staircase. A young deputy was holding his pistol in two shaky hands. He smiled and yelled, "I got her. I got the little Asian piece of shit."

Chung-Cha did not fall right away. She simply stood there as blood poured down her front.

Robie screamed, "No, you idiot!" He lunged for the deputy and knocked the gun out of his hand.

Reel was able to grab hold of Chung-Cha before she fell to the floor. She gently laid her down. She saw the bullet's entry wound and stuck her fingers inside it, trying to close the struck artery, but she couldn't get the bleeding to stop. She tore off her shirtsleeve and pressed the cloth over the wound, trying to stanch the bleeding.

"Come on, stay with me. Come on, Chung-Cha, look at me. Focus right on me." She turned and screamed, "Robie, we need an ambulance. And we need it now!"

Robie had already hit 911 on his phone. And this time the call went through. But as he ordered the ambulance he looked over at Chung-Cha and knew that it was too late.

She was already chalk white and covered in blood.

Reel looked down at her, cradling her head with one hand while keeping the cloth pressed against the wound with the other.

Chung-Cha lifted her hand and touched Reel's face. In a voice that grew weaker with each word she said, "Her name is Min. She is ten. Please help her."

"I will, I promise I will. Min will be fine. But just

don't give up. Help is coming. You're going to be okay. Don't leave. You're going to make it. I know you can do it. You're . . . you're the best I've ever seen."

Chung-Cha did not seem to be able to hear her. She was now mouthing the words over and over. *Her name is Min. She is ten. Please help her.*

And then she said quite clearly with her last bit of breath and a final burst of fire, "I am Chung-Cha. I am young but very old. Please help me."

Then her mouth stopped moving and her eyes became fixed.

Reel just sat there frozen for a long moment, and then gently laid the dead woman's head down on the floor. She looked up at Robie, tears in her eyes. She shook her head once. Then she rose, shoved the deputy out of her way, and walked up the stairs.

76

The attack on the first family had driven the two countries nearly to war, but a diplomatic stalemate was reached that allowed the North Koreans to save face and kept the administration from having to reveal potentially embarrassing and politically damaging facts about the planned coup on the North Korean regime. The Nantucket attack was blamed on rogue elements within North Korea, their actions denounced by the leadership.

There the matter was laid to rest. At least for now.

The North Korean team had infiltrated the town hall by virtue of their Halloween costumes. They had killed a guard near the rear door, entered that way, and then sealed off the building, killing the inner cordon of guards as they went along. The lone deputy who had shot Chung-Cha had finally gotten into the building, seen what had happened, and followed the sounds to the cellar, where his shaky aim had still proved lethal, unfortunately for Chung-Cha.

Robie and Reel had received the heartfelt thanks of the president and his wife, and their children. They were told that they had earned the status of unofficial members of the first family. Tommy was more hero-struck than ever. But both he and his sister were being given counseling to help them cope with what they had seen and endured. Claire was clearly not herself, her brashness struck clean from her. Now it seemed that her brother was supporting her, which might actually have been a good thing for both of them.

Eleanor had warmly embraced Robie and Reel as they were leaving the White House.

"My children and I owe you our lives," she said.

"No," replied Reel firmly. "We all owe our lives to Yie Chung-Cha."

After the White House meeting, Robie and Reel sat in Robie's apartment. They had learned a lot about Yie Chung-Cha, through the information pipeline that was the CIA. What they learned had made Reel even more depressed than she already was.

"She survived all that. All those years at Yodok, having to kill her own family to get out of that hell-hole? Starvation, torture, killing on behalf of that rogue nation. And then saving our lives. For what? To take a bullet from an overzealous cop?"

"He didn't know, Jess," said Robie. "He thought she was the enemy."

"Well, she wasn't," snapped Reel.

"You know Pyongyang wanted her body returned there," said Robie.

She nodded. "But we didn't do it. She's buried here."

"Why do you think she did it?" asked Robie. "I mean really?"

"I took her at her word. She was tired of it all, Robie. Just like I am."

"I guess."

"She was better than us, you know that, don't you?"

"She probably was," agreed Robie. "I've certainly never seen anyone take out five opponents the way she did."

"When she pulled out her knives and looked at us I knew she wasn't going to attack us," said Reel.

"Why? I mean, I thought she looked conflicted, but she told us she was sorry about it."

"Did you ever tell someone you were sorry before you killed them?"

Robie sat back in his chair and thought about this, and then finally shook his head. "No."

"She did it for Min."

Robie nodded again. "For Min."

"Pretty ingenious the way she got the girl out of the country like that."

"Well, if she thought the way she fought she would have made one hell of a chess player."

"Six steps ahead," said Reel thoughtfully.

"Right."

"Blue Man seems to think that tensions will simmer down between us and North Korea."

Robie said, "Until they start to boil again."

"I'll take a little peace and quiet for now."

"Won't we all."

"Which brings us to Min."

"Yeah, it does."

"Do you think they'll go for it?" Reel asked.

"Well, everything is in place, so now all we can do is ask, Jess."

"Then let's go ask."

"You sure?" he said.

"As sure as I am of anything these days."

Robie grabbed his car keys and they set out.

They had had to jump quite a few hurdles and work their way through various agencies, but then an opportunity had presented itself. They had recruited Kim Sook to help them and he had readily agreed.

They made two stops on the way and then completed the drive to the big town house in northern Virginia. Robie had phoned first and they were waiting for them.

Julie Getty opened the door. Standing opposite her were Robie, Reel, and Sook.

And Min.

The little girl was dressed in tights and a long shirt with sneakers. She had a yellow ribbon in her hair.

She was well scrubbed but her face was red for another reason.

She had been crying.

For the loss of Chung-Cha.

And she was scared.

"Hey, guys, come on in," said Julie warmly.

Her guardian, Jerome Cassidy, had recovered from his injuries at the hands of Leon Dikes's men and was waiting for them in the family room. He was middle-aged and lean, with long grayish hair neatly tied back.

He greeted Robie, whom he knew, and was introduced to Reel.

"Julie's told me a lot about you," said Jerome.

"Just the unclassified parts," amended Julie with a smile.

Julie sat next to Min and said, "I'm Julie, Min." Then she said a few words in Korean, some of which Min understood.

Sook laughed. "Not bad. But you need practice."

"I know," said Julie with a wry grin.

Min said, "I am Min. I am ten."

"I'm fifteen, five more than you," replied Julie.

Min smiled but did not seem to understand this.

Julie took one of her hands and counted off the fingers. "Five, this many."

Min nodded and counted to five in Korean.

"That's right," said Sook. "Very good."

Jerome said, "So, Robie, you filled me in a little bit on this. But I'd like to hear more."

Robie explained what he could about where Min had come from. And then what they had come here to ask. Could Min live with them?

"She can't go back to North Korea," said Reel.

"And traditional foster care can get a little tricky with her situation," explained Robie. "I know it's asking a lot, but you two were the first ones I thought of. Min can't understand English really. Hell, she can't understand a lot of things. So if you can't do it, she'll never know we even asked you."

Julie said, "I've always wanted a sibling. And being a big sister would be really cool." She looked at Jerome. "What do you think?"

"I think what with all this little girl has been through she deserves some friends. And maybe we're a good place to start."

Reel looked at Robie in relief and then turned back to Jerome. "I can't tell you what this means."

"I think I know. Wasn't too long ago that yours truly needed a helping hand, or I might not even be here."

As they were leaving, they had to explain to Min that she would be coming to live with Jerome and Julie. Sook had agreed to help out until Min's language skills were strong enough. At first Min clung to Sook, but Julie kept delicately enticing Min away from him until the little girl finally took Julie's hand and walked off with her.

They told Jerome that all the paperwork would be completed and then he would officially become Min's guardian.

"Surprised the government is making it this easy," said Jerome. "I thought their motto was the more paperwork the better."

"Well, the government wants to put all this behind them as fast as they can," explained Robie.

On the way back Reel drove, and when she made a turn that would take them away from Robie's apartment, he instinctively knew where she was going.

The place was in rural Virginia. It was small and out of the way. But it had beautiful views of the foothills of the Blue Ridge. It was only about seventy miles from D.C., but it could have been seven hundred.

Reel parked the car and she and Robie got out. The sun was dipping low into the horizon, burning the sky red. The wind was picking up and the temperature was dropping. Rain was coming in and it would soon turn wet and miserable. Yet, for now, right this very minute, there was a simple beauty here that was bone-deep and undeniable.

They opened the rusted wrought-iron gate and made their way down the uneven grass path. They passed mostly old tombstones and grave markers.

Some leaned at precarious angles; others were ramrod straight.

Near the end of the path and on the left was the newest gravestone here. It was white and resembled those at Arlington National Cemetery.

It was simple in design but powerful in its inspiration.

The inscription matched the design's simplicity:

YIE CHUNG-CHA, WHO FOUGHT THE GOOD FIGHT UNTIL THE END

No one knew when she had been born or where. And no one knew how old she was. And while they knew the exact date of her death, there did not seem to be a good reason to mark her grave with that violent fact.

Reel stared down at the white stone and the hump of dirt. "That could be us down there."

"It would have been, but for her."

"We are like her, you know that."

"There are similarities," Robie admitted.

"How do you think she feels, being so far from home?"

"I'm not sure the dead are really concerned with that. And for her, North Korea wasn't much of a home, was it?"

"I'm glad they didn't send her body back. She

belongs . . . well, I think she belongs here. It's sort of just . . . right."

"It's peaceful enough. And after all she'd been through the lady deserved some peace."

"Like you and me."

"Yes," agreed Robie.

"I didn't know her, though I wish I could have had the chance. But I know beyond doubt that I will never forget her."

"She's left a piece of herself here. In Min."

"And now she's given Min the chance to have a life. We can help her with that life."

"We *have* helped her."

"I mean more than giving her to Jerome and Julie."

Robie looked surprised. "Do you want to do that?"

"Yes. And not just because we owe it to Chung-Cha."

Reel knelt down next to the grave and brushed a few leaves off the freshly turned dirt.

"It's because, well . . ."

She rose and placed a hand over Robie's. "It's because it's something people should do." She paused. "Even people like us."

"Even people like us," agreed Robie.

They turned and walked off together as the light gave way fully to the dark.

ACKNOWLEDGMENTS

To Michelle, for more reasons than I can list. To Mitch Hoffman, for being a great editor and an even better friend. To Michael Pietsch, Jamie Raab, Lindsey Rose, Sonya Cheuse, Emi Battaglia, Tom Maciag, Martha Otis, Karen Torres, Anthony Goff, Bob Castillo, Michele McGonigle, Erica Warren, and everyone at Grand Central Publishing for doing your job so well. To Aaron and Arleen Priest, Lucy Childs Baker, Lisa Erbach Vance, Frances Jalet-Miller, John Richmond, and Melissa Edwards, for supporting me in every way. To Nicole James, best of luck in your new adventure! To Anthony Forbes Watson, Jeremy Trevathan, Maria Rejt, Trisha Jackson, Katie James, Natasha Harding, Lee Dibble, Stuart Dwyer, Stacey Hamilton, James Long, Anna Bond, Sarah Willcox, Geoff Duffield, and Jonathan Atkins at Pan Macmillan, for continuing to keep me at number one in the UK and being so bloody good! To Praveen Naidoo and his team at Pan Macmillan in Australia. To Arabella Stein, Sandy Violette, and Caspian Dennis, for taking care of me so well. To Ron McLarty and

David Baldacci

Orlagh Cassidy, for your outstanding audio performances. To Steven Maat, Joop Boezeman, and the Bruna team, for keeping me at the top in Holland. To Bob Schule, for always being there for me. To auction winners Linda Spitzer and Andrew Viola, I hope you like your characters. To Roland Ottewell, for a great copyediting job. And to Kristen, Natasha, and Lynette, for keeping me reasonably sane!